THE CRITICS LOVE
NIGHT VISIONS . . .

"This excellent anthology series showcases the work of three talents in each volume . . . Horror fans should find this collection well worth looking into!" —*Publishers Weekly*

"Innovative . . . A sturdy collection." —*Kirkus*

"Vivid . . . powerful, unexpected . . . Reading these books, we can savor the multi-faceted talents of some of the best writers of modern horror." —*Fantasy Review*

"Delightful . . . delectable . . . twists and turns." —*Locus*

"Excellent . . . Stories run from moody pieces to more overt horror . . . Quite good!" —*Science Fiction Chronicle*

NIGHT VISIONS

This thrilling new volume is edited by acclaimed author Alan Ryan, and features: the artful chills of Charles L. Grant . . . the quiet but powerful terrors of Tanith Lee . . . and the brutal and poetic horrors of Steve Rasnic Tem. Enter their darkest nightmares—if you dare . . .

The NIGHT VISIONS series published by Berkley

NIGHT VISIONS: DEAD IMAGE
  edited by Charles L. Grant

NIGHT VISIONS: THE HELLBOUND HEART
  edited by George R. R. Martin

NIGHT VISIONS: IN THE BLOOD
  edited by Alan Ryan

◄NIGHT VISIONS►

IN THE BLOOD

ALL ORIGINAL STORIES BY

CHARLES L. GRANT
TANITH LEE
STEVE RASNIC TEM

Originally published as <u>NightVisions</u> 1

Edited by Alan Ryan

BERKLEY BOOKS, NEW YORK

This Berkley book contains the
text of the original hardcover edition.
It has been completely reset in a typeface
designed for easy reading and was printed
from new film.

NIGHT VISIONS: IN THE BLOOD

A Berkley Book / published by arrangement with
the author

PRINTING HISTORY
Dark Harvest edition published 1984
Berkley edition/April 1988

This book is dedicated to

Frank Belknap Long

*who, in 1984,
celebrated his sixtieth anniversary
as a writer of
outstanding short stories.*

The publishers would like to express their gratitude to the following people. Thank you: Cathy Moran, Georgiann Schwartz, Kathy Jo Mikol, Dana Sykee, Robert B. Cole, Lisa Eisenberg, Paul Talwane, Betsy Wollheim, Dick Spelman, Luis Trevino, Debra Vance, Jesus Vasquez, Robert and Phyllis Weinberg, the people of the Skokie Houlihan's, Bob Garcia, Susan Johnson, Karl Edward Wagner, David Morrell, Joseph Payne Brennan, Mike Murray, Harry Mapes, and George R. R. Martin for starting us on our way.

And of course, special thanks go to the five most important people to this book. Without them *Night Visions: In the Blood* would not exist. Charles L. Grant, Steve Rasnic Tem, Tanith Lee, Alan Ryan, and Gregory Manchess.

Introduction

WE USED TO hear all the time that the short story was dead or dying, and we used to hear great and terrible laments for the passing of *Scribner's* and *Collier's* and *The Saturday Evening Post* and *Story Magazine*.

The only one of those I ever really lamented—because it was the only one I'm old enough to remember in its glory—was *Story Magazine*, a handsome monthly package in digest size, edited by Whit and Hallie Burnett, aimed at a general fiction-reading audience, and constituting a monthly tribute to the powers of the short story form.

Some years ago, there was, for a while, a quarterly magazine descended from Burnett's legacy, called *Short Story International*, filled with short fiction from all over the world. I discovered a lot of writers there, and I lament its passing too.

But the short story has, of course, survived. The university journals are filled with them, pale though they often are, and the "quality" magazines, like *The New Yorker* and *Atlantic*, still publish the most important literary short fiction. There are still two annual volumes offering the best short stories of the year, and the O. Henry Award is still—among writers, at least—a highly respected prize.

Even so, publishers have always been reluctant to issue volumes of a writer's short fiction. Such books do not sell as well as novels, and publishers often accept such a book only to retain a desirable author on their lists. Then, a couple of years ago, the publishing industry discovered, rather to its surprise, that collections of stories *could* be sold, and so now we have large volumes of the short fiction not only of Hemingway and Faulkner, standard volumes for years now, but of Doris Lessing, Nadine Gordimer, Bernard Malamud, Donald Barthelme, Hortense Calisher, Ray Bradbury, Elizabeth Bowen, William Trevor, Katherine Ann Porter, Eudora Welty, and many others.

So the short story—even if a little tentatively and with modest expectations—has regained some of its former dignity and is seen now to have commercial value.

Much of the doubt and worry could have been avoided if publishing observers had only looked at the genre markets, where the short story has always flourished. The best of the science fiction and mystery magazines are now many decades old, and are still doing essentially what they were doing when they started: providing half a dozen to a dozen or so short stories every month to an audience of readers who wait eagerly for them, who follow a writer's progress over months and years, and who truly appreciate what they are reading.

Happily, the same sort of thing is true too in the realm of dark fantasy and horror fiction, although, in the absence of a magazine specifically devoted to it, most of the concentrated activity here is in anthologies.

Most of us—those of us, that is, who regularly read and write short fiction that can properly be called horror or dark fantasy—feel very strongly about it. Certainly, for the writers, short fiction is not cost effective, even when previously published stories are collected in book form. At the same time, much of the best work of writers in the field is in their short stories. And many readers and writers hold that, for horror fiction, the single most effective form is the short story. Writers who speak on panels at fantasy conventions very often find that their audiences are most knowledgeable and most vociferous when the subject is short fiction.

In this field, a writer can make a reputation and win a following by writing only short stories. And some of the most respected writers in the field are, in fact, known primarily for their short stories, though they may also write novels. Among the authors of the best short fiction in the field, only some of whom are also novelists, are Frank Belknap Long, Manly Wade Wellman, Fritz Leiber, H.P. Lovecraft, Robert Bloch, Ray Bradbury, John Collier, Gerald Kersh, Charles Beaumont, William F. Nolan, Ray Russell, Joseph Payne Brennan, Roald Dahl, Harlan Ellison, Charles L. Grant, Dennis Etchison, Ramsey Campbell, and Karl Edward Wagner. It would be a lot less easy to construct an equally respectable list of writers in the field who write only novels.

For most of us, the stories come from some other, possibly deeper, source than the novels. They appear in the mind—a word, a title, an image, a line of dialogue, an opening line, a closing line—and they insist on being written. And we write them. We may not tell our agents we're writing a short story, because our agents always get upset, but we write them anyway. And they are ours, often in a way that a novel is not. With a novel, because more money is at stake, everybody wants to get in on the act: agents, editors, editors-in-chief, publishers, art directors, copyeditors, buyers for major bookstore chains, everybody. And they do, in varying degrees. But the short story, for the most part, belongs to the writer. He may work closely with the editor of an anthology, he may agree to take the editor's suggestions for changes, the writer and editor may puzzle out together the proper shape of a sentence, or the right choice of a word, or the most effective rhythm for the closing lines . . . but, in the end, the story belongs to the writer.

Night Visions was conceived as a showcase for the outstanding work being done today by the best of the established writers and the most talented of the new writers in the fields of horror fiction and dark fantasy. Three writers are included in this volume, each represented by approximately 30,000 words of new short fiction, so the reader has a wide opportunity to see a writer's work.

For readers interested in the book's provenance, it came about thus: In the fall of 1983, Paul Mikol of Dark Harvest Books, who was then planning a hardcover edition of my novel, *Cast a Cold Eye*, asked me about the feasibility of doing an anthology of this sort. I had been thinking of something similar myself, and we discussed possibilities over the course of two months or so. We did arithmetic and tried to make it work. We did some educated guesswork. We talked about short stories. We talked about writers we'd like to see in a book like this. We did more arithmetic. Finally, on the last night of the World Fantasy Convention over Halloween weekend in Chicago, we sat in the bar of the Marriott Hotel at O'Hare Airport, took very long drinks from our glasses, and with the anxious support of Beverly Berg, Scot Stadalsky, and Kathy Jo Mikol, decided to go ahead, aiming for publication one year later.

Since then, there have been plenty of tense moments, restless nights, frayed nerves, urgent phone calls . . . and, about to go into production as I write this, the book we had in mind from the beginning.

Charles L. Grant is acknowledged as one of the finest writers of short stories working in the field of dark fantasy. He has won a wide array of awards for his short fiction, and in 1983 won two World Fantasy Awards, one for the four novellas constituting *Nightmare Seasons*, and another for "Confess the Seasons," a novella published in my own anthology, *Perpetual Light*. For many years he has been a frequent contributor to *The Magazine of Fantasy and Science Fiction* and his stories appear often in a wide range of magazines and anthologies. His story collections include *Tales from the Nightside*, *A Glow of Candles*, and *Nightmare Seasons*. His total number of published stories is currently nearing a hundred.

He is also, of course, well known as editor of the *Shadows* anthologies. His novels include the Oxrun Station series, *The Nestling*, and most recently, *Night Songs*.

Both as editor of *Shadows* and in his own fiction, Grant is a proponent of what he calls "quiet horror." Most often, his stories focus on the psychological violence experienced by his characters. That violence is frequently a product of their isolation—a parallel to the small-town settings he favors—and, often, a single, fatal quirk of personality or circumstance. He insists to me that, although his characters are very often alone—children, outsiders, the elderly—they are seldom lonely.

Lonely or not, his characters are faced with a world that, in one way or another, demands their attention. Those who turn away from the confrontation often look inward, only to find within themselves some things much darker than anything threatened by the world outside.

Steve Rasnic Tem is a widely published poet who sold his first short fiction to Ramsey Campbell's *New Terrors*. Since then, he has quickly won a reputation among readers of dark fantasy as one of the most prominent new writers of short fiction in the field. His stories have appeared in all the major anthologies and innumerable magazines. "Firestorm," which appeared in *Perpetual Light*, was nominated for a World Fantasy Award. *Night Visions*, with seven new stories, offers the first substantial presentation of his work.

His stories, the natural product of a poet's imagination, are usually very short, very terse, and visually powerful. The surrealistic nightmares he paints are disturbingly vivid, with the kind of intense and tactile reality most of us only experience in frightening dreams. His characters move in a sometimes shadowy world, a world that, page by page, grows ever more threatening, until things get entirely out of hand.

Yet, for all the unpleasantness he reveals in the world and within the people he writes about, one of the strongest qualities of Tem's fiction is his love and compassion for his characters, a compassion that grows greater as their nightmares grow even darker.

Tanith Lee's reputation rests most prominently on her novels of fantasy and science fiction, yet many readers feel that her best book is *Red as Blood*, a collection of her own dark versions of familiar fairy tales. She is a prolific writer of short stories and her latest book, *Tamastara*, is another collection. In 1983 she won a World Fantasy award for "The Gorgon," which appeared in Charles L. Grant's *Shadows 5*.

Lee's prose, perhaps used to best effect in her short fiction, is rich and allusive, suggestive of much more than it says, and filled with a high quotient of emotional content. And when she turns her attention to dark fantasy, the effect is powerful, producing stories that only she could write.

Her work is widely varied. One of the stories here moves like a chamber music quintet. Another uses the familiar vampire legend with powerful psychological effect, while another exploits fully all the elements, both sensual and deadly, of the unicorn legend. And another is in a great English tradition, a story that I think both M. R. James and Robert Aickman would have approved.

Night Visions is a book of short stories. I love short stories. I hope this book shows why.

As usual with any project of this sort, I owe thanks to a large number of people who, in a wide variety of ways, helped to bring it about. They include the people of Dark Harvest, Ellen Levine, Betsy Wollheim, Charles L. Grant, Steve Rasnic Tem, Jill Bauman, Whitley Strieber, Douglas E. Winter, Craig Shaw Gardner, and Kathy Jo Mikol.

New York City
March 23, 1984

CHARLES L. GRANT

Friends in Dark Places

IT'S NO FUN having friends who don't want to be dead. They always spoil everything. It takes a long time to sneak around the house on the corner, hiding behind that big porch until the bad guys come out into the yard. And you have to be careful because Sammy, the dog that lives across the street with Harry Devon and her mother, he's always trying to play with us and telling the bad guys where we are because he barks so much. And then there's Mr. Smith, who doesn't like us to play near his yard at all because we might squish his roses or put holes in his hedge. So after you do all that stuff and you're really careful about not making any noise, when the bad guys don't fall down when you kill them it's no fun playing.

We were in the cherry tree out front of my house when I said that, and Greg said I was right, that we shouldn't let anyone play with us who wouldn't be dead when he was supposed to. Then Dickie, he says that suppose the mother said not to get the kid's clothes all dirty. I was going to say that it was all right, but Greg said that the kid shouldn't be playing then because we always get dirty when we play, or it really isn't playing.

I know why he said that.

He said it because Dickie was talking about Harry, and Harry never ever falls down because her mother is always telling her not to get her good jeans with the picture of the

9

horse on the back dirty or she'll get a spanking when she gets home. Greg doesn't like Harry, but I do, I think. She's neat. Her real name is Harriet but no one ever calls her that except her mother, and her mother doesn't like anybody, not even the father which is why he ran away from home last year. At least, that's what Harry told us. But Greg doesn't like her anyway because she kissed him once, when she fell out of the cherry tree and he picked her up—she gave him this real big silly kiss right on the cheek, and he never talked to her again after that.

"Well, I think it's okay," I said when Greg was done. He was on the branch just above me, riding it like a horse and getting his long hair in his eyes. He was always having to blow or push it away, and sometimes we kidded him about looking like a girl it was so long.

"Well, I don't care," he said.

"Well, I don't care that you don't care," Dickie said. He was standing where he always does, near the ground where the trunk broke apart into a lot of different trunks. He never climbs very high. He doesn't want to fall like Harry did and break his glasses.

I guess we would have started fighting then if my mother hadn't come along. We were fighting a lot all of a sudden and I didn't know why and I didn't like it because I thought I was going to lose my friends if we kept it up. I was even going to ask why it was changing, how come we couldn't have fun anymore, but my mother came to the front door and told me to get out of the tree, I was going to hurt myself, and how many times did she tell me, a million?, not to do that.

I heard Greg call her a real bad name real soft, and Dickie said we'd better do it, and anyway it was time for supper. So he held out his hand, and I found it and he helped me down, and then I went to the walk and counted the steps until I reached the porch. I climbed up by myself, and the guys yelled goodbye, and I waved and went inside.

"Honestly, Zach," Mom said, putting me at the dining

room table while she finished making supper, which smelled like roast beef. "When are you going to learn?"

"I was all right, Mom," I told her. "I wasn't going to fall."

She groaned and walked away, and I could tell by her footsteps that she was kind of angry with me. But it wasn't my fault, not really. Just because I can't see like other kids doesn't mean I can't play with them. It would be nice, I guess, to play ball and stuff, but I can't do that so I climb trees and play cowboys and soldier and I play cards with Mom and Dad and things like that.

I even this summer learned to play hide-and-seek, though it has to be around my house so I'll know where everything is. It sounds hard, but I can hear real good, and I can catch Dickie because he breathes so loud, and Harry moves around a lot no matter where she's hiding. Greg cheats, though. I know he's there, but he won't do anything until I come right up to him and touch him. I don't think he really believes I can't really use my eyes, and Harry told me once that he's a little afraid of me. I guess it's because there are some times when you can't tell me from a real kid.

Like playing dead.

And like climbing trees.

But most of the time you can, so I don't go out an awful lot because when my three best friends in the whole world aren't around it's not good for me. I might make a mistake and walk into the street and get hit by a car, or fall off the curb and break my leg, or something like that. That's what Mom says, anyway, and so I have to be extra special careful until we can afford to get me a dog that will help me and won't be too big and won't drag me to the North Pole if it starts running.

See, I'm not very big for my age. Which is nine going on ten. The sickness when I was a little baby that made me not see made me also not very strong all the time too. That's a pain. I don't get sick anymore, but I can't always run as fast as I want to.

And I can't have a pet like I want, either.

So mostly I hang around the house and the yard a lot, like that day in the cherry tree. And that night Dad came home and when Mom told him about me climbing again, he laughed and took me into the living room and sat me on his knee. He made a funny noise, like I was too heavy to sit there, but I didn't laugh until I put my hands on his face, just to be sure he hadn't shaved off his beard or grew new lines around his eyes or on his forehead. And when I was done seeing him, when I knew it was really him, I giggled and jumped around until he held me tight, and then I knew he was going to be serious.

"Zach," he said, "you know your mother doesn't like you to climb trees. Especially that one. It can be very dangerous, you could hurt yourself badly."

"But, Dad, I don't do it alone! The guys are always there to watch out."

"I know, I know, but you'll have to trust me on this one, son. It worries your mother too much, and I don't want you to do it again."

"Aw, Dad!"

"You heard me."

"Aw, please?"

"Zachary!"

When he called me that, I knew he meant it. He said he was only trying to protect me and keep me okay, but I don't need protecting. I needed friends, and I wouldn't have any friends if I couldn't play with them. They don't want to sit around all day and watch me like they were babysitters or something. They want to play. I want to play.

"They'll understand, Zach," he said.

"No, they won't!" I said, almost yelling. Then I climbed down and went as fast as I could to my room, which was on the other side of the kitchen. It used to be upstairs, but Mom thought I might walk in my sleep one time and fall down and break my neck, and she didn't like it when I told her I couldn't tell night from day anyway when I was inside so what was the difference? She spanked me for that, crying the whole time, and the next thing I knew I was in a new room. Downstairs. Where I could hear the refrigerator talking to itself late at night, and the oven cooling off, and the furnace right beneath me in the cellar blowing like a dragon when it got cold outside.

Mom didn't try to stop me when I ran away from Dad like that. I guess she heard us men talking, and when I closed the door real hard she didn't yell. She just broke a dish in the sink, and soon Dad was talking low to her and I could tell she was crying again.

I wanted to cry too.

I was going to lose all my friends just because they thought I couldn't climb a stupid tree.

Not fair. Not fair at all.

No pets, no friends, and Mom and Dad were talking like they were keeping a secret.

When I was asleep that night I had funny dreams. I didn't remember them when I woke up, but I got dressed real fast because I couldn't stop thinking that I wasn't alone. I looked around real good, and everything was where it was supposed to be, but I still had that feeling. Like when you're standing someplace and you know deep down in your heart there's somebody standing right behind you. It doesn't make any difference if you turn around and see that you're wrong; it doesn't make any difference at all.

For a littie while there, just for a little while, you weren't really alone.

A lot of days went by, then, and the weather got colder, and Dickie and Greg wanted to play football with some other guys so they didn't come around much. I wanted to play with them, though, so one day on a Saturday when I was tired of being all by myself I followed the sidewalk down the street to the fence that was in front of Greg's house. I walked real slow because I hadn't been there very much, and I went up to the door and knocked, and Greg's mother came and said that Greg couldn't play with me, he was at the football game. I didn't want her to, but she walked me home anyway, and

Mom was really mad this time and wouldn't let me out of the house until Dad came home from the store.

He was mad, too.

He made me stay in my room because I went off by myself, and he said I needed to learn a lesson. He wouldn't listen when I told him I wasn't a baby anymore, and why couldn't I go when I knew the way? He wouldn't listen. He just closed the door and went away.

I had the dreams again that night.

I woke up in the middle of them, and I listened. I listened very hard, but I didn't hear a thing.

But I wasn't alone.

The next day was Sunday, and when I got up I put my hand on the window to see how cold it was. Not very, I found out, so I got dressed and put on my jacket and went out onto the front porch. Mom and Dad were still in bed, but the sun was up. I could feel it on my face. I walked down to the sidewalk and stood by the hedge that was all around our yard, and I was wondering if Dickie would come by even though we couldn't climb the tree anymore.

Suddenly, I thought there was someone nearby.

I turned my head slowly, listening for breathing, or a footstep, or something.

Then I knew it wasn't on the ground, so I looked up, hoping I was looking in the right direction.

"Dickie? Greg? Hey, guys, that you?"

Nobody answered.

"Dickie?"

Nobody said anything.

"Where are you?"

I was getting scared now. I didn't like it when people snuck up on me. I couldn't tell who they were, if they were my friends or what, and Mom had told me a hundred million times about these really bad people who came up and stole little kids away and never brought them home again.

But somebody was there.

I could feel it.

"Hey, come on, please?"

"Hey, Zach, who are you talking to?"

I bet I jumped ten miles into the air when Harry came up on me like that. I must have looked real silly because she started laughing and laughing, and I was real mad at her for doing that, but her laugh was so funny that I started to laugh too. So we both laughed so hard that we fell on the ground and rolled around and kicked, and I got tears in my eyes and my stomach started to hurt, and then we bumped into each other and stopped. For a while we just lay there in the leaves, trying to get our breath. Then we sat up and kneeled so that our knees were almost touching.

"Zach," she said, "are you mad at me?"

"No," I said, crossing my heart and shaking my head. "I'm not mad at you, Harry. How come you think I'm mad?"

"Well, you don't come out much anymore."

I put my hand along the ground until I found a leaf, then picked it up and started pulling it apart. "Dickie and Greg won't play with me anymore."

"Yeah, I know," she said. "Big jerks."

"Yeah."

"All they want to do is play football."

"Yeah."

We didn't say anything for a while, and then she kind of moved closer. "I'm still your friend, you know."

"Yeah, I know."

"I don't care that you can't see."

I knew that. She was, I think, the only one who wasn't afraid of me.

"Sometimes," she said then, real quiet like she was telling me a secret, "I pretend I'm blind, y'know? I put a handkerchief around my eyes and try to walk around my room without bumping into anything." She stopped. "It's scary, Zach. It's real scary."

Boy, I sure liked her.

And I didn't even think about it, I just reached out my hands to see her again. I touched her hair, and very slowly moved my hands over her face. She giggled. So did I. There was a bump on her chin that was ticklish, and her eyebrows were bigger than mine, and her mouth was too.

When I was done, she kind of held her breath and said, "Can you really see with your hands, Zach?"

I shrugged. "Sort of. Kind of, I guess."

"It feels funny." Then she pulled away. "Zach, what do I look like?"

I blinked fast. "Huh?"

"Come on, Zach, what do I look like?"

"Like Harry."

She hit my arm and I grinned. "No, silly. I mean, am I fat or skinny or what?"

"I don't know." I reached out and grabbed her arm before she could move away, and I held it while I touched her face again, and her neck, and across her shoulders. "Skinny, I think."

She hit me again, this time not so soft.

"Then I guess you're fat."

"Hey!" She hit me hard this time, and I didn't hear anyone on the sidewalk until someone suddenly grabbed me from behind by the arm and the neck and jerked me to my feet. It hurt a lot, and I started hitting at whoever it was because it wasn't anyone I knew, I didn't think. I hit and I yelled and I kicked, and I could hear Harry yelling too, until all of a sudden Dad was there, and it was quiet.

Not a nice quiet. A mad quiet.

"Mr. Lyme, I'll thank you to keep your son away from my little girl from now on."

Harry's mother. It was Harry's mother!

"Esther, I'm sure Zach—"

"Mom, he wasn't doing anything. He wasn't—"

"I *saw* him, Mr. Lyme. I *saw* him pawing my poor little Harriet. You keep him away or I'll call the police."

"Now wait just a minute," Dad said, but it was too late. I could hear Harry and her mother walking away so fast they were almost running, Harry crying and her mother yelling at the top of her voice about the police and dirty little boys who shouldn't be allowed on the streets. I didn't know what she meant, but I was scared and I guess I was a baby then because I started crying. Dad picked me up and carried me into the house, and when I stopped he asked me what had happened.

"I was just seeing her, Dad, honest."

"Seeing? Oh. Oh, for god's sake, is that all?"

Then Mom came in and Dad told her what had happened, and she didn't say anything. She just stood there until Dad told me to run along and play, but don't leave the house, and just before I closed my bedroom door I heard her say, "This is getting to be a problem, Frank. We're going to have to do something about it."

So Harry wasn't allowed to play with me anymore, and all I did after that was sit on the top step on the porch and listen to the houses and the trees and the cars and the dogs, and I tried to imagine what it was like to sit in the top of the cherry tree and see the whole world. Really see it, I mean, and not pretend I do when someone tells me what something looks like.

But how do you know what's red when everything's black?

How do you know what a mile is when you can't hold your fingers apart to make an inch?

That night I was lying in bed and thinking about this stuff and thinking about all my friends who weren't really friends at all because they hurt me and they knew it—and just like that, for the first time in a long time, I wished as hard as I could that I could see. I didn't want to be blind. I didn't want to be different. I wanted to be just like everyone else, and it wasn't fair that I couldn't even see the stupid Christmas tree.

Well, Zach, I guess it's time we got acquainted.

I think I almost screamed.

"Who . . . who is it?"

There was no answer.

"Mom? Dad?"

No, Zach, just me.

It was a quiet voice, not a bad one when I thought about it, but it wasn't my parents. It was someone else. A dark voice right there in the middle of my room, right when it was night and Mom and Dad were upstairs in their bed.

"Who . . . who is it?" I said again, getting ready to duck under the covers in case I had to hide.

Just a friend.

"I don't have any friends. And you're not one either."

Are you sure about that?

"Sure I'm sure."

Then I sat up real quick and reached out my hands, but all I felt was the wall and the covers. I sat on the edge of the bed and reached out again. There was nothing there.

Maybe soon, Zach, maybe soon.

"Dad, is that you making a joke?"

I knew it wasn't, though, and I quick got back under the covers and pulled them up over my head and waited until I was sure I was alone. I mean, I was alone before but not really alone because there was that voice talking to me. But I was alone now. I knew it because I could hear it.

Just the wind knocking at my window, and the refrigerator getting ready for breakfast in the morning.

The next day there wasn't any school because it was a holiday, somebody's birthday but I forget whose, and while I was on the step and pretending I was the captain of a ship on the ocean and hunting for pirates, I heard Mom and Dad in the living room. They were talking, not loud but real hard, and they were talking about me.

I didn't deliberately listen, but I hear real good.

"He'll only be there during the week, Margie. He'll be home on weekends, I told you that. And it won't be forever, the training only lasts for about three months. With all those tutors there, he won't lose a bit of schooling."

"But he's only a baby!"

"Marge, for god's sake, he's nearly ten years old! He has to learn more, a lot more, if he's going to get along."

"I don't want to hear it."

"Well, you're going to have to. We can't do any more here, we just don't know enough. And you remember what happened yesterday. Granted, that woman's an idiot, but we can't protect him by ourselves any longer."

Mom said something, Dad said something else, and a chair was pushed so hard it hit the wall.

"He will not fall behind," Dad said.

"His teacher says he's not getting good grades."

"Because he's bored, damnit! He's compensating for his eyesight by studying three times as hard as anyone else. You know that. My god, you see the way he eats up those books. But he's bored!"

"I want him home, Frank. I want him home where I can take care of him."

"Great, Marge. That makes a lot of sense. You just keep him here like he was a cripple, and when he gets bigger he won't be able to do a damned thing but sell pencils on a streetcorner."

There was a noise, then, and I was afraid because I knew Mom had hit Dad in the face.

I don't know if they talked anymore because I got up and went to the cherry tree. After making sure there wasn't anything different I climbed as high as I could and sat down and held on as tight as I could, turning my head so my face was in the wind that smelled like smoke and made the leaves whisper to me.

I didn't feel so good.

I didn't have any friends, and now I wasn't going to have any home.

I sat there for a long time. The sun went down. The leaves rattled and hissed. I could hear cars going by, and some kids laughing I didn't know. Dad came out once and called for me, but I pushed myself hard against the branch and I guess he didn't see me because he went back inside. Then he came out again, telling my mother he'd check my friends' houses in case I went there. But he knew I didn't have any friends anymore. He knew that.

Zach.

I wasn't scared. I was cold. And I was brave as could be when I reached out.

And touched it.

Warm. So nice and warm and soft like the shaggy rug in the living room.

What do you see, Zach?

"You," I whispered.

Right.

And the voice wasn't all in my head sort of anymore, and I smiled so hard my cheeks started to ache. He didn't ask me anything else, not like Harry. He knew that I knew him, and that was all that mattered.

A big wind came up then and shook the tree like a giant was down at the bottom, trying to shake me out. I grabbed hold and waited while the leaves hit me on the head and scratched at my face. My teeth chattered, and my fingers were so frozen I couldn't feel them.

Go down, Zach.

"Why?"

Go down, Zach, and wait for me.

I didn't want to go—he was so warm and soft—but I started to climb down like he said I should; halfway there I looked up and said, "Do you care that I can't see?"

But you can, you know. You can see the dark.

"Damn you, boy!" And Dad grabbed me right out of the tree, tucked me under his arm and carried me like a bag into the house. Mom was so mad she was crying again and Dad didn't bother to take me to my room. He just went to the sofa and put me across his legs and gave me a spanking so hard I could hear him grunting.

But I didn't cry.

I bit on my lips and held my breath until he pushed me off and shoved me toward the doorway.

"Go to bed," he said, as if he was so tired he was ready to fall asleep.

"Dad, I have a new friend!"

"Zachary, go to bed."

I did. My bottom hurt and it was hard to walk, but I went to bed without taking off my clothes, using just the blanket to keep the cold away. And I lay there all night waiting to see if my friend would come and tell me what to do. He didn't. But I figured he had to sleep sometime, so I did too, and didn't have any dreams like I was afraid I would; and first thing the next day I got up and put on my heavy coat from the closet under the stairs and went outside. Before the door closed I heard Mom calling, and Dad yelling, and I knew that they hated me then.

No, that's not right.

They didn't hate me. They weren't even afraid of me. They were tired of me. Dad was tired of yelling at Mom because of me, and Mom was tired of crying all the time because I wasn't like any of her friends' sons. I could play cowboy, but I couldn't play ball; I could read, but I couldn't watch TV.

I was different.

And they loved me a lot, but they were tired of having me around all the time.

There must have been a lot of clouds because I couldn't feel the sun. It was cold. Very cold. And a cold wind was blowing, wet and stinging, and I knew there'd be snow before school got out that day.

I almost ran to the tree, and was halfway to my spot near the top when Dad ran out after me. His feet were like guns on the porch, and he was breathing so heavy he frightened me. I climbed faster, and I knew when he reached the trunk because he ran right into it he was going so fast.

"Damnit, Zachary, you come down here this instant!"

"No!" I shouted without looking around.

"Boy, if I have to come up there to get you, you're going to regret it."

"You're gonna send me away!"

"Oh for Christ's sake, Zach, don't be a baby. It's for your own good."

"That's what you always say. And I don't like it because it never ever is."

I climbed higher, almost missed a branch once and cut my hand a little but I didn't fall. I kept on climbing until I pushed through a bunch of leaves and found a place to sit down.

Zach.

He was warm, and soft, and when I found his head I could feel his teeth.

"Zachary!"

The tree shook.

Who's your friend, Zach?

"You," I said, nodding once to prove it.

"Zachary, damn your hide . . ." And I could hear him climbing. He was my Dad but I was afraid of him now.

It s all right, Zach. You're with friends now.

Then he was gone.

Then I heard Dad say something like, "Holy god, I don't believe it!"

Then he screamed once, and there was a kind of growling, and a loud noise like something heavy falling.

And then there was quiet.

Until Mom came out of the house, and I knew by the way she yelled and screamed for help that my friend was just like me—he was different. So different that people didn't like him. And because he was so different, they hated him.

But he could do something I couldn't do.

And he did.

And Mom didn't scream anymore.

I cried then because I didn't want my Mom and Dad hurt the way they were. And I cried because I was a little scared that I was going to be all alone now, with nobody to play with.

But after a while, after my friend came back and we talked and talked about all kinds of things, I decided it was okay. They couldn't see my friend the way I did. They couldn't hear his dark voice, couldn't feel how warm and soft he was.

And that's really too bad.

Because the next thing we're gonna do is go down to the tree in front of Greg's house and wait for him to come home.

And after that we're gonna visit Dickie and Mrs. Devon, and then we're gonna stay in the trees and see the world, me and my friend, up here in the dark parts.

And if you're real lucky when you're walklng alone, in a dark not like my dark but a dark just the same, you'll think it's the wind that's making the leaves move.

And if you're even luckier, you won't look up and you won't have to be dead.

Family

THE DEAD GIRL sat on the edge of the bed and said, "Grampa, Grampa, tell me a story."

He lay without moving, arms on top of the stiff white sheet, head propped on a pair of fringed pillows that braced him against a plain pine headboard. His hair was combed carefully, his face carefully washed, and his white flannel pajamas had been ironed just that morning.

"Grampa, Grampa, won't you talk to me today?"

He looked down at his hands—large, still strong, the nails manicured and buffed. They stirred when a part of him ordered them to move, to lift and encircle the dead girl's neck. But he didn't lift them, only flopped them over, back to palm.

"C'mon, Grampa, Mommy said we're leaving today." She leaned a bit closer and gave him her best pleading smile. "Please? Pretty please?"

The voice, when it came, was soft but not tired. "No, Ally, not now."

She struck the mattress lightly and pouted, a curl of blonde hair falling over one eye. She was eight and tall for her age, just a little heavy though by no means plump. "That's mean," she said with a smile. "That's real mean."

His eyes closed as he willed her to vanish, opened again and saw her still smiling. White teeth that made her red lips much darker, that matched the white of the room and the white of the sun's glare in the window by the bed. The only color he could see without moving his head was an empty picture frame on the wall by the door. It was wood, and it was black.

"Ally," he said, "I didn't sleep well last night."

"Aw," she said with a shake of her head. "I'm sorry, Grampa. I didn't know. Did you take your medicine?"

He nodded.

"And you still couldn't sleep?"

"No."

"Well, that's all right," she said brightly. "You'll sleep better tonight. I'll take care of it, okay? I'll be your nurse and make sure you get your rest."

He gave her a smile, and she leaned over to kiss his forehead. Lips like ice. Breath like December.

"Are you going to see Miss Grovner today?"

He frowned without showing it—how did she know?

"Perhaps."

"Then you have to get better, okay? Miss Grovner won't like it if you're not feeling very good."

"You're right, Ally. I'll do what I can."

Then the bedroom door opened and the dead girl blew him a second kiss and ran giggling from the bedside, ducking around the skirts of her mother on the threshold.

"Good morning, Father," the woman said with a nod.

"Good morning, Ellen. Ally says you're leaving."

She walked briskly to his side, took a wrist and checked his pulse against the tiny gold watch she wore on her blouse. Her lips pursed, and she sighed without a sound, then pulled at the red blouse too snug for her figure. She wore slacks the same way, and around her neck a gold choker spun to a single fine strand.

He watched her as he always did, for signs of some change, then turned his head away and looked out the window. At the empty lot next to the house with its tall weeds still green, its struggling grass, the infrequent wildflower that added a sad touch of color. Beyond it was another house, clapboard and two stories and virtually indistinguishable from the one he was in. If he pressed his head into the pillow he could just see the street—cars parked and rusting, wagons and skate boards on the pavement, every so often a gang of children Ally's age running silently down the faded white line.

"Ally said—"

"I know what she said," Ellen snapped, dropping his wrist and pulling down the sheet. She prodded his legs, poked gently at his stomach, all the while searching his face for signs of any pain. "We're going up to the cabin for a couple of days. Bert thinks it will do us good to get away. He's been working too hard, and he needs a rest."

"You're right," he agreed. "It's been a miserable summer. I don't remember having such a hot summer, not in all my life. And that," he added with a wry smile and a wink, "has been quite some time."

The smile wasn't returned. Ellen pulled the sheet back to his waist, beckoned him to lean forward while she fluffed his pillow. "You'll have to get up. I'm not leaving if you're going to stay in bed all the time. You'll starve."

"I'll get up," he promised. "I just like to lie here in the morning, remembering all the times I had to get up when I didn't want to. I'm making up for lost time."

Ellen grunted, neither a laugh nor a sneer, and went to the door, held the knob and turned around. "You're being stubborn, you know."

He shrugged. It was, at his age, his right to do any damn thing he pleased.

The dead woman sighed, loudly this time. "Father, you're just making it hard on the rest of us. Don't you think about us at all?"

"All the time," he admitted. "All the time."

"That's not what I meant," she said, almost angry. An argument was stirring, but she let it settle down, closed the door instead and left him alone.

He waited five minutes to be sure she had gone, then threw aside the sheet and swung his feet to the floor. He closed his eyes. He took a deep breath slow and easy. He sniffed, and rose, and opened the closet door—grey slacks, pin-striped white shirts, a half-dozen sweaters, two suit jackets, two pairs of shoes, one pair of slippers. The faint smell of moth balls, and of the dry cleaners he used to use.

Dressing took no time at all, and when he peered into the hallway, he saw no one, heard no one, and nodded his head. If they were gone, that was fine; if they weren't, they wouldn't miss him. They never did. They couldn't.

He paused for a moment on the front walk, taking in the fresh air, checking the neighborhood for hints of alteration. But it never changed, and probably never would. It was a development that had sprung up in a farmer's field just over twenty years ago, and in both those decades, though the trees had grown and the houses had been repainted, it still looked and felt and sounded like a development. No character, he thought; sticking a porch on a raised ranch only makes it a raised ranch with a porch.

With his left hand in his pocket he started to walk, only once looking behind him to see if he was being followed.

It was hot, the sky hazy, but the air still pleased his lungs and the sense of freedom he had still teased his dreams. He grunted. He was beginning to sound as if he were a prisoner in his own home, which he wasn't. But neither was it his. His home, his real home, had been taken and eventually sold by his daughter when she decided he was too old to fend for himself. At the time he hadn't minded because he had just finished a hospital stay for a bout of pneumonia. The weakness frightened him. The nurses terrified him. The doctors and their refusal to give him anything but generalities nearly drove him insane. Ellen, then, had been a godsend for the time.

But the time had passed, and he was anxious to be on his own once again.

He stopped at the park and fed a few of the squirrels, stopped at the river and fed a few of the ducks. There were sailing boats in the currents, and he watched them covetously for well over an hour, leaning slightly when the wind blew to lend them a hand, his fingers clenching and relaxing as he handled the ropes, the wheel, the water-slick tiller. His hair tangled, and he brushed it back. His shirt billowed, and he shivered. Coughed, scratched his cheek and realized he hadn't shaved.

Damn, he thought, you're getting old, you old bastard. Next thing you know, you'll forget to get dressed. They'll pick you up buck-naked and gibbering like an ape.

He found an empty bench by the water and sat down, stretching out his legs and crossing them at the ankles. The clock on the town hall steeple behind him struck eleven, then noon, and his stomach began to rumble just as Doris Grovner walked up.

"Are you practicing to be a statue?" she said, dusting off the bench before sitting down.

He grinned shyly and patted her hand in greeting. She was more plump than Ellen's mother had been, and prone to conservative dresses and tiny white hats she wore above her bun. But her laugh was constant and infectious, her dimples still firm in the firm flesh of her round face, and she knew what it was like to have lived with a dream—her husband had died five years before Ellen's mother.

But she still had a family, while he had only *them*.

"Marsha's coming to visit today."

"What?" He was delighted, then dismayed. "Good heavens, Doris, why didn't you tell me?" He stood and jammed both hands in his pockets, took them out and rubbed the sides of his neck. "Good heavens, I'll have to go to the bank, get some money. Good grief, what is she now, Doris? Ally's age at the accident, I guess. Yes, Ally's age." He turned to stare at the water, thinking as fast as he could. The zoo, a light dinner, maybe a movie if there was something appropriate playing. Tomorrow they could—

Doris shook her head. "Good heavens, good grief, good *night*, John Danning, my granddaughter's not the Queen, you know. Sit down and calm down." She patted the bench beside her, and he sat, but not still.

"I promised her the zoo, Doris," he said. "The last time she was here I promised her the zoo."

"So take her, that's no problem. Just take it easy." Her smile softened, became sad. "She isn't Ally, John. She isn't, you know."

He knew that. He knew that all too well.

"It's funny," he said, leaning forward, watching the river. "Ally asked about you this morning. She said I had to take care of myself or you'd be mad."

Doris was silent, and he groaned and closed his eyes tightly at the mistake he had made. She was a wonderful woman, but she didn't know what he'd done, and thought when he talked like this he was losing his mind.

"Sorry again," he said. "It slipped out."

She kissed his cheek and rose, holding her purse at her waist. "You go to the bank," she whispered. "Marsha and I will meet you here at three."

He got to his feet quickly, and watched as she walked away, thinking that he was damned lucky, and luckier than most, to have this second chance. Most of the old idiots he knew spent half their time on a park bench, or sitting in front of the television, and the rest of the time in bed, remembering what it was like when they didn't live alone.

He had seen it from the time he was a child, and the old folks had filled his father's small waiting room. There was nothing wrong with them, usually, but they needed someone to talk to who would listen, and understand, and his father never once turned one of them away.

It was worse than pathetic, it was sad.

And when he'd married Ellen's mother, he had made her promise that when any of their four parents needed help, needed a bed, they would have it.

As it turned out, they didn't need any of it—one by one, and all in less than two years, they had died in hospitals before they had a chance to know about the lonely.

He thought them lucky, and he thought now that he had done the right thing in not letting his own family, his own flesh and blood, get away from him that easily. The accident had been bad enough, the calls from the police professionally sympathetic, the standing in the church, the waiting at the graveyard while the dirt was thrown in. Bad enough, but when he'd thought about all those others wasting away because they were lonely, he knew he wasn't going to let his family desert him.

And they hadn't.

One day gone; the next day back.

It was as if everything he had suffered had only been a nightmare.

How it was finally done he wasn't sure yet, but he was working on it, working hard every day so he could pass it on to his friends. Part of it, he knew, was memory, part of it love, and a third part . . . something else, the missing link, the invisible man.

He clapped once and laughed aloud, and much louder when a group of teenagers stared at him as though he were ready to drool and drop his pants. Then he rushed home and shaved, changed, dug his checkbook out of the dresser drawer and went down to stand in the kitchen doorway.

Ellen was at the sink, washing dishes; Bert was at the table, reading the paper; and Ally, dear Ally, was sprawled on the floor amid her crayons and paper, drawing pictures of the animals she loved in the zoo.

His daughter saw him first, and scowled: "It's too hot for that suit, Father. You'll have a stroke."

"Pop," said Bert, shaking out the wrinkles after turning the page, "you'd better check to be sure you have your key. I'm locking up when we leave, and I'm not turning around just because you can't get in."

Ally ignored him.

He nodded, and left, determined not to let them spoil his day, more so when he saw Doris and Marsha waiting at the park bench. They could easily have been mother and daughter, and when he joined them, he waved his hand like a magic wand and they were a family. They laughed at his terrible

jokes, endured his streaks of nostalgia, and chided him whenever he grew testy at the crowds jostling them at the zoo.

After dinner at the best restaurant he could afford, he paid
the check with a flourish; after the movie, he walked them
home with a sword at his hip and a cloak over one shoulder,
and a great white plume streaming back in the wind.

It was perfect, even to the loving goodnight kiss and near
shoving of Marsha through the front door so they could be
alone, on the swing, on the porch.

"Lovely day, John, thank you," she said, resting her
cheek on his shoulder.

"Careful there," he warned with a glance to the window.
"Your son sees us like this, he'll call the cops."

She laughed silently, and took his hand. "John, are you all
right?"

"Fit as a fiddle, and twice as bold."

"You know what I mean."

He pushed gently with his feet and set the swing in motion,
listening to the steady creak of the chains in their hooks, the
boards at their back. A bat swept out of the darkness, and
swept back again. He could feel the softness of her hand, the
softness of her cheek, and he could easily imagine having that
forever.

"I'm getting old, Doris," he said quietly, at last.

She nodded.

"I've done a few things . . . that is, I've tried damned hard
not to be lonely and alone at the same time, if you know what
I mean." She did, with a squeeze. "I think, though, folks
don't mind as much anymore when two old—" He stopped
himself, and blushed. "That is, when two venerable senior
citizens decide to . . ." He stopped again, and snarled at the
street. "Damn."

"Yes," she said. "I know what you mean."

A sigh that lingered long after the sound.

"We'll have to talk about it," he said.

"Yes."

"Your kids seem to like me."

"More than you know, dear."

"I'm not about to drop tomorrow, you know."

She squeezed his hand again. "Like you said, we'll talk."

He saw her to the door, kissed her lightly, and was delighted that a kiss never changed.

Free, he thought as he nearly ran home; oh god almighty, I'm free, damnit, I'm free.

When he got home and unlocked the door, they were waiting—Ellen in her chair, Bert in his, and Ally in her nightgown standing on the stairs. He almost cried.

"Damnit, you were supposed to go away for the weekend," he said angrily.

"I changed my mind," Ellen told him.

Ally nodded.

Bert only looked at him as if it were his fault.

"But you were supposed to go!" he insisted, stomping into the living room to stand in front of Ellen. "Who told you you could change your mind? I never said anything about changing your mind. Damnit, Ellen—"

"Father, don't swear."

"But damnit—"

"Pop, not in front of the girl."

Bewildered, he looked at each of them closely, thinking that perhaps someone had finally believed him and had brought in doubles to play a joke on him. But no, they were there. Right there. Just as he'd decreed when he refused them their dying once the funeral was over, just as he'd ordered when he demanded that his life not be lonely anymore.

His family. Doing what they always did, for as long as he'd known them. Doing what *he* wanted, because he was in charge.

"I've changed my mind," he said suddenly, thinking of Doris and Marsha and the fun that they'd had. "You can leave now. You can really leave, go where you have to. I . . . I don't want you anymore."

"Father, go to bed."

"Pop, it's late. Don't you think you ought to get some rest?"

"Come on, Grampa, I'll walk you up."

"Damnit," he shouted, "didn't you hear me? I don't need you now. I've got someone else!"

"Grampa, come *on*! I have to sleep, too."

Ellen turned her face to the TV screen, Bert picked up his book, and suddenly the house was quiet, and cold.

He followed the girl up the stairs in silence, followed her down the hall and into his room. Stood dumbly while she took off his jacket and unbuttoned his shirt; shifted only when she nudged him to take off his slacks, his shoes, and his socks. Then he sat on the mattress and watched her pick out his pajamas, fluff the pillow, and push him down slowly until he stared at the ceiling.

The light went out.

The door closed.

He lay on the bed and watched the stars come out, watched the streetlamps flicker on, watched the windows across the way wink out to black.

A tear in his eye, a lump in his throat.

He was crazy, and he knew it at last. He had to be, because his family was changing. They had been wonderful when alive, were growing horrid in death; they had been caring, now didn't care; they had structured their lives around him, now didn't give a damn.

If he was sane, that wouldn't happen; if he was sane, and simply a little lonely, they would be the same as always, ready to fill his time when he wanted it; ready to fight with him when he was cranky, love him when he was sad, be tender to him when the holidays came.

A tear in his eye, and his hands clenched the sheet.

He was losing his mind, because they couldn't change, they were dead.

And the following morning the dead girl sat on the edge of his bed and said, "Grampa, Grampa, tell me a story."

What Are Deaths For

WHEN MILT HEARD the crash in the front yard, he was sitting in the kitchen, wearing his old plaid bathrobe, old brown slippers, old white pajamas, and basking in a rare sunlit morning that made the room seem less a manufacturer's showcase than a place where someone could sit down, get a good cup of coffee, and reflect on the way things were going in one's life. It wasn't, he admitted when he'd had a few too many, the greatest kitchen in the world, and it wasn't the greatest house in the world, but it was, on this morning, very much his home.

The crash, then, was less alarming than it was intrusive.

"Oh, my heavens, good Lord," Evelyn said without much alarm, "what was that?" She was at the sink, rinsing off the breakfast dishes and listening to the local classical music station. Milt didn't mind; he simply tuned the music out until the network news came on.

"What do you think? Damned fools knocked over the damned garbage cans again," he said without rancor. A snort for a laugh, and he leaned back in his chair, looking to the back door where the sun was gold and the grass was green and a pair of squirrels were fighting over an acorn. "That's the third time this month. Must be some kind of record. I should send them a letter, tell them how proud I am, the city ought to give them a raise so they'll do even better next time."

"Milt, don't be silly," his wife said absently. "You know, maybe you should get one of those plastic ones, they come in green, I think. Maybe they'd be better."

With a loud and satisfying groan he stretched the sleep from his legs, from his arms, and shook his head. "Nope, I won't do that. Things are so cheap they'd crack, split like a melon, and then I'd have to replace them. The tin ones are loud, but they're cheaper in the long run."

She turned off the faucet then, herded the water to the drain with the side of her hand, and peered down the hall toward the front, as though she'd just remembered the sound they had heard. After a moment, Milt did the same, half-rising with a puzzled frown because this time the crash seemed different. There was a silence now, not the bang and clatter that usually came when the garbage truck ground its gears and backed away from its damage.

A silence he wanted suddenly to fill, and didn't know how.

"I think," said Evelyn with a nervous flutter of her hand, "I'll wax the floor. I haven't done it in ages. It must be filthy, and that's not healthy."

"Yeah," he said, still looking down the hall.

She bit down on her lower lip, put a hand through the hair once a soft brown and now brown-and-grey.

He started for the door.

"Milt," she said, "do you think it's—"

"I don't know." He paused, and wiped his hands on his robe. "I don't know."

"It probably isn't," she said, her tone falsely bright, a smile at her lips that lasted only a second. "I mean, it's been a while since last time, hasn't it? Four or five weeks, as I recall. It's probably over, right? I think it's over, don't you?"

He gave her no answer. He only stood there, breathing deeply, one hand slowly brushing his cheek.

Evelyn half-turned, not sure whether to sit or follow. "I

wish we'd never done it." Her voice was low, and touched with regret, dusted with fatigue. "It's a terrible thing, Milt, to say it, but I wish—"

"Yeah. I know."

"But you'll go?"

"I have to. Suppose . . . suppose someone needs help."

A sigh, barely heard. "Be careful," she said, drying her hands hard on her apron.

He waved a *sure I will stop worrying* behind him, and when he reached the front he pulled aside the flimsy curtain that covered the door's leaded double panes. The sun's early glare blinded him, and he swore without opening his mouth, blinked away a tear the light drew from his eye. Then he took hold of the knob, hesitated again, and went out to the porch.

For the briefest of moments he held his breath—the neighborhood seemed the same.

Then a loud popping sound made him blink, made him look again at the place where he had heard the crash.

There was a car in his yard, its rear tire flattening one of his new garbage cans, its front bumper slammed into the willow he'd been trying to grow. The windshield was cracked, there was steam drifting from beneath the hood, and the passenger door was open, a hand dangling red beneath it.

Hell, he thought wearily; oh, hell.

He yelled for Evelyn to get the blankets and first aid kit, then hurried as fast as he could down the steps and across the grass. He paid no attention to the fact that the houses across the street, that the corner only five houses down the way, that the sky, the sun, the very air seemed lost in a dim yellow haze. Instead, he took a glance at the five-year-old tree (damn, what a mess, that'll never come back), then flinched when something sparked and crackled inside the engine. An arm up as if warding off fire, and he walked around the door, looked in, and shook his head.

The driver was a stout woman, middle-aged, and thrown against the steering wheel, her white-gloved hands clutching the dashboard. Blood ran freely down the side of her face, and her left foot jerked in spasms on the brake pedal. As far as he could tell, she wasn't breathing.

The hand belonged to another woman, maybe younger than the first, he thought as he knelt and touched the wrist for a pulse. She was spilled into the well in front of her seat, her hair thrown over her face, and he couldn't be sure that the blood on her hand wasn't from the driver.

"Christ, get 'em out of there, Lowe," a harsh voice ordered behind him.

He looked over his shoulder at Ben Grapinski and scowled.

"Suppose she's hurt bad," he said. "I could kill her if I move her, hurt something inside."

Grapinski rubbed a large hand over an unshaven jaw. "I guess you could, at that." His suspenders were hanging at his waist, and his waist was hanging a good five inches over his trousers. He was a retired steelworker, and the furnace still showed in his cracked and stained face. "But it don't seem right, you know what I mean? We oughta be able to do something, y'know?"

Milt turned away, and moved a bit closer, holding his breath when the engine sparked again.

The woman jammed in the well was still, and he laid a gentle hand on her shoulder. Her blouse was cream silk, the feel of it cool and slippery. He brushed back her hair and saw that she was indeed younger. A teenager; by the look of her, no more than sixteen. Her face where it wasn't bleeding was mottled with freckles.

Maybe, he thought, Ben's right. Maybe we ought to lift her out and put her on the lawn. Get a blanket. Get a pillow.

Maybe this time—

"She dead?" A different voice. Elena Martinez, of the black mole on the chin and the black dye in her hair and her late husband's shirts she always wore over a bosom that defied the laws of nature.

"She looks dead to me."

"She looks unconscious," he said, faintly scolding, "and I don't know if I should move her."

Water hissed out of the radiator, dropped onto the engine and hissed louder. There was the stench of warm gasoline, and the flat odor of spilled oil.

"Heard the crash while I was putting in my teeth," Ben said to Elena. "Thought it was one of them idiot kids finally doing us a favor and doing himself in. They deserve it, you know. Racing to school like that, using our block like it was a speedway or something. They deserve it."

"They gotta have their fun," Elena said without arguing.

"Yeah, I suppose."

Milt perched as best he could on the doorsill, pushing the tail of his robe out of the way, feeling the damp grass tickle his ankles. He couldn't bring himself to take hold of the blood-reddened hand, so he tried to find a pulse in the younger woman's neck. Then he tried to put his hand over her heart, but she was twisted away from him, and besides, it wouldn't look right; he wasn't a ghoul, he only wanted to help. He lowered himself to the ground then, and crouched, trying to get a good look at her face.

Someone opened the driver's side door.

"Good lord! Godalmighty, I haven't seen this much blood since the war."

"What war was that?" Ben asked, an elbow nudging Elena. "The Spanish-American?"

Lace Pepper glared myopically through the car over the dead woman's head. He was wearing a dark pin-striped suit, a muted red tie, and in his left hand he carried a tan leather briefcase. He hadn't been in an office in nearly twelve years, but habits, for him, simply didn't die. "You know damned well what war I mean, Benjamin. And isn't anyone going to help her out of there? This is disgraceful."

"She's dead," Elena said mildly, pulling a cigarette out of her hip pocket. "A blind man can see that."

"Disgraceful," Pepper muttered. "Milt, don't you think it's disgraceful?"

The car creaked, parts of it snapping softly while the steam rose more thickly from the hood and clung to the air like a fog refusing to leave at the warning of the sun. In the back seat a single flame poked out of the upholstery.

"Fire," said Ben calmly while he pulled up his suspenders.

Milt was almost forehead to forehead with the young woman, and his right hand was slowly, painfully, turning her face to his. When at last he could see it all, from the deep scratches on the brow to the fist-sized bruise on her left cheek, he blinked rapidly and almost pulled his hand away.

I know this child.

A quick look to the dead woman, but there was no recognition. She was a complete stranger, yet this other one, this one with the freckles and the blond hair and the faint shadow of a dimple in the middle of her chin . . .

I know this child.

"Impossible," he muttered.

"Suit yourself," Grapinski said, "but it looks like the car's on fire to me."

"I shall fetch an extinguisher," Pepper said indignantly, "since none of you seem eager to do anything but stand around and gawk."

"I ain't gawking," Elena said, lighting her cigarette from a match she accepted from Ben. "I'm just an innocent bystander."

"Me, too," Grapinski said. "Me, too."

Then Elena, grunting and mumbling, hunkered down as best she could behind Milt and stared hard at the girl's face. He looked at her, an eyebrow raised in question, and Elena's complexion paled just slightly. For a moment he saw the glitter of a tear in one eye, a tic at the corner of her mouth; just for a moment, and then they were gone. The woman puffed on her cigarette and rose, walked away slowly and stood with her back to the car. Grapinski watched her, puzzlement on his face until he too crouched down and examined the passenger.

"What do you think, Ben?" he asked without taking his gaze from her face.

"Jeez, it's . . . no."

"Yes."

The old steelworker turned and stood beside the widow.

Milt took his hand away, put it on the small of his back and stood, groaning slightly at the sudden ache in the muscle. Then he let himself check the street.

It was still empty.

There was no one on the sidewalks, no one on the porches. He looked behind him, and Evelyn was standing in the doorway. He beckoned, and she balked; he beckoned again, insisting, and she came, hesitantly, eyeing the car as though it were about to leap away from the tree and crush her. When she reached him, she put an arm around his waist and forced herself to look inside.

"The phone's dead," she said dully. "I tried to call an ambulance but the phone's dead."

He nodded, and made her look again.

"My god," she said, with a hand to her mouth.

Elena and Ben joined them; Lance Pepper returned with the fire extinguisher, put down his briefcase at a safe distance, folded his jacket on top of it, and rolled up his sleeves. Then he stepped forward, aimed the spray first into the back, then at the hood which steamed even more, thickening the fog that now hazed the sun. When he was finished, he threw the canister away, redressed, and walked over. A nod from Milt, and he looked inside.

"She's dead," insisted the oldest man on the block. "She's dead."

"She's right there, Lance," Milt told him. "She's right there in that front seat."

"Nope. She's dead. I am certain that she is dead because I was at the funeral with the rest of you. She is dead."

"Well," Elena said, "she's dead again in Milt's front yard."

Ben rubbed her shoulders until she jerked away, looked to Lance and shrugged with a grin. Looked to Milt and said, "Where is everyone? Where'd they all go?"

"Well, where the hell were they the first time?" Milt said angrily, so close to shouting he could feel the heat bloom on his face. Evelyn took his arm and squeezed it gently. He closed his eyes, blew out a breath, and waited. "It's okay. I'm okay." He turned to Ben and pointed across the street, toward the neighbors they couldn't see. "They didn't help the first time, right? They just let the girl lie in the car and bleed to death. We were the ones who called the ambulance. We were the ones who made the tourniquets and brought out the bandages and blankets. We were the ones who tried to save her, not them."

Elena daubed a tissue against each eye. "It ain't fair, though, you know? It ain't fair they don't help."

Ben nodded.

Lance sniffed, knelt by the car and touched the young woman's hair. "She's still alive."

Milt stared, then rushed to help the old man as they gently, so terribly gently, eased the trapped girl out of the car. Sparks flared and showered from under the dashboard. The fog thickened until they could barely see Milt's house. Elena tore off her shirt and shoved it into a pillow to put under the girl's head; Evelyn raced inside for a blanket and the first aid kit; Ben knelt on the grass and felt for the girl's pulse; and Lance rose, dusted himself off and stared at the battered willow.

"That thing'll never grow now, Milt."

"No kidding," he muttered, brushing the golden hair away from the girl's face. Younger than he thought, he noted as he felt her skin beneath his fingers. Much younger. He looked up at Elena.

She leaned close, and raked a hand over her scalp.

Ben was puzzled.

Lance Pepper marched around to the other side of the car, pulled open the door, and dragged the dead woman out without so much as a grimace, skipping to one side quickly when a brief spurt of blood threatened to stain his shirt. A shake of his head in sympathy, and he loosened his tie, scowled, and took it off and stuffed it in his back pocket.

Evelyn returned and they did what they could, Ben hovering while the women administered and Milt stood away from the steaming hood with Lance.

"She's younger," he said.

"So I noticed," Lance said.

"Younger than last time, I mean."

"Yes. I know."

He pulled his robe more snugly over his chest, shivering at the mist that settled over the yard. "If this keeps up, she'll be a baby."

Lance only nodded.

Elena rocked back on her heels and sighed loudly, reached down and pulled her shirt from under the bloodied head. A stare, and she slipped it on. Evelyn sobbed once, then took one of the blankets and placed it over the girl's face. Ben muttered something and stalked away a few feet, his back to the others, his thumbs hooked in his suspenders. Then suddenly he turned with a groan, and they watched him.

"How many times?" he demanded, hands out in anguish. "How many goddamn times?"

"I don't know," Milt said.

"Why, then?"

Evelyn pushed herself to her feet and brushed off her apron, helped Elena up and they all walked toward the porch. "I think I know," she said.

Milt smiled. His wife probably did know, and was probably right, and what good would that be if this was going to happen for the rest of their lives?

"Good Samaritans, or fools, are hard to come by these days," she said, settling into the rocker while Ben and Lance leaned against the railing and her husband stood behind her and Elena stayed by the steps. "Lawsuits and things keep people from helping. We did. And the family knew it and they didn't sue when the girl died.''

''So?''

''So . . .'' A shudder made Milt hold her shoulders tightly, and she looked up at him gratefully. He winked, and she nodded; there was no need to go on. If the others didn't get it now, they would, sooner or later. Sooner or later they would know how it is with people who need help.

They search for it until they find it.

And when they find it they don't let go.

The engine snapped, the tires settled, and the girl on the ground suddenly sat up, groaned, screamed as though she were being strangled, and slumped back. A streak of blood ran from the corner of her mouth, and her left leg spasmed, throwing off her shoe.

Then she was still, and the fog soon covered her—her, her companion, and the hissing, snapping car.

''Damn,'' Ben said softly, angrily. ''Damn.''

Milt looked at him, and was horrified. There was an expression on the steelworker's face he'd never seen before, not in all the times he thought the garbage cans had been crushed by the truck, not in all the times Ben had gently swabbed off the blood and laid the girl's head on the pillow.

He looked to Elena, and saw the same.

Lance Pepper refused to look at any of them.

''Milt?''

He wouldn't look around. He saw her expression in the tone of her voice, and he couldn't believe it, wouldn't believe that his wife of thirty years was thinking the same thing—that they should have let the girl die without offering any help.

He was cold, then, deeply and deathly cold.

And it had nothing to do with the light breeze that came up, that swirled through the fog and husked the branches on the willow, that soon cleared the yard, the sidewalk, and the street.

When it was done, the willow was alone.

"Gotta make lunch," Elena said with a clap of her hands that made the others jump. "Hungry, y'know?"

"I," said Lance Pepper, "have the morning paper to read."

"Going bowling," Ben said, nodding to Evelyn, smiling at Milt. "Half-price until six." He mimed casting a ball at the pins, snapped his suspenders and grinned. "Average is up this year. Still got the old half-alley curve, you know what I mean?"

They left, skirting the place where the car and the blood had been, not looking at the grass where the young girl had died. Lance seemed older; Elena didn't look back, Ben got as far as the sidewalk before he turned around and came back.

"Listen," he said after looking around to be sure the others had gone. "Listen, I . . . I don't want no help."

Evelyn swallowed, and gripped Milt's shoulders.

"I mean, we know each other a lot of years, right? We know each other pretty good."

Milt nodded, still cold, wanting to go inside and forget the little girl, forget what will happen when she returns as a baby.

"If . . ." The steelworker scratched his neck fiercely. "If I need help, I don't want it, okay? I just want to die." He glared then, accusingly. "You keep your goddamn morals to yourself." His eyes filled, and he turned away sharply, almost running to the pavement. "Let me alone," he called without looking back. "Just leave me the hell alone."

Milt waited for ten minutes more before he pushed himself out of the chair and followed his wife into the kitchen. He wasn't liking himself very much, and wasn't liking her either. Not for what she had thought, nor because he was cold because he agreed, but because he wished to hell that once, just once, he could punch through that girl's pain and tell her to find someone else. That he was tired. That he couldn't do what she wanted, he couldn't bring her back. That he refused to accept the cup she thrust into his hands.

He refused, but she wouldn't leave.

She was too soon dead, she didn't like it, and she wanted him to do it again.

She wanted him to play savior, just one more time.

He knew how Ben felt, and didn't blame him a bit.

Evelyn fussed a bit at the sink, then pulled off her apron and hung it on the knob of the cabinet underneath. Then she took the chair opposite him and divided the paper, sports for him, front page for her.

"How long between?" she asked finally. "I forget."

"I don't know," he said, scanning the box scores and shaking his head. "It varies, I think." He managed a brief smile. "At least there's something about it that doesn't let us remember all that time between."

"Ben does," she said, tracing headlines with a finger. "I don't know why."

Neither did he, and he wasn't going to call the man and ask. All he knew was, sooner or later they'd be out there again, the girl would be younger, and they'd still be unable to call any professional help. It would be up to them. Only them. Trying to save a girl who continued to die.

They ate lunch, cleared the dishes, and Milt helped his wife with the waxing of the floor. Then they decided to dress up a little and spend some time in town, have dinner out, see a movie, come home late and sleep until noon. They laughed quite a bit before they were done, only a faint disturbance at the back of their minds, something not right, something out of place they couldn't pin down.

The moon was up. So was the wind.

Milt had the key in the lock when he heard the crash behind him, felt the brief blast of hot air.

"I'm not going to do it," he said to the door. "I'm not going to do it!"

Evelyn closed her eyes. "Milt? All that talk this afternoon . . . I mean, suppose it's Ben? Suppose it's Ben and he needs us?"

He didn't care. Suddenly, and completely, he just didn't give a damn. Ben was right. They were all right. And he didn't hate himself a bit when he wished that damned girl had died right away.

Jesus, he thought, what the hell were deaths for if not for dying? How the hell could anyone find peace when there was some doddering old do-gooder waiting to ruin the only certain thing left?

"No," he said. "No, I'm not going to do it."

Evelyn turned around.

"Oh, Milt," she said, her voice filled with despair.

Elena was already there, and Lance in his suit.

The girl was in the well, no older than twelve.

Ben was in the back seat, twenty years younger.

"Get the blankets," Milt said, weeping. "I think we'll be here a while."

Poor Thing

THE SILENCE WAS born of the fall of the snow, muffling in dead white the sound of passing tires, smothering in dead white the wind in the trees; it settled over the streets and laid a shroud on the lawns, prettified the houses like waxen corpses in coffins; no birds flew, no dogs barked, the cats in their prowling were confined to the porch; a soft silence, a gentle one, that increased as the snow did, to bury the town.

Deeper as the night deepened, until radios were turned on and televisions blared and not a few fights were started just to make a little noise.

Peering through the tall windows, breath fogging the panes, watching the snow as it slow-filled the gutters, spilled over the curbs, erased all the drives and the sidewalks and steps; wiping off condensation with the heel of a hand, smearing the inside and smearing the white and smearing the face of the man standing in the yard.

Tall. Thin. Black, and waiting.

Robin stepped away with a denying shake of his head, bumped into his father's chair and spun around to apologize, caught himself before he woke the old man and restarted the argument that had been cooking for years. His lower lip curled under, his teeth came down, and he nipped at himself to feel the pain, and the shame.

Damn, he thought with a slow shake of his head, it wasn't the old guy's fault that the stroke hadn't been stronger, or hadn't been weaker, but perfect in its effects to numb the once clever brain and palsy the once steady hands. He could walk with a cane when he felt like walking, and he could feed himself when he felt like eating, use the bathroom, once in a while with the aid of a glass read one of his favorite books when the mood and the light came. But he forgot where he was, and he forgot what he was saying, and half the time he forgot that son Robin was the only one left with him in the house.

He fingered a cigarette from his shirt pocket, lit it, and turned back to the living room window. The room was at the side of the house, two windows square to the wall and facing the street, two others angled outward so he could see, if he wanted, the front yard and back just by pulling the drapes aside.

The snow was fine, barely disturbing the streetlamp on the corner; the snow was steady, having covered the grass at noon, most of the shrubs by sunset. It piled on the outside sill, and it caught in the cracks of the clapboard and the stone foundation

There was no one in the yard.

He crossed his arms over his chest and hunched his shoulders, made himself shudder in order to feel warm, then reached down to brush a finger over the radiator. It was warm, but the room was still chilled, and would be for some time. The house was old, twice as old as his father, and neither the first owner nor the old man had bothered to install insulation or new thermal windows because other expenses were too great and more urgent too much of the time.

Upstairs it was a freezer, and he dreaded the thought of going to bed. The sheets would be ice, the blankets too heavy, and the feathers in his new pillow were already working their way through to stab at his temples and scrape at his ears.

A glance to the mantel, and the clock told him ten. Local news, and with a look to the sleeping man, he turned on the television, sat in his own chair and watched for reports of how deep the snow would be.

After fifteen minutes, he was almost convinced the second Ice Age had arrived. The roads were blocked with snow and snow plows and snow-bound cars; schools and most businesses were to close the next day, and no one was promising that the buses would be running, much less on time.

Damnit, Dad, he thought, why the hell couldn't you live in Florida with the rest of the old farts.

Someone tapped on the window.

Robin turned quickly, so quickly he felt something catch in his neck, and he grabbed at it, wincing, while he peered over his father's chair. The standing lamp to one side blinded the pane, but he wouldn't get up.

And someone tapped on the window.

He frowned in self-disgust, at the jumping in his stomach, and pushed himself to his feet, checked his father for signs of stirring, and hurried out to the kitchen. Either it was the taxus beneath the window tossed by the wind, or it was someone whose car had stalled and needed the phone to get a tow.

But he left the lights off, leaned over the sink and looked through the window to see who was there.

A man in a dark coat, standing in the snow.

Tall. Thin. Black-shadow, and waiting.

Robin stepped away before he could be seen, looked to the wall phone with the brief notion of calling the police. He dismissed it at once. Prowlers in the middle of a blizzard were improbable; besides, the police would have their hands filled with accidents and true emergencies.

A weapon of his own, then, in case the man tried to break in.

He rummaged through all the drawers, and the best he could come up with was a dull carving knife whose blade was scarred with ill-use. He hefted it, and leaned over the sink again.

The man was gone, and there were no footprints in the snow.

All right, he told himself, sniffing, scratching his brow, squinting in the half dark, all right, you're not going crazy, it's just that you're tired. You've been up since dawn, remember, since Dad called out in his sleep. A nightmare. Muttering about things that had happened sixty, seventy years ago. He had heard his grandmother's name, his uncle's, the name of the Irish setter the family had owned. A snatch of lullaby, and a few nursery rhymes he hadn't heard since his mother had died in her sleep.

He yawned, then, and stretched, and saw the knife's blade reaching up toward the ceiling, catching the light from the living room lamps and spearing it at his eyes. He turned away and lowered his arm, walked to the front door and looked out with caution.

The hedge was a white wall, the street indistinguishable from the sidewalks and lawns. What shadows there were, were grey and unformed; the air sparkled, the snow glittered, and a garbage can had been transformed to a headstone at the curb.

The house grew colder.

With a string of impotent curses aimed at the storm, he stalked back to the kitchen and flung open the cellar door. Switched on the light. Tramped down as loudly as he could in a childhood game to drive off the demons. Another light, this one dangling overhead midway to the back, and he stood with hands on his hips and glared at the furnace.

He could hear nothing.

The damned thing was dead.

The back of the hand that held the knife pressed to his brow and he distinctly remembered paying the last oil bill, seeing the delivery truck only last week pull into the driveway and fill up the tank. Wishing he'd listened to his father and had learned something about how it worked, he poked, peered, slapped at the cold metal sides. Nothing worked. The gauges were still. There was no comforting rush of fire, no hiss of warm air as it entered the pipes.

He kicked it, then, and slapped at the light and set it

swinging, kicking his shadow in a frenzy side to side, making him dizzy as the walls closed in and the walls drew away, and the steps to the kitchen multiplied and faded. He barely made it to the top. And when he did, he slammed the door, and heard the old man grunt in his sleep.

A quick rush of guilt replaced by slow anger.

Dumb, he thought. There had been warnings of the storm for nearly four days, plenty of time to have someone in to check on the heating. His father, however, had said nothing about it, and it hadn't occurred to him that the house didn't run on its own. It always had before. The water in the faucets, the radiators clanking and banging, the food in the refrigerator, the screens and the storm windows, the toilets and showers and bathtubs when you needed them.

The old man's doing, of course. The magic old man with the magic old tools, swallowed by the sink when a washer wore out, scuttling in the cellar when a pipe threatened to break, stomping around the attic when a shingle worked loose and he claimed he could fix it without climbing outside.

Everything, he thought, boiled down to the old man.

A draught chilled his ankles, and he skipped away from it, to the stove where he put the kettle in its place and turned on the burner.

God, it's cold, he thought, and after dropping the knife on the counter he hurried back to his father, still deep in sleep. His face, once round, was now gaunt and sagging; his hair once black, was now unpleasantly grey. Cheekbones and jaw clearly part of a skull, hands clasped against tremors were gleaming and thin. He muttered for a moment, shifted his head, settled down. His eyelids were fluttering, a dream not to share.

Robin unfolded a lap robe from the couch and placed it over the man's knees, tucked it in, smoothed it out, thought of waking him and asking him how to fix the damned heat.

But that too would start the argument again: *Robin, when are you gonna learn to do things on your own? When are you gonna learn I won't live forever?*

The wind picked up, soughing now and testing the windows, finding the cracks, bold enough to slip down the chimney to spin the ashes like dust devils without leaving the hearth.

Someone tapped on the window.

Robin swore and ran to it, shoved the drapes farther aside and leaned on the sill, his forehead pressed to the glass.

His father mumbled.

The snow rode the wind and carved *things* in the street, smoothed out the drifts, and not once touched the man who stood in the yard.

Tall. Thin. Black-shadow, red eyes, unmoving, and waiting.

The house, colder still.

He slammed a fist against the pane, pulling his punch just in time not to break it. Whoever that fool was, and whatever he wanted, he wasn't going to force him into doing something stupid. If he wanted to play games while he froze to death out there, that was his problem, not Robin's; he could stay there until spring for all Robin cared.

The old man mumbled, the dream starting to surface.

Robin headed for the kitchen again, to check on the kettle and to call the police and the hell with the snow, but a glance at his father stopped him in mid-stride. His lips were turning blue, and his lower lip was quivering; his right leg was jumping slightly, and in his sleep he had pulled the lap robe to his chin.

Christ, Robin thought, he's freezing to death; and he gaped when he saw his breath fogging the air.

Well, at least he won't have to show me how to freeze myself to death.

He raced upstairs, into his room, and pulled on a heavy sweater, grabbed one for the old man and started back down the hall. Stopped. Turned. Looked into his parents' room, and remembered the days when the lamps were always lit and the music box played Strauss and the smell of lavender seemed to waft from the deep cedar drawers of his mother's low dresser. The old days, that was, before he had left for college, had left to study law and establish his own firm. Before he knew that the law was not what he wanted, before he had changed his mind at thirty to try banking instead.

To try insurance.

To try sales.

To stand by his mother's grave and have his father turn around with a baleful glare: *You didn't kill her, don't worry, but you might as well have, never knowing your mind, letting me do it all for you.*

Like working for the old man in construction, in design, not really good, but good enough to live and see tangible proof of what he had done with his hands, and his father's constant help.

He supposed, as he headed back down the stairs, that he should resent his father for guiding his life as closely as he had, but he knew that sometimes plans didn't work out. Parents didn't get the geniuses they ordered, and children didn't get the instant riches they wanted. He supposed, too, that he could make a case for interference, that the old man never truly let him have his head, never really let him go in spite of the degree and the moving out of state and the marriage that didn't work and the grandchild stillborn. When he reached the landing, he supposed a third time that he could have told the old man there were plenty of others like his only son, men who searched through their lives for the one thing to sustain them, finding it on occasion and sometimes not all.

He supposed.

But it didn't do any good.

The last thing his father had told him before the stroke was that Robin, for all his training, for all his books, for all his unproductive dreams, was like the namesake bird in his mother's favorite rhyme, hiding from winter in an unheated barn.

Y'know, his father said, *when it comes time t'die, I'll probably have to show you how.*

Someone tapped on the back door.

Robin froze, looking down the length of the house, through

the foyer, the dining room, and into the kitchen where he saw the man on the back steps.

That, he thought, is damned enough of that.

He strode toward the man, heels hard on the hardwood floors, his arms swinging, his expression as grim as he could possibly make it. As he passed the counter he grabbed the knife; as he passed the sink he glanced out the window and saw the snow coating the glass with the beginning of frost; as he reached the door to the service porch he saw the man back away. Straight away. As if the steps weren't there.

The brass doorknob was cold.

The wind shook the house now, bearing down out of the north and whipping the storm into lashes of white.

His ears began to sting, and his nose began to run, and when he heard his father cry out, he ignored it and opened the door.

The service porch was tiny, cluttered with mops and brooms and buckets and dusting rags. A shovel was propped against one wall, a rake against the other. The outer door to the steps was narrow and mostly glass, and he could see perfectly the man standing in the yard between the house and the garage.

Tall. Thin. Black-shadow and red eyes, and a great slouched hat that didn't move in the wind.

His father cried out again.

He raised the knife in clear warning, cursed the old man for having a crisis now, and spun around, slammed the inner door and ran into the living room.

There was mucus on the old man's upper lip, spittle on his chin, and his eyes were opened wide, cataract white. His slippered feet were drumming on the floor, his hands were strangling the lap robe, and as Robin approached him, the old man screamed.

And stopped.

And tried to stand up, his left hand groping for his cane, his right scything the air in front of his face.

Robin reached for him to press him down, telling him urgently he had a sweater here for him, that the furnace was

out, that the house was too cold and there was some nut
outside, they were going to have to leave as soon as he could
get hold of the emergency squad and would he please, for
god's sake *please* shut the hell up!

Someone tapped on the window.

The wind. The snow.

Robin dropped to his knees and put his hands over his
head, willing the world to get away from him now, he'd
learned his lesson, he knew he couldn't make it, couldn't
even start up a fire to keep the old man warm. He knew it. He
was ready. He wanted to die, he was tired of playing the
game.

Someone tapped on the window.

The old man sighed.

Robin looked up, his eyes filled with tears, and saw the red
eyes in the window, saw the white eyes in his father, saw the
smile on his face.

And what will the robin do, poor thing? the old man
whispered.

Robin backed away on his hands and knees.

He'll sit in the barn

Robin stood and clenched his fists, and told the old man for
the first time in his life exactly what he thought of him,
exactly how he felt, and told him with a venom he didn't
know he had, that he was going to leave the old bastard to die
here, in the dark.

Where he can keep warm

He ran into the foyer, to the closet where he punched into
his coat, swung a scarf around his throat, and grabbed his
gloves from the shelf where his father's gloves lay. Then he
locked the front door, turned the thermostat up as far as it
would go in case of a miracle and he really wasn't insane,
and returned to the living room where the old man was
smiling.

"Go to hell, Dad," he said. "You're not running me this
time."

He left through the kitchen, not bothering to check for the

blackshadow man. Plowed through the snow to the garage, and had just opened the car door when he stopped, cocked his head, and listened.

There was silence born of the fall of the snow, nothing moving, only waiting. The air sparkling, the trees glinting, the streetlamps gone out to add to the night.

The cold or a wind-slammed branch must have broken a pane in the house; as he slid in behind the wheel he could still hear his father.

With his head tucked under his wing.

Robin started the engine with a laugh dry and bitter.

Poor thing.

And looked up when he heard someone tap on the window.

To Laugh With You, Dear

THE LIVING ROOM was always too warm for comfort. Heat pulsed from the grilled vents set into the baseboards, and clouded from the fireplace where the logs were piled high. The bay window was sealed with transparent plastic, and the windows flanking the mantel were behind heavy drapes. The sliding doors to the foyer were kept closed. The lights were all on.

There were three places to sit in the rather large room—a dark leather club chair studded with dull brass, a love seat in crushed velvet whose cushions were worn like the knees of serge suits and whose springs were sagging almost down to the floor, and a padded deacon's bench in front of the bay window, facing the street through a haze of hanging plants.

The wallpaper was cluttered with fading vines of pink roses, while the trim and the ceiling were long-ago white. By the loveseat was a scallop-edged table that held an empty ashtray once a seashell. An ottoman by the club chair with a fringe mostly missing. A poker lying on the hearth, grey with cold ashes.

Over the mantel was a portrait, a man sitting down and a woman standing behind him, their faces long buried by a powdering of dust.

Bremer sat in the club chair and lowered his gaze from the

portrait to stare at the flames. His cardigan was grey, open, and frayed, and though he knew he should take it off, he knew he'd feel naked without it. His white shirt was gaping at elbow and collar; his trousers were corduroy and loose at the cuffs, bagging at the knees, snug around the waist, sagging in the seat whenever he stood; his green-and-brown argyles had slipped almost down to his ankles, and the soles of his slippers had two holes each.

The living room was always too warm for comfort, and he was getting tired.

"I think," he said with a decisive shake of his shoulders, "it's time I died."

There was no response, and he frowned, cleared his throat and said it again, more loudly: "I think, damnit, it's time that I died."

"Don't be silly."

"Well, why not?" He plucked at his trousers, at his sweater, at his shirt. "Have you looked at me lately?"

"You look all right to me."

A smile. Brief, not quite bitter. But it stirred his lips and set a tremor through his cheeks and made his pale blue eyes narrow to a squint.

"That's typical of you, you know," he said with just a trace of scolding. "You'd say that even if you saw me in my grave ten years from now. The worms, you'd say, set off nicely my natural coloration."

No answer; and he looked to the couch, looked to the bench, decided she was standing just behind the chair where he wouldn't be able to see her. She did that a lot, now as well as then, hiding from him in case he should see the truth in her eyes. He could always do that, see what she was thinking when he looked in her eyes. Nothing was ever hidden. Ask the proper question and all was revealed, and no amount of protest could swing the argument out of his reach.

"I'm not fooling," he said. "I really do think it's time I got quit of this place."

"That's not the same as dying."

"But that's what I meant."

The laughter began as a shadow that crawled out of the fire, scuttled to a corner where he couldn't see it at all, and rose until it filled the room with dusk. Not mocking, but teasing, tickling him under the chin and under the arms until his lips quivered again and he had to join in, in spite of the pain like a rose in his chest. A tear in his right eye; his right hand jumped on his thigh; his left hand tried waving the laughter away as it increased and had him gasping.

And when it was done, when the flames settled down and the smoke drifted toward the flue, he took a deep breath, sighed, and snapped his fingers.

"That's not fair."

"Why not?" she said blithely. "Isn't all fair in love and keeping you alive?"

"Not this time. This time you're being a pain in the—"

"Karl!"

"—neck," he finished with a large foolish grin.

On the mantelpiece, more ornate than anything in the house, a round, glass-faced clock struck the hour; it was two.

A glance to the window and there was confusion beyond the plants—the fire was reflected in each of the dozen small panes, and behind them a backdrop of shimmering black. The other houses on the street were unlighted, he could tell, but he wasn't sure if he was seeing stars or spray from the logs. A car sped past, but its headlamps were dim; if the moon had risen, he couldn't see its shadows.

Two in the morning, then, and he ought to go to bed.

Two in the morning, and try as he might he could not remember where the bed was.

She would know, of course. She had always known where the bed was when they were younger. She knew where it was when he came home exhausted from work, and knew where it was when he was trying to do the wash, and knew where it was when they were expecting company in ten minutes, and she knew where it was when he was too tired to care. In the beginning it was a slap-and-tickle game, and he felt an embarrassed pleasure in being seduced by his wife every time he turned around. But the beginning had ended, and he tried to explain that it was just remotely possible that his needs were not hers. Amazingly enough, as he had braced himself to wince at her tears, she agreed. The excitement of being married was the excuse that she gave him, not having to sneak into the back seat of his car, or having to wait until her parents weren't home, or having to drive to that little motel they liked down the shore. The novelty, she said, of not having to sneak around like a couple of sexual thieves.

Life, she told him as she kissed and seduced him, was not worth the living if you couldn't enjoy.

Which he did. Which he definitely did, and she never argued with that. The problem was one of whose definition. She liked to move, and he liked to sit; she liked to mingle, and he liked to watch; she liked making love, and he liked to sleep. A compromise was in order, and they finally made it, and the next thirty years passed more swiftly than he liked.

They changed houses three times, they changed jobs twice, they even changed countries for one decade back when, and when they returned they couldn't believe how things had become more like her than like him.

"Are you sleeping?"

He shook his head. "No. Just thinking."

"Good. It's still early, you know."

"It is not early," he said, his temper ready to snap. "It's for god's sake after two in the morning. Most sane people are in bed, in case you've forgotten."

Giggling in the corner behind him. He set his hands on the armrests and readied himself to turn, then gave it up as a lost cause—she wouldn't be there. She was never there when he wanted to see her, never there when he wanted to fix her with a look without having to scold.

The giggling continued, sounding as though it were muffled by a hand.

"Do you want to watch television?"

Oh god, she was getting on his nerves!, and his eyes opened wide when he mouthed the thought without speaking. He couldn't believe it. After all this time she was finally getting on his nerves.

"I asked if you wanted to watch some television, Karl. I won't ask again."

"No," he said looking over to the corner where the television was. A blank dusty screen, and dust on the top where a milky white vase of dead yellow mums blended with the wall. He couldn't remember how old the flowers were. Old enough, he thought: they'd long since turned brown.

The screen flickered.

"I said no."

A movie came on—black-and-white, gangsters, long cruising Buicks and longer rattling guns, the sound low the way she liked it so he couldn't tell what was going on.

"It's one of my favorites," she said. She had moved, was now on his left. He glanced over quickly and saw only himself a dozen times peering back through the bay window, through the sparks, through the fire.

"Shame on you," she said playfully, and something bumped the back of his chair hard.

"Don't kick," he ordered sharply. "You'll split the leather, and that's hell to fix."

Her silence told him she didn't really care.

The slight lowering of the film's volume told him she didn't really care at all.

His eyes closed and he prayed for patience. As he had done the day she'd come home just after turning fifty and told him bluntly she had thought it over very carefully and was leaving him for good. When he'd said nothing, she repeated her announcement. For good, he had explained then, implied there might have been other times when she'd left and this, to his certain knowledge, was the first occasion of this sort. She'd screamed at him then, her resolve unable to stand before his calm, and he'd only barely been able to keep the laugh down. She'd yelled, she'd shouted, she'd thrown a few glasses, and once threw a punch he didn't bother to block, just to add to her guilt. She told him that try as she might, and god knew she was trying, she had had it with his infernal sitting, his interminable waiting, his insufferable peace of mind. Challenge, she said, was a stranger in his life because he refused to take chances, refused to make more than ripples on the lake. When they travelled, he contemplated instead of letting go; when they made love these days, it seemed more like he was remembering than getting into the act. She had tried, she'd said, to make him understand that one just doesn't find a comfortable chair and watch the whole damned world go by without once trying to get in on the fun. He was an old man at twenty, an old man at forty, and now at fifty-five he was practically a mummy.

He had listened, and after a while he had even admitted that he had never been the life of the party. That, however, was his nature, as she well knew. And he reminded her of their compromise, and reminded her as well that he had never once tried to stop her from enjoying herself.

That was true, she'd told him.

So, he had asked, what is the problem?

Jesus, she'd muttered, and she'd walked out the door.

He waited.

She didn't come back.

He had made himself dinner, read the paper, watched some TV, went to bed, and couldn't sleep because she didn't come back.

Lord, he thought, those were miserable times.

The gangster film ended, the commercial sold dog food, and another film began, this one about the jungle and a safari and a lost city filled with pearls. Despite himself he grew interested, and once almost urged the hero aloud. Almost. He caught himself in time, and scowled when he heard her giggling again.

"Got you," she said softly, just above and behind his head.

"No, you didn't," he said quickly. "I was just clearing my throat."

The giggle burst into a short laugh. "Karl Bremer, you are impossible."

"I am what I am, and I can't be anything else."

"Oh yes you can, if you try."

A truck rumbled past with yellow running lights hazed, and dust settled from the ceiling in languid grey streams. The television flickered, then steadied and grew louder, considerably so.

A slip of perspiration made its way past his collar, and he rubbed at it angrily. "I'm hot."

"So am I, but I like it. I've always liked the sun, you know that. Tanning and things."

The log split on the andirons, and the flames rose like dragon's breath into the chimney.

"Stop it!" he said.

"Say please."

He clamped his mouth shut, almost closed his eyes.

"Karl. Say please."

The fire began to roar, and a pink rose wilted on the wallpaper by the hearth.

"Karl?"

"All right, please. And while you're at it, will you *please* turn down the damned TV?"

The flames settled, the volume lowered, and she kicked the chair again.

"Goddamnit, Estelle!" And he pushed himself out of the chair and turned around. "Goddamnit, Estelle, will you please leave me alone!"

His voice cracked, and he coughed, and two of the five lamps went out with a snap. He reached for the chair to balance himself, but he would not sit down. She had gone too far this time, and now he was going to assert himself again.

As he had done so manfully when she'd returned two weeks after her leaving. Contrite, and loving, and more than willing to renegotiate the compromise they'd had. Perhaps, he thought later, years later, he'd been wrong. Perhaps he had been too hard on her that day, too inflexible when he should have been understanding, should have been kind. But she was the one who had deserted the nest, not him; she was the one who at a full half-century wanted to feel young again and kick up her foolish heels when there was no time or energy left to do it; she was the one who had given him all those horrid nightmares about her dying someplace strange without him by her side. It was her fault, not his, and whatever guilt there might have been at being so righteous and so stubborn was buried beneath the ground rules he'd laid down for her that night.

Sobbing, near to telling him the hell with it and leaving again, she had accepted.

And the rest of their marriage had been his own heaven on earth.

"If I can't die," he told her, "I want to go to bed."

"Oh, you'll die," she said, coming out of the corner where the shadows were born and the night held its cold. "You will, honest. But only when I say so."

He passed a hand over his face, through the strings of his dead hair. "We made a deal," he said weakly. "Estelle, when you came back we made a deal."

"As far as I know, all deals are off when one of the dealers dies."

She crossed the room slowly and glared until he turned around, reached for the armrests and lowered himself in stages back into the chair. For a brief moment he felt as he had that night when he awoke and heard odd noises in the next bed. Estelle groaning and weeping, and by the time he roused himself and went over, she was no longer breathing.

Instead of feeling sad, he felt cheated; instead of remorse, he was angry. And that, he had decided later, must have been the reason she'd opened her eyes less than a minute later. Too soon for the grief, she latched onto the others.

"I love you," she said then, in a voice without a tone.

"I love you, Estelle," he said softly now.

"I know, dear, I know. And you must know that I love you, too." And she reached out a loving hand to caress his cheek with a bone.

The tear returned, and was joined by another. "Then please let me die."

"Not," she said, "until you learn to enjoy what you have. You never did." Her voice hardened. "You will now."

And he sat there while the hero hacked his way through the jungle, and the flames rose behind the screen, and the plants in the window swung to the sound of her laughter in the room.

He sat there, and he watched, and when the hero saved the girl he refused even to smile.

"You're going to lose," she whispered when the television switched off and the radio switched on.

"No, I'm not," he said sternly. Because he knew that the moment he admitted to having fun, she would do as she promised—she would finally let him die.

"That's right," she said. "That's absolutely right."

He stiffened when the hand brushed through his falling hair, when it rested on his shoulder, when it followed his jaw and took away a piece of skin. He stiffened as he felt her dead cold breath cover his ear. And he stiffened when he saw the knuckle of his left forefinger finally break through the yellowed skin.

But he said nothing. She had made a deal, and he would hold her to it. No one, not even Estelle, was going to take his principles away.

Karl Bremer will not lose when principle and right are at stake; she'd grow tired of it, he was sure, and he was willing to hold out even if it took another hundred years.

Then the bed appeared in the middle of the room, and he felt her slowly pushing him out of the chair.

"What are you doing?" he said. "I'm not tired now. I've changed my mind, I don't want to go to bed."

"I know," she said, giggling again. "I know. You never did."

"No," he said in sudden disgust, reaching to fend off what was left of his wife. "My god, Estelle, no!"

But the living room was always too warm for comfort, the fire too high, the television and radio too low to enjoy.

And: "Relax, Karl," she whispered, "we're going to have fun."

In the Blood

THE WIND IN its guise as the dead who fly—whispering harshly, down in the dark gutters where the dead leaves are trapped, flapping and quivering on the bars of a storm drain; whistling low and steady up between the trees where the wires sag and tremble, shimmering like thin ice and humming high-pitched before they snap apart; cracking branches together, snapping sheets on a clothesline, raising dust into smoke and smoke into cloud; taking a hat and flinging it away, sailing it, coasting it, slamming it hard against the side of a dark building and kicking it in gusts back into an alley.

The wind in October, now and then howling across the mouth of a chimney, moaning in a doorway, sighing beneath an awning that puffs against its weight.

Then resting, not gone, crouching invisible in the black panther night that sighs and grunts and waits for movement on the sidewalk.

Red and white neon in the luncheonette's wide window hissed and popped softly, reminding Jake of how his mother used to test a griddle by flicking water on it to see if it would bead, and if the beads would jump. But his mother was dead and so was everyone else, so he pulled his head down, raised his shoulders and moved on up the long empty street. His hands were gloved but still in his pockets, his greying hair atangle since losing his hat and so much for the effort to keep his balding head warm. At the corner he stopped and looked both ways.

But there were no cars, no pedestrians, no one in the world but him close to midnight, and what he thought was a cat crouched in the gutter across the way was only a paper bag huddled against the wind. He sighed, and checked the street again for movement, peering hard into the night as though his eyes gave him trouble. But except for the neon that still sizzled behind him, the streetlamps were so dim he couldn't read any names, not on the shops or the signposts or above the high arch of the library doors where a ladder stood on the stoop, bucket and sponge beside it, waiting for someone to come along and wash the windows.

He hesitated, patted his side once, and crossed Williamston Pike in a hurry, turned right, turned left, and he was walking a dark street whose only houses were opposite him, peaks and porches and gingerbread at the eaves, hickory and maple and birch in the front yards, oaks by the curb that buckled the sidewalk. Driveways that led to blackened garages. Hedges that penned the black on the grass.

He had no idea how late it was and no idea how much he had drunk, but it couldn't have been nearly enough because he wanted to drink more before he got on with the job. But the Mariner was long closed, and so was the Chancellor Inn, and he'd not thought to buy a pint before he'd started for the Park.

"Jake, love, you really ought to think about cutting down a little," Mandy had told him just before the end. It was said and meant almost kindly, as kind as she'd ever been over the last five years, and he'd almost wept at her bedside because she knew what it was—it was the dying he saw every day for a year, the wasting, the shrinking, the growing into the grave from the inside out. But she said it again, and he'd tried to make a promise, silently blessing her when she didn't hold him to it.

The cemetery wall—blocks of grey stone perfectly fitted without a trace of mortar, and, along the top, teeth of stone that rose from a cement bed to make lovers and vandals think twice about climbing. They had walked this way once in a while, just for the walking, and she'd joked about how it was too imposing for a graveyard, that such a wall couldn't possibly keep the dead from escaping.

He reached out and touched it, feeling the cold through his gloves, the same cold, he thought, that used to permeate his shop when his shop was still open.

Just a month before the end he'd stayed late at work, and she'd smiled as best she could through the tubes and wires. The smile this time was neither kind nor gentle. "Still at it?"

"What else is there to do?"

"My father has friends. You know they could give you something better."

"Don't want anything better, thank you."

Another smile, this one weaker. "Ah, Jake. Once a butcher, always a butcher, is that what you mean? Your father and your grandfather, and now you carry the flag?"

"Carry the flag," he muttered bitterly. "Carry the damned flag."

Easy for her to say, he thought, as he pushed through a gap between the high iron gates, noiseless on their hinges and shadowless on the path. Easy for her to say. She's not the one who finally lost the business to the competition, trying desperately to keep himself from being buried by the giant chains whose corporate gods didn't include a single one dedicated to personal service. She's not the one who had to charge higher prices because a butcher shop carries little else than the meat that it sells and the people behind the counter and when you need the best you save the supermarket for last. Unless you don't have the money. Unless you don't have the time to watch the butcher choose the beef and make the expert cuts.

His step was automatically light as he walked the narrow path between the headstones that glowed despite the fact there were no stars, no moon, no lampposts along the way. A faint glow, white with a tint of pale green, shimmered just below the marble's surface. He'd seen the phenomenon before and had always ignored it. There was no time to be made nervous by what he didn't understand. There was only time to take the right-hand path and walk deeper into the shadows of Memorial Park.

"For heaven's sake," Mandy had asked after they had been married too long, "why would anyone want to be a butcher in this day and age?"

"My family," he'd said, and with the tone said it all—the hard work seven days a week and no holidays to count on, the lack of money for college, the lack of ambition when there was a ready-made job waiting just for him after high school.

He passed an angel whose wings were flared, and he winced as if it had made to strike him.

And after a while, the pride of owning your own business, being your own boss, controlling your own life—until control slipped away.

He'd not asked her why she'd married him in the first place—they were high school lovers and that's usually all the reason lovers ever need.

He wanted his hat. His hair, thinning rapidly, wasn't enough to keep his head warm. And he should have brought a warmer jacket, but when he'd left home this afternoon the sky was an autumn blue and the sun was warm and there was no reason to think the wind would come to the village tonight, out of the valley, down from Pointer's Hill. He shivered violently, deliberately, to start his blood moving, and paused for a moment at a fork in the path.

"I think," Mandy had announced before she'd gone to bed with the cancer, "that I don't want to spend the rest of my life with a man who smells like blood and bone. And I especially don't want to live with a man who looks at me as if I were one of his pretty little steaks."

But it wasn't the looks, and it wasn't the smell; it was the money they seldom had. Even in Oxrun Station there was a certain amount of economizing now, and people had also grown suspicious of his wares. They wondered if he were cutting corners, and they wondered if he'd somehow rigged the scales, and they wondered why he had occasion to once in a while take an extra-long lunch hour at a certain widow's house on a certain street below the hospital.

His jacket billowed at a wind gust, and he held his left arm closer to his side, clutching beneath the coat a single red rose whose thorns nudged the fabric of his red plaid shirt. When the gust died he started again, to the right, deeper into the Park, past older headstones worn smooth by the weather, here and there canted, once in a while fallen. His shoes scuffed loudly on the blacktop, but he didn't dare lift his feet too high or he'd lose the path, get lost, end up cracking a kneecap against marble and spending the rest of the night limping around like some creature loose from a bad movie.

When he stumbled over what must have been a tree branch, nearly fell and sidestepped a dozen paces before his balance returned, he decided to leave. It wasn't worth it. His toe hurt and it was too damned cold and it just wasn't worth it. Besides, she wouldn't know the difference anyway. Putting a rose on her grave each anniversary of her death had been her idea, not his, and promised to her the night she died—and, he learned three days later, put in the will to make sure he neither forgot her nor spent all her money. He could have ignored it, and the attorney's blustering threats; he could have directed the pompous little man to a warm destination and her memory to perdition; he could have treated it as a morbid, melodramatic joke and proceeded with his life.

But he hadn't.

Despite the fact that she would have left him had she lived—for the money, for the looks, and for the widow on King Street—he loved her. He had always loved her. The rich sable hair and the boyish figure and the heavy lips; not beautiful, but lovely, and in spite of his friends' jibes, he hadn't really married her for the money. He loved her. And he missed her—but the years were fast dimming the reasons why he did.

Every year, then; eight years now and still counting, he

placed the rose on the grave, and cursed her for things he barely understood himself, then he went home and got drunk.

He heard an odd sound behind him, a soft sound, something soft on the path, but he ignored it. Here in the Park there were always noises to contend with, from the hunting owls and ravens to the creaking of trees. Eight years he'd been listening to them; he'd had no choice, and less of one as the years slipped out from underneath him. Mandy had had the money to keep the business afloat; less than a year after her death he had sold out. He'd had enough of struggling, had enough of seeing his customers grow old and not be replaced by a younger generation, had enough of people telling him he couldn't do anything but slice and weigh and wrap meat up.

He'd had enough, after twenty years, of holding on to the shop because she thought he couldn't do it.

He wasn't stupid. He could have worked anywhere if he'd wanted and had been given the incentive. But with Mandy gone, gentle at the end in her hatred of him and his, all he'd wanted to do was change it all over. Be a new man. Find a new woman. Maybe even get the hell out of Oxrun Station.

Another branch fell, and he scowled into the dark, cursing the prankster kids who sometimes plagued him.

Living off a dead woman's inheritance was an accusation he'd heard several times, though not to his face. So what, he thought; he enjoyed eating, enjoyed the house with the paid-off mortgage, and enjoyed the occasional vacation that got him out of town and into the real world.

Miss one year, though, and it was all gone.

But when the wind toppled him, spun him around so that he had to walk backwards, he finally decided it wasn't worth it. After the first few times, the attorney had stopped having someone follow him to check. The rest was his conscience, but his conscience had finally died.

Mandy was long dead, he was out here freezing in a cemetery, and there was no reason in the world why he couldn't hire someone to do it for him to keep the lawyers happy.

After all, hadn't she come right out and told him on the day she left him that she knew he'd sell? He'd denied it, but she'd insisted, telling him gently, so falsely lovingly, that after all was said and done, Jake Zelchek was a quitter. Instead of fighting the big chains and improving his stock and customer relations, instead of coming to her for sympathy rather than a damned whore, he'd grown sullen and self-defeating and had quit long ago.

"It may be in your blood," she had said, "but your blood has gone thin."

That's why she was going to leave him, and that's why he'd pulled the plugs before he'd left the room, thinking that at the last she'd been right all along—she looked just like the slabs of meat he kept in the freezer.

What she hadn't known, of course, was how bored he would become, how he began to walk by the old shop once or twice a day and look in the window, and sigh, and walk away.

My blood may be thin, he thought, but damnit, it's still blood, Mandy; and there in the dark he realized at last that he wanted to start again. Take what was left of Mandy's money and open a new shop. A better one, and fairer, and continue family tradition, by god and thunder and the hell with you, Mandy.

"The hell with it," he said, and started back.

And stopped.

The clouds had begun to shred, and the moon laid winking patches of grey over the ground. Graves expanded with the shadows they cast, trees became cracks in the night's black ice. The path seemed darker now that there was light, and he stared at the branch that had only just tripped him.

"God," he said, and wasn't sure it was a prayer.

His arm clamped hard to his side, and the thorns pressed through his shirt, pricking the skin coldly taut around his ribs.

The branch he had tripped over wasn't a branch at all. It was a leg, a human leg severed at the hip, bone and inner flesh exposed to the wind that made it twitch as if it were somehow still alive.

"God," he said again.

A look down to see if there was blood on his shoes, and a searching look to either side, hunting for the maniac, or the ghoul, or the victim, anything that moved.

The wind died, and the leg rolled over.

He gagged and started to run, a stumbling trot that veered him off the path into the marble forest. He tried to run quietly, listening for the murderer who would surely give chase now that he'd discovered the evidence, and would surely use that cleaver on him as well.

Perspiration drenched his face, dripped under his collar.

He tried to tell himself that he'd seen meat before, had used knives before, and there was nothing done to that leg he hadn't done himself in the shop, and wouldn't do as soon as the new shop had opened.

But the leg was human.

And it moved.

And it occurred to him as he ran that it belonged to a woman.

A sudden sharp shadow made him gasp and swerve to the left; a pillar of ice-smooth marble forced him to one side; an angel loomed and beckoned, a granite vase quivered; he found the path again, had run a dozen yards before he saw the arm.

It was dangling from a tree lightning had once bent over the blacktop. The leaves were gone, and the fingers of the hand gripped the branch's middle. Bone, and flesh, and the moon saw it all.

He whirled around and saw the leg, propped against a low copper marker.

Bone. And flesh.

He bolted off the path, heedless of direction because sooner or later he would reach a wall, a fence, or if luck were with him, the gates he had opened.

His arm clamped harder against his ribs, and the thorns

broke the skin; he thought for a moment he could feel a few drops of blood cooling on his side.

Ten yards, and he fell with a short scream when his foot sank into a depression and pitched him forward. His hands weren't quick enough to stop the fall, and he landed square on his shoulder. His lungs emptied, and there was fire along his arm, sparks before his eyes. Old, he thought; too damn old for all this running, and he rolled onto his back to gasp and catch his breath. Spread-eagled on the grass, he found himself looking between his shoes at a tall narrow headstone topped with a pair of doves carrying olive branches in their beaks. For a moment, when the shadows moved, he thought they were alive.

Then recognition made him smile—he knew where he was.

After a deep inhalation he jerked himself into a sitting position and draped his hands over his knees. The rose was still in his jacket, the thorns still jabbing his ribs, but he ignored them and concentrated on getting back his wind. Listening for footsteps of the killer, listening for his breathing. He had heard of people like that, read about them in newspapers and magazines, men and women who got their kicks not from the actual murder but from the dismemberment after.

But not in the Station. There were other things here, but not killers like this.

His panting slowed, and he turned around to kneel, the doves behind him and Mandy ahead.

A simple grave, the stone horizontal and raised on a stone platform, her name and dates etched deep and dark. Polished. Glinting. Flecks of mica reflecting the moon.

Quickly, as long as he was here, he grabbed the rose and tossed it at the grave, telling her silently how dreams are born new. Then he swayed to his feet and looked down at her name . . . and at the arm that lay across the engraved rose at the bottom.

His shoulders slumped—I'm too old, I can't run—and he did not move when he heard a rustling at his side. Only a sideways glance. The moon found another gap in the swift-moving clouds, and on the bed of his shadow he saw the leg, saw another, looked to his right and saw the other arm.

Bone. And flesh.

He belched and tasted scotch and told himself he was drunk, and feeling guilty for even thinking of abandoning his wife. Especially when he looked back before running, looked at the arm and knew it was hers. By the curve of the elbow, by the softness of the skin, and by the diamond band around her third finger, he knew it was Mandy's.

He was drunk.

The hand closed into a fist.

He was drunk.

The legs moved again.

The diamonds flared moonlight stinging and harsh into his eyes, and when he lifted a hand to block the blinding flares he heard her say, *jake you're a quitter.*

He screamed, and he ran, and he stayed on the path all the way to the gates.

jake

He jumped off the curb when the arm dropped from the tree and reached for his ankle.

jake

He kept to the center line and didn't look for traffic, wheeling around corners, not listening to the soft thuds on the road behind him, not watching when a leg torn and bleeding broke through a hedge in an effort to trip him.

jake

He considered only briefly stopping at the police station to have them lock him up until a doctor could be found; he was drunk, and they would know it, but when they let him out the next morning the arms and the legs would be waiting there for him. So he ran past it, across Chancellor Avenue and down toward his home.

A hand, fingers bare to the bone, scraped itself out of a storm drain and followed.

A leg, tatters of flesh veiled in fresh blood, swung out of an open manhole and followed.

He bulled through the gate and ran up the walk, almost kicked in the front door and locked it behind him.

"I am not a quitter," he said to the empty house. "I'm not a quitter, Mandy. I just got tired of fighting."

He staggered into the front room, was almost in his chair when he heard the thumping at the door. Knocking. Kicking. Flesh and bone against wood.

I'm drunk, he thought; I'm drunk, I'm drunk.

Knocking. Kicking. The door rattling in its frame.

"Damnit, Mandy, I'm starting all over! Goddamnit, woman, leave me the hell alone!"

The door shook and the hinges creaked and a window broke loudly somewhere in the house.

He dashed back into the foyer, turned to watch the door.

"The hell with you, Mandy! I'm not going to quit!"

He stood to one side and cautiously pulled away the white curtain that covered the pane.

The pounding continued, slamming up the staircase, echoing through the cellar, footsteps and fists of someone twice his size.

I'm drunk. I'm drunk.

His eyes blinked away perspiration, and he angled his head so he could see outside.

There was no one on the porch.

Only the moon, and the silvered yard, and the wink of tiny diamonds from the band on the finger of the hand turning the knob.

"Mandy, for god's sake, I left the damned rose!"

He backed away, swallowing bile, reaching out blindly until he found the basement door. Without thinking, he flung it open and plunged down the steps, switched on the bare lightbulb and fell hard against the table where he had left all his knives. They were coated with dust, and dust coated his hand when he snatched up a cleaver and turned to face the stairs. It was stupid, and he knew it, but maybe limbs hacked once could be hacked again.

jake

"Aw, Mandy."

jake, i understand

He sagged against the table, closed his eyes, and wept.

jake

"Mandy, please."

There was silence. The wind stopped, and the moon was in the window by the furnace, and all he could hear was the house talking to itself.

"Mandy?" he whispered.

He was sorry. Sorry he'd thought he could ever leave her, even in her grave, sorry he'd sold the business, sorry about the widow; and he was sorry for dreaming he could start over again.

"Mandy?" It was a whimper.

i understand, she told him from somewhere in the dark. *i understand and i want to help you.*

"Mandy, look—"

it's in the blood, she said, *but you're going to need some practice.*

Light again, he thought.

And he started with his hand.

And We'll Be Jolly Friends

NOTHING HAD CHANGED.

It was almost frightening, but as far as he could tell, not a thing had changed.

The houses, most of them built a century ago, were still set comfortably back from the street behind their gently sloping lawns, under their attic-high oaks, behind their five-foot hedges twice-monthly trimmed; the windows were high and washed every season, white curtains, white shades, and open in summer to let the air in; a few of the porches still sagged, a few of the drives were still gravel, and at the curb a few of the older trees still kneed roots through the sidewalk where faded lines of chalk marked forgotten hopscotch games.

The light, too, was the same, sifting through the leaves in sprays of mint and gold, rippling on the blacktop, flaring off the cars parked in front of low garages, so bright above the trees that the block was cut off—not even the houses behind the houses could be seen from the road.

He knew he was grinning from the growing ache in his cheeks, but he didn't care, not now, not concerned in the least that he was tempting a careless motorist by standing astride the same white line where he'd learned to ride his bike. No one would dare run him down, not on his block, not after all these years.

His block, his white line, and from here he could see the ragged rose garden that belonged to the neighborhood witch, the pickup that belonged to the neighborhood drunk, he could see an old stunted magnolia in bloom in front of the minister's house, a pair of dachshunds scampering after their tails and each other on the schoolteacher's lawn.

All sound was muted.

His eyes began to water from the brilliance of the light.

Rubbing a sleeve over his face cleared his vision and turned him around, sent him into the car idling at the corner. He sat gripping the wheel, and took a deep breath.

There was still time, he reminded himself. He could still turn around, go back to the motel and call the lawyers. They would fume, no doubt, and remind him that the house would be lost to taxes if he didn't act. He knew that. He had been avoiding a return for the last two years, after his mother had died in her hospital bed while he was in transit. Always in transit, and no place between. General Delivery, odd jobs, and his dreams. They always caught up with him however, somehow managed to keep sending him notices, demanding to know what he was going to do with the estate—a few hundred dollars, a garage, and a house. They wanted it settled, off their books, out of their hair.

They wanted to know what was taking him so long.

Fear had kept him away, and the fear of wondering if he'd been wrong all this time had brought him back.

He sniffed, blew his nose, and called himself ten kinds of a fool, and a jackass besides.

It wasn't wrong to come back, he was sure of that now, and the only regret was that he hadn't done it sooner, hadn't done it right away, hadn't taken his separation pay and gotten straight on the plane and flown right back to what he knew best. But he had been, he understood now, unreasonably afraid. It had all boiled down to *i don't want to die.*

tough shit, mac, that's what you're here for
but you don't get it, i don't want to die
who the hell does, stupid bastard
i wanna go home
you figure out how let me know, i'll go with you

All right, he said, a pep talk to himself, all right, kiddo, let's get it done.

He turned off the air conditioner and rolled down the window, put his elbow on the ledge and drove slowly down the block. He'd forgotten his sunglasses, and he had to squint to see the road, telling himself nervously that the light had always been this way, always this bright and blinding.

Maybe it was; maybe it wasn't. But he cursed when he nearly drove past the driveway. He braked, backed up so he wouldn't run over the curb, then sped up the gravel to the one-car garage in the back, and sat there, trembling, finally clapping his hands and laughing.

Now what the hell was so hard about that?

You did it, pal. You did it. You're home.

The door worked smoothly, the extra housekey was still rusting on its hidden hook under the lefthand track, and as soon as he stopped gawking at the junk piled on the shelves and propped against the walls, he walked around to the front, giggling when he saw the rain barrel by the downspout, giggling again when he peered into it and saw his reflection in brackish water. He would have to empty it first thing in the morning; for now, though, he'd let it be, recalling the time his grandfather had hoisted it out of his trunk one Sunday afternoon, rolled it into place and announced that they'd never have to pay for water again.

The evergreen shrubs lining the porch and the foundation were in need of a trim—something to do when he was moved in and living; the slanted cellar doors were padlocked, the hinges rusted and in need of replacement. How old had he been when his father made him stop climbing up them and sliding down? Eight? Nine? Fearing, he said, the wood would split and the boy would crack his head open on the concrete cellar stairs. Eleven? It didn't make any difference; when he looked close, he could still see the heel marks.

Beautiful, he thought; nothing has changed.

He stood on the front walk then, and stared at the house, at the peels and chips and flakes of white paint, at the film of dust on the windows, at the dark front door with its brass letter slot in the middle.

"I'll be damned, it *is* you."

He turned so fast he stumbled backward, his heels catching the bottom riser and dropping him on the step.

"Yep, it sure is you. I'd know that stupid look anywhere."

The light was haloed behind the woman's head, but there was no mistaking the short black hair brushed back behind the ears, the faintly olive skin, the large black eyes without a wrinkle around them.

"Sue? Susan Pallante?"

She curtsied. "None other."

He shaded his eyes against the light, and shook his head in slow wonderment. "Susan. Incredible. Jeez, you don't look a day older than when I left, you know that?"

"You're a liar, McCorey Danning, but if you stop I'll shred your lips."

He laughed, and shifted to make room for her when she sat beside him, smoothing her damp-spotted jeans as if they were a skirt, absently patting her hair which was held away from her eyes by a blue cloth headband. She held a rag in one hand, and when he looked at it she nodded across the street, toward her house—three down, red trim, a marble birdbath in the front yard the birds never used.

"Washing the car," she said. "It's Saturday, you know. And since you left, I don't have anything better to do."

"Susan," he said in mock scolding, "that was years ago, c'mon. You can't blame me if you're still single. Which I don't believe anyway, not someone as pretty as you."

She hit him with the rag, and they laughed, sat watching the block for several minutes without speaking before she asked if he were back to stay. He told her he was. She asked if he needed help moving in. He admitted that he wouldn't mind a little company for the first time in; it was, he said, a bit spooky, coming back here alone.

"Never married?"

"No," he said. "Never wanted to."

She slapped his arm. "Always the soul of tact, Corey. C'mon, let's go."

She hauled him to his feet, fairly pushed him up the steps to the door. The keys were cold in his hand, and he hesitated, finally turned the bolt and opened the door.

And couldn't move.

Susan, however, stepped right into the vestibule and had her hand on the knob of the glass-paned inner door. A look over her shoulder. He smiled bravely. She beckoned with a wink, and it wasn't as bad as he feared.

His first steps were timid, until he was in the foyer and could smell the smells that had once filled his life. Then he exploded with laughter and ran with her through all the rooms, snatching sheets off the furniture to use as dusters for the counters, for the walls, for the pictures still in their frames; for the mantelpiece, for the tables, for the wide seat in the bow window that made the living room look larger. Upstairs, they opened all the windows they could, opened the doors, tried the faucets, flushed the toilet, and checked the closets and cupboards for signs of mildew.

His parents' room still smelled of lavender and pipe tobacco; his room still smelled of modeling glue, clay, and baseball mitts; the bathroom smelled of soap, the guest room smelled of nothing at all.

They hauled in the cartons and oversized suitcases he had in the car, and she insisted on cleaning out his dresser drawers before he dropped his clothes in. When he protested, she reminded him that for a while, back when, she was in this house a lot more than he.

That almost sobered him, because it was true.

When he had left, drafted six months out of high school and not bothering to try for any sort of deferment, she had come over to sit with his parents, to watch the news for signs of him, word of him or his battalion, to read the reports in the newspapers from which his father had already cut out and burned the lists of the dead. She was there when his father died of the heart attack from shoveling snow, and he hadn't come home for the funeral because he couldn't stand the thought of having to go back to the jungle.

She was there so much his mother in a letter once called her his sister.

They finished far more slowly than they'd started, and after he had gotten himself a drink of water in the kitchen (smelling of cake and bacon and floor wax and cleaner), he found her standing at the living room window, hands cupping her elbows, staring out at twilight.

"You okay?" he said, though he didn't stand beside her.

She nodded. "Tired, that's all. I didn't expect to work this hard today. And I didn't expect you, either. Not so soon, anyway."

"So soon?" He dropped onto the sofa and propped his feet on the oval coffee table. "God, Susan, it's been nearly ten years since I got out."

"I know."

"Jesus, don't tell me you've been counting the days."

She laughed, a hollow, melancholy sound, and shook her head. Then she turned and headed for the door. "Listen, I'll see you tomorrow maybe, okay? The car isn't going to put itself away."

Before he could move she was gone, the doors closed. The streetlamp over by the driveway was out, as usual, and he couldn't see her once she'd left the walk.

Unrequited love, he thought with a lift of an eyebrow; too bad, Sue, but life isn't flowers that live forever.

He had called from Seattle where the Army had let him go, and had told her he wasn't coming back, not for a while. He wanted to travel, see the country now that he had a few bucks in his pocket, and he had no plans now or ever to get married. He hated himself for doing it that way—cold, distant, words clipped and cruel—but knew that if he had returned to say it in person she would have wept, he would have relented, and he never would have had the chance to get his mind into gear.

That was important.

He had to be able to think clearly so he could tell them the truth; he had to get it all out of his system so there'd be nothing left but the truth. His truth, not the truth of the movies or the novels or the breast-beating sermons that filled every television show he saw. The truth as he knew it, not the truth as they were told.

And in thinking of it and the work to be done, he rushed back up the stairs and into what had once been his mother's sewing room. The typewriter was there, and the reams of paper, the notebooks, and the letters. All the letters his mother had sent him. All the letters *are a pain in the ass.*

they keep you sane, man, they keep you sane
sane is not dying, and i don't want to die
christ, when are you gonna learn a new tune
when i get on the freedom bird for home, that's when
jesus, corey, you homesick or something?
shit, yeah
good, then you'll be okay
homesick is okay?
man, the day you stop being homesick and start liking this fuckin place, that's the day they gonna send you back in a box

That night, someone threw a brick through the bow window.

"Welcome home," he muttered as he swept the broken glass into a dustpan. He was angry because he didn't think the neighborhood supported creeps and hoods; and he was unnerved because he hadn't heard a thing. Sleep had come quickly once he recognized the feel of his own room, and he hadn't discovered the damage until morning, when he had walked to the front with a coffee cup in hand.

The day was warm, though, and the house needed airing, and when he couldn't get a glazier, he decided not to tape up some cardboard until he'd done his shopping. A quick check of the house to be sure nothing else was broken, or broken into, and he was gone for nearly four hours, much of the time spent parked at curbs and staring.

Everything had changed.

Few of the stores he remembered were in their old places, none of the clerks were familar, and hardly any of the names he saw painted on the windows were the same as those painted there when he'd left. He knew that progress was one thing, but this was something else again—this was uprooting virtually an entire town and moving it someplace else he couldn't find . . . except for the neighborhood, and the people who lived there.

After a while, after sitting and thinking, he guessed it was probably the same all over the country. New facades, new owners, new products, new everything. Even the town hall had been given a facelift, and there was a police substation where a Hamburger Heaven had once been. It made him nervous, he didn't like not knowing where everything was, like a blind man in a room with all the furniture rearranged; and as soon as he filled the trunk with groceries and the back seat with bedding and office supplies, he drove back as fast as he could, cursing the fact he'd forgotten sunglasses again when he pulled into his street and nearly jumped up the curb.

The light was still bright, but somehow too mellow, like a gauze-covered lens shooting a wedding.

He finished unpacking, cleaned and stocked the pantry, and washed the dishes; he spent a couple of hours in the sewing room study, flipping through the files he had accumulated, sitting at the typewriter and watching the blank page remain white. He wasn't worried. The truth, his truth, would come sooner or later.

He shivered, then, and realized the house was cooling off. A sigh for another day gone, and he walked into his parents' bedroom, pulled up the shade and looked down at the street. He heard an engine gunning, and pressed closer, tilting his head left until his mouth opened in a silent gasp.

My god, he thought; my god, that's Archie!

A polished and black, '57 chrome-finned Chevy was parked

in a driveway two houses down on the other side of the street. The hood was up, and a man leaned under it, in a black T-shirt, black jeans, and engineer boots whose studs were nearly pointed in their elaborate patterns. Archie Lamonica, spending his Sundays the way he always did—trying to get that stupid deathtrap to run.

The man backed away, and Corey straightened quickly as if he might be seen.

No, he told himself, patting away sweat from his brow; it's not Archie, it must be his son. Good god, Archie was a year older than me.

The engine gunned again in a growling, and he looked out in time to see the Chevy back swiftly out of the driveway and belch exhaust down the street. When it was gone, the block was quiet; Sundays as usual.

He reached out a trembling hand to touch the pane—I wonder who the hell would want to marry old Archie?—and remembered the broken window downstairs. Thinking that he'd forget his head in the morning if it wasn't screwed on, he hurried off to cut up some boxes, find the tape, and lug it all to the porch where he cleared out the shards still clinging to the frame. Then he measured, fit, and was losing his temper again at the thought of the vandals when he heard footsteps behind him.

"I have to admit it, I am in awe of the man's versatility. A jack of all trades, no question about it."

He turned, and squinted through the golden bright light.

"When you're done, Corey, you could come over and fix my old man's garage door. It hasn't worked since World War I."

They were standing at the bottom of the steps, and his hand was already out before he started to move. It was Susan, and beside her stood a tall, gangly man whose trousers and shirtsleeves were always inches too short.

"Glenn?" There were tears in his eyes he brushed away with the backs of his hands. "Christ, Olanski, it took you long enough to come over and say hi."

There were handshakes and manly embraces, and they strung themselves out along the top step, Corey in the middle, feeling Susan warm on his left. Glenn smelled like bubble gum, a wad filling his cheek, and Corey didn't mind at all when his best friend from high school did most of the talking, mostly about the old house and how glad he was to see someone in it at last.

"I think," said Glenn finally, "this is a clear call for a celebration. I accept the post of chairman for the gala, thank you all for all your confidence in me."

"Hey," Susan said, nudging Corey with her elbow, "don't go so fast."

"He doesn't care," Glenn said. "After all, he's the refreshment chairman, and is charged with filling the fridge with beer and pop, bowls with whatever he can find, and we haven't seen him in a hundred years, so don't worry. Right, Corey?"

He nodded, unable to speak, unable to believe his incredibly fine *luck has nothing to do with it, danning.*

but jesus, how do you stay alive?

you pray a lot, and you hang on, man; you just hang on

that's it?

well, i have a trick, some of the other guys use it too, you could i think, with all those letters you got

"Letters? What letters?" Susan asked.

He looked at her, frowning, then realized he must have been thinking aloud. A wave to dismiss it as nothing, and a look to Glenn who, like Susan, was keeping wonderfully fit. Unlike himself, who could see in the morning, could see at night, the way his hair was turning dull, the way his face was taut and lined, the way he was increasingly growing to resemble his father.

"Then it's settled," Glenn said, slapping his knees and standing. "We'll take care of everything else, pal. You just be ready to feed us."

They were gone, striding into the light, before he remembered to ask them when.

But he didn't care.

He was back, and his friends were back, and he'd even had a glimpse of old Archie's son. What the hell more could he ask?

He ate a hastily-made dinner and went to work at the typewriter, remembering how it had been, remembered how it should have been but he had been taken away without anyone asking if he even wanted to go.

The truth.

About dying, about killing, about *hanging on, man, you hang on the best way you can*

like how?

like this spoon here, see? my old lady gave it to me, it was my old man's baby spoon. it's for luck. i look at it, i think about the way it's gonna be when i get back, and . . . i hang on

i don't have anything like that

you got your letters

shit, all mom ever does is cut up my high school yearbook and send me the pictures, tell me what everyone's doing

so use the pictures, you asshole. you think they're dumber than a dumbass little spoon? use the pictures, corey, use them and hang on, right?

you got it, man, you got it

That night, someone broke into the garage and slashed all his tires.

It was raining, the street was empty. He stood on the porch with his hands in his pockets and watched the water spill over the clogged gutters onto the bushes. He had wanted to go for a drive today, to check out the rest of town to see how much more time had ruined his home. Then he saw the tires. He had almost screamed.

A black Chevy hissed past, slowed, and backed up. He couldn't see inside, but there was more than just the driver. Archie's kid, he thought, and his eyes widened in revelation. Archie's kid! Who else but the son of a sonofabitch would bust a newcomer's window and slash four perfectly good tires, just for the hell of it. It was beyond vandalism; it was a marking of territory, a warning that he'd better not think himself king of the hill around here.

It was kid stuff.

He stared, and the Chevy reflected the dim streetlamps, rain sheeting off its sides to slide into the gutter.

Well, he thought, make your move, stupid.

It drove off at less than a walk, brakelights demon eyes when it reached and turned the corner.

A sigh, a shudder at a damp breeze. He walked to the end of the porch and leaned out, looked down the side of the house to the apple tree at the corner. The leaves were bright green, and the fruit was already growing; on the ground were the blossoms, battered into the grass.

A reluctant smile before he looked in the direction the Chevy had gone, and he chuckled. The hell with you, Archie; as he remembered the times he used to climb that damned tree to his bedroom window. His mother professed imminent heart failure, and his father showed him the way it should be done so he wouldn't break his neck.

Tomorrow, he decided, he would climb it again.

Why the hell not? He was home, wasn't he?

A glance up to see if the rain clouds were breaking, and he returned inside, fussed in the kitchen for a while, in his study for a while, then headed downstairs to find a book, the sofa, and maybe some logs for the fire. It was summer, but it was cool, and the only thing missing was a beautiful woman to bring him his slippers.

He reached the last step, and the doorbell rang.

Susan, of course, and Glenn, and whoever else they'd managed to dig up for the party. Whoever else, he amended, was still living in town.

The door opened before he reached it and Archie Lamonica stepped in.

The T-shirt seemed painted across a chest well-defined from lifting weights and pounding enemies; in the rolled-up left sleeve a pack of cigarettes and a book of matches. The tight jeans were black, blacker where grease and oil had merged with the fabric; the boots were polished, the studs glinting, and the heels were slightly higher than normal, to give his punch extra weight.

Hair curly, eyes narrowed, chin almost to a point. An unlighted cigarette in the corner of his mouth.

"Hey, McCorey, you're back!"

Corey reached for the newel post so he wouldn't slide to the stairs. "Archie," he said, keeping his voice low. "Good to see you."

"Like hell."

Lamonica sauntered into the living room and sprawled on the couch. The ashes he flicked to the carpet; his boots went up on the coffee table. He grinned, and blew a smoke ring.

Corey moved to stand in the arched doorway, then reached around to the wall and switched on the lights. When his eyes adjusted, he felt his mouth open slightly.

"Neat, huh?" Archie said, thumping a palm on his stomach. "I ain't gained a pound. Shit, it's better than any exercise, that's for damned sure."

"What is?" he said.

Archie blew another smoke ring. "Y'know, Danning, you're one hell of a pain in the ass. I mean, you're a real scab, you know that?"

Corey drew in his chin. "Now wait a minute, Lamonica—"

"Oh, shut up," Archie said mildly. "You got any beer?"

He couldn't believe it. The man had more nerve than a drunken Irishman, for god's sake. Who the hell did he think he was, walking in here like he owned the place, ordering beer like he was king, probably the one who busted his window and ruined his tires. It was just like the old days—Archie playing the tough bastard while all the time keeping Corey from having the crap beat out of him by the bullies at school. A hardnose. A pal in the oddest sense, but nevertheless a pal. Now he pulls this. Who the hell—

"You finished staring, jerk?"

Corey blinked.

"I asked if you got any beer."

"Archie," he said, trying to keep his voice from cracking, "you look . . . great!"

"No shit," Archie sneered. "What did you expect?"

"What?"

"Oh, for Christ's sake, will you just get me a beer?"

There was no sense refusing; Archie wouldn't leave unless he got what he wanted, and Corey was in no shape to take on a guy like that. He took one step toward the kitchen, then, and heard someone else on the porch. He whirled, thinking it might be the rest of Lamonica's gang, but when the door opened he almost dropped—it was only Susan and Glenn.

Archie called to them, and they greeted him with laughter, ignoring Corey until he cleared his throat loudly.

They turned, his three best friends, and he almost screamed when he saw them.

It's happened, he thought, feeling the perspiration walk on spiderlegs down his sides; the goddamned Army's finally made me crazy. They finally did it, the sonsofbitches, they finally made me *go crazy.*

no, you ain't, you're just scared man, that's all

yeah, well, i don't wanna die

then stop bitching and hang on

jesus, i'm tryin, i'm tryin

then try harder, mac, 'cause there ain't nothin else

hang on

you got it

as hard as i can

you got it, man—as hard as you can

He grabbed the banister and swung himself around and up the stairs, stumbled down the hall and into his study. He didn't bother with the lights; he dropped to the floor and pulled out the drawers of the cardboard filing cabinets he had. Folders were opened on his lap, were tossed aside with curses until, at last in the last one, he found all the letters. Twice a month his mother wrote him, with Pop adding little notes where he could in the margins, and each time she did she snipped those photographs out—from the high school year-book, from the newspapers, from the scrapbook she'd started keeping when Pop gave her a camera.

The envelopes fell to the floor, but he didn't care; all he wanted were the snapshots, and when he found them he raced back down again and stood in the middle of the room. Glenn was on the sofa, Archie was leaning against the mantel and Susan was with him.

Corey looked at the pictures, up, and back again.

"Go ahead," Glenn said. "Tell us how great we look."

It was a joke, of course. They knew someone who knew make-up and had themselves redone the way they used to be.

It was a joke, and a bad one.

"You get shot in that war, creep?" Archie said, lighting another cigarette.

"I think so," Glenn told him. "Seems to me his mother said something about it."

"I was going crazy over there," Corey whispered.

They ignored him.

"In the leg," Susan reminded them. "I think it was a sniper, if I remember it right."

"Crazy," he whispered, the pictures falling from his hand.

"Ah," said Glenn.

Susan picked up the poker, hefted it, and held it to her shoulder like a baseball bat.

"Y'know," Archie said, examining the end of his cigarette with care, "I always wanted to know what it was like being shot. Weird, I guess, all that blood and shit."

Corey spread his hands. "I had to hang on, don't you get it? A guy had to hang on or he went crazy!"

Susan walked up to him, patted his cheek, kissed his brow, and smashed his left kneecap with one swing of the poker.

He went down screaming, and screamed again when Archie's boot put a dent in his spine and Glenn stood on his hand and ground the knuckles to pulp.

"Life's a bitch," Archie said.

Susan broke his left ankle.

The pain and the tears left him as shock set in while Archie kicked the back of his neck and snapped his head forward. It was almost as if he was feeling nothing at all.

"Tell ya, fella," said Glenn, "it ain't fun being eighteen for the rest of your life."

Archie grabbed him under the shoulders, lifted him, slapped him to keep him from fainting, and dropped him on the couch. Susan immediately sat beside him and used his handkerchief to mop the blood from his neck where one of Archie's studs had gouged through the skin. Then she smiled sweetly, and jabbed a long nail into his cheek. Jabbed him again, and kicked his broken ankle.

Corey licked his lips, and said, "I had to hang on."

"Oh, hey, we understand, man," Archie said, taking Glenn's arm and walking him to the door. "I mean, we all gotta do it, right? We all gotta hang in there one way or another. You just fucked up, that's all. You just screwed us through to forever."

The door closed.

Susan opened the draperies and positioned him so he could see outside. Then she slipped a throw cushion behind his head, and patted his chest.

"Comfy?"

The pain was there, working into a firestorm.

"Sweet eighteen," she said coldly, "and never been laid. Just because you couldn't hack it like the rest of the men did. I take it back, Corey—you weren't a man, you were a boy, and you grabbed what Mommy sent you like it was a Teddy bear or something."

"Susan, please."

She stood, picked up her purse and reached inside it.

Please, he thought, let it be a gun.

It was a camera.

She checked the viewfinder, checked the lighting, then took a whole roll. Twice, she had to straighten him when he started to slip over, and propped him with more cushions when he groaned and a trace of blood slipped from under his tongue.

Then she walked to the door and took one last picture.

"For me," she whispered, blowing him a kiss. "So I can remember you forever. Just as you are."

STEVE RASNIC TEM

The Men and Women of Rivendale

THE THING HE would remember most about his days, his weeks at the Rivendale resort—had it really been weeks? —was not the enormous lobby and dining room, nor the elaborately carved mahogany woodwork framing the library, nor even the men and women of Rivendale themselves, with their bright eyes and pale, almost hairless, heads and hands. The thing he would remember most was the room he and Cathy stayed in, the way she looked when she curled up in bed, her bald head rising weakly over her shoulders, the way the dark brocade curtains hung so heavily, trapping dust and light in their intricate folds.

Frank thought he had spent days staring into those folds. He had only two places to look in that room: at the cancer-ridden sack his wife had become, her giant eyes, her grotesque, baby-like face, so stripped of age since she had begun her decline. Or at the curtains, adrift constantly with shadows. They were of a dark, burgundy-colored material, and he never knew if they had darkened with dust and age or if they were meant to be just that shade. If he examined the curtains at close range he could make out the tiny leaf and shell patterns embroidered over the entire surface. From a distance, when he sat in the chair or lay on the bed, they looked like hundreds of tiny, hungry mouths.

Cathy had told him little about the place before they came— that it was a resort in Pennsylvania, in the countryside south of Erie, and that it used to have hot springs. He hadn't asked, but he wondered what happened to the spring water when it left such a place. As if somebody somewhere had turned a tap. It didn't make any sense to him; natural things shouldn't work that way.

Her ancestors, the family Rivendale, had run the place when it was still a resort. Now many, perhaps all of her relatives lived in the Rivendale Resort Hotel, or in cottages spotted around the sprawling grounds. Probably several dozen cottages in all. It had been quite a jolt when Frank walked into the place, stumbling over the entrance rug with their luggage wedged under his arms, and saw all these Rivendales sitting around the fireplace in the lobby. It wasn't as if they were clones, or anything like that. But there was this uneasy sort of family resemblance. Something about the fleshtones, the shape of the hands, the perpetually arched eyebrows, the sharp angle at which they held their heads, the irregular pink splotches on their cheeks. It gave him a little chill. After a few days at Rivendale he recognized part of the reason for that chill: the cancer had molded Cathy into a fuzzy copy of a Rivendale.

Frank remembered her as another woman entirely: her hair had been long and honey-brown, and there had been real color in her cheeks. She had been lively, her movements strong and fluid, an incredibly sleek, beautiful woman who could have been a model, though such a public display would have appalled her and, he knew without asking, would have disgraced the Rivendale name.

Cathy had told him that filling up with cancer was like roasting under a hot sun sometimes. The dusty rooms and dark chambers of Rivendale cooled her. They would stay at Rivendale as long as possible, she had said. She could hide from nurses and doctors there.

She wouldn't have surgery. She was a Rivendale; it didn't fit. She washed herself in radiation, and, after Frank met these other Rivendales with their scrubbed and antiseptic flesh, the thought came to him: she'd over-bathed.

She never looked or smelled bad, as he'd expected. The distortions the growing cancer made within the skin that covered it were more subtle than that. Sometimes she complained of her legs suddenly weakening. Sometimes she would scream in the middle of the night. He'd look at her pale form and try to see through her translucent flesh, find the cancer feeding and thriving there.

One result of her treatments was that Cathy's belly blew up. She looked at least six months pregnant, maybe more. It had never occurred to either of them to have children. They'd always had too much to do; a child didn't have a place in the schedule. Sometimes now Frank dreamed he was wheeling her into the delivery room, running, trying to get her to the doctors before her terrible labor ceased. A tall doctor in a brilliant white mask always met him at the wide, swinging doors. The doctor took Cathy away from him but blocked Frank from seeing what kind of child they delivered from her heaving, discolored belly.

Nine months after the cancer was diagnosed, the invitation from the Rivendales was delivered. Cathy, who'd barely mentioned her family in all the years they'd been married, welcomed it with a grim excitement he'd never seen in her before. Frank discovered the invitation in the trash later that afternoon. "Come to Rivendale" was all it said.

One of the uncles greeted her at the desk, although "greeted" was probably the wrong word. He checked her in, as if this were still a resort. Even gave her a room key with the resort tag still attached, although now the leather was cracked and the silver lettering hard to read. Only a few of the relatives had bothered to look up from their reading, their mouths twitching as if they were attempting speech after years of muteness. But no one spoke; no one welcomed them. As far as Frank could tell, no one in the crowded, quiet lobby was speaking to anyone else.

They'd gone up to their room immediately; the trip had exhausted Cathy. Then Frank spent his first of many evenings sitting up in the old chair, staring at Cathy curled up on the bed, and staring at the curtains breathing the breeze from the window, the indecipherable embroidered patterns shifting restlessly.

The next morning they were awakened by a bell ringing downstairs. The sound was so soft Frank at first thought it was a dream, wind-chimes tinkling outside. But Cathy was up immediately, and dressing. Frank did the same, suddenly not wanting to initiate any action by himself. When another bell rang Cathy opened the door and started downstairs, and Frank followed her.

Two places were set for them at one of the long, linen-draped tables. "Cathy" and "Frank," the place cards read. He wondered briefly if there might be someone else staying here by those names, so surprised he was to see his name written on the card in floral script. But Cathy took her chair immediately, and he sat down beside her.

There was a silent toast. When the uncle who had met them at the desk tapped his glass of apple wine lightly with a fork the rest raised their glasses silently to the air, then a beat later tipped them back to drink. Cathy drank in time with the others, and that simple bit of coordination and exaggerated manners made Frank uneasy. He remained one step behind all the others, watching them over the lip of his glass. They didn't seem aware of each other, but they were almost, though not quite, synchronized.

He glanced at Cathy; her cheek had grown pale and taut as she drank. She wasn't eating real food anymore, only a special formula she took like medicine to sustain her. Although her skin was almost baby-smooth now, the lack of fat had left wrinkles that deepened as she moved. Death lines.

After breakfast they lingered by the enormous dining room window. Cathy watched as the Rivendales drifted across the front lawn in twos and threes. Their movements were slow and languid like ancient fish in shallow, sun-drenched waters.

"Shouldn't we introduce ourselves around?" Frank said softly. "I mean, we were invited by someone. How do these people even know who we are?"

"Oh, they know, Frank. Hush now; the Rivendales have always had their own way of doing things. Someone will come to us in time. Meanwhile, we enjoy ourselves."

"Sure."

They took a long walk around the grounds. The pool was closed and covered with canvas. The shuffleboard courts were cracked, the cracks pulled further apart by grass and tree roots. And the tennis courts . . . the tennis courts were his first inkling that perhaps he should be trying to convince her of the need to return home.

The tennis courts at Rivendale were built atop a slight, tree-shaded rise behind the main building. He heard the yowling and screeching as they climbed the rise, so loud that he couldn't make out any individual voices. It frightened him so that he grabbed Cathy by the arm and started back down. But she seemed unperturbed by the noise and shrugged away from him, continuing to walk toward the trees, her pace unchanging.

"Cathy . . . I don't think . . ." But she was oblivious to him.

So Frank followed her, reluctantly. As they neared the fenced enclosure the howling increased, and Frank knew that it wasn't people in there making all the noise, but animals, though he had never heard animal sounds quite like those.

As they passed the last tree Frank stopped, unable to proceed. Cathy walked right up to the fence. She pressed close to the wire, but not so close the outstretched paws could touch her.

The tennis courts had become a gigantic cage holding hundreds of cats. An old man stood on a ladder above the wire fence, dumping buckets of feed onto the snarling mass inside. Mesh with glass insulators attached—*electrified*, Frank thought—stretched across the top of the fence.

The old man turned to Frank and stared. He had the arched eyebrows, the pale skin and blotched cheeks. He smiled at Frank, and the shape of the lips seemed to match the shape of the eyebrows. A smile shaped like mothwings, or a bite-pattern in pale cheese, the teeth gleaming snow-white inside.

*　　*　　*

Cathy spent most of each day in the expansive Rivendale library, checking titles most of the time, but occasionally sitting down to read from a rare and privately-bound old volume. Every few hours one of the uncles, or cousins, would come in and speak to her in a low voice, nod, and leave. The longer he was here the more difficult it became to tell the Rivendales apart, other than male from female. The younger ones mirrored the older ones, and they were all very close in height, weight, and build.

When Cathy wasn't in the library she sat quietly in the parlor or dining room, or up in their own room catnapping or staring up at the ornate ceiling. She would say every day, almost ritualistically, that he was more than welcome to be with her, but he could see nothing here that he might participate in. Sitting in the parlor or dining room was made almost unbearable by the presence of the family, arranged mummy-like around the rooms. Sometimes he would pick up a volume in the library, but invariably discovered it was some sort of laborious tome on trellis and ornate gardening, French architecture, museum catalogs. Or sometimes an old leather-bound novel that read no better. It was impossible to peruse the books without thinking that whatever Cathy was studying must be far more interesting, but on the days he went he never could find the books she had been looking at, as if they had been kept somewhere special, out of his reach. And for some reason he hesitated to ask after them, or to look over his wife's shoulder as she read. As if he was afraid to.

This growing climate of awkwardness and fear angered Frank so that his neck muscles were always stiff, his head always aching. It was worse because it wasn't entirely unexpected. His relationship with Cathy had been going in this direction for some time. Until he'd met Cathy, he'd almost always been bored. As a child, always needing to be entertained. As an adult, constantly changing lovers and houses and jobs. Now it was happening again, and it frightened him.

The increasing boredom that was beginning to permeate his

stay at Rivendale, in fact, had begun to impress on him how completely, utterly bored he had been in his married life. He'd almost forgotten, so preoccupied he'd become with her disease. When Cathy's cancer had first begun, and started to spread, that boredom had dissipated. Perversely, the cancer had brought something new and near-dramatic into their life together. He'd felt bad at first: Cathy, in her baldness, in her body that seemed, impossibly, both emaciated and swollen, had suddenly become sensuous to him again. He wanted to make love to her almost all the time. After the first few times, he had stopped the attempts, afraid to ask her. But as she approached death, his desire increased.

Sometimes Frank sat out on the broad resort lawn, his lounge chair positioned under a low-hanging tree only twenty or so feet away from the library window. He'd watch her as she sat at one of the enormous oak tables, poring over the books, consulting with various elderly Rivendales who drifted in and out of that room in a seemingly endless stream. He'd heard one phrase outside the library, when the Rivendales didn't know he was near, or perhaps he had dreamed his eavesdropping while lying abed late one morning, or fallen asleep midafternoon in his hiding place under the tree. "Family histories."

The pale face with the near-hairless pate that floated as if suspended in that library window bore no resemblance to the Cathy he had known, with her dark eyes and nervous gestures and narrow mouth quick to twist ugly and vituperative. They'd discovered it was so much easier to become excited by anger, rage, and all the small cruelties possible in married life, than by love. They'd had a bad fight on their very first date. He found himself asking her out again in the very heat of the argument. She'd stared at him wide-eyed and breathless for some time, then grudgingly accepted.

Throughout the following weeks their fights grew worse. Once he'd slapped her, something he would never have imagined himself doing, and she'd fallen sobbing into his arms. They made love for hours. It became a delirious pattern. The screams, the cries, the ineffectual hitting, then the sweet tickle and swallow of a lust that dragged them red-eyed through the night.

Marriage was a great institution. It gave you the opportunity to experience both sadism and masochism within the privacy and safety of your own home.

"What do you want from me, you bastard!" Cathy's teeth flashed, pinkly . . . her lipstick was running, he thought. Frank held her head down against the mattress, watching her tongue flicking back and forth over her teeth. He was trapped.

Her leg came up and knocked him off the bed. He tried to roll away but before he could move she had straddled him, pinning him to the floor. "Off! Get off!" He couldn't catch his breath. He suddenly realized her forearm was wedged between his neck and the floor, cutting off the air. His vision blurred quickly and the pressure began to build in his face.

"Frank . . ."

He could barely hear her. He thought he might actually die this time. It was another bad joke; he almost laughed. She was the one who was always talking about dying; she could be damned melodramatic about it. She was the one with the death wish.

He opened his eyes and stared up at her. She was fumbling with his shirt, pulling it loose, ripping the buttons off. Maybe she was trying to save him.

Then he got a better look at her: the feverish eyes, the slackening jawline, tongue flicking, eyes glazed. Now she was tugging frantically at his belt. It all seemed very familiar and ritualized. He searched her eyes and did not think she even saw him.

"*Frank . . .*"

He woke with a start and stared across the lawn at the library window. Cathy's pale face stared back at him, surrounded by her even paler brethren, their mouths moving soundlessly, fish-like. He thought he could hear the soft clinking of breaking glass, or hundreds of tiny mouths trying their teeth.

* * *

The thing he would remember most was this room, and the Rivendales watching. They had a peculiar way of watching; they were very polite about it, for if nothing else they were gentlemen and ladies, these Rivendales. Theirs was an ancient etiquette, developed through practice and interaction with human beings of all eras and climes. Long before he met Cathy they had known him, followed him, for they had intimate knowledge of his type. Or so he imagined it.

Each afternoon there was one who especially drew Frank's attention: an old one, his eyebrows fraying away with the heat like tattered moth wings. He walked the same path each day, wearing it down into a seamless pavement, and only by a slight pause at a particular point on the path did Frank know the old man Rivendale was watching him. Listening to him. And that old one's habitual, everyday patterns were what made Frank wonder if the world might be full of Rivendales, assigned to watch, and recruit.

He was beginning—with excitement—to recognize them, to guess at what they were. They would always feed, and feed viciously, but their hunger was so great they would never be filled, no matter how many lives they emptied, no matter how many dying relationships they so intimately observed. Like an internal cancer, their bland surfaces concealed an inner, parasitic excitement. They could not generate their own. They couldn't even generate their own kind; they had to infect others in order to multiply.

Frank had always imagined their type to be feral, with impossibly long teeth, and foul, blood-tainted breath. But they had manners, promising a better life, and a cold excitement one need not work for.

He was, after all, one of them. A Rivendale by habit, if not by blood. The thought terrified.

The thing he would remember most was the room, and the way she looked curled up in bed, her bald head rising weakly over her shoulders.

"I have to leave, Cathy. This is crazy."

He'd been packing for fifteen minutes, hoping she'd say something. But the only sounds in the room were those of the shirts and pants being pulled out from drawers and collapsed haphazardly into his suitcase. And the sound the breeze from the window made pushing out the heavy brocade curtains, making the tiny leaf and shell pattern breathe, sigh, the tiny mouths chatter.

And the sound of her last gasp, her last breath trying to escape the confines of the room, escape the family home before their mouths caught her and fed.

"Cathy . . ." Shadows moved behind the bed. It bothered him he couldn't see her eyes. "There was no love anyway . . . you understand what I'm saying?" Tiny red eyes flickered in the darkness. Dozens of pairs. "The fighting is the only thing that kept us together; it kept the boredom away. And I haven't felt like fighting you for some time." The quiet plucked at his nerves. "Cathy?"

He stopped putting his things into the suitcase. He let several pairs of socks fall to the floor. There were tiny red eyes fading into the shadows. And mouths. There was no other excitement out there for him; he couldn't do it on his own. No other defense against the awesome, all-encompassing boredom. The Rivendales had judged him well.

Cathy shifted in the bed. He could see the shadow of her terrible swollen belly as it pushed against the dusty sheets and raised the heavy covers. He could see the paleness of her skin. He could see her teeth. But he could not hear her breathe. He lifted his knee and began the long climb across the bedspread, his hands shaking, yet anxious to give themselves up for her.

He would remember the bite marks in the cool night air, the mouths in the dark brocade. He would remember his last moment of panic just before he gave himself up to this new excitement. The thing he would remember most was the room.

Dark Shapes in the Road

IT WAS DARK when he reached his mother-in-law's house. Charlie hated driving in the dark—he *hated* it. But this had to be done in the dark if it was going to be done at all.

The fact was: Charlie hated driving any time. It was a fear of the automobile that had come so early in his life he thought he might have been born with it. Maybe it had become, since the car's first invention, a *universal,* almost a genetic fear. He was sure that most people experienced this anxiety at one time or other, after being in bumper-to-bumper traffic, after witnessing a terrible accident. The car had established its martyrs: James Dean, Albert Camus, Jayne Mansfield, Harry Chapin, Jessica Savitch. And even its own version of ultimate hell: the gridlock. Charlie found it easy to theorize about the nature of the automobile. Or, rather, he found it necessary; it kept the machine at a safer distance. But he knew that in the final analysis the theories were irrelevant. He knew that all his obsession with automotive safety was ultimately futile. The bottom line was: the automobile killed.

He cut the lights as he turned the station wagon into the driveway. Then he switched off the engine and let the car drift. It rolled forward: huge, dark, almost silent. Like a great shark. Without the lights it was hard to see, and for a moment Charlie imagined the wagon drifting over an embankment in the dead of night, or into a concrete pillar. All because he had forgotten to turn on the lights.

His wife had never understood his fear. She didn't drive herself, so she had no conception of the risk involved, and Charlie believed that made her a danger to their children.

"It's not safe, Ellen."

"You worry too much. Other people let their kids ride like this all the time. You can *overprotect* kids, you know."

"This is a station wagon. Children shouldn't ride in the back of a station wagon with no seat belts. What if there's an accident?"

"Oh, Charlie. You just like to make rules . . ."

"How are you going to feel if we're rear-ended and their little heads go smashing through all that glass? How are you going to feel to see your own kids ripped open and lying in the road?"

Ann and Timmy were crying softly, apparently frightened by their father's loud voice. Charlie wondered if it was just his shouting, or if they understood what he was talking about. He hoped they did; he hoped they got afraid enough to always be cautious.

"See now . . . you've scared them! You're sick, you know that, Charlie? You're really a sick person."

But Charlie had only the vaguest notion of what she was so upset about. He was too busy imagining his children's deaths, underneath the inexorable wheels or behind them, and already he grieved for them. How could he stand it? How could he ever bear up under the weight of those awful wheels?

Thoughts of Ellen's carelessness angered Charlie even now, when he needed to concentrate. There was too much at stake. Leaving the lights off as he entered the driveway was incautious, but necessary. Charlie bit into his lower lip and let the car drift on. He turned the wheel when he figured he'd reached the spot at the corner of the house where the driveway curved around back. He was beneath the window he wanted almost immediately. He got out of the car and climbed up on the hood, then onto the roof of the station wagon.

This had been Ellen's room originally, and the kids always slept there when they visited. He was in and out within minutes, Ann bundled sleepily into his arms, Timmy staggering as he dropped from the windowsill onto the car. Timmy began to whimper.

"Shhhh."

"But my feet hurt, Daddy."

"It's okay—I'm sorry, son," Charlie whispered. "You can go back to sleep once we get into the car." They climbed down and Charlie put them both into the back seat.

"Is Mommy coming? I'm scared, Daddy."

Charlie gunned the engine and raced backwards out of the driveway. "Don't be afraid. Daddy's here." Ann was awake now, crying. Charlie gripped the steering wheel until his hands hurt. The car squealed backwards onto the street. *It can't happen now.* Lights were going on all over the house. He could hear his wife and mother-in-law shouting. "Daddy's here and it's going to be fine." He could barely control the tremor in his voice, but he didn't want his kids to be afraid of him. "We're all going to have a good time." He sideswiped several trashcans as he roared down the street. He could hear Timmy starting to giggle. Then Ann joined in.

When Charlie was a child the road itself had delivered up to him the perfect image for the true horror of the automobile. The highways around his hometown were mostly gravel, and a trip down the mountain was a steadily increasing series of bone-rattling shakes and dancing auto parts. Charlie was terrified, imagining the car careening off the edge of the road and down an embankment at any of a dozen different curves. The fact that the accident had never occurred just made it seem all the more inevitable.

On one such trip into town the family came across an accident at a narrow place in the road. An old pickup had tried to squeeze past a larger truck with a load of dead horses for the rendering plant. The rendering truck turned over. A dead horse sprawled over the hood of the pickup, pink and gray entrails decorating the radiator. Corpses covered the road and leaned against the wreckage. They looked uncomfortably like huge human corpses, dead giants dropped from the sky. The two drivers climbed over the mound of bodies, shouting at the tops of their lungs. The dead had been forgotten. Charlie imagined that things like this must happen daily. The road and the automobile made it be that way.

Charlie watched as his mother-in-law's house finally vanished from his rear-view mirror. Ellen would be frantic. He hated to put her through the worry—Lord knows Charlie could identify with that kind of desperate worry for the kids—but she'd given him no choice. What finally finished things was a shopping trip Ellen insisted they make the day after Thanksgiving, the busiest shopping day of the year. He'd argued for two hours. But she'd insisted—they would save money.

Traffic was bumper-to-bumper to the shopping malls. People were sticking their heads out and screaming at the drivers ahead of them. One man was ramming a car that had cut him off. Several cars had stalled.

Charlie wanted to just stop the car in the middle of the road. Maybe the other vehicles would steer clear and he could escape once the traffic died down. Or a tow truck might tow them to safety. But there would be an accident if he stopped. They were only a half-mile or so from the mall when Charlie swung rapidly onto an access road.

"Charlie! What the hell are you doing?"

"Traffic's too tough, Ellen. This road will take us home safely."

"The hell it will! We've got shopping to do! Are you crazy?"

"I'm just taking the best care of you and the kids. I don't want anybody killed or crippled in this family. Now . . . now you listen to me . . ."

"Stop the fucking car!" Ellen jammed her left leg over the top of the transmission hump, forcing it far enough for her shoe to catch the top of the brake. The car jerked suddenly and began to fish-tail.

"Ellen!" The car seemed to be rocking. His children's screams filled Charlie's ears. *It's happening! It's finally happening!*

But then the car stopped dead. The motor stalled and died.

"You could have kIlled us! You could have *destroyed* our babies! Torn 'em apart! Is *that* what you wanted?"

Ellen flung open the door and was sliding the kids out before Charlie quite knew what was going on.

"You're crazy, Charlie. We're not going to be riding with you anymore."

"Ellen!"

But she'd already slammed the door. In a few minutes they were just dark shapes in the road behind him.

Ellen and the kids didn't come back that night. Or any other night. Two days later she called from her mother's to tell him she was filing for divorce. She'd seen a lawyer.

"But I *love* you and the kids. Ellen?"

There was a long pause on the other end. Then a soft voice. "I used to love you, too. But you need help, Charlie. Honestly, I think you do. You scare me and you scare the kids! Not *one* more day of it."

Charlie didn't like driving the turnpike at any time, but especially at night. It was poorly lit and poorly maintained, and he'd always suspected that some of the cars out there late at night drove without their lights on. He wasn't sure why they would do that, unless they didn't want to be seen until the very last second. Predators driven by predators. He imagined dark vehicles passing him in the night, their only sound the wind rushing by and rocking his car.

But he couldn't go home; Ellen would have called the police by now. There were several towns to the north where he might find an out-of-the-way motel room.

So he pressed the gas pedal harder than he could remember ever doing before, the fear of being stopped momentarily more pressing than the terror of mindless automotive speed. The station wagon took the curves naturally; Charlie was too tense to turn the wheel very much. The Plymouth seemed to be practically driving itself.

Occasionally his headlights would pick out an unidentifiable bit of crumpled metal, a stray hubcap, a licorice-like piece of tire. He'd move the wheel ever so slightly, just enough to avoid it, and wonder how they cleaned this stretch of road of such debris. Did they close it down for sweeping? The logistics of this simple operation seemed almost mystical to him.

Sometimes another pair of headlights would appear suddenly in his rear-view mirror, like two blazing eyes looking down at him. He'd slow a little and switch lanes. Sometimes the other car switched lanes also, and Charlie's anxiety seemed uncontainable. After a while they would be forced to pass him and he'd be reassured it wasn't the police or someone else following him.

As it grew later Charlie grew worried, and afraid. He really didn't like to be on the road this long. And it was so difficult to gauge his speed. It was easy to drive too fast on the turnpike, especially in the dark. He'd heard other people say this and it was true. You could not believe the speedometer. You could not believe you were going that fast.

He'd waited a long time to get his first driver's license, until he was almost twenty-two. But then it was time to move, to find a job. He couldn't put it off any longer. He passed the written test easily—it was just a matter of study, of automotive rules and techniques. But just thinking about the driving test brought out the cold sweats. He did pass it, but driving like a robot, wishing the other vehicles out of existence. He was lucky there hadn't been a serious accident.

There were some advantages to the daze. It kept him from thinking about the other automobiles—the Buicks, the Nash Ramblers, the ugly Packard/Studebaker wagon—approaching him, following him, coming after him in his thin metal shell of a car. His car was all that stood between him and a bone-grinding, body-rupturing death under their wheels.

Each morning when Charlie strapped himself into the family station wagon, he saw how he was going to die. Because of his own inattention the wagon would creep off the roadway, as if in slow motion. It would slide, then roll down the embankment. It would roll over once, twice, and come to rest on its smashed-in roof. Charlie would be dead inside, still hanging from his seatbelt, his neck swollen from the break.

It seemed ridiculous to be driving at this speed on the darkened turnpike, against all the cautions he'd always believed in. But he had to get to another town, to a motel, to some place safe. The faster he went, the less time he would have to drive. That made perfect sense. Driving faster would get him off the turnpike more quickly.

The wind roared in his ears. He looked around frantically, trying to see if any of the windows were down. Everything was sealed tight. But the wind continued to roar in his ears.

Charlie twisted in his seat. He was going to change lanes; it would be a little safer in the center lane. But he had to check the traffic first, see if anyone was coming up behind him, and he knew he couldn't trust the mirror completely. There were blind spots. Driving was full of little traps.

Timmy was sitting straight up in the seat. Charlie stared into the boy's pale face, transfixed.

"I had a dream, Daddy!"

"Timmy, you're blocking the window!"

"The car was coming apart . . ."

"Timmy, I can't see!"

"There were all these . . . *things* coming in after us."

"Timmy!" Charlie jerked around and wrestled with the wheel. A low, brown shape seemed to dive from the side of the road into his left front tire. The car rocked and Charlie felt the two thumps on the car's underside, as if whatever it was knocked to be let in. He glanced into the rear-view mirror and had a momentary glimpse of the large brown dog spinning on its side like a top on the road behind him.

"Daddy?"

"It was nothing, Ann. Go back to sleep." Probably belonged to some child his own kids' age. *I'm sorry, but Fluffy won't be coming home tonight*. It looked as if the dog might have committed suicide, just dived under his wheels. He wondered if humans did it that way. A high dive into flying metal.

The pavement had gotten rougher; the kids were complaining as they were knocked around on the back seat. It was incredibly bad driving for a major highway. The car was hard to control at this speed. Charlie leaned forward against the windshield trying to make out what had happened to the road, but the headlights seemed to have loosened and were jiggling too much for an accurate line of sight. Charlie made out numerous low, dark shapes. Nothing more.

The station wagon felt like an antique, much older than the miles on the odometer indicated. Maybe that dealer had rolled it back on him. He'd read about it—they used a bent piece of wire. The car seemed to be falling apart, in a Hodgkin's dance. He thought he felt pieces dropping off, and suddenly one of the jiggling headlights failed.

The car squealed, more metal flew past. There was a clatter and a sudden roaring behind him, as if all the beasts had been loosed from their cages. In the shaky illumination of the one headlight Charlie could see the dark shapes that covered the highway. They were writhing in pain. Or pleasure. He could not know.

He hoped his children were seeing all of it, however awful. He hoped their eyes and ears would be filled with it. Ellen would never understand; Ellen didn't drive. But it wouldn't be that long until his children did, and maybe his children had a chance. He was making this trip for them. And thinking that, he realized again how very important they were to him. They were more important than anything else. Particularly more than his own worn-out and neglected life. A car wasn't a toy, it was a death machine. Always had been. It destroyed the incautious.

The car leaped forward as if to pounce on the dark shapes, leaped violently, and it was as if the back of his head had blown out, trailing bloody hair and exhaust, his face roaring, his eyes blazing.

And then he knew. He knew. *It's happening now, right now*!

And he turned to check on those sweet children, but the car doors were gone, they'd been ripped off the car like wings from a tortured fly, and his beautiful children were gone, pulled back into the endless miles of black asphalt night behind him.

He twisted back over the wheel with the scream pushing out of him, roaring in unison with the engine as it pulled itself apart. The dark shapes edged closer, and he saw in the rough yellow light that they were of many different sizes and shapes. But all of them dark as the night, highlighted in red. So many dark shapes in the road, waiting to take him at last.

Spidertalk

"REALLY . . . THERE'S nothing to be afraid of, Amie."

The child curled into the corner, making herself as small as possible. Her thin arms were so rigid Liz couldn't pry them away, even using all her strength. The child seemed paralyzed, in shock, as if she'd been bitten by something poisonous.

"Amie, it's all right. They're not going to hurt you."

Amie turned her head stiffly and looked up through a mop of thick, black hair. "Everybody's always talking spidertalk! Always trying to make me afraid. I can't stand it, Miss Malloy!"

Liz thought that a strange way to put it. But then Amie was a highly nervous, anxious little girl; the tension in her often made her word choices, and even her tone of voice, sound strange. They'd been studying spiders this month in school, and Liz had gone to the trouble of setting up a terrarium with two tarantulas in the classroom. Today the other kids had been teasing Amie—Amie was terrified of spiders, even when they were just talking about them. When Liz lectured the class Amie would lay her head on the desk. Of course, most of the other children were a bit nervous around the terrarium, but Amie had always been an easy target, and she served ably to help the others forget their own fears.

"It's okay, Amie. The other kids are gone now; it's just you and me. Your mother will be here to pick you up soon. Let's get up and wait for her. Okay?"

"Okay . . ." Amie said into her arms. With a great deal of effort she unwound herself and stood unsteadily. Liz moved her gently by the shoulders, maneuvering her around the table with the terrarium, to the windows beyond. Amie pressed against her firmly as they passed the table, both arms wrapped tight and monkey-like around Liz's thighs. For some reason the desperation in the child's grip, the completeness of the child's embrace, gave Liz the creeps. Liz suppressed a tremor until they reached the windows, then delicately but forcefully removed the child's arms.

Liz would normally be home by now, but since Amie's parents had undergone a rather messy divorce she was under strict instructions from Amie's mother, and her principal, that she was to wait until Amie's mother picked her up. Amie's father wasn't permitted on the school grounds. Liz wasn't aware of all the details, but she did know that the father had been denied visitation rights, which was unusual in their small community.

"He hurt me sometimes," Amie had told her once, out of the blue, in response to some questions Liz had asked her totally off that subject. The child did that at times when she was really agitated; you had to make her slow down and think before you could follow what she was talking about. Liz had never met such a high-strung, fearful little girl. She wanted to reach out to the child while, at the same time, she was vaguely repelled by her. Perhaps she reminded her somewhat of herself—as a girl Liz had been painfully thin, and afraid of almost everything. No wonder the other children didn't like Amie. They hadn't liked Liz either.

"That's not my mommy's car." The child's voice was so unusually flat, so emotionless, that Liz at first couldn't understand what she was saying. Then the child was suddenly screaming, "It's not! It's not her car!"

"Amie! Calm down!" Liz looked out the window. It was near dusk, the sun had just begun to set, the worst time of the day for visibility. Especially from these windows facing the sun, filling with red and orange light. Trying to see through these windows into the gray-filled space between the school and the trees beyond was almost impossible in the late afternoons.

But she could just barely make out something today: a squat black car, a Volkswagen, she thought, slowly circling the visitors' parking lot. It stopped about ten yards away from their window. A tall, thin figure stepped out dressed in gray sweatpants and a stained, darker sweatshirt. She couldn't make out the face. The figure stood very still, staring at the window.

"Daddy," Amie gasped.

The figure walked slowly forward. Again, Amie began to scream.

The girl's rising screams panicked Liz. She turned and ran out the door, the strength of the little girl's voice terrifying her, spurring her on. There were only two entrances to the small school building. In a few minutes Liz had locked both and returned to the classroom. She locked her classroom door and went back to the window. Amie was silent now, staring out the window, her forehead pressed against the glass.

And then Liz had to stop and wonder why she herself had become so frightened. She'd never met the man personally, and she certainly had no evidence that he might harm either one of them.

The black car was gone. Liz started to pull away, to go to the other side of the building and look there, but she hesitated to leave Amie alone. She felt like a fool—she'd gotten so scared when Amie screamed, and hadn't realized she could have called the police from the principal's office.

"Come on, Amie. I'm taking you to another room." Liz pushed her past the terrarium, noting how agitated the normally placid tarantulas seemed. She watched their legs rising and falling in the still air of the terrarium; so many legs, it seemed, many more than eight, she might have thought. She found herself pulling away from them as she passed. She'd always been frightened of spiders herself—one of the many unreasoning fears that still clung from her childhood. That was the main reason that every school year she'd done this lesson on spiders. Although the fear was still there under the surface, the lesson helped her control it. And yet now, with that black Volkswagen moving slowly through the dusk out there, perhaps even now circling the building, searching for a way in, she could not believe she had so calmly held one of these creatures in her hand that very afternoon.

They reached the door, opened it, and Liz pushed Amie out into the hall. Amie began to scream. When Liz rushed to the girl's side, she found her staring at the end of the hallway, at the glass entrance doors there. Which were now filled with the glare of headlights. A car had pulled up head-on against the door, only a few inches away. The glare obscured its form.

Liz expected the car to come crashing through those doors at any moment. She grabbed Amie and pulled her back into the classroom, again locking the door. Once inside, she shoved one of the work tables against the door, as well as several of the children's desks. She grabbed the table holding the terrarium, began to shove it, then saw the glass case begin to rock simultaneously with Amie's loud sobs.

She stopped. The terrarium settled into place. Amie flew into her arms, trying to wrap wiry legs around her thighs, both bony arms around her neck. Suddenly Liz couldn't breathe—she felt attacked by the child's small limbs, trapped. "Amie!" she gasped, and struggled to pull her off. The girl was crying. "Amie, please!" She slipped her arms around the girl's shoulders and jerked down. Amie fell at Liz's feet, almost hysterical now, her hands clenching and unclenching, needing something to hold.

Liz picked her up and carried her to a bench by her desk, and sat down with her, holding her, stroking her dark hair. She stared at the tarantulas, now calm behind their walls of glass. She felt exhausted by her own fear, and drained by this fearful little girl. She remembered she had a date with Roger tonight, Roger with the sure hands and fierce embraces, who wanted to marry her, to—as he often said—*make her his forever*. It didn't bother her that he might be worried; she wasn't even sure why she continued to see him. She had thought she loved him. But somehow he made her afraid. Chilled, Liz began to speak slowly, softly, trying to think of lullabies as she talked about the spiders. She held Amie tight as the child began to pull away from her spidertalk.

"No, Amie. It helps you know about what you're afraid of. No . . . please, Amie. They can't hurt you—we've fixed them so they can't bite. Besides, even in the wild their bite won't kill you. That's just a story. People are afraid of them because they look so ugly. We're all afraid of ugly things with lots of legs that grab and hold on.

"All spiders are like that. And when you're afraid of them, it seems like you see them everywhere . . ."

They were standing by the terrarium now, Amie transfixed, gripping Liz's hand. Liz opened the lid and inserted a long rod beneath one of the tarantulas, turning it over. It immediately righted itself, making unbroken progress in its cage-crawl, inexorable, driven, mindless in its movements. Liz found that appalling. "See how it rights itself? It wants to be left alone, not bothered, just like we do." She removed the rod, careful not to touch the end that had touched the spider. "The smaller one there is the female. See how she crouches in the dirt, Amie? There's a tunnel under there where she keeps her babies." Amie looked up at her. "Yes . . . you never thought about spiders having babies, did you?" Amie shook her head.

"Can I see them . . . the babies?" Amie asked.

"No, not now—we wouldn't want to disturb them, But we will later in the class. I promise." The talk about babies seemed to have done it. Amie looked much more relaxed. She didn't even glance at the windows anymore. Liz, however, continued to stare at the larger male spider, its hairy, bristly legs, the too-rapid way it moved. Spiders were damn fertile things, and they wove such beautiful webs. To trap insects, to kill them. It seemed as if they produced life only in order to bring about death. But wasn't that the terrible truth about all life and birth? Maybe that was the real reason they appalled and frightened her so. They were a perverted reminder of the human condition.

When she was a girl in Texas, some of the neighborhood kids had doused a tarantula with lighter fluid, and set it on fire. The enormous spider had staggered a minute, blazing brightly. Finally the legs gave out, it collapsed on the ground, and then the fire went out. The other kids poked it—and the shell broke. It had burned from the inside out, all the softness melting away, leaving just that terrible mask.

"They eat birds, small mice sometimes . . ." she continued. "But they're not dangerous to people. There's no reason to be afraid, Amie. No reason at all."

But her fear was a living thing with a mind of its own, that would not respond to her own sense of reason. She was afraid of these spiders, as she was afraid of Roger, afraid of little Amie, afraid of the black Volkswagen outside circling the building so slowly, penning her in, trapping her, wrapping its long bristly dark legs around her thighs and shoulders, embracing her so roughly, needing her so much. She'd always been afraid as a small child, and as she had grown so had her fear. Now it was bigger than these spiders. No one had been much help to her with it; most of her friends just made fun of her. Or made it worse, talking spidertalk all the time, spidertalk about spiders, snakes, the dark, and withered old men with ugly eyes and rough hands. Hideous talk.

She could sense the small grey spiders in all corners of the room, building their webs, listening, all these small fears lying in wait for her wherever she went. Once you're afraid of them, they seem to pop up everywhere. It was true.

She'd behaved illogically, irresponsibly, this afternoon, and she'd always prided herself on being a responsible teacher. It was because she had been so afraid. Her fear had paralyzed her, as if she'd been bitten.

She went to the window. The sun was setting rapidly. Broad threads of silk were floating down out of the darkening sky, the setting sun making them glisten a blood-red color, thousands of them, each silkstrand bearing a spider. When Liz was a child they called it gossamer.

Amie's father stood in front of the black Volkswagen, his dark figure hard to see because of all the spidersilk. He had raised his hand; a red and green scarf hung from it like a trophy. Liz had seen that scarf many times: Amie's mother wore it often when she picked up Amie in her old Chevy convertible.

The scarf floated to the ground. Then Liz saw the convertible parked nearby, the shadowed form sprawling half out the door, the door light on, the bright red interior rapidly filling with silk, the spiders, traveling.

The tall, narrow shape of Amie's father, draped with silk, was strolling toward the building. Crushing hundreds of the quick-legged spiders beneath his feet. Everywhere.

"Look! Miss Malloy, look at the spiders!"

Liz turned to Amie to reassure her, ready to deny her own vision of the spiders floating down from the skies, when she saw that Amie wasn't looking out the window, but into the terrarium containing the two tarantulas. Liz stumbled against several desks in her haste.

The female tarantula was moving slowly, as if reluctantly. "The babies!" Amie cried gleefully, as all the glass in the room began to break, the terrarium, the windows, the cupboard, as the hundreds of bone-white infants spilled from the cocooned cavity in the dirt, each wearing a mask of Liz's fear.

Punishment

JENNIFER WAS DRIVING me crazy. She had been hanging around the house all day, pacing, restless. Picking up a book or a magazine, glancing at it a few minutes, then dropping it again. Nibbling at television segments, switching channels every few minutes. Not bothering to check the paper to see what was on, or forthcoming, content to indulge in this frenetic inventory of random images. I'd warned her about the TV before, and about how she'd wear out the tuner. I'd been lecturing her for years about how a television set was *not* a toy, and that she'd have to use it correctly or she wouldn't be permitted to use it at all.

But I couldn't correct her now. I found it difficult to say anything to her. When she looked at me, she looked past me. She was distracted, thinking about something, and it made me very nervous because I could never figure what she really thought about anything. Everything she did was unpredictable. Things would be missing, things would break or become rearranged, strange bills would come to the house or strange people would show up on the front steps, and there seemed no other explanation except that Jennifer had had her hand in it. Although I can't say that we ever caught her at anything she couldn't explain her way out of. That made it all the worse, however—we knew she had been doing things and yet we couldn't confront her directly about them.

"I'm going out now, to Marcie's."

I was relieved. She made me uncomfortable hanging around like that. And, unaccountably, afraid. But I couldn't forget that I was still her father. I had responsibilities. A duty to my daughter. "You'll be back by bedtime, Jennifer. Am I right?"

Again, she stared past me. When she looked like that I would have sworn that, deep down, she hated me. But who could know? I had no idea what she felt about anything; I didn't even know if Marcie was her best friend, or just a casual friend. "Of course," she said. "I always am."

The uneasiness she'd caused me made me angry. "I don't like that tone. You're my daughter; I have a *right* to expect you home on time."

She stared past me.

"Do you hear me, Jennifer?"

"Of course, Father." She looked bored; I felt silly. "I promise I'll be home at the *correct* time."

Five minutes later she left.

She didn't come home until late the next afternoon. We'd been frantic. And she'd sneaked into her upstairs bedroom and gone to sleep. We didn't even know until my wife opened her door to put some of her laundry on the bed. My wife came running down the stairs, insisting that I go wake her, have a talk with her, "throw the book at her." She was afraid to do it herself. But then so was I. I was afraid of what might happen, and yet I couldn't even imagine what that might be.

I thought my daughter might try something awful, and yet I had no idea why I would think such a thing. So I convinced my wife we needed to give her some space, some time to work out her own problems. And I used that as my excuse for not going upstairs and talking, confronting my Jennifer.

The baby watches you, and yet you don't have the language with which to admonish her. You shout at her; she can't look at you this way. But she maintains her cool control. Everything you can do will not change her.

My wife and I have always put great stock in being good parents. We decided early on that we would bend over backwards to be fair to our daughter. We would always listen to her, we would not unfairly accuse her, we would give her plenty of chances to do the right thing.

Punishment, if it had to come to that, would be logical, suited to the infraction. If she stole something, she had to give it back and apologize. If she broke something, she had to replace it. If she violated the rules while playing outside, the following day she would not be allowed to play outside. If she was careless with the TV, she could not watch the TV for a logically-arrived-at period of time. If she wasted someone's time and energy, she owed that person an equal amount of time and energy. We didn't want to be too harsh, or too easy.

"You are not allowed in our bedroom when we're not here, Jennifer! You've no business here! We don't go in your bedroom, ever. That's how much we bend over backwards to respect *your* privacy. Most parents don't do that; they go into their kids' rooms."

"I know." She was so calm it infuriated me.

"As a consequence you won't be allowed upstairs for a week. Of course, that also means you won't be using the upstairs TV room, either."

"Okay. I understand." Then she turned and went back downstairs.

I couldn't believe it—no reaction at all. She spent most of her time in the upstairs TV room. My wife and I seldom used it, and perhaps it was a more neutral place than her own room for getting away from things. Although what it was she needed to get away from I had no idea. But I respected her right to have such a place, whether I completely understood it or not. After all, I was trying desperately to be a good parent.

I knew that room was terribly important to her; she shouldn't have been so calm about the punishment. What it was, I concluded, was that she was pretending that the punishment

didn't matter, that we couldn't do anything to her that mattered. She was in control. That was the way she walked the
line without tipping over into outward disobedience: she just
made herself not care. It was maddening.

And what had she been doing in our bedroom?

Children had obviously changed since we had grown up.
By the age of eight they were hardly children anymore. They
didn't respect people's property, and they had lost their fear
of the police. Their childhood innocence had been replaced
by a tangle of resentments. My wife and I agreed on that
point. It was a frightening thing, what children had become in
recent years. It was difficult, trying to imagine what they
might be thinking. We weren't sure how things had arrived at
such a state, but all the books said it was the lack of punishment, or the lack of logic or consistency to it. So it seemed
that punishment was the thing to work on with our Jennifer.

She had been a beautiful baby: silky blond hair, great green
eyes. Her lips were exquisitely sculptured, divided neatly in
half by a subtle fold. I remember her beauty startling me at
the time; I hadn't realized a baby's looks could affect me so.

"What do you suppose she's thinking?" I asked my wife.
Our daughter Jennifer stared up at us, practically unmoving,
her green eyes drinking us in.

"I don't know; do babies *think,* really?"

"I'm not sure. I suppose it's something like thinking . . .
maybe 'reacting' would be a better word, though. But somehow, from the look of her, I don't think their reactions are
really all that simple."

Jennifer's eyes didn't track, I found it discomfiting to
watch them. I wondered if she could possibly understand
anything we were saying, or perhaps babies naturally *mis-
understand*. They don't know the language yet, so they imagine what the adults must be trying to communicate. God
knows what they must think. Jennifer seemed to be listening,
but do babies listen? I think they do—I really think they do.

The baby stares at you, and it makes you so uncomfortable you want to leave the room. But you can't leave the room. After all, you're the parent. You become frightened that you might be tempted to strike such a child, if it doesn't stop. There seems to be something willful in the stare. You're not sure what you should do about that. After all, you're the parent. And it's your responsibility to both civilize this child and yet encourage it, allow it to be what it really wants to be. But what if it wants to be a monster? And you start thinking of logical consequences that will get rid of that stare that makes you so uneasy.

Deciding at what age to instigate this program of logical punishments was our first difficult parenting decision. Many parents start shortly after birth—mistakenly, I think. They ignore the baby if it cries excessively—they don't want to spoil the child. They restrict its movements; they lecture it, using their harshest tones. And some few actually spank the baby. All these punishments indicate a basic misunderstanding of this stage of life. This is the animal stage, the beast stage, I think. And if the baby isn't allowed to live its bestiality to the fullest there will be that much more difficulty when it is time to civilize the child and bring it into the human community. You wouldn't cage a squirrel, or lecture a badger. So why use punishment on a baby?

"You haven't been to school all week. Where have you been?"

"Just around."

"Around where?" I realized I'd shouted; she'd gotten to me. Bad technique. I wanted desperately to take it back; I couldn't afford any mistakes with my daughter. Everything counted.

"The park, mostly. Sitting, you know? Catnapping. Once or twice down to the drugstore. And once over at the video parlor."

"I want you to write down dates, times, places."

She just looked at me; I watched her closely for any indications of a smile. Then I'd really "throw the book at her." But she was good with that face of hers; you couldn't tell what was going on. I realized I'd just made a very parental-sounding and impossible demand. And she knew I'd realized that. Once again she retained control over the situation.

"I can't do that," she said. "I can't remember that exactly." I was trying to think of a way out of my impossible, guaranteed-to-lose demand, when she added, "No one could."

I could have hit her, and she knew it. And she knew I wouldn't let myself. "What can I do to make you stop? How bad a consequence does it have to be?" I was shaking.

"I don't know, Father." She stared right through me.

My wife and I were convinced that you should start using punishment around the age of two. This is the time when the child can truly be manipulative, can hide its true motivations from the adult.

Jennifer always made us a little uneasy with this punishment schedule, however firmly we believed in it. For even as an infant she seemed manipulative. She'd scream and we'd come running only to see her lying there peacefully. Or she'd be obviously so tired she was nodding off in your arms, but still wanted to wander off when you set her down. When she was old enough to walk she was constantly running for the road, then stopping just as suddenly before she got into any real danger.

"What is it with her? She just stares at you, like she knows she's in complete control."

"She's just a baby."

"Is she? What's a baby supposed to be like, anyway? I never knew any babies who acted like this, did you?"

Later we would both wonder if we should have been firmer when Jennifer was a baby. But how do you ever know? Adults are basically afraid of children, I concluded. I never shared the idea with my wife; it would have upset her too much. Because she was even more frightened of Jennifer than I was, I'm sure. The fear comes, in part, from the amount of responsibility a parent has. You have to civilize this creature, make it a contributing member of society. But it's alien, essentially, and doesn't share your values or goals. It's as if you're trying to take a native of some other planet and force it into a mask so that it will pass for a human being. And maybe after a few years, if you're lucky, it forgets it ever was an alien and truly believes itself to be a human being capable of programming other new arrivals on our planet into a human resemblance.

Often I tried to remember what it had been like when I was Jennifer's age. For the longest time I thought I could remember. Then I realized it was an adult myth of childhood I was recalling. I couldn't remember my own childhood accurately at all.

We wouldn't make things easier for her. She would be exposed to whatever consequences the real world had to offer. That was the way it was supposed to work. But after a time we began to wonder if our daughter was impervious to those consequences.

The baby watches you discussing her, and knows—you are convinced—what you are saying. What you are thinking.

When the baby moved away from us, crawling on the floor, she was all back and head in her roomy flannel nightgown. I'd swear she was a crawling torso, born without arms and legs. And when I finally saw those little hands and feet I'd swear they were prosthetic appendages, so unnatural they seemed.

"She's gone again." My wife poured the orange juice that morning, her hands trembling. But her voice sounded as if this were an everyday occurrence. And that was almost true.

"She's probably in the neighborhood."

"I hope the weather is okay today." My wife always said this. Practically whispered it.

"I hope so, too. But she's the one choosing to be out, just remember that. I guess I don't even worry anymore. She always comes back, so I guess I figure she must be capable of handling it out there. One thing, though."

"What's that?"

"Lock the doors, and the windows. I won't have her sneaking around, the way she's acting. It's like we're under siege here, subject to sudden assault. There's no telling what she might do, and I won't have that worry hanging over my head anymore."

"But how's she going to get in?"

"She'll come to the front door and knock like a decent human being, or she won't come in at all."

There were periods—six months in the middle of Jennifer's sixth year, three months near the beginning of her seventh—in which she was a real terror. Every few minutes she'd whine or yell or hit or disobey us concerning some minor issue. You couldn't allow her out of your sight during those periods—she might walk into someone else's house and steal food out of a refrigerator, or strike another child to take a toy, or throw rocks at a passing car. She became uncharacteristically unkempt—she always looked as if she had slept in her clothes. I would have sworn her face had grown wrinkled and brittle that year, as if whatever had caused her behavior was a disease that also aged her.

"You can't do things like that, Jennifer! You're not the only person in the world! How is anyone going to like you when you act that way?" She stared right through me. "They're just not, that's the answer! No one's going to like you, or trust you, Jennifer!"

The baby drank it all in, with no reaction. Sometimes you just wanted to beat the lesson into her. But that would be an awful thing; you couldn't think about that. You wanted to be a good parent. But the baby was in complete control.

Raising children, trying to help them become civilized

human beings, was the most frightening thing in the world. It was a horror.

"She's been in the neighborhood. I think I saw her coat in the distance." My wife looked as if she hadn't slept in days.

"She'll come around eventually. I'm through chasing her."

"But it's been four days!"

"And you know she's okay. You said yourself she's been in the neighborhood. So she must be okay, right?"

"But we're her *parents* . . ."

"I made the police report, didn't I? What more can I do? It's up to her when she comes back. She's in control of that."

My wife just shook her head and lowered her eyes. I was thinking of Jennifer's presence, wandering the outskirts of our neighborhood. I looked out the window; it was starting to snow. But Jennifer being out in that kind of weather wasn't what was chilling me so thoroughly then. It was the image of her trying to break into our house after we'd gone to sleep, our guard down, our lives so vulnerable. And her succeeding.

As Jennifer grew older she was subject to terrifying outbursts of violence with little provocation. All you had to do was tell her to do something she didn't want to do. With every action she begged us to hit her, to match her violence with some of our own. But we resisted. We shook inside, but we resisted. She seemed inhumanly stubborn.

We watched her behavior for a very long time, obsessed with it until our vision of her pressed farther and farther into the future. A criminal teenager. A criminal adult. I found myself reading about the frequency of women being executed for murder in our state.

Punishment made no difference at these times. The awful behavior persisted. Was there some mysterious factor in the way we treated her that had caused it all? It was a cliché to say the problem had originated in the family dynamics themselves, a cliché that we'd always thought terribly unfair. But we had to wonder if, in this case, there was some truth in it.

She seemed totally unaware of the feelings of others; she didn't care whom she hurt. "Sociopath" was a word we dared not use in each other's presence. Was there something hereditary in her behavior? My wife and I could not discuss this aspect, but we watched each other's behavior carefully, and wondered.

A few times while she was missing in that storm I thought I saw her in the distance, but of course I couldn't be sure. And it made me feel a little guilty, not racing across the blanket of snow to find her and drag her back home with me. The blue color of her coat, that candy-striped scarf she always wore. Her heaviest clothing—as if she had known it was going to snow.

"What if she dies?" Each night when we turned out the lights and crawled into bed my wife would start talking about her. She'd drone on about the same points night after night.

I had no reply for that one. We're all going to die, and there was no reason, in any case, to think that Jennifer was in a great deal more danger than sitting in her own home or walking to school alone. But I couldn't say any of that to my wife. It wouldn't have reassured her. It would, in fact, have made it worse. "She'll be okay," I said lamely.

"She's punishing us," my wife said for the hundredth time. She always sounded as if she blamed me for it.

It worried me—it was well-known that the parents of demanding babies were more likely to argue, to experience various crises. Most of our arguments had been about Jennifer anyway, ever since she was born.

The baby stares at you. You will never understand why, but you are convinced the baby knows far more than you, or at least it knows a great deal about things you never even knew existed. Secret rules operating upon the world. It's a very different creature from what you've become. That's why it so often seems to stare past you, at the darkness behind you. That's why it smiles when you offer up your meager, self-serving punishment.

It snowed off and on for four days. We continued to see what we thought were glimpses of her in the distance, but nothing ever definitive. The police were becoming irritated with all my calls; they made me promise I wouldn't bother them anymore, but they promised to call me as soon as they uncovered any leads. It was clear from their tone they were pessimistic about the possibilities—they kept suggesting that Jennifer was just another runaway. But I knew better. I didn't know if I was more concerned about her safety or about her sneaking up on us unannounced. Surprising us.

I didn't tell my wife I'd been calling the police like that. I suppose I still wanted her to think I intended to follow the "logical consequences" philosophy of leveling punishment to the end. Jennifer's being out in this snowstorm was a logical consequence of her running away. The real world was therefore punishing her, not us. I thought the police half-understood that also.

But they'd asked me several times why I hadn't gone after Jennifer when we thought we caught glimpses of her in the distance, a sudden apparition in the breaks of the storm. Each time I explained to them my ideas concerning punishment and they seemed to understand, and yet they continued to ask this question again and again. I knew I was telling a different officer each time, but it still seemed to me they shouldn't be asking that same question all the time.

I asked myself repeatedly if perhaps my wife and I had overreacted to Jennifer. When I talked to the police I found it difficult to recall specific incidents to explain why we had to take the disciplinary measures we did. It all seemed a little silly and overblown now. But when they removed their pressure and weren't questioning me it was clear how extreme Jennifer's bad behavior had become. She refused to accept our authority in any form. What could we do? She was denying our role as parents and we had to get that role back. She had to learn to accept our punishment.

Sometimes you wonder if you are totally unqualified to take care of the baby. This is a frightening thing for you. But the doubts are always there, and become more prominent the more you discover how alien the baby is from you, how very different. How could you be expected to raise a creature of an entirely different species?

I knew Jennifer had been in the house for a couple of days. I could feel her presence, but although I searched everywhere I could not find her. Our things were rearranged. Some things were missing. She had brought a chill into the house with her.

She was there, somewhere, in the house.

She decided I couldn't leave the bedroom at night. When I'd get up to use the bathroom in the middle of the night her cold hands would be on me, restraining me. She decided I was reading too much, or spending too much time in the TV room. When I stayed more than five minutes in that room she made it unbearably cold, or she'd shadow the TV screen, or she'd blow the pages back and forth restlessly in my hands.

At night she would whisper in my ear, then pretend she hadn't said a word. She stared right through me; I could feel her eyes.

Occasionally I caught glimpses of her—turning a corner or rising up the shadowed staircase. I wondered if she was having boyfriends over—I could hear other teenagers in her room some evenings—but she didn't give me the opportunity to admonish her. A few times I ran into her in a darkened room, face-to-face, but she continued to stare through me, punishing me. I loved my daughter, and needed desperately to understand her. But when I tried to embrace her she was gone, and I was embracing the dark.

I began to worry about physical punishment. I could see my daughter's hands in the dark—the daughter I knew I still loved, no matter what—and I could no longer sleep the night completely through.

The baby stares past you, into the dark. You cannot know what it is thinking because its mind is very different from yours. You love it without considering and yet you have no idea what it is you're loving. Its mind is alien. It knows things you will never know. It cries and waits for you to react. It wets its bed and makes you feel inadequate, and waits for you to react. It throws a tantrum and waits for you to react. The punishment it has devised for you is both straight-forward and logical.

The Overcoat

WHEN I FIRST saw the overcoat I thought it was a man slumped there, in the alley between Ellison's Deli and the Apex Pool Hall. A warmly-dressed, elderly man, the collar and shoulders of the gray and black tweed coat pushed up over his neck and half-concealing his small, white head. The angle and the lighting had deceived me—the coat was neckless and headless. Yet it seemed to be propped up there, sitting in an unnatural way.

It was an elegant coat for all its age and wear. A subtle blending of black and grey weaves, with here and there a touch of white. The seams and shoulders had maintained their positions well. The buttons were large, black, old-fashioned; they appeared to be wooden, and each bore an ornate cross, like something from a crusader's armor, the crosses highlighted in silver in the dim morning light that spilled over the high walls of the alley. The lapels were wide, as were the shoulders; the coat would have come down to about mid-thigh if I had tried it on. All in all, it was the kind of garment I could really become attached to.

Actually, I had once had a coat very much like it, passed down to me from my father, who had worn it almost every day for the last years of his life. Even during the summers, much to my mother's annoyance.

But now I couldn't bring myself to touch it.

I never saw my father touch my mother. I never heard him

say more than commonplaces to her. But he loved that coat. It kept him warm, however shabby he and it might have become together.

"A good coat is all a man needs, really," he'd say. "Hell, get a big coat, I always say, big a one as you can find. My daddy had one that'd sleep a family of four pretty comfortable." Then he'd horse-laugh. It was my father's favorite joke, and he repeated it often.

"A man's inners get soft and raw as he gets older." That was another of my father's theories. "A good coat protects 'em, keeps your guts from sloshing around, hanging all out if you know what I mean." I didn't, but it would have been foolish to say so. I used to wonder how my father came to be convinced of such craziness. That particular theory gave me nightmares. I'd dream of my father standing in the doorway all bundled up in his old coat. Then he opened it. Each time in the dream I'd want to believe he had brought home something from the butcher's—they just hadn't bothered to wrap it. But then the raw red and grey lumps started to fall, and my father was screaming soundlessly, like a fish. There were bleeding horrors beneath that old coat.

My father died of consumption, but by that time he was eaten up by cancer and other nameless ills. Too much drinking, smoking and carousing, the doctor said. That and passing out in the street and having to sleep there all night. No help for someone like that, the doctor said. Just another drunk. Just another bum. No help for those kind. Nothing you could ever do for them would save them. Everything you did for them became a dangerous drain on your own life. They were determined to crap out on you.

I never got to say goodbye to my father. But I got his coat "for my protection." Just like it had protected my father. My mother said it was the only thing he ever wrote down by way of a will.

When I put that big old coat on I'd find myself unbuttoning it every few minutes to see what I looked like beneath it. Or I'd run a finger under the front of it, then check my finger.

I had my father's coat for a year before I met the tramp in the diner. He wore a baseball cap and a light-weight summer shirt, even though it was late fall. The cheap radio he carried—held closely to the ear because, he said, he'd lost the earphones, or they'd been stolen but he didn't want to accuse anyone—had British flag decals pasted all over it. "The British Invasion!" "The British Are Coming!" He was probably fifty years old, maybe fifty-five. His hair was extremely short and missing in spots, as if he'd had scabies that had had to be cut out.

He sat down across from me, our knees touching under the cracked formica table. "Nice coat," he said.

"Thank you." I felt incongruously formal. I noticed the liver spots like birthmarks on his hands.

"The British are coming," he said, pointing to his radio with a knowing look.

"I see." I smiled, feeling ridiculous.

"My name's Frank," he said. And smiled back.

"Steve," I said. And smiled again. But then his liver-spotted hand reached out and touched me under the table.

I reached down and removed his hand then, just as I had scolded my own father many times during his last years, when he'd been childish or mean with my mother. I held the tramp in my eyes. "You shouldn't do things like that, Frank. Someone else might have really hurt you bad for doing a thing like that."

Frank looked down, ashamed. "I'm sorry. I'm *bad* sometimes."

Again surprising myself, I reached over and touched his sleeve. "It's all right, Frank. Just be careful about that sort of thing."

He looked up at me, and then I knew he thought of himself as the consummate con-artist. And maybe some days he actually was. "I'm awfully cold. No place to go. Could I have that coat?"

Part con-artist and part child. I've never quite understood my actions that night. I gave him my father's coat. Maybe it would protect him, keep his raw "inners" safe. It was much too big for him. Walking away, he looked like a clown. He stuck the radio inside, and said out loud that it tickled, singing into his chest. I was cold walking home.

This coat propped up in the alley was very like that one. But I couldn't touch it, couldn't try it on.

The next day the coat was still there. The garbage around it had a slightly different arrangement, and for some reason that bothered me. Partially opened cans lay around the coat, but they certainly hadn't been touched by your standard electric can opener. They were bent lopsided, the tops twisted as if they'd been punched, crushed, chewed, the contents sucked out. I picked up a can; blood spotted the bent lid.

I stared at the coat. Blood dotted the cuff of the right sleeve. At least I was pretty sure it was blood. I was also pretty sure that it hadn't been there yesterday. In all my admiration for that overcoat, I would have noticed.

I looked at the bulges in the cloth about where a stomach and chest would be. They weren't very large, and about what you'd expect in a coat left bent that way, stiffened with age or filth, and beginning to lose some of its shape. There was a mild breeze in the alley, no doubt concentrated because of the high walls and the ever-so-slight slope of the building that dead-ended the alley. That, I was sure, was what made the bulges seem to stir, to breathe as I stared at them.

I turned to leave. I was feeling sad, and frightened, and something else not quite explainable.

Nor can I explain what I did next. I reached into my jacket pocket—I'd bought it at Sears, a short corduroy jacket with what I hoped was a reassuringly dull history—and pulled out the chocolate bar I was carrying there. I dropped it behind me, by the overcoat. Then I walked out of the alley without looking back. Perhaps I do too many things I can't explain.

I lived then in a poor, run-down section of the city, the kind of neighborhood I'd always gravitated to. Old tenements

with architectural character crumbling to plasterdust in the
corners, peeling off the walls. Plumbing and electricity working haphazardly in buildings not designed for them originally.
Cheap, roomy apartments, and frequently someone passed out
on the steps in front of the building, or on the hall steps
inside. You stepped over them, or picked them up and carried
them if you knew them a bit and they lived there. Dogs and
derelicts would come in to relieve themselves, sometimes
together. It made my few friends crazy, but none of it ever
bothered me.

There was something about those people. Their needs were
naked; there was little point hiding them. It made me wonder
if I would become that way if I lost the little I had. A child
again, with no need to pretend, asking without hesitation.
Whether deserved or not, those people let you love them.
They couldn't help letting you love them. In that regard they
were quite different from my father. Maybe I could do something, and maybe my effort wasn't wasted. I wasn't a saint,
but I carried them to their rooms. I wasn't even a very nice
person at that time—I was much too full of myself—and yet I
bought them meals, gave them rides in my car. I had no
illusions—they didn't give a damn about me—but they let me
love them.

The ones who actually lived in the streets, who had no
homes nor even an occasional rented room, were nearly
invisible most of the time. When the weather got cold—when
you began seeing the large boxes erected over gratings, the
sections of plywood and sheet metal and plastic dragged into
dark backalleys, the spaces under the overpasses turned into
rough-made caves—you realized how many of them there
were. A city within the city seeking its own kind of shelter. It
made you wonder where they had all come from, and I was
convinced I didn't see most of them during the course of a
normal day, even if we lived on the same block. I began to
wonder if there might be some you never saw at all, who
didn't want to be seen, ever, except by their own kind.

I wasn't a saint. And I wasn't their own kind, although
sometimes I dreamed I was.

In ancient times, the unwanted were cast out to die from exposure, without the modern miracle of the cardboard box or the plastic grocery bag.

Each day I left a few more groceries in the alley, an offering to the overcoat. Which altered itself slightly each day, lost more of its shape, as if it were shrinking from within. Starving itself no matter how much I fed it. Its lack of progress frustrated me. Malnutrition is a terrible thing; the coat's persistent ill health enraged me. I wasn't their kind, never would be. Each day the food I had left the day before had been ripped from its packages and devoured.

A pack of dogs could have done such a thing, but they would have disturbed the coat as well. And although the coat was collapsing a bit, it still retained its luster, and any movement of the overcoat was no more than that a body might make after being forced to sit in one place for too long a time.

People screamed, hit each other, abused each other all the time. Sometimes in the streets, to a stranger, but most of the time it would be a couple, or someone and their kid, screaming and pounding and snapping and slapping right on the other side of that rotting panel of plaster, only a few feet from your nose. It was always a question of when to call the cops. Most of the time you didn't, else you'd be calling them ten times a night. Usually if there was a gun shot, or if the context of the screams indicated there might be a knife or club involved, then you called. Lots of people got badly hurt, but what were you supposed to do? Even the cops couldn't tell you when you should call. You shut your door and turned up the TV. Pretty soon it was just white noise. I wasn't a saint.

An old man sprawled on the sidewalk near the opening of the alley, sobbing and spitting up into a metal can, a crumpled bit of paper in his hand. He said somebody went and tore up his million dollar lottery ticket, now how was he going to get right?

The coat was quite sunken now, but still splendid, a beautiful piece of goods. I still secretly wanted to slip it under my arm, take it home and maybe even wear it, protect myself from the cold for a change. The jacket from Sears always seemed too thin for the city winds; the high buildings and narrow street-canyons resulted in a ''wind tunnel'' effect. I really needed a heavier, old-fashioned coat. But I was still afraid, wondering if the wrong person might see me, and if there was a wrong person to see me.

Some of the groceries from last time were untouched, unopened. I gazed at the coat, now looking slumped in defeat. It seemed much thinner than I remembered, more like an autumn jacket, as if some of the lining had been eaten out. What had I been thinking of? There was nothing here but an old coat, and groceries a fool had left for the dogs and cats and rats to rummage through. I kicked at one of the unmolested cans.

It thumped and clacked against pavement, a harsh metallic sound, coming to rest against one sleeve of the coat.

A long, wormlike finger, followed by something like an eye, webbed skin shrouding something unrecognizable, darted out and snagged the can. Sucked it back so quickly the sleeve looked empty again, like after an amputation.

The coat began to dance, a waltz and then a jitterbug.

There was the sound of metal warping, then a moist sound.

I don't understand why I didn't run then. But I'm not the only one who's ever missed a chance to escape.

More pale worm-ends shot out of sleeves, collar, and open waist, unrecognizable pink and gray flesh. In the flurry the can was ejected, empty.

And in the flurry I saw my father open his old, bloody coat, and his pink and gray entrails falling loose. Disease-ridden, worthless, and all because he was careless, irresponsible, depending on an old coat to protect him from everything. Dying and leaving us alone. Didn't even get to say goodbye. And then he leaves me that goddamned coat. As if that's what's going to protect me, keep me safe and sane as I grow older.

And now here's this thing, itself so much like a mass of diseased entrails, some new mutated breed of homeless derelict in the city. But it's no better than any of the rest of them. It pretends to be helpless, and then it rips cans apart. It lets me give it food, but gives me nothing in return, not even its improved health. There's no helping them. They'll drain you if you let them, and then they won't even let you say goodbye. They'll leave you a filthy old coat, good for nothing but to hide the disease, letting it eat you to raw hamburger if you don't open the coat and look in time.

I turned and left there. But slowly.

Somehow my neighbors knew a truce had been broken. Somehow they knew I was on to their manipulations.

During the next two weeks someone stole two books of checks out of my apartment. The police found the kids who did it; their father, a fellow tenant, had ordered them to climb over the transom. The police stopped me for urinating in public. I hadn't done it—a man was sick and I had turned my back on the street and gone over to the corner to see if I could help. He ran away. The police let me go with a warning. Someone drew a nail down the length of my car; someone else—or maybe it was the same person—slashed the left front tire. The hotel where I lived was noisy all the time; there were parties, fights, and party/fights late every night.

Someone groped me in the hall. Someone spat on me. Someone whispered endearments I couldn't begin to understand. Before, they had always let me love them. I had needed them to let me love them.

When I went back to the overcoat the material was nearly flat. Just in case, I had brought a loaf of bread and a can of peas. I scattered the slices of bread all around. Like leaves over a drunkard sleeping under a tree. There was no response. I threw the can into the middle of the black and gray folds. Nothing. I kicked at the beautiful overcoat.

The coat turned on its side. Something long, pink and gray drifted out of one sleeve. It stirred ever so slightly.

I picked up a brick at the side of the alley and dropped it on the pink and gray thing. The coat spasmed, but only minutely. I picked up more bricks and dropped them over various parts of the coat. I emptied a barrel of trash and rolled the barrel up and down the length of the coat, pressing it flat. I did a silly dance on it. If I'd had a match I would have set the whole thing on fire, like a schoolboy dumb to evil with a stray cat.

I turned and left the alley. Again, I did not run.

I gave away all the things I didn't need. The other tenants were overly thankful. I gave away my food too, and some of my clothes, to the mission down the street. But no jackets, no coats.

When I moved back into my mother's house for the first time since my father had died, she was very happy to see me, but also very surprised.

My friends were pleased that I lived at last in a respectable place, but I think their sudden victory caught them unaware, and they didn't enjoy it as much for that.

Some people said I was a really good person to have helped the poor the way I did. I cut those people off rudely, sometimes saying the worst things I could think of to get them to leave me alone. I couldn't stand to hear anyone compliment me. "I was never one of them," I'd say sometimes. "Do I *look* like one of them? You can't do anything for people like that. I didn't even say goodbye."

And even more than before, I dream about an overcoat, opening slowly, like bat wings, showing off the bloody mysteries inside.

Rider

BLACK SAND, PURPLE waves, golden moonlight. Reay knew the cove didn't really have those colors, but they were so intense in her imagination that sometimes it was difficult to see it any other way. She liked to see the world as a series of pretty pictures, herself the young maiden or small girl in the foreground. In this particular picture she felt she must look much the dark Indian doll: her long raven-black hair, narrow face in shadow, bright red blouse and heavy quilted skirt checkered in yellow, green, and blue. She was wearing her new black boots, all laced up, the leather well-shined.

As she did every night about this time she found a place on one of the logs forming the border between wood and beach. She pulled the cloth-bound notebook out of her bulky purse, then the stub of candle fixed to one of the miniature china plates she'd saved since childhood. She lit the candle, musing about how her mother used to complain she'd go blind this way, and set it by her side. Her mother couldn't understand how a candle was so much nicer than any other source of light; did she really expect Reay to use a flashlight? She was thirty; she could make such decisions. She opened up her notebook to a blank page and wrote:

> *Her tears were like little lakes in which the birds,*
> *the fish, the frogs, and even the reeds were invisible;*
> *it made her sad to see these little worlds slip away.*

She was pleased; she loved the suggestion of delicate, ephemeral little worlds. She was so pleased, in fact, she decided she could not write anymore that day. She felt as if she might cry.

Reay thumbed back through the pages, rereading the previous week's entries.

> *dear god—the plant—the surprise of the water drop on its lower leaf . . . green-yellow centers like the spot that appears when eyes are closed. The spiderweb—like a face, an elf? Ah, heaven. Who are you?*

> *Talk with John—his mentioning my quiet disturbed me—I was feeling quite pressured. He helped, joked, got a loud laugh out of me—startling—how spontaneity breaks me. Fish net? Can the fish ever be free? Can he ever escape his death?*

She looked out toward the water, hugging herself, and she thought she was seeing a fishnet hanging like a coat on an invisible hook before her, thousands of strands. She leapt up out of her reverie with a small cry, startled and fearful, so much did it seem like a spider's web.

But it was a man, tall, dark, moon glistening off his wet hair. He must have been taking a swim, but why hadn't she seen him earlier? He was walking up the beach, straight toward her. She had the feeling he was watching her, but couldn't make out his features, his head a black oval.

As if to escape him, and her rising apprehensions, she looked quickly, self-consciously, back into her notebook, took up the pen and in agitation began to write:

> *the sea—so restless tonight—I was seeing it as if for the first time. The way the waves grope forth in large curves in places, but only small fingers in others, so much like a living, breathing thing. I visualize a great, heavy, sweating beast beneath the sea, its laborious*

*breath giving the waters this restless quality. Or per-
haps a vast, steaming, and sparking machine, but I so
hate to think of it as a machine—*

She looked up into clear, almost transparent blue eyes;
never had she seen such eyes! The hair was dark, almost jet,
with small strands of weed entangled here and there; no doubt
he had been in the shallows.

It suddenly occurred to her that she had forgotten to be
startled. And although she had never seen him before, and
was a little frightened by his dark good looks, she realized too
that some part of her had expected him, expected him since
the first evening she came to this beach to write.

*earlier a dark illustration made me think of being lost
in the Miami streets and accepting help from the old,
gentlemanly Englishman—*

His lips flattened out, the line of his mouth extending in
what she took to be a smile. She knew she must look comical
out here, with her notebook, the candle sputtering out, and
the way she had so obviously ignored him.

"I've seen you before . . ." he said, in a voice like a slow
wind over water.

She started to shake her head, not knowing what to say.

" . . . by the beach, here . . ." He gestured at the logs
with a smooth, sweeping motion of one hand, his head angled
toward her as if he were going to dive.

—clear sparkle of water from the drainpipe—

She began to giggle, unable to stop herself. She had just
visualized this tall, handsome man diving over her log and
headfirst, awkwardly, into the sand. She looked up, embarrassed.

But he had not moved, and she could see no signs of
irritation in his features, no signs of anything. He stared at

her so, it seemed uncanny, his features like a gray cliff overhanging the sea. With the candle out she couldn't see the whites of his eyes, although she would have expected to. Now they seemed gray, blending into the shadows.

"You . . . you say you've been here before, seen me here?" She busily rearranged her skirt, looking away from him.

"I'm here every evening . . . about this time."

"Swimming?"

"Yes. I also ride."

"Oh, that must be wonderful! Exhilarating, galloping up and down the length of the beach. But aren't you afraid the sand might throw you?"

He looked down at her, angling his head that strange way again, and this time it seemed to her as if he were trying to hear something. Perhaps he was reading her mind this way, gaining a better approach angle into the stream of her thoughts. She shivered.

He remained silent. For some reason this didn't bother her. She seemed to be able to sit quietly within his presence with no trouble at all.

> *now, hearing the lovely sea chantey on the record player— icy and billowy, pastel & heavenly—and books on the peach quilt—*

Reay didn't know when he left her that evening; he had been so quiet. She had been sitting still, meditating, had not even been aware of his presence for a time. She'd been daydreaming about being a little mermaid, and living with an old sea captain in his cottage, where he had kept care of her. Then she had swum home one day—she'd suddenly felt greatly alarmed, only to find him dead, drowned, and it seemed from his body he had been dead for years. She had snapped out of this, shocked that she could ruin one of her favorite fantasies this way, and discovered the stranger had gone.

She looked around her and saw that some of those worms in the little curled shells had come out, as they often did after a rain, and she noticed the beach around her was damp. When had it rained?

In any case she walked a long stretch out of her way to avoid the little worms; she was too frightened to walk near them.

my sea man—so dark and quiet—I'm sure it betrays a kind of gentleness. So many of us afraid to show ourselves, afraid to be vulnerable—and we all go off to our lonely little rooms—I should have spoken to him more, been kinder—

John today—touched my arm asking for some tissue— his face had a very gentle light in it—his eyes bigger and clearer than usual—then amazement—he put his hand gently on my head as he left the room—I thought I dreamed it I was so surprised and touched—I know I brushed my head with a jolt, expecting the messed hair to be straying—feeling a kind of shine—felt like crying and telling him how soothing the gesture was—I must look very sad, I thought—

Last night—fierce bright dreams—I awoke twice with a parched throat—draught of sweet cider so refreshing— then back to soft bed amd more dreams—

twice today people in the laundry have turned to watch and follow my progress—the snow has begun to fall—

Reay didn't return to the beach the next three nights because of the snow. She knew that many people would have been surprised at her going there at all in winter, but the beach, in winter, gave her wonderful feelings.

the beauty of the snow—I felt like an old peasant

woman as I walked through the soft crispness—ah how
it fell on me gently and entrapped me—I love it when it
snows, I feel so less lonely—I felt as if I were walking
under a great featherduster—no, a flower duster, and I
was tiny within it—

It was whiter at the beach than during any other winter she
could remember. The trees looked so much more barren than
they had only a few days ago, the trunks so dark against the
brilliance that they seemed burnt, all the life gone from them.

She was surprised to see the first footprint, so obviously
fresh, but then not so surprised as she followed the trail up
the beach. She'd expected him to be here, after all. Then she
came to a place where the snow and the sand beneath were
quite disturbed, torn up, as if there had been a struggle. Reay
was afraid. But out of the tangle came the prints of a horse,
and she knew her sea man had mounted his horse here, then
gone sailing away, his dark hair streaming, strong shoulders
moving much as the horse's beneath him. She hadn't seen the
horse's tracks until then, but perhaps he'd been leading it
through the lap of the surf. But those frigid waters! How
could he? These thoughts were forgotten when she caught the
flash of dark up ahead. The snow was coming down quite
thickly now, the visibility poor, but she hadn't been mistaken. Between gusts she could see that fluid black flash.
What a gorgeous horse it must be! She began to jog, difficult
in such snow, but the frozen sand beneath began to give her
purchase, and then she was running, laughing, chasing the
horse off into a sky and shore bleached white.

the mountains in mist this morning—old chrysanthe-
mums in snow—

The cold wind hurt her throat and lungs terribly, but still
she continued to run, so excited she was by the flash of that
wonderful beast. Where was its rider? Because of the speed
and the snow she couldn't make out any figure astride its

back. Such speed! How did the horse manage it in these conditions? She was never quite able to see the entire animal, mere bits and pieces, flashes which tantalized. It seemed thin, as if it had no flesh at all really, just black hide stretched over bone. And the shoulders so sharp, so angular, moving alternately into the currents of snow as if the horse were swimming through it, so rapid, the black hide, the tangled hair, the wild eyes . . .

Reay suddenly fell into the snow, her nose filled with cold, her skin burning. She began to cry, not so much from this insult as from the knowledge she'd never be able to catch him now.

She sat up and held her face. She was hearing . . . what? Faintly at first, a thumping? Pounding? Then, unmistakable as it grew louder, the sound of hooves thundering all along the beach, like a herd of horses. The sound of hundreds of hooves, thundering as if on a dry and dusty prairie.

Thundering all around her, the heady smell, loud breathing, snorts, beginning to close in the circle . . .

I remember being very tense and very frightened last night—afraid somebody was under my bed—

That next night the beach was a cold, lonely place for Reay, the horse nowhere to be seen, nor the stranger. She had had a long, unsatisfactory phone conversation with John that day; they really didn't seem to be getting anywhere. The talk had upset her, so she had tried to make up for it by doing some things to the house. She got out all the tin-foil from the candy and gum wrappers she'd saved, and in the middle of them pasted pictures she'd taken from some second-hand fairytale books. She looked over at the far corner—she remembered that moment distinctly—and had thought how she liked the wheat-colored wild grass on her white table there, the red goblet nearby.

—the weeds on the hill barely lifting with faint pale

*life—turn my head and the rich green in the stubble—
the silver strand of hair crossing my eye—*

Tonight she was wearing her lemon-lime shirt with the
delicate strawberries, her hair up. She felt pretty in it. Too
bad no one was here to see it.

*my tangled hair—I will be brave about this! I won't let
the tears distract me—melted tracks of water from the
cars, tears—*

How could John be so stubborn? It seemed as if he really
wanted to be lonely; he certainly seemed to do little to
alleviate it. For a moment she thought of bringing John to the
beach some night, but no, that couldn't be! The beach was
her place.

*with John—unbearable memories of men not knowing
what to say and making me feel I've got to take the
lead—I hate this sensatlon—I hate the frustration—it's
an area where I've exhausted my patience—oh I hate
myself sometimes—*

She'd felt so uncomfortable in her house today; she couldn't
wait to get out. It disturbed her; before she'd enjoyed the
solitary moments in her rooms so much. Now it seemed she
craved the excitement, the thrill of looking at the great black
beast, feeling the thunder all around her, and within.

*so many people—pounding down the years, achieving
nothing but boredom—*

Reay remembered the book she'd been reading that morning, about the sea, and those who lived there. Such smooth,
capable creatures. She fancied herself a delicate mermaid.
Playing, sliding through the cold and dark. Undying. What it
must be like!

*dream of the child giggling somewhere, invisible—afraid
I'd be struck at any moment—living in an old mansion—
trapped beneath the blankets—deep sense of alarm
about to be sprung—such human suffering—Rilke calls
sorrow a source so often of blessed progress—*

Reay was greatly disappointed in her next few trips to the
cove. Each day she'd sat in her rooms alone, determined not
to yield, but finally driven out by John's persistent phone
calls, by her own self-conscious gesturing before the mirror,
by boredom itself.

But each time her anxiety and excitement had been unre-
warded; the stranger, her sea man, and his horse had not been
there. The cove was white, deathly still, completely iced
over. Nothing moved, not even the usual animals she saw
there. There was no reason to stay; it was like walking into a
dream of death by mistake. She didn't want that at all.

So she returned to her rooms each day to sit quietly, read,
and jot thoughts into her notebook. Sometimes she tried to
dream about spring, about green growing things, but the
fantasies always went wrong somehow, became cold and wet.
There seemed no escaping the winter.

*a vision—thinking back to our old house in Virginia—a
dark hillside—with cabbage-like flowers that I have to
till daily. I work in the darkness but there's dew on the
flowers—I've got to work as hard with these spindly
flowers as one would with a full flower garden in a
sunny field—but my flowers! They look like the souls
of animals—crystal & fragrant—a smell much like
chrysanthemums—diaphanous, snow-flake complexity—
wafting like plants underwater—all this within the heart
of a petalled flower—*

For the first time she thought to ask herself where her
stranger might live, if he were married, where he must keep
that gorgeous horse. She would keep it in the house, she was
sure, no smelly stable! She'd give it a real bed to sleep in . . .

*the need to punish & be punished; god, how it drives
lovers—*

Reay woke depressed, but the energy which had left her
body seemed to have collected in her fingers, so she wrote
fast and furiously in her notebook for two hours. Only when
her fingers began cramping did she realize she'd not yet
turned the heat on in the house. She felt the coldest she'd ever
been. She held her hands under hot water, grabbed her coat,
and started out on her walk

*ah heavens—the death scene of the child in my new
book—holding the beautiful mother and father—oh the
eyes of Marion—oh heavens, the lift of her neck—such
spiritual beauty*

*the boy's smile—like a pebble-struck brook, goes out
into the open after travelling the body—*

Although she hadn't gone that route in several days, she
wasn't surprised to find herself making the turn toward the
cove. The sky was the gray of old lead this morning, made
darker by the brilliance of a fresh layer of snow on the fields.
There was no one else in sight; she appreciated that. The
houses looked abandoned, not even dogs barking. No birds in
the sky. As if she were the last creature alive on the planet.
As she took the long trail bordering the beach, and the
houses dropped behind her, the gray of the sky seemed to
blend with the ground. That, and some low patches of fog,
made her feel as if she were walking into a bank of clouds.

*the remarkable beauty of the candled rooms—so like a
religious place, a sanctuary, mortuary—the triple deck
porcelain pearl bracelet around the still wrist—the arti-
ficial flowers against the pale neck—the feathers—the
satiny chestnut dress, with piled hat and matching ribbon—like a display case, as beautiful as any flower bed—*

There were a few leafless trees in this part of the cove: tall, white, thin, bowed like old ladies, their stiff strands of hair frozen and weighted earthward by the snow.

the shadow of hair all flying in a tangle—and I can testify that I smell flowers under the ground—

I tell you I smell chrysanthemums—

Suddenly she grew rigid, as if violated by the cold. She jerked open her eyes; she was in his long, dark arms. He rubbed his chin, startling, against her cheek in an almost animalistic gesture. Then he showed his long teeth, his full mouth . . .

—my love's teeth are white geese—

Then they were moving, quickly, the landscape jiggling by her. She realized he had taken her up in his arms and was now carrying her as he ran. It astonished her . . . such strength. His heavy odor began to rise; expecting to be offended, she was not, but was excited. She let go of her fear. She began to giggle. She laughed out loud. They were going faster and faster, so fast she thought he must have mounted the horse with her, and her so groggy she hadn't known it. But the movement wasn't that of a horse, and she was held so she couldn't look down.

my world turns so rapidly—how can I have the stable land to walk on? perchance I must learn to dance on a small square of it?

She laughed again. He turned his face to her this time, and again made that stretching of the mouth she took to be a smile. Of course! She was sure of it.
"Why do you laugh?" he asked.
"Oh . . . well." She chuckled again. "Actually nothing

. . . no, let's say I was wondering about mermaids, especially mermaids in winter. How do you suppose they manage with the inlets and northern seas all iced over?''

He made a sound much like a bark, which she took to be a reciprocation of her own laughter. Then he gestured to the cove. She could vaguely make out a large crack in the ice; it hadn't been there a few days ago. *"They work their way . . . from beneath. Otherwise"*— he moved his arm sweepingly— *"they stay beneath, in their homes . . ."*

Her sea man turned his head forward again, angling it into the wind, and they went faster and faster down the shore. Her skin prickled, blood stirred in its deepest, stillest wells. Unaccountably she thought of John, and wondered why things weren't like this with him. She thought there should be an excitement between lovers, a higher energy, an intensity. The intensity had never been there with John. But perhaps she could do something about that. She'd never had a lover, but suddenly she was convinced she held the key. The stranger filled her with sudden power. She felt she could do anything. She could be the active one now . . . the thunder in her ears drowned out all thought.

the dogs barking—made me think of a duck filled with bells—the cracked amberglass of my feet memorable for some reason—

somewhere between striving for a goal and accomplishing a routine comes a moment of pure beginning—where within the world does this happen?

Reay was buying blouses, the delicate one making her feel like a perfume phial, the orange dress she wore reminding her of quilts from childhood, the undies she once had. Or that baby sweater in violet—buy that? Hood too. Made her feel like the sugar plum fairy. She could put cinnamon in the pockets. She finished and strolled to the library, where she wrote:

I felt like a magic dwarf in the store—my speckled lantern socks unmatched when I tried on the rose—slit, tight cold skin—Ha!

last night making love to John—so delicate, the light tickle, sensation as of a feather—I thought I'd pass out—ah, feeling so warm—as the poets said, such a gentle death—

Also, babe, you have as much height as depth—

Reay went back to the cove early in the afternoon this time, wearing her new outfit, her notebook in hand. She brushed the snow off one of the logs and sat down. Her excitement building she began to write:

—the fire in my sea man's eyes—it's deadly!—his approval so important to me that I don't—I'm not sure what this is I'm feeling—the excitement when he held me!—John's so nice, but—

She could feel his breathing behind her, the rise of his animal smell. She climbed to her feet and began to turn, arms outstretched to embrace him.

The jet horse snorted at her loudly, then nuzzled her roughly with its nose. It whinnied. It coughed. Fire in its eyes. Hot, fetid breath.

Reay put her arms around it; she began to stroke the mane.

And before she knew it she was off, dragged up onto its back, her hair flying, bones already aching, eyes tearing from the icy blasts suddenly racing in from the white-encased sea. She tried to scream but could not, could not even whimper. The cold air silenced her, took her breath away.

She was smelling the perfume of flowers, thinking strangely of old, decrepit mermaids, when the horse leapt out on the ice, and as the ice began to break she could feel the change beneath her: the jaws shortening, the back falling, the cold greeting of those blue transparent eyes.

And as her sea man embraced her, she thought back to her
notebook lying now on the snow-covered shore, the pages
turning open to the winter wind, when he exposed his long
white teeth, and she could think of no more images, so
overcome was she with thunder.

*I am so unsure of myself—certain only that I have a
very tender youthful imagination—and a great sense of
being assaulted by fate—*

—chrysanthemums dark in glass bowls underground—

Worms

ELLA STOOD BEHIND the heavily-gauzed parlor windows, watching the neighbor's dogs—German sheperds, or maybe they were those vicious Dobermans she'd heard so much about on the T-and-V—defecating all over their ill-kept lawn, the lawn that had once been part of her grandfather's estate—the part where the stables had been, or maybe it had been the guest house—and it was a pain to her, a pain gnawing at her insides, to see those dung-encrusted animals with their long pink tongues and wormy hides defecating all over Grandfather's memory.

Papa had been a fool to sell that part of the inheritance, even if times had been bad. Her grandfather—a fair man with no snobbery in him—had just the same always believed in preserving a respectable distance between the "classes." He never would have allowed neighbors like these. Would have had them shot if nothing else had worked. He wouldn't have tolerated such defecations.

The woman came out the back door and stepped into a patch of earth made muddy with her animals' leavings. Fat, ugly thing. She screamed. Such language! She kicked one of the dogs and almost fell over backwards, her bermuda-bound thighs wobbling obscenely. Ella turned away, afraid she might grow ill. How could she bear such people living next door? They'd lived there six months and already the fine old residence—her great-grandfather had added that particular dwell-

161

ing to the estate—was a shambles. It could never be the same again.

As if she couldn't help herself, Ella turned back. The dogs came up to the fence between the two properties, an ugly wire affair the neighbors had erected two weeks after moving in. Their narrow pink tongues fell loose, licked the wire, tongue-tips probing into Ella's yard space. She stepped back involuntarily. The dogs seemed to be staring right through the window, as if they knew she was watching them. Of course they couldn't know. But they began to bark, and snap their jaws, staring right at her.

Their teeth terrified her, and yet brought her an idea.

She walked over to the hall closet, slowly so as not to lose the thread of this new thought. With careful deliberation she donned her heavy winter coat and, after further consideration, her thickest pair of gloves. She stepped out onto the back porch and opened the gardening cupboard. The tools inside were grey with dust; her arthritis had been so bad the past two years she'd had to let the grounds go a bit. She chose a pair of hedge trimmers, almost too rusty to open, but then it wouldn't be necessary to open them.

When she entered the back yard the dogs resumed their howling with a new ferociousness. As she stepped closer to their side of the yard they began to attack the fence, chewing at the post. The smell of dog feces was overpowering to her, but although she squinted she wasn't able to see any through the fence. The dogs began to croon together in a terrifying way. Ella held her breath.

Someone could very well be bitten by such dogs. It was quite believable that such a thing could happen to an innocent passerby.

She came as close as she dared to the fence. She looked up at her neighbors' house. Or the house they lived in; she could never think of it as truly theirs. There was only one window on this side, heavily shaded, and her neighbors hadn't raised that shade to see if anything was wrong. The dogs barked so much anyway, they'd never know if there was something out of the ordinary. But to be safe she crouched with the clippers, poising them over a dead rose bush. She felt a momentary regret, thinking how beautiful the blooms had been once; then, recalling why she was here, she edged even closer to the dogs.

With all its pounding, her heart seemed to hurt her frail chest. The presence of the dogs, the smells and the awful proximity of their long slimy tongues, was almost over-whelming. But she had to be sure. She bent still further over the bush. She could feel the dampness of the dog's breath across the top of her head. Anyone looking would see an old woman innocently trimming her rose bush.

She looked up once more into the dogs' foul-smelling mouths, obscenely filled with snake-like tongues. Then she began to scream.

Once she started she feared she might not stop. That in itself almost halted the charade. She let herself fall to the ground and squirm there, writhe and raise her voice into one piercing note. In fact, the loudness of the note made her feel proud. Then she added words to the scream.

"I'm bit! I'm bit!" she cried. When no one came immedi-ately to investigate she returned to the scream, pushing the scale upward until she thought she might faint. Her neighbors still did not show their faces, again impressing Ella with the extent of their irresponsibility. She was aware of the dogs' silence now. They hovered by their house, looking somewhat bewildered.

A middle-aged man from across the street was suddenly at her side, kneeling. "Are you all right?"

"I'm bit! Those vicous dogs! They bit me, attacked me right through the fence!"

The man seemed surprised, and looked over at her neigh-bors' yard. "That's odd. They seem so quiet, not vicious at all."

"I tell you they attacked me! Now what are you going to do?"

He looked serious then; it was obvious to Ella he was

trying to hide his embarrassment. "We'll just get you inside. I'll call the dog warden and report the bite."

"Yes, yes. The dog warden. That's the thing to do." He helped her to her feet and started her toward the back door. She faked a limp. It surprised her how naturally it came. "Thank you. Thank you kindly."

She turned her head slightly, just enough to see the woman at her back door watching, her husband beside her. And still in his undershirt. It was disgusting. His face was pink and swollen, as if ravaged by some sort of skin disease.

It took the dog warden only a half hour to arrive. Ella usually found much to be desired in the city's services, but in this case she couldn't have been more pleased. She imagined it was the boldness of her idea; it had caught everyone quite off guard.

"You say the dogs bit you, ma'am?"

"Yes. Attacked me. Viciously."

"May I see the bite?"

Ella felt the blood rushing into her face. Her nervousness was easily converted into outrage. "I am a *lady,* sir! I cannot show you where!" She purposely glanced down at her hip. The warden was young; she stared at him deliberately. He hastily looked back down at his clipboard.

"I understand, ma'am. You just better get that looked at by your doctor. Have to be careful about the tetanus, you see. We're a lot more worried about that than we are about rabies."

"I should think so!" The warden looked at her oddly, but Ella ignored him. He was so young. The very idea of a member of her family having rabies! "You'll take the dogs then?"

"They'll be quarantined two weeks, just to make sure they have no diseases. Then the owner can get them back."

"Oh."

After the dog warden left Ella stared out the window again, watching him arguing with her neighbors, the neighbors pointing at her house and shouting, and the warden loading the stinking animals into his truck. He should have taken the owners as well! She thought them much more likely carriers of rabies.

Just before sunset Ella went out to retrieve her clippers. Stooping to pick up the tool she found herself staring at several piles of dog feces right by the fence, no doubt deposited there by the animals during all the upset.

Something blurred her vision. She tried to focus, then saw it was the dung moving, crawling with white worms, some of them falling over into her yard. They were short and curled, like nerves cut apart and turned ghost-like. She could sense the electricity they emitted. They hurt her teeth and squeezed her stomach until it spasmed. She imagined them getting into her shoes if she were to step in the wrong places.

This time she stifled her true scream and ran inside.

One morning five days later Ella was surprised to look out her parlor window and see a truck backing over the front lawn next door. The woman and her husband helped two men load their few pieces of tattered furniture and several boxes full of clothes, cooking utensils, and miscellaneous junk. Last to go on the truck were three large boxes marked "movie magazines." Ella snorted in derision.

Without even a backward glance the couple climbed into the truck with the two men and left. Ella was stunned by the extent of her victory. She supposed they just didn't want any more trouble. Perhaps they sensed her determination.

She wondered if they would even bother to retrieve their animals once the quarantine was up. She doubted it. Those kind weren't capable of showing loyalty even to a pet.

Late that afternoon Ella was still basking in the radiance of her success—her first real success in a long time—when the doorbell rang. It was almost exactly four o'clock. She knew because she had been watching the clock, trying to think of something appropriately celebratory to prepare for dinner. Perhaps a nice hen. Or an eggplant. Thoughts of food always made her feel contented. But they ill prepared her for her first meeting with Alfred Sanchez.

She could feel the smile draining from her face once she opened the door. She was struck by a definite physical sensation that almost made her faint. The man at her front door—the clearly *Mexican* person at her front door—was carrying a bucket full of worms.

She grew rigid, choking the doorknob. The man smiled; at least, she thought he smiled. Her attention was riveted to his face, desperately avoiding his hands. Two rows of enormous teeth filled the space between his yellowed-gray moustache and beard.

"Alfred Sanchez, ma'am. Your new neighbor. I brought you these, with my compliments."

"You have no accent."

He frowned slightly. "What do you mean?"

She shook her head. "You haven't an accent. I . . . it surprised me."

He smiled again. "We don't all have accents, ma'am. You don't have an accent, now do you?"

"But I'm . . ."

"I'm American too, sure am, Miss Wills."

Ella grasped her throat. She was aware of hundreds of worm ends stroking the metal sides of the pail. Stroking, sliding, sticking to the metal. It was a hot day; they must be sticking. "How did you know my name?"

"It's on your mail box. And the Carters, the people who lived there before, they told me."

"They told you *what?*"

Again he looked at her doubtfully "Don't know what you mean, ma'am. I just asked them who lived next door, and they gave me your name."

"Then you don't know them?"

"Just met 'em this once. I saw you out in your backyard, and I asked 'em, I says, 'Who's that *fine*-looking woman next door?' and they told me, that's all."

Ella felt herself blushing. "I . . . I didn't see you."

"Well, I was just there for a quick looksee before I decided to take it."

"You were able to decide that quickly?"

"Hell, ma'am, all I care about is the size of the basement and the backyard, providin' the backyard's got the proper shade so it don't get too hot."

Ella tried to ignore the man's obscenity, so intrigued she was by his house-buying criteria. She had trouble tracing his line of logic. "I'm afraid I don't understand, Mister . . . Sanchez."

He grinned too widely for her, seemingly far more than experience had taught her was possible, and held the bucket of writhing worms aloft, practically shoving its hot, slippery grey surface into her face. For a moment time stopped for her, and the room swelled with the knotty mass of rotting brown string, of decaying rags in dark oil, of gray intestines freed from an aging body, of male genitals probing through mud, of pale serpents feasting on a corpse, of slick, stinking, vile worms. She began to gag, and turned away.

"Why, it's for the *worms*, Miss Wills!" His belly laugh had a strangely liquid sound, as if his lungs were diseased. "I raise 'em! I just brought this bunch over for you!"

Ella swallowed and managed to turn partway back to answer him. Couldn't he see that they sickened her? "Whatever . . . would I need . . . *worms* for?"

"Why, they'll be good for your yard an' garden! I could see that your ground hasn't been worked with for a while, understandable what with your being a single woman and all, and these worms'll just loosen all that hard dirt up so's somebody can help you work it this spring."

"I really don't think . . ."

But he'd already opened the door and started down the front steps. "See here?" He began to tip the bucket; she could see the reddish tide of liquid worms beginning to spill off the lip.

"Wait!"

"This is a *ferocious* bunch of worms, I tell you! Raised them myself!" The mass of worms landed with a muted plop on her front lawn. For a moment they looked like leftover spaghetti; she suddenly tasted the horrible softness in her mouth. "Watch 'em scatter, now!"

And incredibly, that's what they did. Slipping away faster than worms could possibly move, faster than Ella *knew* any worm had ever traveled, the worms separated several at a time from the football-sized mass, blending so quickly into the brown-spotted lawn Ella was able to detect none of them after a couple of minutes. She'd never seen such worms; it seemed unnatural that there should be such worms. "So quickly" was all she could say.

Mr. Sanchez grinned. "That they are! Breed 'em that way—they're something special, you see."

The thought of the worms making their way through her lawn and, God forbid, working their way toward the foundation of the house, brought the cold weather right into her bones. She desperately wanted to close the door. But there was something she had to ask him.

"Mr. Sanchez, do you know whatever happened to my neighbors' dogs?"

He continued to grin, but it seemed to her the size of the grin suddenly diminished. "Why, I believe they're dead, Miss Wills. I do believe they're dead."

She stared at him, not knowing whether to believe him, trying to see something in his face that would reveal his true purpose here. But she kept thinking about those worms, and knew she just had to close that door. "Well, good day, then. I suppose I will be seeing you again."

"Oh, I'm sure you will, ma'am. I'm sure you will, good-lookin' lady like yourself."

The man was dirty, sweaty, vile in every way. His smile was slick, too-bright, and evil. His shirt was sweat-stained and he had holes in his pants disturbingly close to the front. And a foreigner on top of all that. But what bothered Ella most was her own feelings. She was not completely unflattered. She was not completely uninterested.

Ella spent most of the next two days, and evenings, poised

behind the parlor curtains, watching Mr. Sanchez and two workers move his belongings into the house next door. The workers looked disturbingly similar to the ones who had moved her previous neighbors out. But she was more concerned with what they were carrying into the house this time: heavy crates full of earth, all manner of industrial shelving units and enough lumber to build many more, boxes full of chemicals, wire mesh, plastic sheeting, dozens of metal pails similar to the one Mr. Sanchez used to bring her those horrible worms, and hundreds, maybe more than hundreds, of tall cylindrical containers. She knew what they contained; there was no fooling her. Enough worms to encircle the block, perhaps the city. Enough worms to cover every inch of you if they were to escape, if they felt inclined to attack, to turn. Ella giggled, thinking of all those worms turning. She giggled more loudly than she had intended, and struggled to contain that frightening laughter that escaped unbidden, unnaturally, from her lips. She'd read somewhere, or heard somewhere, that some worms bite, or sting, she wasn't sure which. She wondered if you could contract rabies from a worm.

The second day she went to the phone to find out about zoning. "What? You mean there's nothing you can do? Well, I think some people should lose their jobs over such zoning!"

There was also nothing Sanitation could do, unless Mr. Sanchez kept a bad house, and Ella's argument that a worm farm in and of itself was pure filth and pollution did not appear to impress them. She discovered the animal control people to be of no help either; worms were not considered animals, it seemed.

And so Ella was left to sit and watch through her parlor windows, hoping to catch Mr. Sanchez in some illegal activity or other, anything she might be able to use as an excuse to call in the authorities.

He was actually a rather handsome man, she was forced to admit after watching him working shirtless in the back yard for several weeks. Unusually fit for his age, which she guessed to be somewhere near her own. He did get rather filthy hefting those old crates about, and erecting shed-like structures which she imagined to be the worms' "homes." The back yard next door was looking more and more like a shanty town, which did bother her, and if he built many more of those sheds she wouldn't be able to see much because of their roofs.

But the dirt really didn't look so badly on him, after all. It highlighted his handsome tan, and made his beard seem whiter, more stark. Her own grandfather used to say that sometimes a man had to get his hands dirty if he was going to accomplish anything in this world. And perhaps, in his own way, Mr. Sanchez was accomplishing something, building his own business empire. She had no idea if there was any money in worms, but she supposed there might be. For research, and fishing, perhaps even for food in some backward countries. Let them eat what they wanted; she didn't care.

After a time Mr. Sanchez would break for lunch, and sit down by the fence, near the same spot where she had had her dog "attack." That incident seemed a long time ago now. Now there was Mr. Sanchez, who would sit shirtless by the fence, leaning back with his eyes closed, although sometimes he would turn and look up at her parlor window, and she would feel vaguely agitated, thinking he might be seeing her, but it was a pleasant sort of agitation, for a change.

This particular day she could feel spring in the air; there were patches of green in the lawn now, a few leaves on the trees, and even signs of budding on a couple of the old rose bushes. Ella wondered if it might not be a productive spring this year after all, and was beginning to think of things she might do to bring the grounds at least partially back to their previous splendor. Perhaps Mr. Sanchez would provide some aid toward that goal—his vague offer of future assistance hadn't gone unnoticed.

The ground around the old house had softened a bit; it was almost springy underfoot. She wondered if that was due to the action of the worms Mr. Sanchez had let loose, but it seemed much too short an interval for the worms to be the cause. No doubt it was the change in the weather, and the unusual amount of snowfall they'd received this past winter. Besides, since they were first released Ella hadn't seen a single worm around the place. Perhaps they'd died, or found their way back home to Mr. Sanchez's. Surely worms possessed some sort of rudimentary homing sense; everything else seemed to.

Mr. Sanchez was asleep there by the fence, his snoring a soft, not unpleasant hum. It had been a long time since there'd been a man around the house, not since 1965 when Papa ran Horace Gilliam off the place. Said he wasn't right for his daughter. What did Papa ever know anyway? He was the one who sold the place next door. Wouldn't he have a fit to see Mr. Sanchez moving in with all those worms!

Ella began to notice that Mr. Sanchez's beard was not the pure white she'd remembered it to be. It was streaked. In brown, it seemed.

She held her breath. Periodically the streaks lengthened, as if to kiss Mr. Sanchez on the mouth. Ella touched her own lips with the tips of her fingers, felt the softness there, tasted the slight saltiness of dirt. Then looked again at Mr. Sanchez's handsome tanned face with its white beard where the streaks were wriggling, wriggling, and Mr. Sanchez was beginning again to grin the grin that would fill his face with teeth.

When spring finally did come Ella was anxious to begin her rejuvenation efforts on the yard, but Mr. Sanchez appeared to be even busier than before, so busy she hesitated to bother him. Every day she would awaken to the sounds of his working in his back yard. If she looked down from her second-story bedroom window she could see his broad shoulders, the supple way he moved as he worked. The work seemed mindless much of the time; it appeared as if all he did was to move piles of dirt from one shed-like structure to another. Getting himself filthier and filthier as he worked, and the dirt spilled over the sides of his shovel and covered him. He seemed almost careless in this, as if he enjoyed getting dirty. By mid-morning he was slimed head-to-toe with a mud made from his sweat. And he grinned constantly, the grin brighter the dirtier he became.

Ella began the work on her own, her meager efforts doing little to alleviate the poor condition of the grounds. She managed to dig up two of the bushes and replace them, and she struggled with a fertilization device attached to her waterhose—the man at the local greenhouse had recommended it—but she never could tell if she was using it properly. It leaked, and gave her a good soaking by the time she decided to quit trying.

Never once did she see any worms, and after working with the ground for several hours she concluded it wasn't that much softer after all. She'd developed this fascination—this foolish schoolgirl fascination—with Mr. Sanchez. She could admit that now. It had clouded her judgment, made her imagine all sorts of fantastic possibilities.

Ella developed a spring cold, and that sidelined her from spying on Mr. Sanchez for a while. She could admit that too, now; she had been spying on the man. But it didn't make her quit. Now she was more determined than ever to find out something useful about him, something she could relate to the authorities.

When that thing came, she was ill-prepared to use it. She would have been too embarrassed.

The last few days there had seen a considerable decrease in hammerings and sawings and the miscellaneous thumps that had always characterized Mr. Sanchez's activities. Ella assumed his construction work was finally over, and so she might have a period of peace with her new neighbor. Perhaps she'd hardly see him at all, making his ownership of her family's old property somewhat more palatable.

She'd gotten out of her sickbed and gone down to the kitchen for tea. She had to pass through the parlor to get to the kitchen, and so, just out of habit, she happened to glance out the parlor window.

Mr. Sanchez was standing in his back yard, between two of

the sheds. He was plastered heavily with mud; there wasn't an inch of him that hadn't been covered. And although she had to look at him very carefully in order to convince herself, he was quite unmistakably naked.

This time Ella didn't even gasp. Somehow it wasn't completely unexpected.

As if her recognition of his state had become a signal, Mr. Sanchez began a dance. The movements were so subtle at first Ella hadn't been sure he was moving at all. She thought maybe she had developed a slight tremor of her own, and that was what had created the sense of movement. But the movement became more and more pronounced, and Ella was able to see that it was Mr. Sanchez moving up and down, then wiggling ever so slightly side-to-side.

As the movement increased Mr. Sanchez began to grin that bright, impossible grin.

He stooped, then rose up on tip-toe. His arms fell down at his sides, and it seemed as if they continued to fall. The dance made it seem as if he were . . . elongating, his muddy hide become elastic. His teeth flashed. His muddy skin grew muddier. His flesh turned color. The worm ends bobbed obscenely. He inched through rotted meat. He bored through bellies bloated with gas. He covered every inch of her with his wet cool, moving flesh. Her throat gagged on the mud.

She opened her eyes again. For the first time she noticed the Spanish music playing in the background. The man was quite drunk. He bobbed, weaved, sometimes shouted things unintelligible. The man was quite sodden. The worms crawled on him. They climbed on at his feet and worked their way up the mud that was his only clothing. She turned away as they started up his neck. She pulled out the sherry decanter hidden in the good china hutch and carried it back up to bed with her.

It took a number of drinks before she could forget about the mud, and the wet sounds she thought she could hear coming from that other yard. But she fell asleep still thinking about the worms.

She didn't think about any of that the next day when she walked outside and approched him from her side of the fence. She thanked God he was clothed today; she had checked through the parlor window to make sure before going outside. She wondered if he had ever been naked in the first place; maybe it had just been the mud, and she had been sick and not thinking too clearly. But she really didn't think so.

"Mr. Sanchez?"

He turned with a frown, and his smile seemed to begin a bit too slowly for comfort. "Why . . . Miss Wills! *So good* to see you. I haven't seen very much of you lately, around the yard I mean."

Ah, but I've been seeing you, Mr. Sanchez, she thought.

"That's what I wanted to talk to you about," she said, "I'm afraid I can't manage it very well on my own. Too much for an elderly lady, I suppose . . ."

"Why, you're still in the prime of life! And look it too!" He winked. Ella caught a quick glimpse of brown mud on the eyelid before he raised it again. "And I *did* kind of promise you some help with it, now didn't I? I'm sorry, just had so much to do around here, you know? Those old neighbors of yours really let the place run down, you know?"

Ella started to agree wholeheartedly, then realized how ridiculous his statement was. What had he been doing besides playing in the dirt and dancing naked? At least her previous neighbors hadn't done that. "Yes . . . I suppose they did, Mr. Sanchez. I *would* appreciate your help, but I don't want to interrupt your work. I know you must have a great deal to do here, with all those worms, I mean."

"Well, 'course, there's lots to do, ma'am, but I tell you—I got these worms now to the point where they're pretty much taking care of theirselves. Don't need me so much anymore."

Ella tried to force words through her sudden shudder. "Then you *will* help me?" She kept seeing him muddy, and naked. Moving.

"Be a pleasure."

"Fine, then." He looked clean today, but she knew that he

must be dirty under those clothes. Dirty, and naked. She tried
to walk away, but he was grinning so at her. She tried to walk
away, because now she could see that something was squirming in his pants pockets, making the khaki move frantically.
But he was grinning so. "Could you stay for dinner?" she
finally asked, and some of the tension was gone.

"Why, Miss Wills! That'd be even more of a pleasure!
Been a long, long time since anyone's invited me in for a real
sit-down dinner."

She wondered what his previous neighbors had thought of
him, how they had dealt with such a man. Or maybe he had
lived away from people before, in the mountains or in the
desert, where he could raise his horrible worms and dance in
private.

"Good. You'll come over tomorrow morning?"

"Tomorrow's fine."

"Good. Tomorrow." The worms were crawling out of his
pockets. She had to force herself to leave. But not before she
saw him pick a few out of one pocket, hold them in his palm,
stroke them, hum to them, grin. Several were crawling up his
arm toward his face, worm-ends raised expectantly.

Mr. Sanchez knew his plants. Ella reasoned that that made
the outward crudity of the man more bearable. When he
crouched to work on her near-dead rose bushes half his
buttocks rose out of his pants. He wiped his nose on his
sleeve. He made no attempt to constrain his bodily sounds.
And he looked at her often, many times when he must have
thought she wouldn't notice. No man had ever looked at her
that way before.

She wanted to go inside and go about her other business.
But she felt compelled to watch his every move. She needed
to watch him, she told herself. There was no telling what he
might try to do. He wasn't to be trusted. So she made it her
business to study him.

The silences grew long and awkward. Mr. Sanchez spoke
little while he was about his work, at least one trait that Ella

found admirable in a man. But after a time, what with her hovering over him and him pretending not to notice, keeping his peace, Ella felt the need to fill some of the quiet with her own voice.

"You know, it's funny. I haven't seen any of the worms you released on the lawn that first day."

"Didn't know you looked at 'em that careful, ma'am. To be able to recognize those particular ones, I mean."

She didn't know whether she should laugh, or if he was ridiculing her. Ella had never taken well to jokes. "No, I mean I haven't seen any worms on my property at all since that day."

"Maybe the ones I raised and gave you ate the rest of the worms that were here." He chuckled. "Pretty ferocious bunch, they were."

Ella forced a small laugh, but it came out shakily. "Oh, you don't mean that!"

He turned slightly. She could see his dark eyes over his right shoulder, staring at her. "Don't I now."

She waited until he returned to his work before she spoke again. She didn't feel safe talking to him with his eyes on her like that. "I guess I'm really curious, Mr. Sanchez. Could those worms have died between then and now?"

He mumbled, but the words were clear. "Not a chance."

"And why's that?"

"I raised them. I know. They're just digging around down there, exploring, thinking whatever worms think about. They're waiting for the proper time to come up topside again."

"So how will they know?"

"Same way you and I will know, Ella." The familiarity stopped her; she wouldn't ask any more questions. After a few more minutes of awkward silence she went back into the house.

By the end of the day Mr. Sanchez had finished all the work Ella had waited two years to do. He certainly was a hard worker. He went back to his own house, to shower, he said, while Ella began preparing dinner.

It had been a long time since Ella had prepared a full meal in the old kitchen; she usually just snacked. So there was a certain amount of awkwardness at first. She couldn't find the right pot. The large butcher knife wasn't where she expected it to be. The good dishes were dusty, so she had to wash them. Small things, but they raised her anxiety to an uncomfortable degree. She fumbled with the cucumbers as she tried to wash them. She kept seeing Mr. Sanchez covered in mud, Mr. Sanchez rinsing himself off in the shower, the mud dropping off like molt, Mr. Sanchez naked. She scrubbed the cucumbers vigorously. She didn't know why she was going to all this trouble—the man was a pig. He wouldn't even notice, or care.

She planned to prepare her grandfather's special meatloaf recipe, something she hadn't done in a long time. She hoped she still remembered how. It required a great number of onions, making use only of the small spirals that could be cut from each end, down near the heart of the onion. And there was the special grain filler you mixed with the meat. Her grandfather had developed that as well, and taught it only to her; her mother hadn't been interested. She should still have a bit of that left, in the pantry.

Ella pulled the tall glass cylinder off the shelf, stared at it for a moment, vaguely disturbed by it, then dumped it into a pan with the meat.

She began to blend grain and meat together with her fingers, frail fingers that ached in protest from the effort. But the pain might bring about a fine meal, as her grandfather used to advise.

She stared down at the tan and reddish substances, mesmerized by the blending and swirling of colors. Her vision began to blur.

And at the edges something squirmed, white and out-of-focus.

She stopped and shook her head to clear it. The vision came back, but without the squirming white shadow.

She began to add the onions to the mix, the ones she'd prepared on the cutting board by the sink. As they dropped slowly into the pan she thought she saw some of the tight curls straighten, others attempt to change their course in mid-flight.

She poured the tomato sauce over it all, too quickly, and slid the pan into the oven.

The kitchen curtains rustled. A leaf, several twigs, dropped into the sink. Something soft smashed and slid beneath her shoe as she stepped over to the cupboard where the pots and pans were kept. She'd been dropping vegetables; she had to be more careful. But she had no time to look for them now.

She took out the pot for the carrots, and started filling it with water, when she saw the brown streaks inside. Obviously she hadn't cleaned it properly the last time she'd used it, so she put it back on the shelf and chose another, ignoring the hollow tapping sounds coming from inside.

She chopped up the carrots and dropped them into the new pot, added water, and placed it on the electric burner. Medium heat. When the sizzling and popping began on the bottom of the pot, she was assaulted by a horrible, acrid smell. She tried to lift the pot from the burner, but it was stuck fast. Her vision blurred again, and she could make little out of the viscous, ghastly mass that oozed out onto the stove from the pot.

Ella figured she must be weak from hunger—she hadn't had either breakfast or lunch. It was becoming more and more difficult to keep the lines of the room straight. They wiggled. They writhed. And sometimes, when she watched them out of the corners of her eyes, they dropped right off the wall.

Again, she saw Mr. Sanchez dancing in the mud. She'd better get dressed. She hoped meatloaf and the one vegetable would be enough for a man of his size.

The window was open in her bedroom. Debris blew past her, some of it striking her, latching on, sticking. She had to brush some of it off her bed in order to sit down, but some of it didn't brush very well. It stuck to her hand; she had to scrape it on the bedclothes to get it off.

When she opened her dresser drawer her clothes began to

move. She looked fine, just fine. There was no sense changing for someone like Mr. Sanchez anyway.

Her shoes made small wet noises as she walked back down the stairs.

"Why, this is delicious!" Mr. Sanchez's overenthusiasm about everything Ella did was beginning to wear thin. Particularly when he had a limp strand of onion hanging from one corner of his mouth, bobbing in time to his words. "You are a real fine cook, little lady!"

But Ella did like getting compliments. It had been a long time. If only she felt well enough to enjoy them. Her disorientation in her own home had increased even more since dinner had begun. And to make it worse, Mr. Sanchez had arrived late, in a mud-brown jumpsuit. An outfit much too young for him.

"Could you pass me some more cucumbers, Ella?"

She frowned, but passed them along anyway. Why was she putting herself through all this? Papa, or Grandfather either, would never have allowed such a man into the house.

"I told you those worms would do you some good," he said.

She had trouble grasping what he was saying. She wondered if he might be drunk. She couldn't smell anything on him, but she'd heard about these new kinds of drinks, which were odorless, or something like that. Maybe that was what was wrong with her. Someone had slipped some of that kind of drink into her tea. "I . . . don't understand, Mr. Sanchez."

"The worms, ma'am! They've done wonders for your yard. Your disposition, too, I could say."

"Worms? I told you—those worms you released here have quite disappeared, Mr. Sanchez. I haven't seen them since."

Mr. Sanchez began that awful grin, but before it was quite complete, he broke out into a raucous, howling laugh. It was the most vulgar laugh she had ever heard. She expected him to jump up at any moment and take off all his clothes. Well, she wouldn't stand for it.

"You haven't *seen* them since? Why, woman, they're all around you! Just take a good look!"

Ella sat rigidly, careful not to move her head, avoiding the directions his expansive gestures indicated. "That is a *lie*, Mr. Sanchez. There are *no* worms in this house! My father and grandfather would never allow it. Vile, disgusting things like worms—don't you think I'd move to rid myself of them as quickly as possible?"

"Oh, I suppose so. Worms are pretty low things. Kind of like dogs shitting up the neighborhood, aren't they? You just have to get rid of them."

Ella swallowed with difficulty. "Don't you dare use such language in my home!"

Mr. Sanchez chuckled. "Oh, excuse me. When a woman invites a man over for a little lovin' he just assumes he can speak freely. Could you just pass me those fine Chinese noodles?"

"Chinese noodles? I didn't prepare any . . ."

"Oh, sure you did. There—just a few inches off your left hand."

She saw them and reached, stopping herself just as she was about to touch their slick, cold sides. She looked around—it was as if the entire dining room had been covered with thick streaks of brown, black, grey, and pale red paint.

She thought Mr. Sanchez was laughing at her again. But she could not hear him beneath her own loud thoughts.

Ella spent the night in the parlor, the only place she could see that the worms had not infested. They were everywhere—hanging onto the curtains, spotting the walls, sliming the floors, the floors where she had stepped, had padded barefoot the previous morning. The house would never feel completely clean again.

And as she thought about this, and what it was she must do, her previous neighbors pulled up next door, where Mr. Sanchez greeted them like long-lost friends.

"Sanchez!" She screamed it, with the kind of vulgarity she

had never thought herself capable of before. They were all disgusting, worthless creatures, no better than the inorganic slimes they lived in. But she'd gotten rid of them before, the neighbors and their shitting dogs. She could do it again. Sanchez should never have shown his nakedness to her. Her father and grandfather, they would never have forgiven her for seeing the man that way.

She stepped to the parlor door—carefully; the worms were crawling on the floor near the entranceway—and began to run toward the back door. She felt the countless soft bodies flattening beneath her feet, smearing to a jelly that made her footing unsteady, but all she had to do was make it to that back door, and even with the squirming bodies dropping onto her from the ceiling, filling her hair and slipping under her clothes, she knew she would make it, and once out she could go to the authorities, and this time they would listen, this time her neighbors would have to pay.

She burst through the back door without stopping, stumbling on the grass that covered her back yard so thickly. But she didn't fall, though the grass was so soft it made progress difficult.

Sanchez had been wrong after all. This lawn hadn't been helped that much by all his worms. The ground had softened, and the grass was much thicker, but it was still brown, in fact far browner than it had ever been before.

Sanchez had failed.

The thought made her slow down. She took a moment to gloat, to stop moving. To her surprise and horror, she had a sudden, nearly unrecognizable urge to go to him, to make it better, to swallow him up.

It was then that she discovered the grass itself was moving, undulating around her feet, then her calves, as she began to slip into the slick waves of brown.

It was then that she discovered it wasn't grass at all.

TANITH LEE

The Tree: A Winter's Tale

THERE IS A picture by Botticelli entitled *Venus and Mars*. Mars lies asleep; Venus is wide awake, and watches with a slight, enigmatic, if impervious smile, as the third of four furry-legged satyrs blows the golden conch shell on Mars' lance into the sleeping ear of the god. It is of course possible the shell does not at all act as a real conch, and will emit no sound. But why then the obvious effort of determined blowing depicted in the third satyr's puffed cheeks and screwed-tight eyes? It is equally possible the shell does work, and that one instant later, in the next frame as it were, Mars will leap up bellowing, all his nakedness revealed, hurling howling satyrs for miles in every direction.

No one seems to have remarked on this absurd and perhaps sinister aspect—why is Venus so complacent?—of an otherwise idyllically sensual painting. For centuries the drama has gone on, its quietude hanging by a thread and the sword descending . . .

Jenver woke up and saw, across the darkened room, one long white finger of window. In the window, on the slope of the garden, Marcusine was standing in the snow. And beyond Marcusine, the tree. The tree was immense and winter-black, its huge arms outflung at the sky. Behind it the old orchard ran in parallel to the old house. Stripped and outlined on the snow, the ranks of the orchard had a wonderful medieval symmetry. But the tree was not symmetrical. It was barbaric, and leaning as it did towards the house, seemed about to fall on his sister.

To his relief, at that moment she turned and came back to the window. Jenver stretched with a groan of displeasure. As she walked into the room, he touched the igniter, and a blazing fire sprang alive on the hearth.

"Well, good morning," said Marcusine.

"I wish this damn fire would stay alight. Can't we alter the program?"

"It's a safety device. I doubt it. It always switches off after three hours unless someone presses the button again."

"Damn it."

"You shouldn't," she said, "keep falling asleep in the library. Why don't you go to bed like everyone else?"

"Marsh was playing one of his ghastly cantatas *multo noiso*."

"And you hate sound-proofing your room—"

"Because I don't like the generalized impression that I've gone deaf."

"You could speak to Marsh," said Marcusine. She knelt by the fire. Out of silhouette now, her dress was a winter color, a somber holly-leaf green. From its central parting her dark hair, fashionably unfashionable and timeless, fell to her shoulders.

"I can't," said Jenver, "speak to Marsh. It's his house, too. I couldn't make him feel he can't do exactly as he wants because I don't like it, could I?" He was no longer thinking about his cousin Marsh. The fascinated love he felt for his sister was sweeping over him in waves, as it always did. He was not surprised that she, too, had lost track of their discussion. She raised her pale serious face and he looked at it, exploring every familiar angle, the slender sharp cheekbones, the darkly-polished eyes.

"The tree," she said, "it really will have to come down."

"Is it worse?"

"Yes. The roots are well out of the ground on the other side. In a high wind—or even this snow—it's dangerous."

"Yes," Jenver said. "And even in summer it makes everything impossibly dark."

In summer a thick green treacle of shade invaded the library, and all this side of the house, the tree blotting out the sun so the lights must be used. Once, years ago, Stemyard had insisted on having a tea-party under the tree. She had held it alone. Even her sister Araige had refused to join in, while Stemyard's two cats had hidden in the cellars pretending there were mice to be caught. There was something about the tree. Its wild unstable boughs, its knotted mast. Every year, it had grown a little stronger, every year the old house had decayed a little more, despite all the renovations and the ultramodern improvements. The tree vampirized the house, sucked the life from it more by more along a system of green tubes hidden under the earth.

"How old is it?" Jenver suddenly asked. On the cold blank of the sky, the tree had seemed to tilt a fraction nearer. If it fell now it would at least shatter these three long windows. Its branches would fall on them like iron claws.

"The house computer records it as approximately ten centuries, in the first entry."

"And the computer was put in about seventy years ago. It seems improbable."

"Not when you look at the tree," said Marcusine.

They looked, through the closed glass window, at the tree.

Jenver had slept all night with the tree facing him over the sloping lawn, ready to crash against the house. He shivered.

Marcusine stood up.

"Come to breakfast."

"Let me shower first, and change. I feel glued into these clothes."

"All right." She reached the library door, turned and smiled at him. She was four years older than he, her eyes full of strange wisdom. One could not tire of her gracefulness, the fire catching her one way, shadow another.

"I love you," he said.

"No. I love *you*."

She went through the door and was gone.

Stemyard had three cats now. They sat in a neat line on the wide window sill, looking out at the snow.

Stemyard stood behind them, brushing her fair bob with brisk flat strokes.

From this window, she could only see the edges and tips of the branches of the tree. Beyond, the orchard was a briary of dark silver, dotted with small dark birds which still bravely tweeted through the pitiless cold. Between the tree and the orchard, Araige, Stemyard's sister, the youngest of all the cousins, had had put up a marble bird-table on a tall smooth pillar the cats could not climb. Araige would go out there later today, standing on the circle of the icy gravel, laying out nuts and fats and scraps. The birds knew about Araige. When she went towards them in her wild, multi-colored clothes, crowned by the dab of pink hair, they did not fly away. When she had retreated again only four or five feet, they flew into the feed. Afterwards, they flew back to the orchard.

They never came to perch on the tree.

Very little snow had stayed on the tree, either.

Stemyard leaned over the cats and stared sideways at the tree. It looked aloof today, disdainful. Stemyard had always deduced emotions from the tree. Contempt was the most frequently apparent, and sometimes the contemptuous sorrow of something so very ancient and alone. It had been here long, long before the house, long before the orchard, even, had sprung up. Occasionally, Stemyard sensed rage in the tree, perhaps only rage it could not die. To live such a span, to witness so much so helplessly, immovable . . . The boredom of its colossal life oppressed her.

The cats assumed her proximity was a wish to be near them. Siddi rubbed his face against hers, Shoh purred spontaneously, Set shuffled away and slapped her with his tail. Set was the thoroughbred cat, a short-haired Reverse, a white beast with a coal-black belly, breast and under-chin, and high black socks, as if he had been walking slowly through ink. All the rest was unspotted save for the black insides of his ears and the black highwayman's mask across his eyes, which spoilt his pedigree and insanely enhanced his extraordinary looks. The eyes themselves were yellow. Shoh was yellow-eyed too, another Reverse, with a ginger under-stripe and paws, but his white was freckled all over with orange and calico, as if—his program-breeder had remarked in despair—he had been whirling in the womb. Siddi was not a bred cat but a random stray, a small pewter creature with lettuce-coloured eyes, possessed of great courtesy.

Stemyard loved her cats. It was no psychological accident their names and hers began with the same letter. Of humans Stemyard tended to be fearful and jealous. Stemyard could get no control of this. Araige, for example, had a wanton courage and energy Stemyard utterly lacked. Next year, surely, Araige would be going abroad again, and Stemyard hoped secretly this time she would not come back to the house.

Stemyard liked the house. She respected it, and felt that it respected her, her need for study and for privacy, while the garden and the mildly savage land beyond were satisfying to her tame yearnings for nature. The outskirts of the city were only a mile away. But one could overlook that, even the industrious mechanized golden glow above the city on summer nights could be ignored or explained away.

As for the tree, she could placate it. In childhood, once or twice, sensing its anger, she had taken the tree offerings—a locket buried between the roots under the full moon; a doll. Later, in adolescence, glasses of wine poured amidst its claws as they bitterly gripped the earth. And most recently—the night of a storm half a year ago—she had dashed a flagon of scent against the bole, smelling the sweetness mingling with rain and electricity, afraid lightning would strike both it and her.

For no logical reason, Shoh the womb-whirler, still purring, turned and bit her wrist.

"Blast you, Cat!" Stemyard exclaimed, examining her flesh. This was always happening. Her right arm was covered with tiny bites at various levels of healing. She poked at Shoh, who hissed, and then curled directly into a smiling ball. It was Set who sprang away into the room with an offended squawk. Siddi, a study in puzzled tact, began to wash.

Marsh woke late, hearing Araige fluting to the birds from the bird-table. Winged things were fluting with responsive excitement; this was what had roused him. He had been dreaming of a sinking liner, a dream that seemed always now to haunt his morning sleep. It did not fill him with particular terror or depression, but he was irritated by its sameness. He supposed in some way it was a reminder of the mass parental tragedy that had struck them all seventeen years ago. The others had really been too young to understand what had happened, except possibly for an eight-year-old Marcusine, who had come to him leading a minuscule four-year-old Jenver by the hand. "Are they all dead?" "Yes." "Why?" He had tried to explain truthfully, succinctly, and ungraphically, about the party conducted on the private air-ship which subsequently fell blazing from the sky. He had been forty-four, and had been used to having the house full of persons of all ages, from his own mother, spry and attractive in her eighties, to the latest child of his youngest uncle, born only a few months previously. Suddenly he found himself alone with a quartet of miserable children. Marsh had never been able to cope with children. He left them to their hired companions and the infallible mechanical devices already installed all over the premises. Having grown up they did not like him, he thought, nor did he blame them for that. Nor did it much matter. The five of them owned the house jointly, but it was a massive place, rambling with rooms and individual suites. Two hundred years ago, it would have been unmanageable without servants. Now, of course, it would be unmanageable without machines.

Marsh entered the en-suite bathroom. Emerging twenty minutes later after his usual disgusting confrontation with the mirrors, he sat listening to a sonatina by Cibienzi, letting the shaver cream-shave him, drinking the glass of cold sweet wine with which he began each day, early or late.

He had played the cantata too loudly last night. No, actually at two this morning. He had had an argument with Jenver, and had wanted to pay him out in some way. It had worked. Jenver, who hated to soundproof his own suite across the passage, had gone out, slamming the door, and down—presumably to the library. What had the argument been about? Marsh idly racked his brain, but the orderly, scholarly rows of informative memory gave up no trace. The real problem was, in fact, that his cousin Jenver had turned out so very like the handsome boys Marsh had been keen on years ago. Not that Jenver was of their proclivity. Jenver was quite straightforward, except in his love for his sister, and that, though exceedingly passionate, was also completely physically unincestuous. Mentally, one noted though, perhaps not. Jenver's amatory relationships were few and far between. No other woman had measured up to Marcusine. Definitely not the other cousins, sullen Stemyard with her bloody mad cats, or the soulless woeful Araige, who filled the rooms with scent, smoke, and shed articles of jewelry, scarves, or cigarette papers.

But, if only Jenver were now a little less. Well, it could scarcely be helped. This was Jenver's house, too. One could not drive him away simply because he resembled the carnal ghosts of one's past. Marsh had ended all such affairs when once he began to consider himself decaying and unacceptable. This, as it had not been with his mother, had seemed to happen very quickly. By his late fifties, Marsh found himself sexually unseemly. The sort of men he wanted did not naturally want him any more, and he became afraid of being made a fool of. The pretence that he himself had lost his appetite worked most of the time. Now his solace was music.

It was rather curious that he should therefore use music as a weapon of war against Jenver.

Outside, the birds were quieting down, flying back into the orchard, stuffed with bread like winged sausages.

The shaver finished with him and patted astringent cologne on his cheeks. Marsh refused anymore, where it could be avoided, to touch himself, his own face or body. He hated and resented what time had done to him, and was doing, the flaccidity, the aridity, the decline and fall of the empire of the flesh.

He lay back in the chair, finishing his sweet wine, looking at the lines the tree had scrawled over the sky. The tree was old, too, but it had only grown more vehement. Surely some-one had said the roots were pulling out of the ground on one side? He ought to go and look at that. He would enjoy that. For years, it seemed, he had been wanting the tree to die.

Araige paused on the lawn, and thought about herself for one minute.

Her hair was the colour of a pale pink winter sunset. Her woolen coat was black, white and purple and her boots a crushed magenta. She was wearing hose, jade-green, long green stems of legs going into the boots, and a cream knitted shirt with a crimson rose pinned on the loose collar. She herself could smell the dusky aroma of her own perfume. Why was any of it significant? For whom had she dressed, for whom powdered her eyelids with golden dust and crayoned her lips with soft mulberry? For herself? *She* had wanted to stay in bed and cry and cry until she suffocated.

She thought about Paris-Sur-Ône, and the man she had been in love with. She thought about the carnival on the ice, the spitting, stabilized torches and the sleighs with bells, and how he had rolled across her in front of the others, and to her protest had said, "You're only a whore." The word was obsolete. He and she alone, because of their studies, knew what it meant. He was drunk. She told him to stop. "Do you think I care about you?'' he said. ''Yes,'' she said, her heart gone to water and running away. He said, ''You're wrong.''

How silly it was. It must have been a mistake of some kind. She would never forget the darkness of his eyes as he said it—''You're wrong.''—like black ice, and she slid from him, losing him, as he walked away.

How quiet it was now the birds had stopped squabbling over the food.

Araige liked to feed them.

She seemed to have been feeding them, in just this way, for many years, many times a day. And yet she had not been here, had she, more than a month or so.

''You're wrong.''

She started to cry. Her cosmetics would never smudge, and she could make out it was the cold air, to Marcusine, who had suddenly appeared from one of the library windows. But Marcusine seemed not to see her. She came around and stood beside the tree, looking down at its claws embedded in the snow. Then she walked back into the library and shut the window.

Araige did not examine the tree. It meant nothing to her at all.

She thought about her strawberry nails and the gold crescents on them, enamelled through a little stencil. By the time she reached the conservatory doors she had stopped crying.

The machines had laid out a combination breakfast and lunch: eggs, fish, meats, breads, cakes, on nests of heat; juices and wines, in nests of cold. The tall coffee pots steamed. Only Stemyard was drinking tea. Siddishohset ate salmon close to the hearth. They were accustomed to being served by mechanicals. Only Siddi sometimes still raised a paw to tap the air-borne entity pouring water in his dish.

Jenver and Araige had finished their meal, if they had eaten. He sat reading among the cats. She was rolling a mauve cigarette. Marsh, who was not long in the room, helping himself to eggs and ham, puzzled over her colors. A soft rainbow in the dark chair, tinselled by a long scarf, and now by smoke. Araige had been five months old when the ship exploded in the sky. In Paris-Sur-Ône there had been some man, twenty-seven or -eight, too old for her. Her emotional and sex life had begun early, as his had done. He wondered if she, too, would grow old ungracefully.

Marcusine came in from the conservatory.

She stood at the edge of the room, and their eyes went to her almost inadvertently.

"The tree," she said, without preliminary, "it really will have to come down."

There was, for some reason, something inexplicably tiresome about this pronouncement. Probably they had discussed the tree before. For years it had denied them natural light, blocked their views, threatened the foundations with its crawling talons.

"Oh, the tree," said Araige, brightly, like an idiot, repeating things.

Jenver lowered his book.

"It's worse?"

"The roots are coming out of the ground on the far side. It's dangerous. In a high wind, it could fall on its own."

"I imagine it would be easy enough to arrange," Marsh said. "Some sort of contractor."

"*No!*" Stemyard shouted.

They looked at her. She was white. Set spat by the hearth.

"You can't," Stemyard said. "It's always been there. No."

"I know it's very old," said Marcusine calmly. "But it truly is—"

"I won't let you," said Stemyard.

"Won't let me?" Marcusine gave no sign even of minor annoyance. "Well, perhaps we should—"

"It's always been part of the house. Since we were children."

"Yes, Stemyard. Perhaps we should take a consensus. What do we all think?"

"To chop or not to chop," said Jenver. "Let's get rid of the godawful tree. I've always hated it."

"Of course," said Stemyard, "Jenver would agree with Marcusine."

"I don't," he said. "Or not for the same reasons. Her arguments are logical. Mine are purely superstitious."

"Then you ought to know," snarled Stemyard, "that to cut down a living tree invites a curse."

"Does it?" said Jenver. "How entirely fascinating."

He could be too clever sometimes, Marsh thought. Jenver was the kind who was knifed in alleys, razor-edged, but without the agility to back it up. He slashed mental skin negligently, and then forgot he had. The wounded, of course, remembered.

Stemyard had reddened now. The spotted cat, Shoh, had also begun to spit and hiss.

"It's a very old belief. I still believe it. If you cut that tree down for no more excuse than that you don't like it—"

"Hate it, I said. Not dislike."

"Children," said Marcusine, "please."

Jenver grinned. Stemyard went mad.

"I have as much bloody say as any of you!" she screamed. "If you dare touch that tree—" she stopped herself. "Don't," she said and drank her tea in loud gulps.

"What about you, Araige?" said Marsh. He had finished his food and sought a new distraction. Araige wriggled elegantly and neurasthenically.

"I don't care," she said. "But if Stem doesn't want—"

"No, I *don't* want."

"Well, I think," said Marsh, "it would be an excellent idea to get rid of the monster. You know, I've looked at the damn thing for thirty-odd years before any of you were born. I'm sick and tired of it. Let it go. Stemyard, we can plant something else, something more harmonious."

He occasionally pulled this trick on them, one or other or all of them, his weight of age and experience—what else was it good for? He sat back, watching them benignly, jealous and ill-at-ease.

Stemyard found herself out-numbered and on the verge of tears. She loathed all of them, stupid unaware Marsh, smug Marcusine and spiteful Jenver, and her own sister who cared for nothing but her own pleasure and the savage flights she would take to get it. Stemyard's mind diverted intellectually, in order to escape. She considered arcane curses, druids, tree-cults. The tree was old enough itself to recall all these. She thought of the land eleven centuries ago, open, spare, and the seed in the ground which would be the tree.

"An Apple-Cyrus would be nice," said Araige vaguely.

Stemyard stood up.

"Listen to me," she said. "This house and the land belong to me, too. If I say you can't cut down the tree, you can't. You know it."

"Rubbish," said Jenver. "You're just a silly kid. Now shut up, for god's sake."

Stemyard walked over to him. As he raised his smiling, inquiring face, she punched it. Jenver yelled. His book went to the ground and tapped Set in the ribs. Yowling, the Reverse cat leapt for the automatic inner door, which opened to let him hurtle through.

"I'm sorry," said Stemyard. She was not. But she was acutely embarrassed.

Jenver nursed his face, allowed Marcusine to examine it and assure him he was neither slain nor maimed. Marcusine laughed and shook her head at Stemyard. Stemyard ran out of the room after the cat.

Presently the two other cats followed, Siddi eagerly, Shoh making excuses, searching the veneered wainscoting for beetles all the way, finally inventing one and chasing it upstairs.

The cat-hatch in Stemyard's door let them all in. Soon they were sitting in a neat line along the wide windowsill, staring out at the snow.

Stemyard brushed her boyish hair, swallowing tears.

After a while she leaned forward to look sideways at the tree.

She could placate the tree. She would be forgiven.

Shoh turned, purring, and bit her arm.

Marcusine went into the garden. The sky was misty now, the tops of the orchard dissolving, the sun invisible as it had been all day, and would continue to be until darkness came.

She went to the tree, as she seemed constantly to have to do, compelled.

She stood on the snow, looking down at its roots, up into the inverted roots of its branches. She felt old, far older than Marsh, old as the tree itself, maybe. What type of tree was it? Did any of them know? The house computer would have a record. She should listen to the tape again. It was surely bad manners to destroy a thing of whose name and nature she was ignorant. But it would have to come down. It dominated them far too much. Look at the scene which had ensued. Its shadow fell in their rooms, their lives. There was a foolish pun in it all, somewhere, too: the tree, the *family* tree, *roots* . . .

Marcusine grimaced idly. She put her hand on the damp, impenetrable bark.

''I'm sorry,'' she said to the tree, as Stemyard had untruthfully said to Jenver. Another inch, and she would have given him a black eye, and probably well-deserved.

Their relationship, hers and her brother's, was also unsatisfactory. It had never troubled Jenver. He took charmingly, and besides had experimented successfully with other companions outside their sphere. Marcusine herself found that people bored her. She was not even afraid of them, as Stemyard was, which would furnish a tolerable pretext for avoiding contact. With Jenver, Marcusine was neither bored nor excited. She was alert, comfortable, and at home. He sometimes exasperated but never offended her. She was conscious of his beauty, and occasionally the word-play of outsiders had caused her to wonder if she might ever try to seduce him. The hot revulsion such an idea caused her always inclined her to think that on some level she did desire him, and had evolved revulsion as a safeguard. Her sexual encounters in the world had been many and varied; she was greatly more experienced than her brother. She enjoyed the act, but found the complexities displeasing. She had never been in love, not even infatuated, merely attracted, and never for long. To some extent, then, she remained unfulfilled, not sexually, but emotionally in the sexual area of her life. Only once had she ever discovered herself in the wish that Jenver were not her brother, that the notion of making love with him did not revolt her, that everything had been different. But then, if he were not her brother, perhaps she would not have liked him at all.

Something might be done with the stump of the tree. It would be a high stump. Vines would help to camouflage its nakedness, and then possibly leaves might still grow. A marble shape of some sort could stand on it, something aerial, lifting towards the sky.

Marcusine walked back to the house, and went into the library. It was in darkness, unlit. She hesitated; somehow she had expected Jenver to be seated in the chair facing the window, the fire playing on his face, hands and hair. A kind of after-image persisted. For a moment she almost spoke to him.

Marsh woke with a sense of dull deprecation. He had fallen asleep in his sitting-room—a wasted afternoon; already what had once been called the 'shades of evening' were filming the windows. He touched a button and amber sidelights came on. The windows snapped from charcoal to amethyst.

He went into the bathroom, confronted the mirrors, and ran the tub. He lay in the hot water, trying to relax into wakefulness, but the sudden sleep had deadened and depressed him. Tonight, no doubt, he would have to have recourse to a sleeping capsule, or else read until dawn.

He dressed tidily, refusing to attempt grace. As he came out of his suite, Jenver simultaneously came out of his across the hall. They looked at each other.

"This place becomes more and more like a hotel," Jenver remarked. His velvet jacket was the color of dying leaves.

"A hotel out of season," Marsh amended.

Jenver offered him a cigarette. Inconsequently, they stood in the passage, smoking.

"It's not that I object to cantatas," Jenver said eventually. "Not that I particularly like them, but I don't object—"

"I apologize. Far too loud, I know."

"No, it's my fault. If I could stand the soundproofing—"

"A form of audial claustrophobia. I think you got locked in a cupboard once as a child, didn't you?"

"Did I?" Jenver was fascinated, as always, by details about himself he had forgotten or not known.

"Yes, one of the cellar cupboards. You were playing some game and the door jammed. There was a great fuss. The machines located you, but you would have been badly scared."

"Poor me," said Jenver, with genuine sympathy.

Marsh smiled. The boy really was delightful. One should make more allowances, perhaps contrive to be with him now and then.

"That might be the cause," said Marsh. "A cupboard like that would certainly have been deadly quiet. You must have thought no one would ever find you."

"Yes. I must have."

They finished their cigarettes. It was two hours yet till dinner.

"It's rather odd," said Jenver, "you can remember what happened all those years ago. And yet suppose I asked you what happened yesterday?"

"Much the same as today, I surmise. God knows. But that's one of the penalties of senility, forgetting the recent past."

"Oh, come on, Marsh, you talk as if you're a dinosaur. You look forty, a damn good forty at that. You know you do."

Marsh was grateful, even as he shook his head. He had the notion Jenver was flirting with him, but Jenver flirted with everyone who permitted it.

"In any case," Jenver said, "I didn't mean you, exactly. I

meant me. I was trying to remember what I did yesterday. And I can't quite pin it down, except that substantially it was like today. Oh, and it snowed heavily yesterday morning, didn't it? I recall Marcusine coming in from the garden with fresh snow in her hair, and talking about the tree—which is also odd—''

''What's that?'' said Marsh. He was losing the thread of the conversation, absorbed by the look of Jenver and the musical sound of his voice.

''*Déjà vu*, Marsh, that's all. I suddenly had the feeling we'd stood here like this before and I'd said everything I just said . . . before.''

''It's quite likely you have. Why not? The suites face each other.''

''My god. I knew you'd say that. Or something like it. I probably need to get away from the house.''

Marsh shrugged. It would be a pity if Jenver went away. One man against three women seemed an unfair ratio. And just as he had begun to feel some point in getting to know Jenver better.

They walked out of the passage to the head of the second staircase.

''I don't know about you, but that tree really ought to go,'' said Marsh. ''Although I examined the base of it after lunch, and the roots seem quite firmly fixed, despite Marcusine's analysis. Perhaps the snow misled her when she looked at them. Even so, it's a blasted nuisance, it always has been.'' Had it? He could only remember its worrying him since . . . since when? Quite recently.

''When I was a child,'' said Jenver, ''I used to think the tree would reach right up through the house at night and strangle me, or drink my blood. Or something.''

They laughed, and went down the stairs.

Jenver was slightly entranced. He had just told a lie, in order to be entertaining. He had never, as a child, actually felt anything about the tree, had he? Had he even been locked in a cupboard? That was too classic, was it not?

Poor old Marsh. What would it be like to fall to pieces like this? Stupid, for one thing, with so many preparations on the market, over-the-counter drugs that could have helped. Why did he never try some of them?

Jenver skipped off the last two stairs and offered Marsh a courtly bow. Compassionately, he took the older man's arm, and conveyed him into the billiards room for a game of Shot.

It could well be a good idea to go away for a time. Marcusine should get away, too. They could chop down the rotten tree and sell the timber and do something ridiculous with the unexpected money they didn't need. Separately, of course. Their escapes had always been alone. For the pleasure of returning and being together again?

But it was a long time since either of them had been away or been seriously apart.

Araige finished her letter, read it through, rose and walked about the room.

Yes, I know how we parted, but I refuse to believe—

She took up the letter again.

—to believe that a crazy quarrel on a frozen river—

No, no, no.

She tore the letter into pieces.

She had written this letter so often, torn it in pieces so often.

She sat down at her dressing-table and the soft lights bloomed about the mirror. She brushed dark green glitter onto her eyelids, and then, using a stencil, painted green stars over her nails.

Stemyard closed her book on its silken marker. She preferred the book to a screen, the book's actuality. It was more intimate.

A piercing nostalgia rode her. Why had she been born now, why not then, the teeming, unhygienic, passionate, rose-red past—blind life, romantic bloody death, fearless, cruel and great.

Had there been any choice? Had she chosen to be this, to be Stemyard now, instead of Cesare Borgia in 1501?

Siddi snored in her lap. Shohset had fallen asleep fighting round her ankles.

These were her family. She loved them. After all, love bound her to the present.

Marcusine had changed into a burgundy dress. Yesterday evening it had been dove-grey. She recalled going out to look at the tree in the new snow and the grey dress.

Was she becoming obsessive about the tree, or only about Jenver?

Jenver was becoming horribly bored. It was truly horrible. Marsh was regaling him with anecdotes Jenver knew he had heard a hundred times, or more. Marsh had assumed a dreadful sprightliness. The game had been a mistake.

Marsh scored twenty points and chalked his cue. He felt almost unpleasantly hysterical, drunk, in fact. Jenver seemed, however, to be enjoying his company. Perhaps he really was.

Outside, the tree stood in the center of the winter landscape, the light of day dying all around it.

The machines had laid out a midwinter dinner, roast beef and chicken, sauces and stuffings, the tiny green cabbages that Jenver in his childhood had erroneously called 'hassles', potatoes baked within and without their skins, bowls of peas like green pearls. The carvers whirred. Corks exploded from bottles.

For a while, it was quite festive.

Siddishohset ate carefully-boned chicken by the hearth. At some point, always, with chicken, however boneless, Shoh would pretend, or actually manage to think, he had a bone caught in his throat. Stemyard would rise in panic, and then Shoh would swallow, and indignantly resume his meal.

It was bitterly cold beyond the house. A blast of wicked air had come in with Marcusine from the conservatory.

"The tree," she had said.

"It's worse," said Jenver, drinking rye whisky.

"I examined the base of it after lunch," Marsh said, also drinking whisky, bourbon. "The roots seem quite firmly fixed. Do you think the snow misled you, Marcusine?"

"No," she said amiably. Her drink was generally vodkagne, and Jenver mixed one for her.

As the first pleasures of eating dulled, however, Marsh began to tell old stories they had all heard before.

Stemyard forked her dessert impatiently. Araige was far off, her eyes cloudy, not listening, smiling when the others forced laughter, uninvolved.

Shoh choked. Stemyard started up. Shoh swallowed and resumed his meal.

"Inevitably," said Marsh, "I find I repeat myself."

"I thought you'd never notice," said Jenver, with one of those isolated but snake-like flashes of spite almost unbearable after the charm and courtesy before.

Marsh's face fell. He lost the spurious poise he had acquired during the last two hours. It dropped from him with a sort of clank, embarrassing them all.

"Well," Marsh said. He plucked at his napkin, discarded it, and drank down his wine like medicine. "I apologize for being a boring old fool. Excuse me." He rose from the table and walked stiffly through into the coffee-room.

"Oh, dear," said Jenver.

"You really shouldn't have," said Marcusine.

"I couldn't stand it any more."

"Now he'll sulk all evening," snapped Stemyard. "You are a pig, Jenver."

"Shut up, Stemyard."

"Why should I? Why should you be the only one in this house to do as you like, say what you like, regardless of the trouble you cause? You're useless, a parasite."

"And you are a loud-mouthed little bitch."

"I wish you'd get out and go to hell."

"Children, please." said Marcusine.

"Hell is here," quoted Jenver, "nor are we out of it."

"Don't quote things, you never get them right. When are you leaving?"

"Children," said Marcusine.

"When?" Stemyard shouted.

The cats looked at her.

Jenver turned his smiling, inquiring face towards her.

"Afraid I'll really go?"

Stemyard leaned across the table, raising her narrow fist to punch him. Marcusine caught her arm and held her.

"No, Stem. You've already done that."

Stemyard writhed, red in the face.

"What? What are you talking about?"

She subsided involuntarily and Marcusine let go of her.

"I don't know," said Marcusine. "Let's have some coffee, shall we?"

Stemyard stalked away into the other room.

Jenver and Marcusine strolled after her.

Araige rose slowly to follow, and paused, and thought about herself for one minute. For whom had she dressed, powdered her eyelids, crayoned her mouth? For herself? *She* had wanted to go to bed and cry until she suffocated.

She thought about Paris-Sur-Ône. The vision kept coming back, she could not stop it, nor did it lose its pain. "You're only a whore. Do you think I care about you? You're wrong."

She ran the gamut and wept. Then her tears ended and she walked through into the circular coffee-room.

The light there was harmonious and soft, the hearth blazing. Like every other fire in the house, after three hours, it would die down, and the igniter must be pressed. Then it would blaze again. Then die again. Then blaze again—on and on.

The drapes were unclosed, and on the pale backdrop of the

snow-paved garden, the tree stood immense, its huge arms outflung.

Araige took coffee, and rolled a blue cigarette.

Marsh sat over a bulb of brandy, his eyes hard with scar tissue.

Stemyard's three cats had jumped onto the wide window-sill, where they sat in a neat line, looking out at the snow.

"Isn't this cozy," said Jenver unforgivably. Only Marcusine realized the crack had been made from nerves.

They looked out at the tree.

"You know," said Marcusine, "we never did come to an agreement about the tree. Marsh, how do you feel?"

"You mean I'm permitted to have feelings?" he said bitterly, embarrassing them further. "At least, to have them, if not to mention them verbally."

"Marsh, I think we all seem to be rather on edge," said Marcusine. "Jenver was impossible. He didn't mean to be."

"No, I didn't," said Jenver. "I'm sorry, Marsh, Stemyard. Is there anyone else I've upset?"

There was a long silence.

"I could contact someone about the tree tomorrow," said Marcusine. "If we can all agree."

"But you know we can't," said Stemyard.

"What really is your objection, Stem?"

"It's always been there."

"I know it's very old," said Marcusine calmly. "But it truly is potentially very dangerous. It blocks the light. And the roots are almost certainly damaging the foundations. If it fell—"

"I won't let you—" said Stemyard.

"Won't let me? Well, perhaps we should take a vote. What do we all think?"

"The tree or not the tree," said Jenver. "Let's get rid of the godawful thing. I hate it and I'm sure the feeling's mutual. I have plenty of enemies, without adding a tree to the list."

"Of course," said Stemyard, "Jenver would agree with his sister."

"But not for the same reasons. Hers are logical. Mine are superstitious."

"Then you ought to know the superstition that to cut down a healthy tree invites a curse."

"Oh, Stemyard," said Marcusine, "we've been all through this before."

"Have we? Then did I tell you before the thing I found out about our parents, yours and mine? And Marsh's mother?"

Shoh, the spotted cat, hissed like an erupting pan. Set, usually the hisser, turned his back.

"All right, Stem," said Marcusine. "What strange occult detail did you find out about our joint parents?"

Stemyard took a deep breath, her slight body swelling, rather in the manner of certain birds or lizards, enlarging themselves with air in order to warn adversaries.

"My father kept a diary. When I was about ten I found it, and I read it. The week they planned to make the crossing in the air-ship, and have the party, that week they planned something else, too. They planned to have the tree cut down when they came back."

Jenver rattled his cup.

"But they didn't get round to it, so what happened to them can hardly have been retributive."

"It could have been preventative," grated Stemyard, with unqualified emphasis. Her cheeks flamed, and she looked, Jenver noted, almost interesting. What a weird young woman she was. "You see what I mean, do you?" she rasped on, carried by her tide. "The ship—they burned. It stopped them."

Marcusine poured herself a cognac, hesitated, and poured one for Stemyard too.

"Here, drink that. I believe you're saying that the tree— our poor old monster out there—killed our parents to prevent their killing it. So that we too (oh dear, Stem), will suffer the same fate if we make the same horticultural decision."

"Not necessarily," Stemyard was now morosely defiant.

"It wouldn't harm the house. It's used to the house, respects the age of the house, even though the house is a mere child to the tree. A symbiotic relationship, perhaps, on some level. But if we left the house it might somehow do—something. They were all together, weren't they? And a great distance off, in the sky."

"Good Lord, trapped together for ever and ever and amen," said Jenver. "Unable to leave. But quite able to signal for help. We could call in the tree people, whoever they are, whoever cuts down trees. Just call them, and sit back and wait."

Stemyard bit her lip, staring at him.

"Yes, I suppose so. Then there'd have to be some other way."

"I wonder what. Green tendrils by night, sucking out our blood. Replacing it with green tendrils . . ."

"Marsh," Stemyard said loudly, "do you remember what my father wrote? They *did* agree about it, didn't they?"

"I don't remember," said Marsh. He could hear Araige quietly crying in her chair. He felt uncomfortable now, as well as wounded, and rather afraid. Oh, not of the idiotic tree-curse, not of that. Of real life. He had almost been included in the party on the air-ship. A mild attack of influenza had cancelled his place. He could not recall if they had planned anything about the tree. The tree had not concerned him, then. It was simply there, as the house was, the family. And, outside in the world, the young men with their greeting eyes. In those days, mirrors had not offended him. If he had told the same joke twice, entranced, his companions had still laughed at it.

Old fool. Bloody decrepit old fool.

He should have been more careful. The snake under the stone. It might have been better if he had been on that blasted burning ship, he thought, with abysmal, hopeless resentment, and hated himself the more for this concept of martyrdom.

Stemyard found herself outnumbered and on the verge of tears. She loathed all of them, and herself also, for resorting to fantastic theories before them. Such ideas could only harden their closed minds further against her and her plea.

She was frightened by the thought that the tree might really be destroyed. It was an awful fear. She did not even try to put it into proportion.

"I'm going up," she said. "To read." To re-enter the Renascence, where you are not. "Good night."

She went.

Presently the cats followed her.

Araige lay in her chair, now smoking, now crying, now still, now crying again, miles away.

Marsh lit a cigar.

Jenver poured himself more coffee.

Marcusine stood by the window looking at the tree.

She felt old, far older than Marsh, old as the tree itself, maybe. What type of tree was it? Did any of them know? Something might be done with the stump. Vines would provide camouflage. A marble shape, an aerial statue, might stand on it, making a feature of it.

Jenver opened the book he had brought from the library. He had lost his place. This passage seemed familiar; he had obviously read it before. The next page then . . .

He glanced at Marsh, who was dozing, the cigar dead between his fingers.

Damn. He should have been patient with Marsh. But Marsh was so touchy. What, after all, had Jenver said? Nothing really. Only the truth. Damn.

Jenver probably needed, he thought, to get away from the house, the family. Even from Marcusine, maybe. But both their escapes had always been alone. For the pleasure of returning and being together again?

The fascinated love he felt for his sister was already sweeping over him in waves. Wherever he went, whoever he was with, he would come back to her.

Marsh woke with a dull sense of deprecation. He had fallen asleep in the coffee-room, and been abandoned there. It was the chill of the dead fire which had finally alerted him. He pressed the button with irritation, and the flames sprang to attention.

Yes, they had all gone. A wasted evening. And for sure, he would never sleep in bed now. It was after one o'clock.

He rose, grunting and dry-mouthed. He poured himself a cup of the stale, cooling coffee and drank it wincing, looking about. Almost all trace was gone of everyone; he might have been alone in the house. Only Araige had left her tinsel scarf, as usual, and a scatter of blue cigarette papers, and a scrap of writing on a page torn from a note-pad. *Crazy quarrel* it read. That was all. A comment on the whole evening, probably.

Marsh went up to his suite and ran the tub. He lay in it, trying to relax, aware it was useless.

He considered Jenver, the vicious little beast. There had been a hint of movement as Marsh passed his door, serene preparations for sleep. Well, that could be remedied.

If Marsh must lose sleep, he need not do so quite alone.

He grinned maliciously, catching sight in the mirror of grey loose skin and yellow teeth.

In his sitting-room, he selected a Cibienzi cantata, magnificent and pealing, and set the player.

The glorious paean roared out, and Marsh grinned.

Not long after, the door across the corridor slammed with some violence. Footsteps went towards the stairs.

Marsh grinned maliciously.

Araige dreamed burning birds fell on an icy river, and she ran along it, after a man who forever walked away.

Stemyard dreamed of formlessness, surrounded by cats snoring and twitching, a furry doss-house.

Marcusine dreamed, with an overpowering sense of terror and hot revulsion, that she was making love to her brother.

The sky lightened behind the tree, and the sun rose. The weather had changed. The weather, the world, these were always capable of alteration, progression of some kind. But the tree stood rooted to the earth, grey slush rushing and shifting now about its claws. By midday the snow would all be gone, the sky a smoky innocent blue. But the tree would remain, fixed, living, experiencing perhaps minor varieties—buds, leaves, fall, frost; winds and snows and night and day; the movement of things in the air and on the ground, the growth or decay of time. Yet, throughout such changes, unchanged. Always. Every day, no matter how different, was the same for the tree. The boredom of its colossal life was oppressive.

Marsh, at last asleep, dreamed of a sinking liner.

Jenver did not remember his dreams.

Jenver woke up and saw, across the darkened room, a long white finger of window. In the window, on the slope of the garden, Marcusine was standing in the melting snow. And beyond Marcusine, the tree. The tree was immense and winter-black, its huge arms outflung at the sky.

Marcusine turned and came back to the window.

Jenver touched the igniter and the hearth blazed.

"Well, good morning," said Marcusine.

"Don't ask why I'm here; I'll tell you. Marsh was playing one of his ghastly cantatas *un poco roaro.*"

"And you hate soundproofing your room."

"And he knows I do."

"Speak to him."

"I can't. It's his house, too. Confound him."

He looked at his sister. Her dress was holly-berry red, a winter color. He explored her face, the sharp slender cheekbones, darkly-polished eyes.

"The tree," she said, "it really must come down."

"Must it?"

"The roots are well out of the ground. It's dangerous."

"Yes. Besides, it makes everything pitch black, even in summer."

Marcusine knelt by the fire.

Upstairs, Marsh felt the tugging swirl of water as the liner vanished.

Stemyard was awake, brushing her bobbed hair briskly, leaning to the window.

Marsh heard distant crying, and leviathanic bubbles rose from the water.

Araige lay in bed, thinking of the birds. She would feed them today, on the marble bird-table whose top reminded her so much of a frozen river.

"Blast you, Cat!" Stemyard exclaimed, as one of her loving companions of the night, the purring Shoh, bit her.

Jenver, who had slept all night with the tree facing him through the library window, over the sloping lawn, wondered how old the tree was, and shivered.

Simon's Wife

HER NAME WAS Kristy, and she was his wife. In fact, she was no business of mine, except inasmuch as she was his business, since I was his lover.

Lover. Odd word, really, to describe us, the mutual objects of sexual desire, a word which bore, in our case, no positive relation to love. Oh, he wanted me, needed me, all of that. One can't expect more, for the world is an abject primitive place under its veneer of aspirations. You settle for what you can get, or else you settle for very little. I had tried both states, and I thought I understood what I must settle for. And it's nice to be needed, wanted. When I saw that in his eyes, that's when I started, in turn, desperately to want him. I didn't know about Kristy then, not quite then.

I met Simon in the way of business, which happens. Somehow, one resentfully feels it shouldn't happen, since one can shut one's self off from the social side of things and be safe from the complexities of life, but to eat one must work, you have no choice in the matter. Then, when you are vulnerable with having to be in a certain place, life seizes its unfair advantage by throwing you together with someone, and the contact is made, the fuse lit, and no escape. There had been for me nobody, for a year, rather longer. You struggle out of one situation, bruised, wretched, consoling yourself that you will never let it occur again. Of course, it does. For over a year I'd managed to avoid the trap. The theater is a paradox;

it permits superficially intense intimacies and involvements which somehow miss, by their very nature, any actual entanglement. You can swim through these syrupy currents a very great while, and emerge unscathed, happy even, when you come up for air. Then one morning, standing about backstage with my sheaf of designs, I saw Simon standing at the angle of the corridor.

They were casting for the new production, and people were coming in and out with that bizarre, always attendant aura of impermanence and barely controlled hysteria. This band of actors scattered in the corridor had taken on the unnerving look of the dole queue they always somehow acquire at such moments, as if by sympathetic magic. He had it too, the feigned listlessness of stance betrayed by wide eyes, which would be funny if it weren't so disheartening to see talented people consistently in this predicament. I didn't register much else, except his hair, which was very blond, the wrong sort of blond to be a bleach-job. Then he glanced up and his eyes didn't quite meet mine. I offered him the respectfully distant but rueful smile I keep by me for these occasions. And almost at once, still without looking directly at me, the reaction came from his face—the face of a stranger—I hadn't anticipated, a sort of blatant and emotional interest, a kind of naked quickening that threw me, made me feel physically threatened, queasy, like suddenly touching a slab of alien bare skin in a crowded train. Then my door opened to admit me and my designs and I slid away inside the room, like a crab going under a stone.

Simon was in the production. It was a play full of small dehumanized parts that send the actors off in agonizing spasms trying to learn what the hell they're meant to be doing. The sort of play that's not a play for actors to act in, which can work, strangely enough, given the right impetus. I liked my designs, but again, it was that sort of play—it required accessories rather than people. I saw Simon very often. I saw him looking at me. It was a constant thing, almost a frightening thing. Though not because it was aggressive or insolent. He

was attracted to me, that was all. Yet there was an element of
the inexorable in it. It was worse, because we rarely spoke,
only enough to exchange names, mention peculiarities of
weather, acoustics. When we were face to face, he looked
away from me; it was when I looked away he looked at me.
Which gave me the feeling that when our eyes finally met
some absolute demand would be put to me, not even so much
a demand as an appeal, and I couldn't be sure what answer
was going to well up inside me.

The play didn't work; it folded. Everyone folded with it in
a mute, gray, resigned and cynical depression for which no
consolation is ever to be found. Three days after the closure,
Simon phoned me. I had known he would. When I heard his
voice I experienced that glint of satisfaction at a prediction
vindicated and the horrible terror that always assails me at
such instants. The cause of the terror was simple: I could see
the door of the trap swinging open, and I knew I was going to
step inside.

We had dinner somewhere. God knows what we ate, each
other, probably, in the abstract. Our eyes met, on the third
glass of wine; he was that afraid, or that mistrustful of
himself or me. And the eyes laid out before me all I had
dreaded to observe in them, and with a shudder of revulsion,
I felt myself respond. We do not belong to ourselves, but to
our physical codes and appetites. We do not necessarily want
what we need. By the time we left the restaurant and walked
along the Embankment in the early night, our hands and our
bodies could barely keep themselves apart; we were over-
whelmed by the dismal, fruitless concupiscence that tortures
those with no easy access to a private bed. We were both
poor—the aborted play had seen to that—both presently out
of work. In the great and glittering city of vice, you still need
money to copulate in comfort or security. For myself, de-
prived of funds, I had vacated my flat and moved in with a
woman friend—onto her couch, to be precise, a not auspi-
cious location for sex. As for Simon—clinging to my hand as
if in fear of falling and drowning in the blue-black water,

with its gilded frescoes of lights such an inconsequent distance beneath us—he now made his confession.

"Yes, I'm married. You guessed, of course."

Of course, I had guessed.

"Yes."

"Does it matter?"

"No," I said. It didn't, for I was still naïve enough then to imagine it did not. I am still naïve enough to imagine it does not—except for me.

"There isn't much left of a marriage," he said. "The trouble is, I care, I care a lot. It's a mess—"

"You don't have to tell me," I said.

"It's a relief to have someone to talk to."

"Good."

He glanced at me warily. He was, after all, an actor. It's too easy to suppose an actor always acts, is acting out lies, ploys, cunning scenes to snare and entice. He can presumably do that, it's his trade. But then, you would be suspicious all the time, would never credit anything. I believed him, as far as it went. It was hard not to believe him, when every inch of my skin and flesh and every bone and every nerve ending was primed to his eyes, his voice, his touch.

"It's pretty bad," he said, "but then I meet someone like you, and everything inside me turns over. I don't know how to say this," he said. Naturally, as always, this was the prelude to his discovering precisely how he might say it. His wife was going away. She was going to spend two or three days with her mother. The mother lived in Scotland, as if on purpose to facilitate visits that would take her daughter from the country and leave hearth and home free for the extra-marital sojourning of other women. It was perfectly ridiculous, for this is what he asked me to do: stay with him in her absence.

It seemed to me then, she must know, his wife, whose name I was not yet familiar with, know he was about to make this liaison with me. Probably he had asked her before asking me. Such arrangements are not uncommon, or so one is led to think.

I said: "I suppose you do this quite often."

He looked miserable, and said he had never done it before.

Oddly enough, the same sick disorientation that was sweeping me seemed also to be sweeping over him. It was the sort of mood where one might do anything. There is, for me, this added dilemma, that I am afraid of everything, and consequently sensible fears have no value. A day in some provincial English city I am unused to produces in me the same kind of vivacious head-long panic anyone else might suffer on crossing through the Iron Curtain. I could not assess it, and did not try, but I said I didn't know what to say, and like him, at that point, I was lying.

So we adhered our bodies to each other, that marvelous kissing of new lovers, very like death without death's essential and obligatory deadness. We parted nervously, and next day he nervously rang me, and I nervously told him I would do what he had asked. It seems quite peculiar to me now that I agreed to it. Even then, I thought it absurd. But I was desperately lonely and had not realized it. Life and lust were exacting their revenge for being ignored.

The house was of the tall, narrow, semi-detached variety, and abutting on a wild stretch of London heath. It had a fashionable, delapidated air, autumnal and Victorian. The kind of place that fills me with nostalgia for a past where I never existed, the kind of place, too, that I pine for and admire, but should really hate to inhabit. The other half of the house, the other "attached" portion, was somber, overhung with trees like massive cobwebs. It looked as if the neighbors had died and no one had found out yet. Other dwellings kept their distance, and the road, all bits of stone, came winding up from the raucous High Street as if onto another plane.

Simon met me at the station, standing on the platform like a happy child to greet me, as I came from the train, stiff and chilled with fright. He was rather older than me, but made me feel terribly old, he was so apparently liberated and glad at my arrival. On me, the whole situation had come down like a ton of bricks. It seemed almost nightmarish, and as the train had gathered momentum, I had scrabbled frantically around in my brain, trying to remember what Simon actually looked like, for alarm had dispelled his image. All I could recapture were the hungry eyes, the white-blond hair, and my own sensual longing that had included itself as a weird facet of my terror. Then, meeting him, his innocence, or his insensibility, which made him oblivious of the ghastliness of what we did, its sheer bad taste, seemed to add an extra burden to my back.

"I hope your neighbors are blind, deaf, and dumb," I said.

He said neither he nor his wife had anything to do with neighbors. Defiantly I decided it was not my problem, that I had come to gratify myself and damn him and damn all the rest of it. We got into his car and drove through a welter of streets, eventually onto the gravel road, the rainy green wing of the heath opening on the right, and the gaunt houses with their witch-hat gables and glaring black windows on the left. We reached the relevant drive, got out of one interior, the car, climbed stairs, emerged into another, the house. I had now achieved the stage of no longer really seeing things, except through a sort of fog, a type of fear-drunkenness which can only be eradicated by the real thing, alcohol, or possibly yoga, which I have never mastered. I surveyed the immaculate living room and sat bolt upright in a terse pink chair, letting him pour drink into me like anti-freeze into a reluctant engine. At last a rose haze replaced the fog, a rose haze through which I could, strangely, see very well.

We went into the upstairs bedroom. Temporarily freed of doubts, I gave myself over to the self-conscious yet quite unique joy of lying down in a bed with a man whose naked body filled me with desire and pleasure, even delight. The best is always the first, perhaps, that is the sugar coating; the bitter kernel comes later. The walls turned white, then dull red with the stormy sunset. We made love like two people dying of thirst and coming on a well. It surprised me to find him apparently as thirsty as I. Presently, in a series of twining aftermaths, we began softly to say those things to each other that men and women do say at such a time, when they have got over the limiting fences of good manners, reticence and clear judgment. And gradually the walls turned redder, and more red, then slate, then almost green, then the color of Lucozade from the modern street lamps, which marched up the road in despite of all Victoriana and all the arcane stealth of love.

By now, I was sober again, or rather drunk merely on the loins and liking of a man. At some point we got up and ate in the stern, un-Victorian kitchen below, eating huge random chunks of bread, cheese, oranges. In the pitch black of the night, just the neon shafts on the wall like blades, we went back to bed and coupled—coupled *is* the word. In the black I could not see his face, nor any part of him, or scarcely. No matter; by then I knew him through and through.

"You're beautiful," he said. "A beautiful lover, a beautiful woman. So beautiful."

But when he turned to sleep, he turned also his back to me, the surest sign this idyll was only of the flesh, and only for one night, or two.

When light came in at the windows, I woke up, as in fact I had been waking on and off throughout the darkness. I looked first at him, lover's look, woman's look. He slept soundly, appetite appeased. For the first time, rather stupidly, I accepted the fact we were lying in the bed which normally he shared with her, the unknown, unnamed woman in Scotland. I didn't feel guilty, hadn't really at any point felt that, only vaguely and disturbingly surprised to find myself in such a situation.

I got up quietly, and went into the strange, bright, yellow bathroom. When I returned he was still asleep, but he stirred as I slid back into the bed. "What is it?" he said, and it abruptly occurred to me he had forgotten who I was, and thought I was his wife. His eyes opened and a sharpening of some suddenness in them convinced me this was so. "Nothing,'' I said. He sighed and shut his eyes again, and I said, before I could stop myself: ''Does she know I'm here?'' He laughed drowsily. ''Christ, no, she doesn't.'' The cold primal light of the windows was washing all about the room, irradiating objects, items I hadn't properly seen before. ''She'd mind, then,'' I said idiotically. ''She'd probably stick a knife in you,'' he said. He was nearly asleep again, and people say these things, out of a sort of ugly pride masking insecurity, or a sort of unconscious striving to create drama in their lives. Even so, the frightful tactlessness of the remark made me aware of my own tactlessness, lying beside him in their bed. I watched the light bleach the ceiling and fell asleep not thinking to.

The phone rang about eight-thirty and woke both of us. Simon went cursing to answer it, and came back cursing.

''Fred, my agent. Something's come up. I've got to get back to town by ten. Christ, he picks the most bloody times.''

He had that bewildered appearance people take on who have forced themselves physically wide awake in a matter of seconds, abandoning the brain to catch up later. Two things went through my own mind. Anyone connected with the theater is liable to these calls, with about a day to an hour's notice to make it to some important interview or function. Agents pounce and sink their teeth in whatever gets close enough, and expect the same predatory instinct from their clients. Simon obviously couldn't pass this up. At the same moment, though, it might so easily be a ruse, planned in advance, an excuse to be rid of the adulterous partner.

''I'd better go,'' I said.

''Go where?'' said Simon.

''If you have to be in town.''

''I'll only be two or three hours. It's nothing special. Three hours at the most. No, stay here, I'll be back in time to take you to lunch.''

His eyes were still full of their emotional hunger, not appeased after all. Perhaps he didn't want me to leave. Yet his manner was indefinably not the same, more brisk, less lingering and less happy.

By half past nine he was gone. The car drove off into the rain. And I, as I realized suddenly, with no means to regain access should I once leave the premises, was trapped inside the thin Victorian semi-detached.

The strangeness did not come immediately. To begin with (though this, I see now, was a sort of defense against the impending premonition of strangeness), I gave myself tasks. I washed the stack of dishes, rinsed them and set them to drain; I stripped the bed, and made it. These activities, of the kind which one carries out quite spontaneously in one's own home, gave the place a spurious friendliness, gave my being in that place a spurious correctness. Yet, even those actions somehow have, in retrospect, a brittle quality . . .

Tasks completed, I ran a bath in the yellow bathroom. In the yellow bath, the water was reminiscent of egg yoke. The soap, also like an egg, I did not particularly care for. It slid out of my hand onto the mat. On the wall, above the bath, was a white chip in the paint. I wondered what could have made it. Perhaps it had always been there. Perhaps Simon's wife had come into this bathroom and flung something at the wall and so chipped the paint—this irrational idea half amused me, and half appalled me with its visualization of violence. Just then, precisely then, I heard the front door open, very softly, next softly close, and my body, naked in that yellow bath, turned to ice.

I don't know how long I sat there, frozen in the warm water. I was listening, waiting. I knew that Scotland had disgorged Simon's wife, that she was here. I knew that in a moment she would mount the stairs, walk into this bathroom whose door I had not bothered to lock. And then? She didn't come into the bathroom, and the suspense was so devastating that finally I could no longer accept it. And naturally, rejecting the suspense, I saw the truth at once. She didn't come into the bathroom because she wasn't here in the house. Old houses are notorious for their inner murmurings, creaks and timpani, and this one was no exception. Why, if she had been here, I should have heard other sounds, and indeed, the front door would have shut more noisily, for she did not suspect and would have returned in innocence. Or did she suspect? Was she planning to arrive early, and was this an omen? No, ridiculous. People didn't carry on that way. You could rely on their lack of imagination, their adherence to convention, their fear, which kept them safe within the limits of reason. And Simon was so sure of her, of the day of her return, he had told me so, stressed it. My thoughts made the same whirlpool and disintegration in my head as the water going through the bath through its constricted exit point. I understood perfectly I was being stupid. Even so, to dress my bareness and to camouflage my face with make-up had become imperative.

Clothed, camouflaged and in possession of my external self, I believed I was calmed and altered. I went down into the modern kitchen and made myself coffee, and looked at the rain through the window, and the rain-glaucous heath.

The mug I had picked up, not thinking, had a flowery girl patterned on it. It was probably hers. Well, so what? She would never know. Never know I had walked about her house, made coffee in her mug, eaten from her dishes and washed them (two dinner plates draining, two breakfast plates, two cups, two saucers, two of everything); if she came home early, never even seeing me, just seeing that double act of crockery, she would know, wouldn't she? I'd bathed in her yellow bath, slept in her bed, my head on her pillow, my body coupled to the body of her man. Yes. Well, it was done.

I finished the coffee, washed the cup, and dried it. Methodically, I dried and put away in its proper compartment one of everything that had stood draining. And then a kind of electric urge galvanized me. It wasn't merely crockery that condemned. A tissue thrown negligently in a waste bin smeared with the wrong shade of eyeshadow, a jar of cold cream left behind, forgotten in a last minute rush to leave. Worse, a hair, not the right color, on the pillow or the side of the wash basin. Yes, a *hair*. I was blonde, but not as fair as Simon, and somehow I guessed she would be dark, his wife, darker than either of us.

Bizarre: I could start, if I wished, to build up a picture of her, a very clear picture, simply from the things around me.

The rain dripped and splashed outside, and the house made small noises to itself. Almost like a footstep, just then, in the living room next door. Fool. I went back upstairs, treading quietly, though who would hear? All right, if I wanted to be careful, I would go over the house and destroy every trace of myself.

I began in the bathroom. There were no hairs, but I made certain. Then, on impulse, I packed away my toothbrush, and the other washing impedimenta, into my sponge bag, and carried it into the bedroom where I had left my other things. I even checked the bathroom cabinet, which I had not actually used. There was a glass bottle of bath salts in the cabinet, they smelled of roses, hers. . . . In the bedroom, I stripped the bed again, inspected it, remade it. I took my box of tissues, my perfume and a scatter of other small items, and packed them up. Even an alien scent, of course, could give a warning—I opened the bedroom windows. The rain sheeted in, I banged them closed again. Suppose someone had seen me at the window?

I was being an idiot. I told myself this, but I could not rest. When Simon came back, I could question him more thoroughly about dates and times, reassure myself. He would be angry, probably, at this pedantic terror of mine.

Maybe I should investigate the living room below? Had I been avoiding it? For some reason I didn't want to go down into that immaculate chamber with its pink chairs, where I had gradually and determinedly lost my inhibitions, drinking this woman's drink in order to drink her husband more thirstily.

Eventually, my bag was completely packed, the impression of myself expunged, I thought, from the upper floor. I felt the effectiveness of this expunging in the sense of impermanence which now engulfed me. I wandered this house like a ghost, no familiar possession of mine in sight, a lost traveler without a landmark.

So I noticed, more and more, those possessions, those landmarks of Simon's wife, whose name I did not yet know, whose picture I was forming by irresistible slow degrees.

Why did I suppose her to be dark, almost black-haired? For this was how I most definitely envisaged her. It came to me at last that the flowery-patterned girl on the mug had had black hair; probably the idea sprang from that, yet I could not shake my conviction off. A dark, slim wife, and taller than me. But then, I am not very tall. Her dressing table in the bedroom was littered with personal effects. They now took on the frightful aspect of objects subtracted from the pockets or luggage of someone found dead, because she had left them helplessly behind to my scrutiny. I did not mean to pry, but could not avoid gazing, nervously fingering. The porcelain bowl with its population of hairpins, and little beads presumably rescued from a broken necklace, the blue pomander which no longer had any odor. A large, clean, black and green cotton handkerchief hung three quarters of its length out of a drawer. A postcard was tucked into the angle of the mirror. It showed a view of trees and a castle. I touched it, and it fell instantly from its niche and landed picture down on the table top. As if purposely constructed by a stranger months ago in order that I might find it and learn from it, the neat handwriting on the postcard said: "Dear Kristy and Simon, the weather's lousy but the pubs are fine."

Very, very carefully, as carefully, perhaps, as if handling the wires of a bomb, I replaced the postcard in its corner of the mirror.

Her name was Kristy, then. I knew it now. Kristy, Simon's wife.

The power of giving names. Ancient superstition. By thy name, I conjure thee to come to me . . .

What did I understand about Simon, anyway? Sex is a false reassurance, it shows so much, but still there is so much more that is hidden. No, I didn't really have an inkling of his basic motives, his unconscious mind. Suppose—no, insane notion—yes, but suppose. Suppose he had lied to me about the day of her—of *Kristy's*—return? Suppose she were coming home today after all, and he had meant her to walk in and find me, I merely the pawn in some game of love and hate he wished to play with her.

I was shivering by now, but I switched on no fire to cheer me, and though the overcast sky was darkening all the rooms in a preternatural fashion, I could not turn on a light. What time was it? A quarter to twelve. Well, he'd be here soon, one o'clock, not long.

Anyway, even if . . . even if his Kristy were to stalk through the front door right now, I was packed, I was ready to leave. I could run, snatch up my bag and coat and—my coat. A simple matter, a coat. But where had Simon put this coat of mine? Suddenly it became a problem of panic-ridden intensity to find the coat, penultimate (I was the ultimate) piece of the randomly scattered jigsaw of Me I was putting frantically together.

Be calm, and think. Yes, he had hung the coat on a hanger—or had he? Was the coat merely lying over the back of a chair in the living room? Wait, there was a cupboard in the bedroom, one of those fitted cupboards flush to the wall—I did not, I believe, really imagine my coat was in the cupboard. What was I doing, then, opening the door to bring myself face to face with the garments of Kristy?

I think I stopped breathing as I looked, afraid to breathe her in, some fragrance of miasma of her life. Clothes are very intimate, one does not realize how intimate they are. Slender and shadowy, they swayed there, like the several hanged bodies of the woman herself. They appeared pathetic, desolate. And yet, how curiously terrible.

I slammed the door shut, took up my bag and went down the stairs. The kitchen gleamed in the brackish rain-light. The door was just barely ajar which led into the living room. The house was silent now, cataleptic but not dead.

Don't be afraid, no one's in there.

The room was empty; congealed and uninviting, with an awful dank, pale smell as if it had been recently distempered. I could hardly recognize it, this room, which before had been made dramatic by nerves, and warmed by Simon's presence. My coat lay over a chair back. Because I was so very cold, I raised the coat and drew it on. I set my bag down beside a pink chair.

What time was it? Twelve o'clock.

Only another hour. Perhaps he might come sooner.

How trustworthy was Simon, though? What had he said to me, with that tactless ugly self-aggrandizement: She'd stick a knife in you. Poor Kristy. How much would it hurt her, if she did know? As much as it would hurt me, knowing it was with her he would lie in the future, wrapped in that black-twining pleasure-madness he had shared with me?

There was a book lying on the window sill directly across from me. The rain glitter through the window was flickering on its jacket, like a signal: Come see.

I went to the book reluctantly, dragging my feet.

A quite ordinary volume. I don't even recollect what it was, although I may have noticed, for a moment. I turned the pages, flyleaf, title page. I saw, written there, mundane, unoriginal and entirely horrifying: "Darling Kristy, always my love. Simon."

The house made a sound. It was like a great soft indrawn breath. The stairs creaked, settling from my descent, the way old stairs will.

I could see her now, vividly. She seemed to glow up at me from the grayness inside my brain. Slim, dark, and tall. Her eyes were fixed on me with a sort of blindness that could yet behold me, like the duplicated eye of some fearsome camera.

Kristy. Simon's wife.

Something moved in the window. Not the rain. My reflection.

No, not my reflection. The reflection of something else, a few paces behind me.

I didn't turn all that fast. I didn't have to whirl about to discover, because I already understood.

She was standing just inside the doorway. She was tall, slender, and very, very dark, and her face was exactly as I had pictured it a second before; in fact, so absolute a reproduction that at any other instant I would have questioned it. But not then, oh, not then. She held me in her camera sight, blind, seeing. Her right arm was raised. I had witnessed the stance a hundred times in the cinema, a safe distance from me on a screen: the angle of the elbow, the clenched hand with its knuckle-bones protruding, the searing shine, borrowed from a window, high-lighted and flashing. It was the bread knife she held so securely. Its serrated edge, which last night had cut the loaf, the orange segments, trembled in the air as it waited to cut my flesh.

My heart is strong. It lurched, contracted, seemed to burst, but it kept beating. I didn't speak or cry out; neither did she. She looked pitilessly at me, but with no enjoyment, no tears and no fury. Just with the knife clenched in her thin strong hand.

And then somehow it occurred to me that I could get by her, which was surely unlikely, or impossible. Yet it seemed I could do it, and somehow I did do it. I even grabbed up my bag as I ran under the silver blade of the knife. I ran, and I got through the door, across the hall, flung wide the outer door, found myself darting headlong down the steps. I could not feel my feet, my body, but the rain I felt. The rain pulled me forward into itself, sheltering me.

In fright, I heard her pursuing feet behind me, over the gravel driveway, along the wet pavement beyond. But I looked back, and she had not pursued me. Kristy had not pursued me with her knife.

I never thought to fling myself upon some neighboring door, hammering the bell and shrieking. But then, in any case, all the houses which fronted on the heath had that same blank uncommunicative appearance. I hazard no one would have answered.

I did not continue running. I walked, quickly and steadily, down the hill. Once or twice I looked over my shoulder; only the rain was behind me.

I reached the High Street, found a bus which took me to the station, found a train which would take me home.

I don't know exactly what went through my mind as I did all this, if anything did. I was responding to an impulse to vacate the scene, not merely the house, but the district itself, yet I was not afraid, or did not feel afraid. Even when I had looked over my shoulder, I had already guessed she was not there. I was very dull, matter-of-factly thinking of my brush with a murderess. I slumped on the train seat, an average uninteresting passenger, with no claim to notoriety and no evidence of it in my person.

It was not till I got back to the flat of my friend, whose couch I currently utilized, that my hands started to shake, next my whole body. No one was in, so I was able to throw up in the bathroom and presently weep, all undisturbed, unwitnessed and with no need of explanation. By the time my friend returned that evening, she found me apparently normal and with some casual excuse for my abbreviated absence.

I was washing my hair when the phone rang. It was Simon. I didn't want to speak to him and could not grasp why he should be phoning me. Actually, I had hardly thought of him, hardly thought of anything at all.

At the sound of my voice, he began instantly to shout at me. I couldn't work out what he was saying. He was demanding to know why I had abandoned the house, where I had gone. He said he had driven about for hours in the car, searching for me. He was angry and desperate, and it made no sense. I was quite calm, and when he stopped, I said, quite calmly enough: "Surely Kristy told you why I wasn't there?"

"What the hell has this got to do with Kristy?"

My wet hair dripped on my shoulders as the rain had done. My friend stood in her small kitchenette, making an omelette; I knew she could hear every word I said. So she heard me say:

"Kristy came home early."

"What are you talking about? I told you, she's in *Scotland*, for Christ's sake—"

"Kristy came home early," I said. I smiled as if he could see me. "She found her own explicit way, to tell me to get out."

"What are you playing at?" he shouted. "Have you gone bloody mad?"

"Ask her," I said.

"How can I bloody ask her? She's bloody not here, you stupid bitch."

I put the phone down. It didn't make sense and I didn't want to think about it anymore.

My friend peered at me sideways.

"Sorry," I said. "If he rings again, could you be fantastically kind and tell him I'm not here?"

He did ring, once more, next morning.

"He said where could he reach you," my friend informed me. "I said I didn't know. Bloody rude bastard," she added.

I waited till she went out, to cry again.

He didn't ring anymore, and I cried, on and off, for eighteen days. And then, like getting over 'flu, I suddenly recovered, the whole thing dropped away from me, ceased to matter.

Only one time did I wonder, make an attempt to figure it out. Had Kristy got rid of me, and then left the house before Simon's return? And when she saw him again, did she pretend nothing had happened? Or did she use her shining knife on him? Somehow, I never reckoned that she had.

A month later, I heard, through the theater grapevine, Simon had a part in some playhouse production in the north. I was working myself by then, submerged in that thick buoyant sea which I find so sustaining and generally so danger-free. Professionally, I did quite well that year, actually. Quite well.

It was the year after that I met Kristy socially.

I was at someone's party, in a rambling basement flat in

Kensington, drinking sour white wine under the dim moody
lighting. I'd just been working very hard on some rush designs, and was in that state of worn-out lassitude that will
laugh at any joke and commiserate with any misfortune. I'd
talked to about twenty people, most of whom I didn't know,
most of whom had seemed to pour on me the stories of their
lives, which I'd gratefully lapped up with suitable giggles and
groans, only too happy to let my own brain slumber. Then
there was a plump fair girl, a couple of years younger than
me, who didn't really say anything and looked at me with the
same sort of tired preparedness to listen that I was giving
everyone else. We drifted apart incompatibly, after a brief
audible silence, and I seated myself with a male acquaintance
on the fake Italian cassone in the hall.

"Saw you talking to Kristy," he said. "Must have been
dismal for you."

I got the sort of feeling you get when a car, hurtling from a
side turning, narrowly misses you on the wet road.

"Kristy?" I said.

"Yes, you know Kristy. Simon's wife. He was in that
thing you did those nice red trees for. Folded. What was it?
Couple of years ago."

"Yes, I remember."

My eyes were feverishly searching, searching, but I couldn't
find her. "Where is she?"

"Oh, my God, girl. *There*. You were rabbitting with her
about half a minute ago. Sack dress with the big tits. That's
it."

"No," I said, "that's not Kristy." He was pointing flam-
boyantly, and discourteously, at the plump blonde girl with
the listening look.

"Not Kristy? Of course, it's Kristy. Poor cow. Simon's
pissed off and left her, living with someone in Leeds now,
and she doesn't seem to want to pull herself together. She
always was a well-rounded wench, but she's starting to sag.
My dear, I said to her, you've got to make the effort, can't
you see what you're doing to yourself."

"She bleaches her hair," I said. "That's new."

"No, that's natural, that hair, always was. Used to look weird, her and Simon together. She's nearly as fair as Simon. Quite incestuous. Mind you, I don't say a good hairdresser couldn't improve on nature."

He went on, telling me what a mess she was in, what he'd told her, how her bra needed to hoist a couple of notches. The blonde girl went on standing in the corner, by the lacquer fire screen, letting people come to her, fill her glass with gin and her ears with chatter. Once I caught her name, clear across the room from another mouth: Kristy. Kristy, Simon's wife.

"It's funny," I said at last, my voice perfectly level, because I suppose anyone who has to do with the theater, in whatever capacity, eventually masters some rudiments of acting.

"Funny? It's terribly, heartbreakingly sad, you callous cow."

"No," I said, "I mean it's funny because I met Kristy once, or I thought I did. And she was quite different."

Across the room, Kristy, short, blonde, overweight, tired and deserted, had started to cry into her little glass of gin, simultaneously fumbling from her bag a large black and green cotton handkerchief. And with her plump hand, which patently had never held a knife, she lifted the handkerchief that once I had seen hanging from her dressing table drawer, and crushed the cotton over her eyes.

The Vampire Lover

HE IS WITH HER TONIGHT.

I know it. What shall I do?

Of course, there is no moral dilemma. Those doubts I had—my halting discussion with the priest left me chastened and horrified. Why then hesitate? Can it be—it must be so—the shadow has stretched out to touch me, too? Then I must hurry. It is no longer the single matter of her life and soul, but also my own.

Mariamme, my sister, was pale. But this was no problem, for she was always beautiful. To say her hair was gold, as the singers always did, was not strictly true. She was a blonde, as our dead mother had been. When the sun met her hair—either Mariamme's or our mother's in life—it gleamed more fiery white than gold. She had died, our mother, in trying to bear our father a son. At this time I was thirteen years old, but my sister only five. Her grief was more easily expressed than mine, and the sooner forgotten. Her nurses loved her and each gladly became her mother, and she was my father's favorite. He and I, alike in our darkness, were often in accord over things of the mind, but since intellectual women mystified him, he was also uncomfortable with me. I should have been his son, I suppose. But I was a woman, almost thirty years of age now, to Mariamme's pure two-decades-and-one.

I sat in the sun-arbor on the terrace of the Stone House, and watched her as she wandered to and fro. She seemed preoccupied, and how listless. Now and then she would indicate a flower to be plucked. "Yes, that one." The maid would snip it from the trellis, or perhaps, if she were not quick enough, one of the two or three gallants would break it less tidily. Such young men always provided Mariamme her own court. They were knights of our father's, but he made no objection. Chivalrous love, the woman-worshipped-as-Madonna, it was all the fashion. He had announced no plans to marry her to anyone as yet. She was so lovely, one might imagine he was saving her for some especially expedient match. But he liked her by him, too. For myself, a political marriage had long ago been arranged, actually the second, for I had first married when I was sixteen, by proxy. The union, to the Lion House, would have been helpful to my father, but the prospective husband (he was twelve) died of plague a month later, even as I was on my journey to him. Sent back again, I waited another ten years for my second betrothal. Though unblemished, straight, and healthy—and still a virgin—I was no longer young. My new bridegroom was some twenty years my senior, but, like the first, I had never set eyes on him. He had agreed to me by messenger. We were to wed when he returned from the long northern wars. Providing, of course, he did return. As yet he showed no sign of it. But I too was in no hurry. I would obey, when I must.

"And this?" said my sister, pointing to a smiling rose, with a finger on which three large jewels flashed.

"No, another. That is the thirteenth on the stem." The gallants laughed, but they were in earnest, too, being superstitious to a man.

"Then this?" And the three jewels flashed again, and then more brightly as Mariamme put her hand to her forehead.

Her knights were alarmed. They supported her. But it was

only a momentary weakness. Once she came to sit by me, and had begun to sip the cup of wine one of them poured for her; she was soon merry enough. Yet, she was very pale.

I tried to continue with my reading, but it became more difficult against the chatter, and presently one of the gallants had produced a lyre, and it was to be a singing game. Marking my place in the bestiary, an enormous book I carried with some awkwardness, I said I would leave them. No one stayed me, I did not expect it, but as I rose, I noticed a strange little mark, to the left side of my sister's throat. Pausing, and at the risk of offending with the interruption, I asked, "Why, Mariamme, have you been stung?"

"Oh," she said, and a curious look came over her face, "No . . . I think . . . I scratched myself yesterday evening, when I undid my necklace."

"But your maids see to your jewelry," I said. "They must in future be more careful."

"No. It was my fault. I was . . . hasty. . . . Oh, play for me!" she cried suddenly to the gallant with the lyre. "A happy song, very fast."

They took great pleasure in her changeableness. Only I found it peculiar. But then, I was not courtly-in-love with Mariamme.

Puzzled, I left them in the peach-leaf shadows of the arbor.

The flowers she had picked, or selected to be picked, were on the high table to grace our dinner, and my father was charmed. Despite this, Mariamme seemed excitable, half uneasy, as if afraid she might annoy him inadvertently—something which never happened; I was the one who did that. I gazed at my sister surreptitiously, but with an increasing sense of some strangeness. It came in a while to take my appetite, as plainly it had already taken Mariamme's. Our father was concerned she did not eat, but she lowered her eyes and turned shy, and I saw him make the decision that this was all due to the

"Moon." He began gruff, then jovial, to offset the masculine gaffe. However, her condition was nothing of the sort. Her sister, sleeping as I did in an adjoining chamber, I knew generally when it was that she bled, her seasons and pulses, as one knows weather in a familiar country.

Much later, I went to her room.

She was kneeling at prayer before her icons, in her shift, her hair spangle-veiled by the candles. But when I entered she sprang up as if I had caught her out in some guilty act.

"This is not like you," she said, "to come into my room at bedtime. I remember how I used to entreat you to, when we were children and I was so afraid of the dark—"

"The dark never frightens you now."

"Ah, why should it? Night is as beautiful as day."

I had noted the lower window stood wide open. The evening was mild, but not airless. I asked her why she had opened the shutters.

"For the scent of the flowers on the creeper," she said. "No, you no longer scare me, unkind sister. Do you remember how you used to make me cry with your stories of huge night insects flying in between the sheets, or bats which would perch on me and end all tangled up in my hair?"

I may have warned her of such things when she was little. All I recalled was her own fear of ghosts. But at this moment an odd thing happened. Like a black paper, as if summoned by her words, a bat did go flitting across the window, and up, out of our sight.

"Well, so you see," I said. And I went to the shutters and drew them closed.

Mariamme observed me. She said nothing more.

High above her bed, the inner window of glass, lit by the great three-night candle behind it, blazed a somber rich crimson, and now some draft from the closing shutters caused the light to flutter and cast shadow—as if somehow the bat had after all come in, and hid there, beating its narrow black dragon's wings impatiently.

The disturbance of the red light caused me to see another thing which before I had missed. It was a vague trailing mark among the covers of the bed—pale, as if attempts had been made to erase it. But even countered by water and much scrubbing, I thought I recognized the stain of dried blood.

Now I said nothing and went away to my own chamber.

Two thicknesses of wooden doors separated me here from Mariamme, and the little stone annex between. She seemed removed by miles, by mighty cliffs and forests. I lay awake a long while, and, intuitively, I *listened,* but all I heard was the faintest rustling of the creeper on the house wall as the night-breeze whispered to it; the hunting cry of a nocturnal bird in the woods.

The lights of my inner window—this gift of glass our father gave us; it is an important symbol of status and wealth—were cool and customary blue. They trembled lake-like on my bed and soothed me. My outer window was shuttered. Nothing would get in. This was my last, macabre thought, before I slept.

Next day, about noon, players came to the gates. Our father allowed them in. He was generally indifferent to such shows, as I was, but his household liked them, and Mariamme had adored all spectacle from the time of her childhood—he was in an indulgent mood. They put on their entertainment in the hall, after the evening meal, having fed well themselves in the kitchen court. From the gossip, one heard they had been in the neighborhood some weeks, nor were they strangers to us, having performed in the Mallet House at Mid-Winter, where some of my father's people had traveled to see them. They were reckoned excellent of their kind.

It bored me, I fear, the whole business, but I must not go up to bed or book; my father had brought everyone in for the fun and would be offended. He himself sat stoically, even raising a laugh at some of the idiotic antics. Every actor was masked, naturally, in the tradition, which to me only en-

hances the preposterousness of the situation. There was a
white-masked fool, gymnastic and limber, constantly cart-
wheeling and bending backwards; our father particularly remarked him, and called him out at one point to throw him
some gold, at which we all clapped, the actors prudently
included. But the jollity was marred nevertheless.

If he had meant this treat to rejoice Mariamme, our father
seemed mysteriously to have failed. She had risen late today.
I had not seen her until supper. If she had been out of sorts
before, now she was wan and sleepy. Her face looked white
as the white mask of the jester. When our father was amused,
sometimes she would force a laugh, but otherwise, how
drawn she seemed. Her hands shook, so the jewels spurted
continuous fire, she trembled all over, and bit her lip. I found
I could not take my eyes from her, and what the players did
on their stage of tables mostly I missed.

But then there came a scene with Death in it, the way these
mountebanks invariably show it: a man, black-cloaked and
cowled, with a crown of staring bones. He entered with a
swirl of his mantle, jumping from nowhere, it looked, so
some of the ladies screamed. My sister, too, started in her
skin. Something made me say to her, "But you have seen
them act this before, surely, at Mallet?" And she answered,
"Not Death," and then toppled lightly out of her chair.
One of her retinue of knights caught her before she struck
the floor.

Our father was enraged with the players, and turned them
out of doors immediately. I could have told them, in their
sulks, they were lucky to get off without being ordered a
whipping.

Mariamme was put to bed. She would not consult the
physician, and even the priest was refused. She wept and
clung to our father's hand. "You," he said to me, "must stay
by her." Dismayed at her emotion, he left her to me, and for
a while I sat by her bedside under the ruby flame of the inner
window. I felt myself grow chilled as I sat there. I could not

tell what it was. Finally I said, for she did not sleep, "Why not undo the ribbon at your throat, perhaps it makes you uncomfortable." At once, her hand rose to cover throat and ribbon together. She stared at me with confused frightened eyes. "Oh," she said, "what do you know? Tell me now."

"I? What should I know, Mariamme? It is for you to tell me."

"I can tell nothing. But you are so clever. Do you hate me?"

I flinched at her words. They wounded me.

"I am your sister. How can I hate you, and for what?" Her eyes now evaded mine. "Mariamme," I said, "tomorrow, let the physician come and look at you."

"No," she said, "I am not sick. Only . . ."

"What, Mariamme?"

"Nothing at all," she said hoarsely. And then, with wild desperation, "please go, leave me. How can I sleep when you glare at me all the while? Let me alone!"

I got up. "Very well."

She sighed deeply. She was frantic to have me gone, yet did not seem to understand her own vehemence. As she had writhed, the ribbon shifted on her neck. There, where I had seen the small freckle of blood, a thunderous bruise now swelled the white skin. I said nothing of this. Bidding her goodnight, I went out, closing her door, and presently mine. Now I too trembled, My hands were icy. My head hammered.

In those minutes I already knew it all. But, skeptic that I am naturally inclined to be, I would not surrender to my instincts—or not entirely.

I rarely pray, save from duty. But then I went to my knees and I admit that I required of God a sign. I had some learning, and even in superstition, or those matters I attributed to superstition, I was not uninformed. After a long while, I rose and sought the old volume of supernatural bestiary. There I searched out a particular word, and read again the text and examined again the drawing that lay under the word. Then I laughed at my own imaginings, though my body stayed cold and shivering. Going to my own shutters, I opened them, slowly and cautiously, and leaned out a short distance.

It was a little beyond midnight, dark traveling towards dawn in its long black hourly wagons, silent each as a grave. My window looked from the same stretch of wall, creeper-wrapped, as Mariamme's. Turning my head I saw how the winged shutters of her room again stood wide. They had been fastened when I was with her. She must have risen and seen to them once I had gone away.

Something then made me rapidly draw back, pulling my own shutters almost to, but without a sound. It seemed to me I dared not breathe, dared not glance—but clearly I must see if something were to be visible. What did I anticipate? Only the thing I had read of in a book I did not believe.

As I had kneeled to pray, so now I knelt again, and putting my face close to the slats of my shutter, stared through them, towards Mariamme's window, so open, so much an invitation.

There was a dearth of light, but suddenly from that very window bloomed a blood-red ghost that dewed every one of the creeper's leaves with blood. It would seem she had renewed the three-night candle behind her inner window of ruby glass, even as I had left that behind my window of blueness to go out. A signal? What else? Heaven help her. As the victim so frequently is, she was in collusion now with the creature which slowly murdered and damned her.

And then my heart froze. Peering between the slats, I made out something, in the creeper, there, easing and gliding like a snake *up the very wall of the house.*

At the last moment my courage failed me. I covered my eyes as it began to slide in over the threshold of her room.

Needless to say, as I huddled in the half-dark, I *pictured* it all. How she lay, my sister, voiceless, will-less, and waiting, and the black thing came to her and covered her whiteness with its ink. It seemed to me I heard a small stifled cry—and at that I knew she had again been pierced by the hungry fangs of it. There under the blood-colored window, the vampire which preyed on Mariamme sucked her blood from a cup of pale flesh and gilded hair.

At first, I could not move from sheer horror. Then a sort of lethargy overcame me. Eventually, a stupor . . .

I wakened—and the sun rose! When I forced myself to look out again, the shutters of the other window were fastened closed. Only a slight tearing in the creeper marked the invader's progress. Obviously, demon of the night that he was, he would be long gone before sunrise. I gazed and could not think. My mind was empty of anything. There my sin began.

My sin was, of course, this: I did not speak of it.

I did not speak, and quantities of days followed, quantities of nights between, when I knew. Days of Mariamme moving listlessly about the house, now drooping and ashen, next volatile as if in a high fever. Always a ribbon or a necklace to conceal the tell-tale bruises at her throat. She kept away from me. I did not seek her. She was to me like one infected by plague, she revolted me, yet I was tortured by the image of her subjugation, the pouring in of darkness, the plundering— worst of all, the submission which the vampire inspires in and exacts from his prey. Every night that she went to her bed- chamber, sending out her maids (who sometimes loitered in the anteroom, talking of her pallor and her nervousness), every night then I felt I must run to her door, beat on it or force it open; she locked it when once alone, I was certain. Over and over I rehearsed my plan. The anteroom led into a corridor, barred at its far end by a large door. Outside this, turn by turn, chosen knights of our father's, two by two, stood each a month-long service of guard, and had done so all our lives. We were precious, for our various reasons, my father's daughters. We had only to cry out to bring the pair of champions of that night's watch, fully armed, hurtling to our defense. But I would go to them softly. By the rituals and ordeals of their knighthood itself, they knew that evil existed, and in many forms, to battle with the hosts of God. Generally, I had found them as superstitious as the lowliest peasant, though their phrases in describing the affair were high-flown. Now I might thank all the saints they had kept this innocent wisdom. Once I had told them all I had witnessed, could they prevaricate? From the window of my room, screened by darkness (the candle in the blue window put out), and the creeper's fall, they could behold for themselves that eerie, awful progress the monster made up the stone walls of this house. Even to think of it—I had never again been able to bring myself to regard it—filled my veins with snow.

Then again, it had occurred to me I should seek the priest of our house. He was an old man, also learned, and no scoffer at what I had always called "myths." Though never less than respectful towards him, and steadily attentive to my religious duties, maybe he did not care for me. Mariamme, who lapsed and committed childish sins continually, also burned with an emotive childish devotion to the idea of God, which the priest liked much more than my unfluctuating piety. He had had to set me no proper penance since I was sixteen, just before my first marriage. He seemed ever on the verge of telling me now that my confessions were a lie; he would have enjoyed doing so. But as I had always only told him the simple facts, he could never catch me out. And though not the favorite, I was still the Lord's daughter.

However, in this, surely in this, he would help me, advise me. If not, I must go elsewhere. The Devil worked upon us—and I did nothing.

Nothing, though I had seen the proofs and could communicate them to others, all those dreadful proofs the bestiary, treating the vampire as a submortal, thus a *beast*, had digressed upon. (And had not the hand of Fate been even in this, that I should have chanced on this very passage and read it, only a few minutes before I saw the mark on my sister's neck?) The book related all. First the shape-changing, to a wolf, or to that other vampire thing, the bat—just as I had seen him, going by the window. Next how, though I myself had closed the way, he manifested from thin air behind the lens of red glass—so they did, for no human barrier could keep them out. And oh, the stain of blood, her blood spilled from the wound he had made, on her sheet. And the tiny puncture in her neck which, with his constant *use,* swelled up and blackened in that terrible bruise she must always conceal. Her weakness, her paleness—sure signs—her fainting at the image of Death, which was a cipher for the vampire. How he entered by night, abandoned her before the sun or the crowing of the cock, leaving her ever more despoiled, until, at length, she would die. And worse than die, die and become one of his own, dead yet possessed, a live corpse with my sister's face, but motivated by the will of a demon.

And knowing all this, *I kept silent.*

Why? It comes hard to me. I partly do not believe it—and partly I do. She was so lovely, and I—well, I was not Mariamme. She had so long been before me, the vision of her brightness which captivated all as I captivate none. Let me say it out then. I accuse myself of jealousy, of the sin of Envy. Could it be I would be glad to see her perish, the victim of the Beast? But no—no. How could such a thing be true? She was my sister.

It was this anguish which drove me to the priest tonight. It was before him, having woken him in his bed, that I stumbled through a confession in which I murmured certain things, hinted at others. At one juncture the old man caught his breath and broke in. "Your lord father will ask an appalling payment for it—but not from her. He has always loved her. I would rest my own life on that." Then I saw he had misunderstood me, so I spoke more precisely, if perhaps no more succinctly. Abruptly he too blanched, and crossed himself, whispering a snatch of prayer. At this I left him. I fled.

I returned here to my chamber and paced about.

Soon the moon rose. In terror and trouble I put out the candle behind the blue window. I crept to my shutters and opened them only a crack. When the creeper rustled I ran and hid my eyes. Coward!

He climbed. He reached the window and passed inside.

He is with her now, milking her life and purity . . .

If I have not the wit to go for the knights of our guard, let me go alone and sink my woman's nails in his undead flesh, let me harm him all I can for daring to take her. I have felt his shadow. His shadow has come to me in dreams—a faceless presence—I see now, not my fault—it is his thrall which has corrupted me, made me as compliant as she is—and I shall be his next victim. Yes, he will claim me, too, as his bride of death . . .

No more. I must act swiftly and at once.

She runs along the corridor, Mariamme's elder sister. She opens the door there at its end and goes out to the two nightly guards, astonishing them. Her story, which she tells with a powerful and controlled hysteria, is more energizing than any passion. It turns them from civilized men to embattled warriors. This night is a fortuitous choice—these two knights are founders of Mariamme's inner court. They definitely love her, and grow instantly afraid.

So they go along the corridor, through the anteroom, at a noiseless rush, and flinging themselves against the door of Mariamme's chamber, smash through its one flimsy lock in a few seconds. Then they are in the room, the room of their sacred Madonna, while the dark sister stands in the doorway behind them, still as a post.

The ruby window, bleeding, gives good light. What do they see? What horror, what demoniac extravagance?

Their goddess lies naked, sprawling on the pillows, helpless, with a look of fear beyond any they have ever seen, except perhaps in a deer about to be ripped by the hounds.

At the bed's foot, a man-shaped being, flowing in and out of blackness against the crimson lambency, seeming as if about to dissolve, of which the vampire, as they know, is capable.

Each man stands transfixed, raising against Satan the crosspiece of his sword. *Un*manned.

It takes the other woman, she in the doorway, to cry out; "No—he will be gone—kill him! Look how he has used Mariamme!" And then more terribly: "Or give me your swords. Must *I* do it?"

That shifts them. Both spring, and taking hold of the creature, which even now is in its turn springing, pantherish and abnormally agile, towards the window, they bring it down. It screams as their blades go through it, guts and head—but there is only one sure way with a vampire. Of this they are aware. As one man drags back the head by its hair, the other hacks it off.

Bizarrely, the screaming fails to stop.

No longer the vampire, it is Mariamme who screams. She kneels on the bed, screaming and screaming, her face mindlessly turning its screaming mouth to each of them, one by one.

Suddenly one of the knights falls to his knees before her. He lifts his blood-red sword into the blood-red light, a sort of pledge, dazzled by her nakedness and her defilement. At the gesture, Mariamme's screams die. All at once she is totally dumb, though her look of abject fright remains. And in dumbness and in fright, she steps from the bed, runs to the window and throws herself out of it. Before anything can be done, she is gone into the darkness with a ghastly, striking, wrenching sound that may only be the tearing of the creeper on the wall.

My father summoned me in the last quarter of the hour before dawn. I had been praying with the old priest, who had been very constrained with me, his fear and distress evident in every mannerism. The whole of the Stone House was wracked, in uproar, weeping and wailing. From far off, any who chanced to hear would think us doomed.

He was in the chapel, my father, where the two bodies had been taken. The demon's remains, under its black cloak, had been ringed by in-pointing swords, fragments of the Host, branches of thorn hastily lopped and smelling still of their sap. The arms and legs, the torso, the severed head, all were discernible in outline. My sister's poor pitiful corpse was less well-arranged, so shattered was it by its fall. It lay, a heap, wrapped in a red mantle, and already some flowers were scattered over it. One hand, still whole and perfect, had been allowed to lie out on the robe's surface. The jewels glimmered on the fingers, but only with the motion of the candles.

I told my father, with a bowed head, of my grief and guilt. I was brief, not wishing to inflame his hurt. I had already cut off all my hair, in token of mourning.

"Look up," said my father. I obeyed, of course.

"You wish me to tell my story?" I asked.

"I have heard your story from others." His face was like the house stone, unmarked by any tears. Neither of us had cried at all. I have never found it easy. "I am only interested," he said, "in how you, who have never credited such things, came to credit this."

"I saw the proofs," I said. "My shame is, I waited too long. His hold on her was by then too great."

"These proofs."

"As I have described. Her pallor and lassitude. The wound on her neck. And the stain in her bed, though faded by much washing. Lastly, when I saw him climb the sheer wall."

"There is a creeper on the wall. A strong creeper," said my father. "Even Mariamme's body, striking there repeatedly till all her little bones were smashed, did not tear it away. Firmly rooted, the creeper. And he was very athletic and supple. Did no one tell you? It was the the actor who played the fool. Oh, and he played Death, also."

"In his human form, he was one of the actors?" I said. "Well, I have heard of such things. Did his fellows never suspect?"

"No. Never. They knew he would go out at night. Some girl, they thought. Which was, too, why he wished to return here. Some highborn girl he wanted, who gave herself to him. A silly thing to do, they always guessed as much. It would seem she was afraid of her father, a man inclined to anger. She was pale with fear every next day, though there was also another cause of that, her paleness, her weakness, her fainting at a sudden public sight of her lover, and the premonition of his death. . . . She was with child."

I stood transfixed, bemused. I felt as cold as when I recognized the vampire.

Through the deep windows, as if to augment the rest, it was beginning to get light.

"What are you saying?" I asked him, my father.

"As for the wound in her throat, she caught her skin in the clasp of her necklace, hurrying to remove it so her maids would go, and leave her to the longed-for company of her visitor. And the next night, you see, he kissed the little wound, and his kiss grew impassioned—a type of kiss you know nothing about, since no man has ever kissed you in such a way, nor shall one, I imagine. A bruising kiss. But she hid that from me, too, and all the others. She thought I would be enraged and kill her. *Her*. I would have been enraged. I would have killed him—or perhaps not, if she wanted him, if she had pleaded for him. I could never refuse her anything. When she asked me for the colored window of glass for you, too, not just for her, a blue window for her red window, she said you would feel the slight otherwise. No, I could refuse her nothing. I loved her. When she begged me not to marry her to this one, or that, I always relented. I let go good matches that way, and fine men. Not like the leavings who would agree to take you—and even they have no stomach for you in the end, they prefer the plague or the war. But even so, she never trusted me, my Mariamme. Some flaw there; I never saw it. Nor, it seems, did I ever see you, my scholarly dark daughter.''

I said, ''Her bed was marked with blood.''

He said, brusquely, ''She was a virgin when he first had her. Even *you* must have heard of Showing the Sheet of the First Night.''

We stood almost idly then, and the sun came in through the windows.

It came to the vampire under his cloak, next across the body of my sister in its red mantle. The shape of the limbs, broken or only hacked, did not alter, no stench rose of grave mould and crumbling dust. My father crossed to the sword-ringed corpse. He lifted a corner of the covering. I glimpsed young skin and staring eyes.

''One omission for the itinerary,'' said my father. ''Sunlight, which destroys vampires, leaves him untouched.'' He let the cover fall again. ''And her. I suppose, if she had not killed herself, you would have found some excuse—a fiendish glint in her eyes, a look of the Devil—you would have had to do *that* work yourself. Her knights would never have been able to take blade to *her*.''

''I was mistaken,'' I said. My head rang, as if from a blow. I heard myself say, ''But do you want this blazed abroad? Your younger daughter a whore, lying down under a common mountebank. Better keep to the other tale, it has a nicer flourish. A vampire who raped only her sweet soul, which was then freed by your gallant knights. She died absolved, naturally, and now queens it again, in Heaven.''

''Ah, yes,'' murmured my father. ''*Now* I hear you.''

''Why?'' I whispered, ''what did I say?''

It is a dire time we have of it. The Stone House has more than earned the grimness of its name.

All are smitten by sorrow. I, who can never weep, feel it perhaps more than most. I miss the sunshine of Mariamme.

There is no one to take her place. Her special knights have already begun to find excuses to desert us. My father lets them go on their pretexts of campaigns and crusades. He is, I am afraid, somewhat unhinged by bereavement.

Yes, I do fear for his mind. He will not see me, or let me near him. I keep to my room, therefore, and read the large old books. It is peaceful, though sometimes I grow unaccountably anxious.

Even, sometimes, I admit, I become fearful to eat any of the food which is sent me, or to drink the wine. For a reason I cannot quite fathom, and which is certainly foolish, I begin to think he may very soon poison me, my father.

The Hunting of Death:
The Unicorn

One: The Hunting

IN THE FIRST life, Lasephun was a young man.

He was reasonably tall, of slender, active build, and auburn-haired. His skin, which was to be a feature of all this group of lives, was extremely pale, and lent him an air of great intensity. By nature, the being of Lasephun was obsessive. Charged with fleshy shape, the obsessiveness took several forms, each loosely linked. The first life, the young man who was called Lauro, became obsessed with those things which were unobtainable, and hungered for them with a mysterious, gnawing hunger.

Firstly then, the motive force, which was creative and sought an outlet, drove him from place to place. In one, he would find a forest, and in the forest a shaft of light like golden rain, and the sight of this would expand in him like anguish. In a city, he would see a high wall, and over the wall the tops of crenellated towers, and beyond the towers the sky with thunder clouds, and somewhere a bell would slowly ring and a woman would go by picking up the whispering debris from the gutter. These images and these sounds would stay with him. He did not know what to do with them. Sometimes, like some intangible unnamed scent, there would be only a feeling within him that seemed to have no cause, a deep swirling, disturbing and possessing him, which could neither be dismissed nor conjured into anything real.

At length, he learned how to make music on the twenty-two strings of the lutelin, and how to fashion songs, and he sang these in markets, inns, and on the steps of cathedrals for cash, or alone on the billowing roads and the sky-dashed face of the land for nothing—or for himself. But his songs and his music filled him with blunted anger. And as he grew, by mere habit, more polished, his anger also grew. For what he could make never matched the essence of what he felt. The creation was like a mockery of the stirring and dream within him. He almost hated himself, he almost hated the gift of music.

To others, he was a cause of some fascination. To others he was attractive, phantasmal, like a moving light. They would come to him, and sometimes even follow him a short distance, before they perceived he no longer saw them. He never stayed long in any one place. As if he felt the movement of the earth under him, he traveled, trying to keep pace with it.

Proceeding in this way, it occurred to him one night that he himself did not move at all, but simply paced in one spot, while the landscape slid towards him and away behind him, bringing him now a dark wood, and now a pool dippered by stars, and now a town on a high rock where wild trees poured down like hanging gardens.

It was well past midnight. The morning, disguised as the night, was already evident on the faces of any clocks the town might hold. Lauro leaned on a tree in the vale below the town, not far from the pool which glittered, and the dark wood which had gathered all the darkness to itself as if to be cool.

Was a world so beautiful, so unfathomable, also a disappointment to its Creator? Had the world failed to match the vision of the god who devised it? On his seventh day, not resting but lamenting, had he gone away and left his work unfinished, and somewhere else did some other world exist, like but unlike, in which had been captured the creative impulse entire and perfect?

Lauro touched the lutelin and the strings spoke as softly as the falling of a leaf.

And in that moment a white leaf blew out of the dark wood and flickered to the edge of the pool.

Lauro stared. He saw a shape, which was not like the shape of a horse, but more like that of a huge greyhound, and all of one unvariegated paleness so absolute it seemed to glow. He saw a long head, also more like that of some enormous dog, a head chiseled and lean, with folded glimmering eyes. And from the forehead, like the rising of a comet, frozen, the tapering crystalline finger of the fearful horn. And the horn lowered and lowered to meet the horn of another in the pool. Where the two horns met each other, a ring of silver opened and fled away. Then the mouth cupped the water and the creature drank.

As the unicorn was drinking, Lauro only watched it. To him it would have seemed, if he considered it at all, that the unicorn was not drinking, but only carrying out some ethereal custom special to its kind. For the unicorn was unearthly and therefore did not need to accomplish earthly things. The unicorn had strayed into this world, which was God's disappointment, out of that other world, the second creation God had made, when the form had finally matched the vision.

So Lauro watched and did not move, probably did not even blink, his back against the tree's trunk, his hands spread on the strings of his lutelin. But then the unicorn raised his head from the pool, and turned a little, and began to come towards him.

All creative beings are capable of seeing in symbols, and each will seek analogy and omen, even if they deny the fact. Embryonic though Lauro's creative gift might be, his beautiful voice unrefined and his song-making erratic, uneven, and a source of rage to him, still, presented with this unique symbol, he recognized it. The sorcerous quality of the unicorn was inevitably to be felt. No one, however dull, could have mistaken that, and Lauro was not dull at all, but, if anything, too aware and too sensitized. The sight of the unicorn touched him and he resonated to the touch as the strings of the lutelin had resonated. It was not a voice which spoke to him, and there were no words uttered either in the darkness or within his own heart of brain, yet it was as if something said plainly to him: *Here it is, here it approaches you, that which you require, that which for ever and ever you have pursued, not knowing it. The wellspring within yourself you cannot tap, the jewel in your mind you cannot uncover.* And in that moment the miracle of the unicorn seemed to be that if he could only lay his skin against the skin of it, even so small an area of skin as a finger's tip, everything that burned and smoked within him would be, at last, his to use. He, too, laying hands on this creature of the second perfect world, would gain the power of perfect creation. But maybe also there was a part of him which recognized the unicorn in another way, as that thing which must always *be* pursued and *never* taken, the inconsolable hunger, the mirage which runs before and can never be come up with, since the consolation of hunger is satiety, and the end of the chase is stillness and death.

And so, for one reason or another, as the unicorn moved towards him, Lauro broke from his trance and moved forward one step in answer.

At which the unicorn, perhaps seeing him for the first time, stopped.

At which Lauro took another step.

At which the unicorn became the single blink of a white lid on the night, and was gone.

Nothing natural could have moved so very fast. It had not even seemed to turn, but just to wink out like a flame. Nevertheless, Lauro knew it had gone back into the wood, which must be its habitation. A vague succession of stories came to him which explained how a unicorn's wood might be beset by perils, by phantoms, by disasters. These did not stop him. He ran at the wood and straight into it.

It was like falling off the edge of the night into a black pit. The pit was barred over by raucous branches which slashed his face and slammed across his body, full of earth which gave

way under his feet and the tall columns of the trees which met
his body with their own. He fell many times, and once he was
almost blinded when an antler of branches stabbed into his
face. But presently he glimpsed a white gleam ahead of him,
and knew it for the unicorn, and he shouted with fury and
joy. And then he fell a long way down, as it seemed into the
black soul of the wood, and lying there on the black soul's
floor, where there were decayed leaves like old parchment,
and some tiny flowers that shone in the darkness, he dazedly
saw the white light coming back to him. This time for sure
the unicorn might savage him. He thought of this with awe
but not terror. The touch that would unlock the genius within
himself could not kill. Whatever wound there was, he would
be healed of it. The fall had stunned him, and he was
conscious that the neck of the lutelin was snapped off from
the body.

Then the unicorn came between the trees, and it was only
the moon.

Lauro knew despair then, and a sort of anger he had never
felt before. He lay watching the moon, its light making his
face into a bone in the black cavity of the wood.

When the day came, he was able to climb out of the cavity,
which had not seemed possible before, although conceivably
it had been possible. He put the broken lutelin into his pack,
and walked out of the trees. By day, the wood had a different
appearance. It was very green, but the green of undisturbed
deep water. On all sides the trees, though struck by sunlight,
seemed impenetrable.

It was silent. No birds, no winds moved in the unicorn
wood.

A while before noon, Lauro entered the town on the rock.

It was like many other towns, and he scarcely looked about
him. Others looked at him, and he felt their eyes on him. This
was because he was a stranger, but also because he was
himself and there was that quality to him of the fire, or the

moving light, a quality in fact curiously like that he had noted in the unicorn.

And today, besides, his obsessive intensity was very great. It was like a wave banked up behind his eyes. And when he sat on the steps of the stone church, under the high doors and their carvings of martyrs and demons, his face was like these stone faces, with the reddish autumnal hair falling leadenly round it. His hands were stiffly clasped, without even the lutelin now to lend them life.

After a while, a woman came to him and offered him bread from a basket, and he would not take it, and later another offered him fish and he refused this too. Then a priest came out, and offered him holy comfort, and Lauro laughed, high, and pitched as if he sang. There were others, all eager in their timid solicitous ways to aid him, for they sensed his pain, and they came to him and the cold fire of his pain, like moths to the candle. He refused them all. They could not help him. They knew it and they went away. Even the child who tugged on his sleeve, looking up into his eyes and their black centers, even the child, at whom he briefly smiled, ran away.

The day gathered in the town until it was the color of strawberries, and the rays of the sunset fell through the church windows from within and out upon the steps, and upon the face of Lauro. He could not play or sing what he had known, could only speak it, and had not been able to.

He had been there seven hours when the Lord of the town came riding to Mass in the church, a thing he did not generally do. The strawberry sky was behind him and behind the eight dark horses and the dark forms of the men who rode on them. The horses were not remotely like the unicorn. Even if they had been given crystalline horns that flamed in the sunset, they would not have been like. Someone had told the Lord of the stranger with the lank red hair and the frozen face and hands. They had reported him as a seer or a poet, one who has witnessed some portentous thing; and so he had.

The Lord reined in his horse at the foot of the stair.

He looked at the stranger with his Lord's proud and self-blind eyes, and suddenly the stranger looked back at him with eyes that had seen far too much.

"You," the Lord said. "Why are you sitting there? What do you want?"

Lauro said, "There is a unicorn in your wood."

"A unicorn," said the Lord. "Who reckons so?"

"I do."

"You may be mistaken. You may be drunk or mad. Or a liar. *You*. What are you?"

"I forget," said Lauro. "I forget who I am. I forgot in the moment I saw the unicorn."

The Lord smiled. He glanced about. His men smiled to demonstrate they were of one mind with him. The townspeople smiled, or else lowered their eyes.

"Perhaps," said the Lord, "I do not believe in unicorns. A fable for children. Describe what you saw. Probably it was a wild horse."

Lauro got to his feet, slowly. His eyes were now wise and looked quite devilish. This was because he did not know any more what to do. He turned and walked, without another word, up the steps and in at the church doors.

The Lord of the town was unused to men with devil's eyes who turned and walked wordlessly away from him. The Lord gestured two of his men from their mounts.

"Go after him. Tell him to come back."

"If he will not obey, my Lord?"

The Lord frowned, visualizing a scuffle in the precincts of the church, damaging to his reputation. He dismounted suddenly. The Lord himself, with his two men at his back, strode up the steps into the church after the stranger.

Lauro was standing at the church's remotest end, in shadow before the darkened window. His hands hung at his sides and his head was bowed. The Lord gripped him by the shoulder, and Lauro wheeled round with a vicious oath. Lauro had been in the other, second world, aeons away, where the unicorn was. His eyes flared up and dazzled, luminous as a cat's, and the Lord hastily gave ground.

"Swear to me, on God's altar," said the Lord.

"Swear to what?"

"The unicorn."

"An hallucination," said Lauro. "I am a liar. Or drunk. Or mad."

"Swear to me," said the Lord.

Lauro grinned, with his long mouth closed, a narrow sickle.

"What will you do if you believe me?"

"There were stories before," said the Lord, "when I was a boy. Years ago. I dreamed then I should hunt such a beast, and capture it, and possess it."

Lauro put back his head and laughed. When he laughed, he looked like a wolf. Laughing, the wolf went to the altar and placed his hand on it.

"I swear by God and the angels of God and the Will and Works of God, that there is a unicorn in your wood. And God knows too, you will never take, capture, or possess a unicorn."

The Lord said:

"Come to my stone house with me. Eat and drink. Tomorrow you shall ride with us and see."

So Lauro lay that night in the Lord's stone house with its three dog-toothed towers. Sometimes before he had lain in the houses of lords. His envy and his ambition were not exacerbated by anything of theirs.

Preparations for the hunting of the unicorn had begun almost at once. It occurred to Lauro that the Lord wished to credit the unicorn's existence, that on some very personal level the reality of the legend was highly important to him. But Lauro cared nothing for the desires and dreams of the Lord. The hunt was less convincing to Lauro than the memory of the unicorn itself—which had now become ghostly. He believed in the unicorn rather less than the Lord believed, and yet he knew he had beheld it, knew that it waited for him in the wood. If it was possible to come at the unicorn by means of dogs and horses and snares, then he would accompany the hunt. But he did not believe in this, either, as he had said. It

had come to be that what he believed credible was useless to
him, and that what he did not believe could happen at all he
believed *would* happen—since it had already happened once,
and because it was essential to him. Actually, the hunt was as
his song-making had been, a needful but flawed expression,
inadequate but unavoidable. So he lay in the house, but did
not sleep.

In the morning, the Lord's underlings brought Lauro down
again into the hall. People hastened about there with a lot of
noise, and food was piled high on platters and wine stood by,
just as on the night before. The dogs were out in the yard, a
sea of brown and white that came and went in tides past the
open door.

Presently a girl was conducted in at the door. She was
fair-skinned, and this skin had been dressed in a long green
gown. Her hair and her eyes were both dark as the wood, and
Lauro, looking at her as she curtsied for the Lord, knew her
purpose. She knew it too. She was very solemn, and her eyes
were strangely impenetrable, as if the lids were invisibly
closed not over, but behind them.

The Lord came to Lauro eventually.

"I have only to give the word, now. Are you ready?"

"Are you?" asked Lauro.

"You show me no respect," said the Lord peevishly. "I
do not trust you."

"Did I say you should trust me?"

"You have nervous hands," said the Lord. "I would think
you were a musician, but you have no instrument with you.
Walk with the grooms, in front of me. I want you in sight."

Lauro shrugged. He was not really aware he did so.

They went out into the courtyard, and the dogs began to
bark. Overhead the sky was clear, and all around the air was
sweet. The girl in green was put up on a horse, which she
rode with both her legs on one side, in the manner of a lady.
Because it was the custom of the legends and stories, she had
been set at the head of the hunt, and the dogs, which were
leashed, tumbled after the tasseled hooves of her horse.

Lauro walked with the grooms, behind the dogs and before the horses. The hunt-master, and the Lord and his men, each with their swords and knives, came clanking on. There were three bowmen, and two boys to sound the horns. The hunt-master himself carried a long blade in an ornate scabbard, but he was frowning, angry or unnerved.

The townspeople stood watching in the streets, and they scarcely made a sound, though some of them indicated Lauro to others who had not seen him previously.

As the hunt left the town and began to pick a way down the rock, with the dogs whining impatiently and the green-clad virgin riding side-saddle before them all, everything became, for Lauro, measured as a planned and stately dance. The falling verdure of the trees that flooded round the track as they descended, meshed with the sun and confused his eyes, so he partly closed them, and the noises of the dogs and the metal noises of the men made his ears sing, so he ceased mostly to listen.

Apart from the girl, it was like any other hunt, for meat or sport. He knew, when they reached the wood—day-green and opaque—they would not find the unicorn. The wood was like a curtain or a tapestry. It was possible to thrust through to its other side, but not to discover any substance in it.

They entered the vale under the town. They rode through the vale, between the solitary trees with their caps of sunlight, and over the long rivers of their shadows. The pool appeared, a shallow rent in the fabric of the land, with the sky apparently beneath and showing through it. At this sky-pool, the unicorn had drunk, or performed its ritual of drinking. Behind lay the wood like a low cloud balanced against the earth and the horizon. He remembered the wood and the pool as if he had lived in this spot since childhood, he who had always been wandering. But then, these also had become figments of the second perfect world which, in some esoteric way, he had indeed always known.

The girl cast one glance behind her before she rode among

the trees. As she lowered her eyes, they met Lauro's; then she turned away again.

The hunt trotted into the wood about twenty paces, and then stopped still, while the hunt-master ordered his men ahead to search for droppings and other indications of the presence of a large beast. Lauro moved aside and leaned on a tree, and smiled coldly at the ground. A unicorn could not be taken in such a fashion. His mind seemed to drift out into the wood, searching and searching itself for some permissible, ethereal trace, like an echo, of the unicorn, but the greenness was a labyrinth where his mind soon lost itself. He sensed the girl had moved ahead alone. He closed his eyes, and all of them were gone.

Then—he did not see or sense it, he *knew* it—then the unicorn came, as if from nothingness, and stepped across the turf, ignoring the hunt, the dogs, the girl, looking at him. And Lauro felt the shadow of the unicorn wash over him, like a faint breeze.

Lauro opened his eyes. There was nothing there, where he was gazing. But something was happening to the Lord's men, a susurration not of noise but of silence. There was a great heat in the wood.

The girl had indeed moved forward alone, and she had dismounted or been lifted down. She stood between two trees, and the unicorn stood beyond her. It was like a statue, immobile. It did not look real.

There was nothing to be done. The creature did not move. If the men should move, the unicorn would run. So much was obvious. But the hunt-master, used to his craft, to the unsupernatural deer and starting, panic-swift hares, signaled to one of the boys who carried a hunting horn, and the boy, his eyes bursting, blew the horn—since he had always done so—and the men by the hounds slipped their leashes, again from habit.

The pack flung itself forward and the surge of it hit the girl as she stood there before the unicorn. She was tossed sideways, and would have gone down, but one of the grooms snatched her up and away out of the foam of dogs.

Everyone seemed taken by surprise at his own actions. The unicorn, for an instant, seemed surprised, too. But Lauro laughed again, as he had in the church. He was dubiously glad the hunt had come to defile the unicorn's sanctity and purity and solitude. Glad for the yelping and shouting, and the blundering of hooves. Yet he did not suppose any true defilement was likely.

But the unicorn ran, and the dogs belled and swirled after it. Men and horses rushed by.

There was a long aisle between the trees, tenuously barricaded at intervals by screens and sheer sloping walls of blinding sunlight. Down this aisle the unicorn ran. And suddenly Lauro realized he could see the unicorn running, that it was perceptible to him. Before, the speed and articulation of the unicorn had been quite invisible.

As he noticed this, with a kind of slow searing shock, one of the bowmen let fly an arrow.

The unicorn was so white, so luminescent even by day that it seemed the shaft was drawn after it by magic, magnetized to the shining skin.

Lauro saw, or thought he saw, the arrow penetrate the right flank of the unicorn. It seemed to stumble. It was like a star clumsily reeling in its smooth and faultless flight. Lauro could not now believe what he saw. The unicorn had become a deer, a white stag, nothing more. Lauro was running, with the rest. So he beheld the foremost handful of dogs catch up to and leap on their prey.

The unicorn fell. It was very sudden, and the dogs gushed over it. He saw teeth meeting in the sorcerous skin. And then, something more terrible. The unicorn, like almost anything at bay and pulled down, began to fight. First one dog was spitted, screaming and lathering on the slender tower of the impossible horn, and then another. Each, as it was impaled, was thrown away, its entrails loose as ribbons. And the fabulous horn was red.

A man raced forward shouting, laughing or appearing to laugh. He thrust the tip of his short knife into the unicorn's side. Another was driving a blade in the arching throat. The blood of the unicorn, just like that of the dogs, was only red.

Lauro dropped to his knees, and the hunt went by him and covered the sight of the fallen unicorn which was only a white stag. It had not made a single sound.

Someone, dashing by, kicked Lauro. He felt the blow from a distance of many miles. No blow, no pain, no warmth could come at the cold thing inside him.

The horns were winded, and the hunt-master swore in a businesslike way. They had hunted the unicorn, wounded it, bound it. It was taken. The whole event had been very quick.

Lauro continued to kneel, as if he prayed, on the trampled turf.

At some juncture, he was offered payment. This was after he had followed the hunt back into the town. He had walked a quarter of a mile behind them, then a mile, two miles. He had not seen what had happened as they entered the town, but when he came there the streets were empty. It had begun to rain, gently at first, but with increasing violence. If blood had trickled into the streets from the unicorn's wounds, it had been washed away. The people, too.

If any had watched the hunt's return, they would have seen an animal, slung between staves, its feet obscurely roped, its head hanging down. It had looked dead, dead and bloody and of a surpassing, horrid ordinariness.

But the slung carcass of the unicorn was not dead.

Lauro himself had not looked at it.

Somehow, however, he had followed them all, and come in the end to the three-towered house, and at the door men had been waiting and taken him in.

The Lord sat in a carved chair and drank wine. He was rain-wet, and his clothing steamed. The hall was full of such steam, and the yard full of the steaming, snarling hounds, who had tasted blood and been given no portion of a slain beast to devour.

The Lord stared at Lauro. The Lord was gross and ruddy.

"Well. You will wish to be paid. I have gained a rare animal. I may henceforward collect such oddities. It might amuse me to do so. What price do you ask for your information?" And when Lauro said nothing, staring back with his cold inhuman eyes, the Lord said: "It was worth something, and you know it. I had heard rumors, from my boyhood. Many heard these tales. But it took you, stranger and vagabond, to suss the creature out for me."

"For you," Lauro said.

"For me. What price then?"

Lauro said, "Where do you mean to keep it?"

"Penned. On grass, under trees. A pavilion. Something pretty. The ladies shall tame it. In three months it will eat from my hand, like a lap-dog."

Lauro looked right through the Lord and his hall, and saw a pavilion on grass, and the unicorn gamboling. It occurred to him, with an uncanny frightening certainty, that since the unicorn had only been a legend before, he himself, by his desire and his desperation, had somehow conjured it. Conjured, witnessed, and betrayed.

"By the Christ," said the Lord, growing furious all at once, "name your price, you insolent devil."

The thoughts and the words combined. Lauro smiled.

"Thirty pieces of silver," he said.

With a curse or two, and a clinking of coins like curses, they paid him. Afterwards, he went outside, and around the wall of the Lord's house, from sight. He sat down by the wall, in the rain. He could think of nothing, yet the image of the unicorn remained. After a time, deep within himself, he felt the mysterious formless stirring which tortured him, as always, unable to find its expression. He understood that this occasion was no different. But he was now like a dumb man in enormous pain who could not cry out.

At some point he slept under the blanket of the rain.

When he woke, there were warm and fluttering lights in certain high windows of the house. He wondered where the unicorn was, in some stable or outhouse, perhaps, and he wondered if it would die, but it did not seem to him it had lived. He slept again, and on the second awakening the lights in the house were out. He got to his feet and rain fell from him like water from a bucket. He began to move around the wall, searching for something, at first not comprehending his search. Eventually, he became conscious that he was seeking a secretive way back in, a way to reach the unicorn. But he did not know why he did so, or what use it might be. He did not even know where the unicorn had been imprisoned.

He came to a part of the wall which seemed, even in the wet darkness, to be different. He could not tell what it was. But then the notion began to grow that it was different in some mode of the spirit, because it was connected to his purpose. Almost immediately he found a thin wooden door. He rapped on the door, and received no answer. There were rotted timbers in the door, that sagged when his knuckles met them.

For maybe an hour he worked at the rotten wood, and when some of it gave way, he worked on the rusty bar within. Ivy clung to the bar and insects skittered away from his probing, wrenching hands. The joints of his shoulders jarred in their sockets and sweat ran down his back and across his breast, turning icy cold when it touched the heavy rain in his clothes.

When the door opened he no longer thought it would, and had been working on it from mere momentum, as if hypnotized.

Inside the door was an obscure stone-arched walk. Lauro went into it, and through it, and came out in an old yard framed by the tall blank walls of the house. Another door, this one unbarred, led into a little garden. Beyond the garden, still inside the precinct of the house, was a patch of muddy ground. Distantly a tower loomed up, before the tower several cumulus-like trees rose in a bank of shadow. A lamp burned, showing two men asleep under an awning, an empty wine-skin between them. These things were like messages inscribed on the stones, the earth, the dark. In the very center of the dark, far beyond the scope of the lamp, against the trees, was a dim low smoulder, like a dying fire, except it was white. It was the unicorn.

A fading ember, a candle guttering. The flame of the unicorn dying down, put out by rain and blood.

Lauro went forward, past the drunken sleepers, out of the light. He padded across the grass, and came under the rustling, dripping trees. The rain eased as he did so, and then stopped. He saw the unicorn clearly.

It was seated, with its forelegs tucked under it, like a lamb or a foal. The fringe of its mane was somber with water. Its head was lowered, the horn pointing directly before it. And the horn was dull. It looked unburnished, ugly, *natural*, like a huge nail-paring. He could not see its eyes. Though they were open, they were glazed; they had paled to match the darkening of its flesh until the two things were one.

There was no protection for the unicorn from the elements, but then, it had lived in the wild wood. What held it penned was a fence of gilded posts, no more. They were not even high enough that it could not have jumped over them. What truly held it was the collar of iron at its neck, and the chain that ran from the collar to an iron stake in the ground.

Something glittered in the mud, more brilliantly than the unicorn now glittered. As Lauro came nearer, he saw there were small gems and coins lying all about the unicorn. A ruby winked like a drop of wine. Some man had thrown a jeweled dagger, some woman a wristlet of pearls.

Bemused, Lauro stood about five paces from the gilded fence. There had been no emotion in him he could identify, until now. But now an emotion came. It was disgust, mingled with hatred.

He approached two more paces, and hated the unicorn.

He hated it because it had failed him. It had proved attainable, and vulnerable. It had let itself be dirtied. It was inadequate, as he was.

Its wounds, of course, marred it. There would always be scars, now, from the teeth of the dogs, the arrow, the knives. But its fading was not due to these alone.

He had reached the fence. He waited, in an appalled foreknowing, for the beast to turn to him, to plead with him by means of its lusterless eyes. If it did so, he might kill it. For he knew, at last, it too was mortal, and could die. It had never existed in a second world of perfection at all. His mistake.

It lay like a sick dog and did not look at him, while the night murmured with the aftermath of the rain. Some minutes elapsed before Lauro leaned in across the gilded posts and stretched down to take the rich man's dagger from the mud.

An hour later, when his limbs were numb from standing rigidly in one place so long, and his spine ached and his head and his very brain ached, and the moon appeared over the trees and the unicorn had not looked at him, Lauro threw the dagger at the unicorn.

As he did so a cry burst from him. There were no words in it. Then the dagger struck the unicorn in the neck, or rather, it struck against the area where the chain had been locked to the collar.

Something happened. Something snapped inside the case of the lock. The lock mouthed open, and the chain snaked away and lay coiled on the mud among the scattered jewels. The collar spun from the neck of the unicorn as if propelled.

Lauro took a step backward. Then many more steps.

What had freed the unicorn seemed to be an act of magic, perpetrated through him, and through what had been intended as an act of malicious harm. A theory that the force and angle of the blow might simply have sprung the crude mechanism of the lock did not temper Lauro's reaction. As he stepped back, he examined the fence of posts, expecting it to dissolve or collapse. This did not happen.

Nor did the unicorn respond to its freedom for some moments. It seemed almost to consider, to debate within itself. Then, when the response came, it was complete. It sprang up, deftly, and the night seemed to slough from its body like a skin.

Set loose from this skin, as from the chain, the unicorn began to glow. It altered. Its eyes filled as if from a ewer and were charged again with depth and nameless color. The wounds glared, changed also like peculiar eyes, shot with incandescence—its new skin, or the skin beneath, was white again.

Lightly, and with no preliminary, it leapt the posts of the pen. And then once more, it halted.

Lauro was closer now to the unicorn, or the fantasy which was the unicorn, than he had ever been. He was not afraid, and no longer was he consumed with hatred and disgust or disappoinment in it. These also had been sloughed. The unicorn was renascent, beautifully and totally. The wet mane was like silver. The horn of its head was translucent and the night showed through it faintly, and there seemed to be stars trapped within the horn.

Lauro waited, like a lover who is willing to permit an old love to resume its mislaid power upon him. He waited for his belief in the miracle of the unicorn to come back. And slowly and irresistibly it did come back, flowing in, touching him as before, so he felt the certainty of it in his bones, sounding them like a chord.

The unicorn began to move again. Its head was slightly tilted sideways. It looked at Lauro with one eye which had grown denser than the night.

He had believed in it, betrayed it, freed it. This time, he knew, the unicorn must acknowledge him. Lauro's awareness was unarguable. It was a fact for him. Perhaps it was his sureness itself which would cause the unicorn to do so.

The unicorn hesitated yet again. Lauro gripped the air and the darkness in each of his hands. He tried to memorize the image of the unicorn. Soon, it would be gone. Only the unlocking it would give to him, only this would remain. Twinned, bonded, they would have freed each other of their separate chains. That must last a lifetime. It would.

Then the unicorn moved. It raced towards the little garden

and the walk beyond, unerringly seeking the environs outside the house. And, for a frantic instant, he thought it would avoid him. But as it passed Lauro, it turned its head once more. The silken, star-containing spike of the horn drove forward and to one side, laying Lauro's breast open, cloth and flesh and tissue peeled away, the beating heart itself revealed, and ceasing to beat.

As the ultimate inaudible leaf-sounds of the unicorn's feet died in his ears, Lauro, lying on a bed of blood and hair and mud and rain, understood at last the rhythms and the means of his expression. The feeling like pain, like a death wound, swelled inside him, carrying him upward, and he was able, finally, to give it utterance. His lips parted to speak the glowing exactitude of the words which came. His lips stayed open, and when the rain began again, it fell into his mouth.

Two: Of Death

BUT IN THE second life, Lasephun was a young girl.

She was small in stature and slim. The pale skin was now in her almost white. Her hair was long and very dark, falling to her waist in black, shining streamers. The character of the being Lasephun's obsessiveness, in this, the second life, was muted and quiescent, although still in evidence in particular ways. But this life, a girl of sixteen who was called Sephaina, had been cared for in a unique manner, grown almost like a cherished plant. She had not yet had occasion to seek within herself, and so to be astonished, or to become dissatisfied.

Where Sephaina had been born she did not know, neither her parentage. These things did not matter to her. They had no relevance. Sephaina's awareness had begun in a slate-blue house, moated by brown water. Lillaceous willows let down their nets into the moat, and birds flew by the narrow windows with which the walls were pierced. Such pictures were set like stained glass into each of her days. The calm of the house, certain architectures, certain lights and shades incorporated in its geography, these were the balm in which the years of Sephaina floated. Her companions were several, and choice. The women who firstly cared for and then waited on her, were kind and elegant. The girl children who played with her grew up into beautiful maidens. Nothing ugly came in her way, and nothing more distressful than the death of a bird or a small animal from the meadows beyond the high walls of the house.

Within, the house was a puzzle of rooms bound by winding stairs and carven doors. From its tallest turrets the meadows, pale golden with summer and pale blue with flowers, might be seen stretching away to a sort of interesting nothingness, which was the edge of vision. Sephaina had seldom entered the meadows, then only to picnic beneath a tree, her girl companions spread about her, birdsong and the notes of mandolettes mingling. For Sephaina, the world was no more than these things. She had never been sick, or truly sad. The only melancholy she had known had been slight, and bitter-sweet. She was surrounded by love and devotion, and it was in the nature of this life to accept these gifts, and dulcetly reflect them. To be valued was as integral to her days as her curious adopted state. For she understood that others did not live as she did, while never questioning how she lived. From her first awareness, a sense of her own purpose, though unexplained, had been communicated to her.

Not, however, until the day preceding her sixteenth birthday was her destiny announced, and placed before her like a newly-opened flower.

Shortly after noon, as Sephaina sat quietly with two of her women, a priest entered the room, and a group of men with him. Sephaina had, of course, seen and conversed with men, but never with so many at once. She was not shy with them, but she guessed instantly, and faultlessly, that something of great import was about to happen.

The priest addressed her without preamble.

"Tomorrow you will be sixteen years of age, and on that

day your fate, which has always been with you, governing your existence—although unknown—will be fulfilled.''

Then he extended his holy ring to her, and Sephaina kissed it.

The men nodded. None of them spoke.

The priest said to her: ''Follow then, and learn what your fate is.''

So she rose, and the priest went from the room, up a winding stairway and into one of the turrets. Sephaina followed him, with her women, and the men walked after, the heavy brocade of their garments making a syrupy sweeping noise on the steps.

If Sephaina had entered this turret before, she was uncertain. If she had ever come there, then the turret had since been much changed. There was a long and exotic tapestry, worked in a multitude of colors, which covered every wall. A candle-branch burned in the middle of the floor, flickering somewhat, so the figures in the tapestry seemed to quiver and to breathe.

The subject of the tapestry was a great hunt, which pursued a white beast with a single horn through the glades of a wood, until a girl was found in its way, seated on the grass, and the beast lay down and put its head in her lap. At which the hunt drew close and with dogs and bow at first, and thereafter with knives and spears, appeared to kill the creature. It bled from many wounds but the blood did not reach the grass, which was starred instead by rainbow blossoms.

Sephaina looked at these scenes of cruelty, deceit and death, and she wept a moment, as at any of the few deaths she had seen. But her tears ended almost immediately. She was perturbed, and turned to the priest for his answer. He gave it.

The creature in the tapestry was a unicorn. A thing part fabulous and partly earthbound. It was not necessary that one either believe or disbelieve in it. There had been an era when the unicorn had been hunted, had been slain or captured, cut and roped, demeaned, used to increase some lord's vainglory or pride of acquisition, or bloodlust. But the death of the unicorn was, in fact, largely inconsequential, It was conceivable only a single beast had ever been killed, or that none had been killed. Or that all the unicorns then extant in the world at that time had died—only a dream left behind them capable of seeming life, or that they had been reprocreated by mystical means from some eerie quickening between foam and shore, cirrus and mountain-top. Neither did truth or falsehood rate very highly in this case. The core of the story of the unicorn, its humiliation, in some ways paralleled the history of the Christ and might be said to represent it. And now, as the debasement of Christ had been raised to worship, so the unicorn, ghost or truth or simply dream, was propitiated and adored. The clue to existence was the protean ability of man to alter things. To balance the ignominy of the unicorn's death, whether false or actual, the ritual of the hunt had transformed into a festival of love.

They would advance into the trees of the wood, not with horses, dogs and weapons, but now on foot, unarmed, with flowers and fruit and wine. And to lead the procession there must be a maiden, who would charm by the magic force of her virginity, not in order to betray, but in order that they might do homage. And if it should come to her, laying its long head, horned as if with polished salt, in her lap, then the offerings could be made to it. Or if not, still the beauty of the tradition had been honored, and the spirit of the unicorn with it.

"And you," the priest said to Sephaina as she stood between him and the circling tapestry, "you have been reared in perfect harmony and happiness to be that maiden who will lead the procession into the wood. Your years have been kept lovely in order that you be wholly lovely for him, the white one, so he will wish to come to you and give his blessing to what we do, and his forgiveness of what has been done. Every sixteen years, this is the custom. You are very special. You were chosen. Do you understand?"

"Yes," she said. The men behind the priest murmured then.

Sephaina lowered her eyes and saw the unicorn imprinted on the floor. It was different from the entity in the tapestry. It glowed, and its horn had a light within it like that of burning phosphorus. In some strange way, she remembered the unicorn. To be told of it was no amazement to her. That it might dwell in the world, that it might come to her indeed, did not seem incredible. But, for the first time also, something twisted inside her, a feeling very old, though new to her: It was fear.

They showed her the gown she was to wear. It was the palest green, sewn with flora of blue thread. They showed her the oils and perfumes they would use for her skin and hair, and these were scented like a forest and the most delicious plants that might be discovered there.

Sephaina walked through the house, gazing at everything in it. She had a feeling of loss, as if she could never come back there. No one had told her if she would. Something had prevented her asking.

As the sun began to set, something odd happened in the meadows beyond the house. There began to be fire-flies, dozens of them, scores of them, and then hundreds upon hundreds. They were not, of course, fire-flies, but the flames of torches and of lamps. The meadows, from the far distance to the edge of the moat, were dark with people, and on fire with lights. Bizarre shifting patterns, like those in a weird mosaic, formed and fell apart. Sephaina watched the lights, knowing why people gathered about the house. She had never known her power before, though she had, at some oblique station of her heart and mind, accepted her rarity long ago. To see the demonstration of her power, her influence, her emblematic worth, stunned her.

She brooded on it, pausing for long minutes, transfixed at one after another of the high windows. She wondered if they saw her, the ones who waited in the meadows. She imagined that perhaps they did, although not with their eyes.

Eventually her women persuaded her to the bedchamber where she had alway slept. They washed and braided her hair with herbs, ready for the morning. When she lay down, they drew the covers over her. One read her a passage from a beautiful book which told of enchanting and lustrous things, towers built upon water, boats sailing the air, lovers who loved and lost and refound each other at the brink of violet seas where birds spoke in human voices. Then, her ladies and her maidens kissed Sephaina, and they went away to the antechamber beyond her door. Here, two of them would sleep each night, in case she should want something and call out. This had not happened since she was a little child.

Sephaina lay in the familiar bed, and watched the bedroom in the mild irradiation of a single low lamp. She remembered nights of her childhood, and how the shadows fell at different seasons, or when the moon was full, and how the room would be when the sun rose again. Her window was sheltered, however, by the ascension of a wall, from the vantage of the meadows, and so from the lights of those who stood about the house. And she wondered all at once if this room, whose window, unlike all the other upper windows of the house, was shielded from the meadows, was always given to the chosen maiden for just this reason: To allow her peace on this one night of her life, the eve of her sixteenth birthday.

The words of the priest came and went in her head all this time, behind every one of her other thoughts.

She had only seen depictions of woods, she had never seen a real one. The wood in the tapestry had been very dense, very darkly green, with slender tree-trunks stitched on it, and with blossoms thick on the grass, and yet there had seemed no way to go through the wood. And the unicorn. How would it be to wait for it to come to her, how would it be to know she herself was the magic thing which drew the magic thing towards her? It was curious. It was as if all this had happened to her before, yet in some other distorted way . . .

Sephaina closed her eyes, and was startled that two tears ran from under her lids.

But she had been trained by serenity to sleep easily and deeply, and already her mind moved forward from the shore, slipping into the smooth currents of unconsciousness. A dream rose from the threshold, and greeted her. She beheld a drinking cup of crystal with a long and fluted stem. The drink in the cup was very dark. She stared, and saw the wood and the unicorn inside the drink, inside the cup. Then she swam by the dream into the depths of sleep.

Sephaina woke to a huge silence that was uncanny. It was an actual presence in the room, filling and congesting it. It might have been that her own heart had stopped beating. Or it might have been the heart of time which had stopped, every clock in the house, or the world, stilled. Yet she breathed, was capable of movement; her heart sounded. These things she discovered by cautiously testing them.

At length she sat up, the ultimate test, and so she saw that a shape crouched in the embrasure of her sheltered window, between the room and the starry night.

Fear has many forms. Sephaina's fear burned low as the low-burning of the lamp, yet, like the lamp, pervaded the chamber. Fear was also so novel to her that it seemed quite alien. She could barely control it. The twisting she had felt within herself when they had told her of her destiny, the ebbing and swelling flow of unease and isolation that had mounted as she watched those hundreds of lights swarm upon the meadows, now gained a quiet and terrible dominion over her.

She could not have cried out, even if she thought to do so, and somehow the ambience of her fear prevented her from thinking of it. She was alone, on the whole earth, with the shape, whatever it should be, which had manifested between light and night.

Then the shape altered, melted upward. It slid from the embrasure, and began to come towards her, gliding, taking no steps. The lamp did not in any way describe it, except that, with no warning, its eyes flashed, cat-like and appalling. And in the very same second, dry summer lightning also flashed. It shattered the window and the room together. By means of this freak illumination, she saw the outline of the invading demon. It had now assumed, or perhaps had consistently possessed, the structure of a man, rather tall, physically agile and long-haired.

It seemed to her he addressed her. In the dreadful silence, she replied.

He said: "Would you see me?"

She replied: "No."

At that he laughed. She was sure enough of the laugh. He sang it to her, and it was very cruel. Just then the tinderish lightning ignited again in through the window, and he seemed to catch flame from it, absorbing, vampire-like, colors and equilibrium. She knew him instantly, the demon. His hair was red as rust, his eyes were bleak, and his face like a bone. Across his breast a flap of cloth hung loose and ragged. Under this rent was an incoherent darkness that evaded or tricked her gaze.

She knew him. The knowledge was a facet of her fear.

At last she said: "What must I do to be rid of you?"

"Nothing, yet. I shall step from your window, in the same way I stepped up here. You will come with me."

Sephaina visualized the drop from the window to the moat below.

"You mean to kill me."

"No. Why not put your trust in me? You are willing to trust all others—your servants, your friends, the priest. The unicorn."

Sephaina stared. She began to pray, and fell quiet.

The demon only said, "Give me your hand."

At which Sephaina, without knowing why, gave him her hand.

Immediately she was weightless. The covers of the bed drifted away from her. Linked to the demon, she too now glided across the room, her feet half the height of her own body from the ground. Seeing which, she would have let go of him, but her hand would not leave go.

"Why fear this?" he inquired of her, almost with irritation. "There are other things you should fear."

And even as he spoke, he passed through the window and out onto the broad cool highway of the night sky, and she was taken with him.

The roofs of the house lay below, uncertainly gleaming, like tarnished pearl. The moat had become a circle of mist. The meadows were a great fire which had burned down to embers, for only here and there were the lamps still lit, and these looked very small to one who moved through the air, as if they no longer had any significance for her.

How was it possible to travel in this way? It occurred to Sephaina that maybe she had left her body behind. Yet her form was opaque, though weightless as a feather. The demon, too, appeared physical rather than astral, and as they clove the dark air, sometimes strands of his hair would blow across her face, stinging her cheeks: Both things had substance and were real.

The arc of the sky, like a glorious cathedral ceiling, benighted, swung and dipped above them.

The land below sheered away, amalgamated and no longer discernible. Sephaina, who all her days, as he said, had been able to trust—and so was in the habit of trusting—commenced trusting her devilish guide somewhat. She was not afraid of being suspended in space. In her limited experience so many things were miraculous. Anything different was a wonder. A wonder, therefore, eventually seemed merely different. And besides, she knew hin. Of course, one life ago she had been him, or she had been what he appeared to be. She became relaxed, and it made her impatient that she could not tell what the landscape was that unfolded below them. She wanted to see it; she had seen so little, save in books.

Then the flowing abstract knit together. Sephaina saw they hovered like two birds above an ebony cloud, which as they sank lower grew gilded veins and smoky fissures. A waterfall of leaves brushed her face. They had come to a wood.

Inside the upper levels of the trees they moved with a

darting precision, like that of fish. There was an opening, a glade like a bubble, and the demon drew her into it. They rested on invisible nothingness.

"Look down," he said to her. "Look about. What do you see now?"

Sephaina looked into the slightly luminous black heart of the glade. Enormous sallow flowers dimly shone back into her eyes.

At last he said, "Did you never see bones, before?"

"Yes—the bones of a bird—once."

"These are the bones of other things," he said.

They dipped again, and the grass-heads met their feet. She stood a few inches above the carpet of the glade, and she recalled irresistibly the tapestry of the unicorn, where the ground was strewn by blossoms. Here, bones lay thick as snow.

He led her. They spun over the glade. She was glad she need not walk on the bones. So she looked into the sockets of skulls and of pelvises. The demon drew a thigh-bone from the grass. He examined it and threw it aside with the contempt of some great inner pain. The form of this long bone, as it fell, reminded Sephraina of the spike on the unicorn's forehead.

They came into a second glade, adjacent to the first. Here too there were bones, but fewer of them. In a third glade, the bones were scarce and mostly concealed among the tree-roots, or in the tangle of the undergrowth. Some of the bones were smudged with moss.

"And who do you suppose left their skeletons here?"

"Are these . . ." she whispered, "are these the bones of unicorns?"

"These are the bones of countless young girls that unicorns have killed."

Although she did not want to, Sephaina raised her head and looked into his eyes. His eyes were unkind and clever, and exceedingly honest.

She did not question him. Presently he said, "In reparation for the ancient hunting, for capture and for death. A sacrifice.

The maiden is perfect and her life is also without blemish. No
disease. No sorrow. They have told you, you will wait, and
the unicorn will come to lay its head in your lap. That is true
enough.''

He continued to speak to her, and after a moment Sephaina
screamed.

He was a demon. He told her lies. Yet behind her lay the
snow of glistening bones. The bones of the young girls who
had been pegged out, naked and spread-eagled, awaiting the
supernatural beast from the wood. Which, scenting them, did
indeed come, and did indeed lay its head in the lap of
each—breaching her virginity and impaling her womb upon
the blade of its monstrous horn.

The chosen sacrifice, brought to death by those she loved.
Judas' kiss. The crucificial nailing. A reversal of the image of
Christ and of the unicorn. Animal for god, the female for the
male. The lore of the wood. Of death.

Her hand was still molded to the hand of the demon. When
she cried out, she felt the cry pass into him.

''You think you do not credit what I say. But what I say is
the truth, as the unicorn is also truth.''

''No,'' Sephaina said.

So he made her go back, back through the glades, and he
made her see, again and again, the bones of dead women.
Again and again he murmured to her of how it had been, how
it was. Tomorrow she, like the rest, would lie on the floor of
the wood, and next year, on her seventeenth birthday, she too
would be bones.

At last he drew her away, back up into the night, where the
stars hung, brooding on their longevity. She saw the stars,
and the world below. They meant nothing to her. This fresh
miracle, the miracle of betrayal and horror, she had also
accepted, or so it seemed.

''Now you believe,'' he said to her, ''I will tell you how
you may evade your destiny. Would you like to hear?''

''Is there a way?'' she asked.

''More than one. I can set you down in the meadows

beyond the house. There any able man, ignorant of who you are, can deprive you of your virginity. Without this ceremonial enticement, the unicorn will not seek you out. Or I can carry you to some far-off country where no one will think to search for you.''

''But you are a demon,'' she said. ''And this is a dream. Wherever you took me, I should wake in the house.''

''Should you? Then do only this: Approach those who come for you tomorrow. Reveal your knowledge and your reluctance. They will not press you, for the sacrifice must go willingly. You will, of course, be cast from the house, and will become an exile. No one, anymore, will care for you, and few will offer you love. But you will avoid the agony and death of the sacrifice.''

Sephaina gazed at the stars, which lived forever, or very nearly.

She beheld the land below, so distant it did not seem she need ever return to it.

''I do not know,'' she said. ''Tell me what I must do.''

''No,'' he said, ''my part is played out. I will tell you nothing more.''

Sephaina shivered. Her hand in his was changing into ice.

''Then let me go. Let me go back and wake.''

''This is no dream,'' he said. He smiled. His mouth was a crescent, his eyes were colder than her hand.

Then the night was emptied away. Winds and stars and darkness and the earth, all emptied at a vast and improbable speed, through her eyes and in through her window.

The last thing she was aware of was the separation of their icy fingers, his dead, hers merely frozen.

She did not sleep after that, but rather she ceased temporarily to exist. When once more she grew to a consciousness of her surroundings, the dream remained vivid and actual, as if it lay in shards about the room. She had only to take up these shards, examine them, bring them together. She did so, trembling. She lived again each minute of her flight and her time in the wood of bones. Very little was missing. And she knew it was not a dream, as in the dream she had known it was not.

When this had been accomplished, Sephaina lay like a stone, and gradually the window, where stars had framed the demon, began to pale and grayly glow.

Soon the sun would rise, and they would come for her. They would bathe her and anoint her and dress her in the green gown embroidered with blue and heavenly flowers. They would take her among the trees of the wood. They would strip her and chain her and death would come, white as the moon, with starlight caught even by day inside its killing horn.

Sephaina lay, and she considered how the demon had offered her freedom from this death, and how she had not allowed him to help her, and she wondered if he would have helped her.

To lie with a man—she could not have done that. She had been nurtured in a certain way, and was quite innocent. Never having thought of the sexual union between man and woman, as if knowing she must die a virgin, such an act was now like a myth, and useless to her. But to be carried to safety in some other place, far from the house, the moat, the meadows. How would she live there? And lastly, if she herself were to deny her fate to her attendants, to the priests—crying out when they came to her that she had learned they meant to give her to death—if she did that, pleaded for her survival, won it. . . . How should she fare on the raw face of the world, untutored, unguided? She who had always been cherished and trained to find her cherishing natural, therefore necessary.

Yet to live, to evade pain and horror, and whatever abyss or ascent, hellish, supernal, stood beyond mortality. Surely to escape this was worth all exile, despair and loneliness.

Then she thought in bewilderment of those she loved, and how they had always intended to destroy her. The very shock of it made her, somehow, certain that it was so. Such a thing as this could not have been invented.

But neither had their love been false.

With puzzled wonder, she considered this final absurdity. Love her they did. Simple instinct reaffirmed her belief in their sincerity, just as the same instinct had believed the warning of the demon.

As the warmth of dawn started to powder the grayness, she rose and stood at her window. She watched the birds begin to fly upwards, and the light begin to hang the heads of the willows beyond the wall with thin chains of greenish gold.

When the sun lifted, the sky flushed, blushed with joy. Sephaina felt her own heart lift, despite herself. She felt herself to resemble the sky. She had been cultivated to openness and beauty, and she knew a sudden extraordinary happiness. It dazzled her. She sought for reasons. It had come to her, she was an atom of the whole creative, created landscape, of the air, of the sun. Her course, too, had been fixed: to rise and to go down. For this lovely and poignant day she had been bred. Because of her value on this day, she had been loved. She was the sacrifice by means of which earth and heaven might touch. The hands of the clock might not terminate their progress. The shadow on the sundial could not hide itself. Some things must be.

With a sigh that was like the loss of blood, and yet also like the loss of poison, Sephaina bowed her head. She would not step aside. She would say nothing. If it must be she would be hurt and she would die. But not in negation, not from fear of other things, not out of slavish acquiescence and blindness. She saw within herself, as if in a dawn pool, the reflection of all her years. It had been impossible to think of her life drastically changed, continuing elsewhere, not because she was ill-equipped to live it in such a way, but because her whole life had been a building towards this end. Her death, the last stitch in the tapestry, upon which all other stitches rested. She could not break the thread. Harmony was her familiar. Harmony she recognized, and must yield to.

She remembered the lamps burning out in the meadows. She thought of the burning lamp of faith, contained in herself.

Sephaina shuddered. She had thought of bones. But her resolution did not slip away.

When the gentle rap came on the door, the early sunshine had overbrimmed the window and lay across Sephaina's body. When her attendants entered, she saw their faces in this silken light. Anguish and pleasure were mixed in each face, and a calm, saddened hope.

She was not afraid of them. She could not hate them. *She* was their hope, and her death was what had saddened them. Their hands touched her with love, as if she were very precious. She would not cry out at them. She touched them as carefully as they touched her.

There was a stillness in her, like death already. Yet it was warm.

So they took her through the meadows where the people knelt, and along a narrow road, and through a valley, and came to the wood. They entered the wood, entered its hot, green essence where the sunlight dripped down and the shadows spun like spiders. There were no bones in the grass, and neither any flowers.

They brought her a crystal cup with a dark drink in it, but she put the cup aside. She had already begun to cry, but softly, almost unobtrusively. Her maidens kissed her hands, the priests blessed her. The older women took her away, and drew off her garments, concealing her with their bodies. No one explained to her what they did. Sephaina did not question or protest. Her tears fell noiselessly down onto her own skin.

She lay on the ground between the margins of her black hair. The women put the bracelets of the shackles, which were light and delicate and did not chafe her, on her wrists and ankles. With great decorum, circumspectly, they arranged her limbs, until she was a white cross on the grass. Men pegged the ends of the shackles into the ground, some distance from her, their faces averted so they should not shame her by looking at her nakedness.

Then, every one of them left her.

Through the scent of her own tears, Sephaina could smell the fermentations of the wood, like the perfumes with which they had dressed her. She heard the faintest whispering, also, that might have been the wings of insects, or the leaves brushing one another as they grew. Above, the green roof was burnished by the sun. Rays of sun leaned like spears all about her. Like a fence of gilded posts. It was peaceful. These instants seemed timeless, and might go on forever, and while they did so, she was secure. Then she heard something step through the grass towards her, and the sound was scarcely discernible, not remotely human.

The unicorn leaned over her like a tower.

It was dark against the flaring leaves above, its whiteness curbed. It seemed the largest single entity in the world. The horn on its head was like another shaft of sun.

Sephaina clenched her whole body, but she could not shut her eyes, she could not look away from the unicorn. When it touched her, she would die, in terrible agony, and beyond the agony an unknown whirlpool gaped.

There was a pause. She gazed at the mask of death, and felt a stasis, an unconscionable waiting. And then the birdlike soaring sense of rightness, in fact of perfection, came to her again, even in her fear. Her entire body quickened, seemed elevated. She knew pain could not hurt her, and she smiled, in welcome. The unicorn seemed to read her mind. He swung his gigantic head and the blazing spike of the horn ran down.

There was a rending. Feeling nothing at all, she was confused. Then the rending came again, and twice more, and the ropes of grass which had bound her wrists and ankles lay dismembered. The unicorn stepped across her body, laving it with shadow. The curtain of the trees drew back and the unicorn re-entered the deep of the wood. There was a flash of whiteness, the curtain fell and the unicorn was gone.

Out of the green space, women came and clothed her, and lifted her. A priest came and took her hands. They were ghosts, but the ghostly priest talked to her.

"It is always done in this way," said the priest to Sephaina, under the sun-broken trees. "There is a warning given. For each, it will be unique; the demon within arises. It may take any form, that of some secret misgiving, perhaps, or some awful memory. It speaks the words of death and nightmare. Many of our daughters cannot endure the thought of what lies before them. They are shown the bones, bedded deep in the wood. The bones, you must understand, do not exist, but seem most real, as you recall. Those young women who cannot bear their fate fly to the meadows or the lands beyond, or else fall to their knees before us, begging us to release them. This too is always done, they are sent away, and thereafter without true happiness and without sanctity we must live, until the next sacrifice is due. For almost fifty years, Sephaina, the sacrifice has failed. For she must accept her death, and go consenting, to set the balance right. But to consent is *all*. Then death is not needful. You live, and we are holy, because of you."

Sephaina said, like one waking from a dream, "What now, then?"

And he told her now she would live in honor and luxury in the house, among the women she had always known, who had tended her. And that when the next chosen came to them, a little child, she too would help to care for it and rear it to its purpose, as she had been cared for and as she had been reared.

They carried her back to the slate-blue house, singing, with garlands, wine and laughter. The people in the meadows also sang, and gave her gifts. For today at least she remained wholly special.

But after today . . .

Seeing the house she had not expected to see again, the flowers, the lilies on the polished moat, Sephaina knew disillusion in her rescue as she had known a wild elation in her fear. The shining building of her years had collapsed. She had met death, who had turned aside. Her sunset went unrequired, though like the sun her glory faded. She was to be an attendant. She was to wait upon another. She was no longer the chosen one. Another would be that.

After the vision and the vision's ending, how drained and commonplace and far away the world seemed. A collection of plants and stones and random flesh, now only paintings in another book.

It was true, they had not killed her, but she might still die. Of boredom.

Three: The Unicorn

AND IN THE third life, Lasephun was the unicorn.

In the beginning there had been only something white, white and gleaming as the center of a flame. It moved like marsh gas, a disembodied, cool fire, or a breath of opaline wind. It entranced things to pursue it, may-flies, doves, fawns, but it did not consume them. Nor were they able to pass through it. Sometimes it rested, at others it ran. Its speed seemed dependent upon nothing, not even itself. Its repose was similar. It neither fed nor expelled any waste matter. It was not embryonic. It did not take on the forms of other things. At night, faintly, it emanated a pale, unimaginable glow. It was like the soul of a star, fallen in the wood.

One day, this luminous uncreature drifted from the wood, and skimmed over the surface of a pool. The pool faithfully reflected it for several moments, and then ceased to reflect it. The pool began to show instead another reflection, of something which had once been there, drunk from the pool, and spirited itself away.

This thing in the mirror of the pool touched its long slim horn to the wafting formless whiteness. When the white thing reached the other edge of the pool, it let down slender legs into the grass. A canine beautiful head emerged, an arching body. The starry spike broke from its forehead.

It had no particular memory, the unicorn. It did not know, therefore, if it had been dead and had then existed as a spirit or a fable, or if now it was reborn. The pool had refashioned it in a partially earthly shape, as the eyes of a man would have done. Water, and human eyes, possessed this sorcerous ability.

The unicorn touched the earth with its feet.

The earth knew the feet of a live thing.

The trees, the air, knew it.

The recognition of presences about it solidified the presence of the unicorn. The unicorn was now solid, and externally actual. Inside itself, however, it remained phantasmal and fantastic.

The nature of the unicorn was like a prism, composed of almost countless facets. Each thought was a new dimension. The intensity of Lasephun, the obsessiveness, was demonstrated by the unicorn's adherence to each of these facets as it explored within itself.

Its life became and was self-exploration. It had no other function. It lived *within*, and where the external world brushed it—the scents of the wood, the play of light and shade, day and night, the occasional wish to drink from the pool, it explored these sensations within itself and its reaction to them. It had no gender, no creative or procreative urge. It was timeless, knowing neither birth nor death. It was refined like the purest distillation, and it was totally self-absorbed. So it lived and was happy, learning itself, finding always new aspects of itself and its relation to the objects around it. It was seldom seen, and never disturbed. Possibly a hundred years went by.

One dawn, the unicorn came from the wood as the sun was coming from the horizon. The world was all one contemplative and idyllic pinkness. Pink seemed in that instant the shade of all things lovely, ethereal and divine. As the unicorn lowered its head towards the spangling water of the pool, it sensed, for the first time it could ever remember, an expression of life nearby.

Startled, the unicorn raised its head, and water-beads glissanded from its brow as if the horn wept tears of fire.

The startlement might have resembled that of a deer alarmed at its drinking, but was not of this order. Never before had it encountered a corresponding life signal from anything about it. It had never known that such a note was capable of being sounded.

After a moment, confused and fascinated, the unicorn moved away from the pool, and glanced around itself.

Above the valley, a ruined town rotted graciously on a rock. Some way off in another direction, a slate-blue house sank in a dry moat: this was not visible from the pool. Beyond the pool another way lay the wood, while in the valley there were several trees. Beneath one of these a young girl lay asleep. Presently the unicorn came on her and paused.

Her long dark hair ribboned about her, her skin was white as cream, save where the freckling of leaf-shadows patterned it. A pannier lay beside her; she had been gathering roots and plants perhaps for use in some simple witchcraft.

The unicorn recognized her at some basic inexplicable level, and a fresh facet leapt into being in the prism of its awareness. Decades and decades before, the unicorn had been human and a girl rather like this one. Yet there was more. The girl asleep under the tree was very young, and she was a virgin.

The magic of virginity—for magic it was—was quite straightforward. Its sorcerous value was that of energy stored, and was accordingly at its most powerful not in the celibate, but in the celibate who had never yet relinquished celibacy, and better still in one who had not even known himself. This, as it happened, the girl had not. Her life, just as the unicorn's had been lived inwardly, had been lived outwardly. Her meditation and her senses turning always outwards, she had not yet found herself, knew herself neither in the spirit, nor in the body. In this manner she was strangely asexual, as the unicorn was. While her extreme youth lent her also, briefly, an air of the ethereal. Her birth was close enough she had overlooked it, her death far enough away she had not considered it. Life and death and sex were, for this time, beyond the periphery of her sphere—yet only just. However, for this short season, the sounding note of her existence had paralleled the unicorn's own.

Aside from the sounding note, and despite recognition, the unicorn did not see the girl as what she was, but only as another external object, like a stone or a flower.

After it had observed her for some time, the unicorn pawed the turf a little. The gesture was reflexive, physical, a mere exercise of the muscles which now must be used. It looked nevertheless ferocious and dangerous, and it wakened the girl, who sat up, bewildered and staring, her hand to her mouth in fear.

It seemed she had heard old stories of what a unicorn was. She did not appear to be in doubt, only in amazement and fright. Then these emotions visibly faded.

When she spoke aloud, the unicorn, having no longer any knowledge of the human vernacular, did not understand her. Nor did it seek to understand. It sensed exultation in her voice. It sensed itself the cause of this exultation—and not the cause. What in fact she had said amounted to the words: "You are my sign from God. Now I know the one I love will come also to love me." For in fact the very innocence of her meditation had already, through itself, brought itself to an end. She loved.

The unicorn had forgotten almost altogether the aspirations and the inner processes of men and women. It looked, with its shadowy, gleaming eyes, that were like burned yet burning violets. It watched as the girl obeised herself before the unicorn which had become her omen of love. As she did so, the unicorn felt itself harden once more inside the shell of its physical existence. So all things may be fixed by the regard of others.

But before she could try to touch it—it had some dim memory, perhaps a race-memory of its kind, of such touchings—the unicorn drew away and vanished in the wood.

Then from the wood's edge, its eyes piercing through the foliage which was like curious jewelry, the unicorn continued to watch. Rising and picking up her pannier, with a strange half-weeping sigh, yet smiling, the girl moved away across the valley. She began to climb towards the ruined town, and the unicorn watched.

A village leaned against the walls of the town. The unicorn saw the girl enter the village. It saw her step into a little hovel with a roof of golden thatch. She sat down at a spinning wheel. The wheel spun. The girl whispered dreamily. Magic as well as thread was unfolded from the primitive machine. By now the unicorn felt as much as it saw. It had ceased to view with its eyes alone. Some aspect of itself, still fluid and supernatural, had followed the girl and now hung against a wall. It was reminiscent of a cobweb, pale and luminous unobserved.

Dusk seemed to enter the room suddenly, like smoke. A moment after, the girl raised her head and her face lost all its faint color. A shadow, intensely blue in the evening light, fell across the room, the spinning wheel. It was the shadow of a young man. Even in the gathering darkness, the color of his hair was apparent. It was auburn, as the hair of Lauro had been. The phantasmal cobweb that lay against the wall, the perception of the being which had become a unicorn, clung against itself. It had now recognized, without recognition, the two lives which it had formerly been. The purpose of this representation, its earthly male and female states, filled it with strange longings, a sort of nostalgia for mortality it did not comprehend.

The young man spoke. Then the young girl.

The cobweb essence of the creature which had become a unicorn listened. It began, at last, by some uncanny osmosis of thought—telepathy, perhaps—to distinguish the gist of the conversation.

"I have thought of you all day," the young man said. "I do not know why."

"You are uncivil to say this. Am I not worth recalling?"

And the wheel spun, as if it, not she, were hurt, excited and unsure.

"I think you are a witch, and put a spell on me." But he laughed. His laugh was Lauro's. In this way the unicorn had laughed, long, long ago.

"So I might. So I meant to."

"And why?"

"To test my skill. Another man would have done as well. You are nothing to me."

"If I am nothing to you, why do you sit and gaze at me in church?"

"Who told you that I did?"

"Your own face, which is red as a rose."

"It is my anger," she said.

But he went close to her and sat beside her, following the wheel with Lauro's eyes, as she followed it with Sephaina's.

The light faded, and at last he said: "Shall I light the lamp for you?"

"You are too kind. Yes, light the lamp, before you go to your own house."

"May I not stay, then, in your house?"

"If you stay," she said above the flying wheel, "the village will remark it. I have neither father nor mother, nor any kin. If you stay, you must wed me, they will all say. And the priest will demand it."

"The priest already knows I am here. I took care that he should."

Then the wheel was left to itself and whirled itself to a standstill.

The cobweb clinging to the wall beheld itself embrace itself, the two it had been as one. But the anguish and the urgency of love it did not pause to examine, for some noiseless clamor drove it abruptly away.

As the lovers twined in the hovel, therefore, the unicorn walked delicately to the pool in the valley. It touched the tip of its unbelievable horn to the reflection there. Its calm eyes were two purple globes, shining, and its whiteness was like summer rain.

A human would have been thinking: Ah, I must consider this. I must *know* this. But the unicorn only considered, only *knew*. It returned to the black wood, wrapping itself in the blackness, fold on fold, until it was utterly invisible, even to itself.

The brief mortal kindling it had witnessed—or possibly imagined that it witnessed—held its awareness as its own life and the manifestations of life had formerly held it, and nourished it. It turned about within itself the images of the perfectly commonplace coupling, the commonplace wishes and desires which had heralded it. It turned them about like rare gems to catch the light of the rising moon.

The unicorn lay down in the blackness of the forest. It drank from its own brain.

Sometimes the blackness of the wood grew green or gold or rose. Sometimes there were faraway voices, or thunder, or the velvet sound of falling snow. Flowers burst out or withered under the body of the unicorn, which was no longer perceptible as anything like a body.

The magic of virginity, which had drawn the symbol of the unicorn on the air, both for the virgin and for itself, a virginity ironically almost instantly given up, drifted like a spring leaf on water. Then down and down through the unicorn's prismatic awareness.

At last this floating leaf, a green mote, struck the floor of the unicorn's intellect. It felt a cry within itself, a terrible cry, aching and raging, and full of inhuman human despair.

What was the meaning of *this*?

The unicorn did not know it, but time was also like the wood. As the wood had grown tall and tangled and old, so time had grown, hedging the unicorn round as if with high reeds, or a fence of gilded posts.

When it ran lightly over the pool, it did not notice it ran across water, as in the beginning.

The trees on the rock had also grown old. The unicorn

passed through them, unimpeded, like fluid. The throbbing center of the pain which had somehow reached the unicorn was to be found on the track that ran through the middle of the village.

Under the broken ancient wall of the town, an elderly woman was crying and lamenting, not loudly, but with a desperate intensity. To the human eye, her trouble was immediately quite plain. Two men had between them a covered figure on a bier. One hand, like a parcel of bones, stuck out, and this the woman held and fondled. A man was dead and due for burying, and the old woman, probably his wife, overcome at the final undeniable fact of parting, had halted the proceedings with this eruption of passionate grief. All around, others stood, trying to comfort or dissuade.

To the unicorn, only the outcry and the anguish were decipherable. They needed no explanation. And then it saw auburn hair and black, and recognized, or so it seemed, the lovers from the earlier night.

The unicorn moved closer. It stepped across the broken sunlight and the shadows and drew near to the old woman who wept and softly cried out, endeavoring to distinguish the young man and the young woman who were, in their physical forms, its own self from two other ages.

Then came a separation, of persons, of thought. The young man who resembled Lauro was younger than he had been when last the unicorn looked at him, and his hair was blacker than a coal. It was the girl, older than remembered, older than Sephaina, whose hair hung red as rust all down her back as she held the weeping woman, and took her hand from the dead hand on the bier.

"Mother, my mother," said the girl, "my father is dead and we must let him go to his rest. Has he not earned his rest?" said the girl, gently, calmly, and it was the young man now who began to weep. "Let him be on his way."

The old woman allowed her hand to be removed from the stick-like fingers. She stood in the street, sunken and soulless, staring as the men with the bier moved off from her.

The unicorn sighed.

It had seemed only yesterday, or seven days before, or maybe at most a month, or a season ago, that it had left them, embracing and new and brimmed with life and trust beyond the spinning wheel. But summers had come and gone, winters, years and decades. Their children had grown. The son had his mother's hair, the girl her father's. And the maiden who had slept under the tree was gnarled and bent like a dehydrated stem, and the young man who had wooed her was an empty sack of flesh, its motive force spilled out.

"No," said the old woman tiredly. "How am I to live, how am I to be, now, alone?"

The unbeautiful incoherent words conveyed her desolation exactly. She was rooted to the track. She saw no need to go on, or to return. Meaningless and stark and horrible, the world leaned all about her, a ruin, shelterless. Her poor face, haggard and puckered, the filmy eyes that had been dark as the pool beside the wood, all of her flaccid as the dead man carried away from her. Her mouth continued to make the shape of crying, but now even the tears would not come. She had reached the ultimate lethargy of wretchedness. And tug at her arm as the red-haired daughter might, or try to steel and support her as the black-haired son did, the old woman, who had been young and a virgin, stood on the track and saw her wasted life and the bitter blows of life, and all of its little, little sweetness, now snatched from her forever.

And then something changed behind the dull lenses of her vision. Something seemed to open, some inner eye.

She had seen the unicorn standing not three paces from her.

"Mother—mother, what is it now?" the girl asked anxiously.

"Hush," said the old woman. She was apparently aware her daughter could not see the silver beast with its greyhound's head, its amethystine eyes, its body like a moonburst, its single horn like a cone of stars—that no one could see the unicorn but she. "Hush. Let me listen."

"But what are you hearing?"

"Hush."

So they fell silent in the street. The men and women looked at each other, fearing for the wits of this one of their number. Yet, politely, they waited.

The unicorn stood, a few inches from the ground, visible only to one, fixing her first with this lambent eye, then with that. The unicorn, of course, did not speak. It had no speech. But lowering its neck, it set the tip of its horn, like a silver pin, to the old woman's forehead.

There is no death. Beyond life, is life. Whatever suffering and whatever disappointment, whatever joy, whatever bewilderment, there is more time than can be measured to learn, and to be comforted. Blindly to demand, meekly to consent, inwardly to know, these are the stages of existence. But beyond all knowledge is another, unkown knowledge. And beyond that unknown knowledge, another. Progression is endless. And to be alone is the only truth and the only falsehood.

The unicorn vanished on this occasion like a melting of spring snow. The old woman noted it, and she smiled. She walked firmly after the bier, crying still somewhat, from habit. She was to live to a great age. One evening in the future, she would tell her daughter—then rocking her own child in the firelight—"On the day of your father's burying, I saw the Christ. He wore the shape of a white unicorn. He promised life everlasting."

But that was far away, and now the unicorn ran, like the wind, and as it ran it left humanity behind itself forever. It dissolved and was a burning light.

The light asked nothing of itself, it was content to blaze, which also, surely, was another truth.

The being of Lasephun was presently transmuted, passing into some further, extraordinary stage, the name of which creature is unknown, here.